Vic APR 1 8 2009

D0046808

THE JADE DRAGON

A Story of Ancient China

by Jessica Gunderson

illustrated by Caroline Hu

PICTURE WINDOW BOOKS
Minneapolis, Minnesota

Editor: Shelly Lyons
Designer: Tracy Davies
Page Production: Michelle Biedscheid
Art Director: Nathan Gassman
Associate Managing Editor: Christianne Jones
The illustrations in this book were created with brushed
pen and ink.

Picture Window Books
151 Good Counsel Drive
P.O. Box 669
Mankato, MN 56002-0669
877-845-8392
www.picturewindowbooks.com

Printed in the United States of America.

All books published by Picture Window Books
are manufactured with paper containing at least
10 percent post-consumer waste.

Library of Congress Cataloging-in-Publication Data
Gunderson, Jessica.
The jade dragon : a story of ancient China / by Jessica
Gunderson ; illustrated by Caroline Hu.
p. cm. — (Read-it! chapter books: historical tales)
ISBN 978-1-4048-4735-4 (library binding)
1. China—History—Juvenile fiction. [1. China—History—
Fiction. 2. Luck—Fiction.] I. Hu, Caroline, ill. II. Title.
PZ7.G963Jad 2008
[Fic]—dc22
                                2008006306

TABLE OF CONTENTS

archery—the practice or skill of shooting with a bow and arrow

chi—energy that is used to move the body

Confucius—a Chinese philosopher whose teachings still influence many Asian citizens and others around the world

jade—a green gemstone

jiao di—an ancient Chinese form of wrestling in which players wore horned helmets

Qin Dynasty (221 B.C.–A.D. 206)—the First Emperor of China, Qin Shi Huangdi, reigned during this period; in 221 B.C. the kingdoms of China were unified, forming one country

INTRODUCTION

219 B.C.—Qin Dynasty

Confucius the great thinker once said: "Riches and honors are what all men desire. But if they cannot be attained in a truthful way, they should not be kept."

Once, when I was a boy, I took something that wasn't mine. I tried to tell myself it was mine, because I had found it. But I knew deep down that it was not mine to keep. I wanted to have something that my twin brother, Cheng, didn't have. Cheng and I were alike in some ways, but in other ways we were very different. I was slow, and Cheng was fast. I was weak, and Cheng was strong. When we played, he had more friends. Cheng always had more—that is, until our 10th birthday, a day I'll never forget.

4

The afternoon sun sparkled on the waves of the Wei He. The river was calm that day. Few boats passed by.

My twin brother, Cheng, leaned over the side of our boat. He skimmed his fishing net through the water. When he lifted the net, a large fish danced inside.

"One more for me!" Cheng exclaimed, tossing the fish into the bottom of the boat.

Every year on our birthday, Cheng and I competed. The one who caught the most fish did not have to do chores for a week. Every year, Cheng caught more fish. And every year, I did both of our chores for a week.

I scowled at my empty net and grumbled, "You must be luring the fish with promises not to eat them."

Cheng laughed. "You're just jealous, Zhou," he said. "You're so clumsy! Even if a fish swam into your net, you would drop it."

I leaned over the side of the boat, trailing my hand in the cool water.

"That's not true," I said.

"Shh," Cheng said. "Do you hear that music?"

We both held our breath and listened. The sweet sound of music was rising from downstream. Then we saw a large boat rounding the bend in the river. The boat was like none I had ever seen. It was topped with a shimmering silk umbrella. Along the sides of the boat, small jade dragons stood like soldiers. Rows of elegant girls dipped their paddles into the water. At the front of the boat stood a girl so lovely my eyes watered. She wore a blue and yellow silk robe. She cooled her face with a fan.

"Who is she?" I whispered.

"Zhou, don't you know?" Cheng hissed. "It's Princess Mei-lan."

I couldn't believe the princess was so near! It was the greatest birthday gift I had ever received.

We rowed toward the shore so the princess' boat could pass. Mei-lan tipped her fan at us and smiled. Cheng and I stood and bowed. My gaze was fixed on the princess.

Suddenly, I lost my balance and
tumbled into the river. I made such a
splash that it rocked the princess' boat.
Gasping for breath, I planted my feet on
the river bottom and stood. Horrified, I
looked up at the princess.

Mei-lan clutched the edge of the boat
as water splashed over the sides, soaking
her silk robe.

I looked down in shame. When
Mei-lan's boat was finally out of sight, I
looked up into Cheng's glaring face.

"I can't believe you are my brother,"
he said.

"Let's go home," I said.

CHAPTER TWO

Once I got back into the boat, I reached into the water for my fishing net. I saw that something was caught inside. But it wasn't a fish, like I'd expected. It was a jade dragon. Its jeweled eyes glistened in the sun.

I slipped the dragon into my sleeve
and looked at Cheng. He was leaning
over the other side of the boat, dragging
his net in the water. He had no idea what
I had found.

I took out the dragon again to get a better look. The green jade glinted in the sun. As I stared, the dragon winked its eye and smiled. I blinked once, then twice. The dragon was still smiling.

"What did you catch, Zhou?" Cheng asked. He peered over my shoulder.

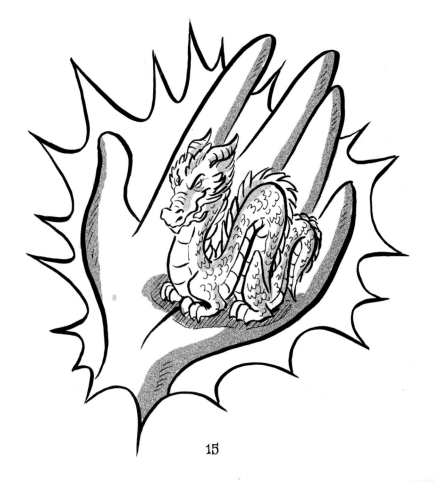

I slipped the dragon back into my sleeve.

"Nothing," I said. "I thought it was a fish, but it's only a stone."

That's not a total lie, I told myself.

"Let's go," Cheng said. "You have some chores to do." He grinned.

"One more time, and then you win,"
I said.

I lowered my fishing net into the
water. Cheng dropped his in, too. Within
seconds, my net jerked. I lifted it. Inside,
a fish flopped wildly. But there wasn't
just one fish. Not even just two fish.

Three fish were tangled in my net.

"Now we're even!" I announced.

Cheng stared, his mouth open in shock.

"The princess' boat must have disturbed the fish," he said. He lifted his net, but it hung empty.

"*Who* will do the chores?" I joked.

"Don't get too proud, Zhou," he snarled. "We're still tied. Let's give it one more try."

We fished again and again. Each time, my net brought up more and more fish. Cheng's net caught none.

Cheng grumbled the whole walk home. And he grumbled as he did our chores. Meanwhile, I smiled. For once, I had done something better than Cheng. Inside my sleeve, I felt the jade dragon. It was getting as hot as fire.

CHAPTER THREE

The next morning, Cheng was scowling in his sleep. He scowled even deeper when I woke him.

"Just you wait until the tournament tomorrow," he muttered. "Then I'll beat you fair and square."

I sighed. He was right. Every year, the boys of Xianyang competed in a tournament. The tournament had three rounds: archery, rowing, and *jiao di*, or wrestling. Whoever was the best at all three won the tournament. Cheng was always the best. And I was always the worst.

21

After breakfast, Cheng and I walked
to the river to meet our friends. I made
sure the jade dragon was tucked safely
inside my sleeve. Today we would
practice jiao di. It's the hardest of the
three sports.

During a match, wrestlers wear
helmets with oxen horns on their heads.
The wrestlers fight like oxen, locking
horns and twisting each other to the

ground. Our horns were curved upward and rounded at the tips so we couldn't hurt each other.

I was nervous about the practice. I still hadn't mastered the skill of jiao di. Siu-liu, the leader of our group, waved. He held a helmet of oxen horns. The helmet was ringed with gold pieces.

"This helmet is unlike any other," Siu-liu said. "It was my father's."

We all knew that Siu-liu's father had been a great warrior. Cheng reached for the helmet and placed it on his head. The helmet fell to the ground.

Siu-liu laughed. "It's too big for any of us," he said.

I bent down to pick up the helmet. I was going to give it back to Siu-liu, but something made me put it on my head. It was a perfect fit.

Siu-liu smiled and said, "Zhou, you
may wear it."

"I am honored," I replied.

Cheng stomped away without a word.

We drew sticks to see who would
wrestle whom. I was paired with
Siu-liu. He was one of the strongest boys
in our group. Only Cheng could beat
him. When it was our turn, everyone was
silent, as was the custom.

Siu-liu and I circled each other. I breathed deeply, controlling my *chi*, or energy. The match was on.

Siu-liu grabbed my waist and tried to pull me to the ground. I kept my feet steady, holding my stance. I would not let him throw me down, even if it took all of my strength. I felt the jade dragon in my sleeve. It was hot, as if luck were steaming from it.

I lifted my right arm and bent it
around Siu-liu's elbow. His elbow bent
sharply, and he released his grip on my
shoulders. He swiveled sideways.

Siu-liu was taller than I was, but that was to my advantage. I knew he would try to lock his horns against mine. He lowered his head and charged. I ducked. I grabbed his waist and twisted. He fell to the ground.

One. Two. Three. He was down!

To everyone's amazement, I had won the match.

"You are a true fighter, Zhou," Siu-liu whispered as we bowed to each other. "You may have to face your brother in tomorrow's tournament."

I grinned. Nothing could make me happier. And nothing could make me more scared. I touched my sleeve. With the jade dragon's help, I could beat Cheng. I could win the tournament.

CHAPTER FOUR

Early the morning of the tournament,
I walked to the river. I was so nervous
I couldn't breathe. I had never been
nervous for a tournament before. But
that's because I had never had a chance
of winning before. Today, because of the
princess' dragon, I had a good chance.

As I neared the river's edge, I stopped. My breath caught in my throat. I was not alone. On the banks of the river stood Princess Mei-lan. I bowed.

When she saw me, she smiled. "Oh, stand up," she said. "I am just a kid like you."

I straightened up and took a step away from the water. I didn't want to risk falling in again.

The princess stared at me, frowning. "I've seen you before," she said.

I nodded. I couldn't speak.

She looked at the waves splashing against the sand. When she looked up, I saw tears glimmering in her eyes.

"Will you help me?" she asked.

"Of course," I squeaked.

"I have lost something very special," she continued, "something that means a lot to me."

My stomach clenched. Suddenly I felt very cold.

"My grandmother gave me a set of jade dragons," Mei-lan said. "She is gone now, and the dragons are very precious to me. I accidentally dropped one into the river."

My heart sank. *What should I do?* I
thought. I did not want to give her the
dragon. If I did, I'd lose the tournament.
Perhaps I could give it back to her
tomorrow, when the tournament was
over. Or maybe I could keep it for good.

A sudden wind made the leaves on the trees shiver. I reached into my sleeve. The dragon was there. But it was no longer hot. It was stone-cold. Before I could stop myself, I had placed the dragon in Mei-lan's palm.

Mei-lan's eyes widened. She clutched the dragon to her heart, laughing with joy. She stopped when she saw my downcast face.

"What's wrong?" she asked.

"The dragon," I said. "It brought me such luck!"

Mei-lan laughed again. "Nonsense!" she said as she placed her hand on my chest. "Luck is here. *Inside* of you."

I shook my head, but she was already walking away into the trees. The jade dragon was gone. Forever.

CHAPTER FIVE

The boys gathered near the river for the tournament. I walked toward them, feeling gloomy. The lump in my throat was gone. My breath was steady. I had no reason to be nervous anymore. I would lose, just like I had all of the other years.

Siu-liu rushed to me when he saw me.
"Are you ready?" he asked. "This year,
you will win the tournament! This year,
you will beat your brother!"

"I will beat no one today," I sighed.

But Siu-liu clapped me on the back and shouted, "Luck is with you, Zhou!"

I reached into my sleeve where the jade dragon used to be. *No more luck,* I thought.

Archery was the first round of the tournament. We lined up with our bows and arrows. The target was a tiny wooden rabbit on top of a tree branch.

Cheng, last year's champion, went first. It was no surprise when his arrow knocked the rabbit from the perch. No one else even came close to the rabbit.

When it was my turn, I closed my eyes to steady my breath.

Then I heard a voice in my ears saying, "Luck is inside of you."

The princess! I opened my eyes and looked around. I saw no one but the boys, waiting for me to aim. I let the

arrow fly. But the arrow did not whiz past the rabbit, as I had expected. It spun toward the rabbit and knocked it off the branch.

Siu-liu held up the rabbit. The arrow still quivered in its chest. I had won the first round!

Most of the boys looked amazed. Siu-liu smiled.

But Cheng glared sourly at me. "Just wait until the next round," he muttered.

The next round was rowing. I gazed doubtfully at my boat. The last time I had been in a boat, I had fallen into the river.

We climbed into our boats and waited for Siu-liu to give the signal.

"Go!" he shouted.

Oars splashed the water. As I rowed, I heard the voice again saying, "Luck is inside of you."

I tried not to pay attention to the boats around me. But I couldn't help seeing who was at the front of the race. It was Cheng, of course. He looked over as I glided beside him.

"Zhou!" he shouted. "You'll never beat me! You'll never win!"

My boat swerved and slowed. Water splashed over the sides.

No! I thought. *Luck is inside of me.*

Cheng was still ahead of me. We neared the finish line. I closed my eyes and paddled hard as we crossed.

"It's a tie!" Siu-liu announced.

Cheng and I looked at each other. There was one round left—jiao di.

"Just wait," Cheng whispered.

CHAPTER SIX

A small crowd had gathered to
watch the final round.

"Cheng or Zhou! One will be the
winner of today's tournament!" Siu-liu
called out to the crowd.

I lowered Siu-liu's father's helmet onto
my head. Cheng and I bowed to each
other. He did not look at me when
I whispered, "Good luck, brother."

The match began. Not a sound could be heard, other than the clash of our horns. Cheng rammed his horns against mine, and I stumbled, breathing heavily. My chi was gone. I tried to remember all that I had learned. But I could not.

Cheng's eyes were on fire as he circled me. He rammed my horns again, and I fell. I tasted dirt in my mouth.

I heard Siu-liu counting, "One … ."

I willed my chi to return. The princess' words floated to my ear. "Luck is inside of you," I heard her whisper.

"Two … ," Siu-liu said.

I pushed myself up and faced Cheng. He rushed at me, but I dodged his horns.

I could see that Cheng was angry. He was forgetting all he had learned. He had forgotten how to calm himself with his breaths.

I rushed at Cheng. He was ready for me and held out his arm to block me. But I was ready for him, too. At the last second, I lowered my head and hooked his elbow with my horns. I turned my head quickly, throwing him off balance.

He stumbled and fell. I breathed once, twice, and a third time. Three counts. He was down.

"The winner!" cried Siu-liu. "For the
first time in history! Zhou!"

The glory of my win faded when I saw Cheng's face. Tears flowed from his eyes.

"Just wait until next year," he whispered as we bowed to each other.

Later, after the tournament feast, Cheng brightened. "I taught my brother all of my tricks," he bragged to the other boys. "And that is why he won!"

I smiled.

Siu-liu saw me and smiled, too. "What tricks?" he asked Cheng.

Cheng frowned. "I can't tell," he said. "It's a secret between brothers."

I patted my sleeve where the jade dragon had been. I felt only my own skin. The princess had been right. I hadn't won because of any tricks. I hadn't won because of the luck of the dragon. The luck was *inside* of me.

AFTERWORD

The Chinese dragon is a mythical creature. It is shaped like a serpent and has scales on its body.

Dragons are important to Chinese culture. They show up in art, literature, poetry, and songs. Ancient builders carved dragons on the roofs and pagodas of houses and other buildings. Known as the "sons of heaven" and the "kings of rain," dragons represent royalty and good fortune.

Dragons were thought to give life. Their fiery breath is called *sheng chi,* or "divine energy." Chinese dragons were not feared. Instead, they were known to be wise and good. They blessed those around them with gifts and good luck. People showed respect for any dragon image. Even the ancient emperors of China admired the creature. They kept statues of dragons in the royal palace. The dragon statues helped protect the emperor and his family from enemies. The dragon also gave wisdom to the rulers.

Chinese people today still respect the mythical dragon. Dragon dances and parades are held throughout China, especially during the Chinese New Year.

Xianyang

Wei He River

QIN DYNASTY
in 219 B.C.

ON THE WEB

FactHound offers a safe, fun way to find Web sites related to topics in this book. All of the sites on FactHound have been researched by our staff.

1. Visit *www.facthound.com*
2. Type in this special code: 1404847359
3. Click on the FETCH IT button.

Your trusty FactHound will fetch the best sites for you!

LOOK FOR MORE *READ-IT!* READER CHAPTER BOOKS: HISTORICAL TALES:

Choong Soon Kim

About the Author

Choong Soon Kim, the author of this book, was born in Haejeo-ri, Bonghwa-eup, Bonghwa-gun, Gyeongsangbuk-do of South Korea. Having completed doctoral course at Yonsei University in 1965, he went to the U.S. to further his study. He received M.A. in sociology from Emory University, Ph. D. in anthropology from the University of Georgia, and taught at the University of Tennessee for 30 years (1971-2001). He was Professor and Chair of the Department of Sociology and Anthropology (1981-1991), University Faculty Scholar (1991-2001), Senior Fulbright Scholar in lecture and research (1989-1990, 1993-1994), and Scholar in Residence at the Rockefeller Foundation's Belagio Study Center, Italy (1990).

Since his return to Korea in 2002, he has been active in many areas, including teaching of Hangeul to foreigners living in Korea. Currently he is President of the Cyber University of Korea and Professor Emeritus of the University of Tennessee.

Books by Choong Soon Kim

- *Voices of Foreign Brides: The Roots and Development of Multiculturalism in Korea*
- *Kimchi and IT: Tradition and Transformation in Korea*
- *One Anthropologist, Two Worlds: Three Decades of Reflexive Fieldwork in North America and Asia*
- *Anthropological Studies of Korea by Westerners*
- *A Korean Nationalist Entrepreneur: A Life History of Kim Söngsu, 1891-1955*
- *Japanese Industry in the American South*
- *The Culture of Korean Industry: An Ethnography of Poongsan Corporation*
- *Faithful Endurance: An Ethnography of Korean Family Dispersal*
- *An Asian Anthropologist in the South: Field Experiences with Blacks, Indians, and Whites*

If you want to know more about him, please visit
http://www.cuk.edu/100122.do or http://eng.cuk.edu/100526.do
(the Cyber University of Korea / the Cyber University of Korea English ver.).

Way Back
into
KOREA

**A New Insight
by a Native Anthropologist
Come Home**

Way Back into KOREA
A New Insight by a Native Anthropologist Come Home

Copyright © Choong Soon Kim 2014
Published by ILCHOKAK

ILCHOKAK Publishing Co., Ltd.
39, Gyeonghuigung-gil, Jongno-gu, Seoul, Korea 110-062
Tel   82-2-733-5430
Fax   82-2-738-5857

First published 2014
Printed in Seoul, Korea
ISBN 978-89-337-0687-9 03300

The Korea Foundation has provided financial assistance
for the undertaking of this publication project.

A CIP catalogue record of the National Library of Korea for this book
is available at the homepage of CIP(http://seoji.nl.go.kr)
and Korean Library Information System Network(http://www.nl.go.kr/kolisnet).
(CIP2014030729)

Way Back
into
KOREA

**A New Insight
by a Native Anthropologist
Come Home**

Choong Soon Kim

ILCHOKAK

Contents

Preface and Acknowledgment

When my book *Kimchi and IT* was translated into Arabic and Vietnamese, I had the chance to read it again carefully. I found that some of the information in it had become out of date, sometimes glaringly so. For instance, Lee Myung-bak was at the time the mayor of Seoul and a front-runner for the presidential election. Today he has finished serving a five-year term as president and has since left office.

This problem of obsolescence is not unique to my book, of course. I recall Max Weber's lament that the fate of scientists or their works was to become antiquated in a relatively short period of time: ten, twenty, or fifty years (Weber 1970). And for a society that has changed as swiftly as Korea has over the past sixty years, any book written about it is subject to accelerated obsolescence.

After contemplating what I might do to remedy this (because I had been asked about revising the book), I decided that what I should do is write a new book, one worthy of its own title, rather than simply update the old one. What required updating was too extensive in some cases to admit of any easy fix. What the book needed was a new addition. On top of this, there were some new interpretations needed as well. Some important socioeconomic and demographic changes had taken place since I wrote the first book. Nevertheless, a few chapters, such as Chapter 1 on the Korean ethos; Chapter 4 on the long road toward democracy; Chapter 5 on Korean marriage, family, and kinship; and Chapter 7 on religions and beliefs of Koreans retain much of the earlier books with a minor changes and up-dates. Notwithstanding, in cases where I am quoting my own writings from the earlier book, with the understanding and approval of the

publisher, I have not made any direct or indirect quotation marks so as to make it easier on the reader.

Of many matters that my earlier book did not mention was Korea's multicultural movement. At the time I wrote it, discussion of *multiculturalism* in Korea was not nearly so prevalent as it is today, and the immigration of 1.5 million foreigners to Korea from 180 different countries had yet to register on people's radars. In fact, the term multiculturalism was not formally introduced by either the government or Non-governmental Organizations (NGOs) until 2006. Today, the number of foreign brides married to Korean men and living in Korea is substantial, and multiculturalism is an idea whose time has come for many Koreans.

In this newly written book, I need to mention another significant change in Korean politics, particularly regarding the role of women in the Korean presidential politics. After Lee Myung-bak stepped down from office in a move unprecedented in the history of the Republic of Korea, a woman president was elected on 19 December 2012. As in *Kimchi and IT,* I acknowledged the struggle of women in patriarchal Confucian Korea, but I would never have predicted that the country would elect a female president, certainly one who had never married. This gives me another reason to write a new book to a degree deserving of its own title.

Kim Si-Yeon, President of Ilchokak Publishing Co., Ltd. and original publisher of *Kimchi and IT,* induced me to write this book rather than to do a minor revision of the earlier edition. Publication of this book has been partially supported by a publication grant to the publisher from the Korea Foundation, to which I am immensely indebted. I owe special gratitude to Han Kyung-Koo, a fellow anthropologist and personal friend, who offered me many valuable comments and suggestions. My appreciation extends to the anonymous readers consulted by the Ilchokak and the Korea Foundation; their constructive criticism improved this book. Ilchokak was essential in its enthusiastic support and expeditious

evaluation. The editorial staff members of the Ilchokak have done a splendid job in shepherding the manuscript stage of this book to the final stage of the book by coordinating between and among the author, readers, and the Korea Foundation.

A special acknowledgment is given to Han Chung-Eun, who did the tough job of reading the first draft of the manuscript word for word and converting my original writings on the Korean names and places in the traditional McCune-Reischauer system into the new system developed by the National Institute of the Korean Language. I am particularly indebted to K. E. Duffin for her meticulous copyediting. Robert Brown assisted me in polishing my rough writing into a readable one. Eom Hae-seon was instrumental in gathering a lot of basic data. For this, I am grateful.

I owe special gratitude to my personal friends, who also encouraged me to revise portions of the existing book and to compose entirely new portions at this late stage of my academic career. Nguyen Hoa, President of the University of Languages and International Studies, Vietnam National University, Hanoi, took the initiative to translate *Kimchi and IT* into Vietnamese and expressed his keen interest in the forthcoming work; Kendall Blanchard, President of Georgia Southwestern State University has been a cheerleader for my work, and as a fellow anthropologist he read this manuscript and offered me many suggestions.

Since this book is not based on a single episode of my fieldwork as a cultural anthropologist, but instead synthesizes my previous research with works of other scholars, I am also indebted to many organizations and previous works. I drew an overall picture of Korea and its culture in 1993 when I was writing a section on Korea for the *Encyclopedia of World Cultures* under the auspices of and with the support of the Human Relations Area Files at Yale University (Kim 1993:144-149). Several chapters of this book draw on previous publications of mine: about the nascent modernization effort by cultural nationalists under Japanese colonial rule (Kim 1998), about

Korean family dispersal during the Korean War (Kim 1988), about recent economic development and industrialization (Kim 1992), about the rhetoric of multiculturalism (Kim 2011), and others.

In preparing this book, I have built upon insights from research made possible by various funding sources, and I am grateful for their support. They are the Asia Foundation (1963-1965); Committee on Korean Studies, Association for Asian Studies (1988); Institute for Far Eastern Studies, Kyungnam University (1988); a National Science Foundation grant for travel (1988); two Alma and Hal Reagan Faculty Development Grants (1993, 1998) from the University of Tennessee at Martin; the Rockefeller Foundation's Scholar-in-Residence Award (1991-1992); two senior Fulbright Research and Lecturing Grants (1988-1989, 1993-1994); a Smithsonian Institution Travel Grant (1978); the U.S. Department of Health, Education, and Welfare (1974, 1978); an E. Hunter Weller Grant (2000) via the University of Tennessee at Martin; the Wenner-Gren Foundation for Anthropological Research (1988); and numerous Faculty Research Grants from the University of Tennessee at Martin (1981, 1982, 1984, 1986, 1988, 1991-1992, 1996).

I owe special gratitude to my family. My wife, Sang-Boon, had to carry a heavy burden when I was away from home doing fieldwork and then again while I was writing this book. My two sons, John and Drew; two daughters-in-law, Karen and Nancy; and five grandchildren, Matthew, Ryan, Jack, Luke, and Caroline, have been inspirational. I am forever grateful.

By now, I have learned that publication of a book is a social production, with the participation of numerous people and organizations. For that reason, authorship of this book could be many times multiplied. As the person whose name happens to be on its cover, I just hope this book will be interesting or useful to anyone desiring to know something about Korea and Koreans. If it is, I will be pleased.

Bukchon-ro
CSK

CHINA

RUSSIA

Hamgyeongbuk-do

Yanggang-do

Jagang-do

Hamgyeongnam-do

Pyeonganbuk-do

Pyeongannam-do

Pyeongyang

DMZ

East Sea

Hwanghae-do

Hwanghaenam-do

Gangwon-do

Ulleungdo

Incheon

Seoul

KOREA

Dokdo

Yellow Sea

Gyeonggi-do

Chungcheongbuk-do

Chungcheongnam-do

Sejong

Daejeon

Gyeongsangbuk-do

Daegu

Jeollabuk-do

Ulsan

Gyeongsangnam-do

Busan

Gwangju

Jeollanam-do

Jejudo

JAPAN

Korea Map

Introduction

If one surveys the titles and subtitles of books that Western scholars have written about Korea over the past several decades, it appears that these works are reasonably accurate in their descriptions of the country's socioeconomic and political situation, at least for the time when they were published. Taken together, these titles trace a miniature narrative of Korea's history as written by others. For example, 1882 was the year William Griffis' book characterized Korea as a "hermit nation" in its title, casting it as isolated and obscure.* When Percival Lowell described Korea as the "land of morning calm" in the subtitle of his 1888 book, the epithet carried Romantic connotations. Such a blithe description, however, is belied by the fact that Korea has been attacked by foreign neighbors many times in its history. In his 1966 book, Shannon McCune corrected Lowell's poetic view of Korea by calling it the "land of broken calm."

Korea's relative obscurity is not, however, commensurate with the length of its history. In fact, Korea has a prehistory stretching back over half a million years, and for much of this millennia-long history, Korea was an independent kingdom with a continuous culture. Despite this, those unacquainted with Korea might imagine Korean culture to be a pale imitation of China's or Japan's. In reality, Korea was never an offshoot of China or a clone of Japan (Nelson, 1993). Even so, Korean studies are given secondary status, if not passed over

---

* Griffis' title was out of touch with the contemporary Korea of his day. Ironically, however, the year his book was published Korea swept onto the international stage for the first time in its history by concluding treaties with the United States, France, Germany, and many other European countries.

altogether.

When Western scholars and writers publish books on Japan or China, they seldom fail to acknowledge the country's national identity and sovereignty in the titles: Ronald Dore's *Taking Japan Seriously* (1987) and Ezra Vogel's *Japan as Number One* (1979), for example. In lionizing the remarkable economic progress of China, Dwight H. Perkins gave his work *China* (1986) the subtitle *Asia's Next Economic Giant*.

Conversely, scholars in the West, in the not-too-distant past, tended to exclude Korea and Koreans from the titles of their books. In fact, more often than not, titles (in the absence of their accompanying subtitles) give no indication that the books are even about Korea. Some examples serve to illustrate this curious exclusion: Nancy Abelmann's *Echoes of the Past, Epics of Dissent* (1996), Nancy Abelmann and John Lie's *Blue Dreams* (1995), Roger Janelli's *Making Capitalism* (1993), Laurel Kendall's *Shamans, Housewives, and Other Restless Spirits* (1985a), Clark Sorensen's *Over the Mountains Are Mountains* (1988), Carter Eckert's *Offspring of Empire* (1991), and Laura Nelson's *Measured Excess* (2000). I, too, must admit that I omitted "Korea" in the titles of two of my books about it (Kim 1988a, 2011b).

However, Korea has not stood still. Its economy, social life, and politics have changed dramatically; so much so that earlier accounts of Korean life are no longer adequate for understanding the country. Consequentially, almost all books with Korea as a major topic identify Korea in the title. Some examples are Donald Clark's *Culture and Customs of Korea* (2000), Bruce Cumings' *Korea's Place in the Sun* (2005), Michael Robinson's *Korea's Twentieth-Century Odyssey* (2007), Boyé Lafayette De Mente's *The Korean Mind* (2012), and Daniel Tudor's *Korea* (2012). The increased presence of Korea in the titles of scholarly books published in the West parallels Korea's increased visibility in the world at large—economically, diplomatically, and culturally.

Why Korea?

Geopolitically, Korea is in the middle of the Far East. Korea's long northern border abuts the vast expanse of Manchuria, China, a land area almost forty-three times Korea's size. A size comparison of Korea with the Russo-Siberian landmass, with which it shares an 17.5 kilometers (eleven-mile) border, is almost ludicrous. Across the East Sea lies the island nation of Japan, with an area almost 70 percent larger than Korea's. As a consequence of its location, Korea has always been vulnerable to attacks from neighboring states. In addition to invasion and domination by Chinese dynasties over the centuries, there have been continual intrusions from nomadic northern tribes such as the Yen, Khitan, Jurchen, and Mongols. Two full-scale Japanese invasions by Toyotomi Hideyoshi in the sixteenth century devastated the Joseon dynasty (1392-1910). While Koreans were living under the constant threat of skirmishes and full-scale invasions, one may wonder how they were able to maintain an independent kingdom for most of their millennia-long history.

The recent expansion of the Korean economy has drawn the attention of Western media, scholars, intellectuals, and ordinary citizens. It is indeed a miraculous tale for such a resource-poor country still bearing the scars of Japanese colonialism of less than seven decades past and the fratricidal Korean War of six decades ago that devastated the country, killing millions, destroying almost one half of the industrial units nationwide, and reducing the peninsula to ashes. To have overcome these adversities to become an economic powerhouse in so short a period of time is a remarkable achievement (Kim 1992).

Korea no longer produces cheap "knock-off" consumer goods but instead today manufactures high-end technology products, such as semiconductors, mobile phones, smart phones, and smart TVs, as well as cars. Koreans possess skills, techniques, and a reputation for building world-class ships and undertaking major construction projects. In carrying out such projects Koreans have employed the

most advanced techniques of construction and have coordinated an international consortium of thirty contractors (Timblick 2010). Richard Steers and his associates (1989:136) state that "It took the United States 100 years to move from an agrarian economy to an industrial economy, and it took Japan seventy years to make a similar adjustment, but it took Korea less than thirty years." Perhaps most remarkable of all, and against all odds, Koreans have succeeded in institutionalizing a democratic political system while achieving a high level of industrialization. What factors have contributed to Koreans accomplishing such a momentous task?

Occupying the southern half of the peninsula, South Korea (99,720 square kilometers or 38,623 square miles) is a rather small country in terms of sheer real estate, roughly equivalent in size to the state of Indiana (94,322 square kilometers or 36,418 square miles), which ranks thirty-eighth in size of the fifty U.S. states. Nevertheless, Korea's gold medal standing at the XXX London Olympic Games in 2012 was fifth out of 205 participating nations. Korea's count of thirteen gold medals was next only to those of the United States, China, Great Britain, and Russia. Except for the 2000 Summer Olympic Games in Sydney, where Korea ranked eleventh, for the last seven consecutive Olympic Games since 1988, Korea has ranked among the top ten in medal standings.

During the London Olympics, an extraordinary thing happened at the quarterfinal soccer games between Great Britain, the host nation, and South Korea. In front of some 75,000 zealous home fans in Cardiff, Wales, the South Korean team defeated Great Britain in a 5-4 penalty shootout. No one in the world who follows soccer could believe the final outcome. Korean players themselves knew that the British had a better team in terms of individual skill and team strategy. The Korean coach commented that it was "mind games" and Korean players' "mental toughness" that led to their win. What then is the nature of Korean minds, and how tough are they? It is interesting and enlightening to learn something about Korea and

4

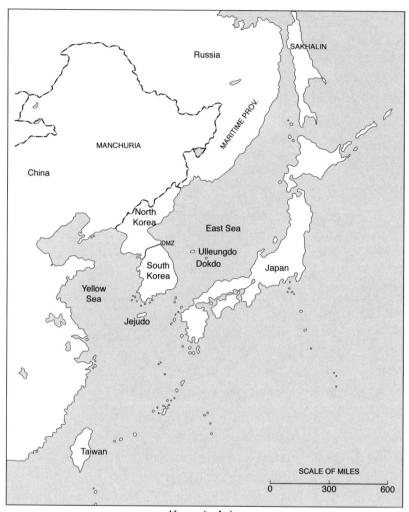

Korea in Asia

Koreans.

Over the course of this book, I address some key related questions. What has allowed South Korea to leap forward economically in so short a period of time, from being one of the poorest nations in the world during the Korean War (1950-1953) to becoming a prosperous nation today? How have Koreans succeeded in building world-

class ships, establishing large automobile plants abroad (in places like Montgomery, Alabama, and West Point, Georgia), and constructing the Great Man-Made River in Libya and the world's tallest tower in Dubai? How has Korea become the world's most wired nation at the cutting edge of information technology? Why are so many Korean students enrolled in the finest universities of America, Canada, Europe, and Oceania? Daniel Tudor (2012:10) explains why he calls Korea "the impossible country":

> Fifty years ago, South Korea was an impoverished, war-torn country that lurched from brutal dictatorship to chaotic democracy and then dictatorship again. Few expected it to survive as a state, let alone graduate to becoming a prosperous and stable model for developing countries the world over—and one with an impressive list of achievements in popular culture, to boot. Quite simply, South Koreans have written the most unlikely and impressive story of nation building of the last century. For that reason alone, theirs deserves to be called "the impossible country."

What are my reasons for writing this book?

Until Korea took a major step forward economically and industrially, it was largely invisible to the Western world. Even many contemporary Westerners who use all sorts of Korean-made electronic products, such as Samsung smart phones, LG high-definition televisions, and Hyundai and Kia automobiles, do not associate their consumer goods with Korea. To have some understanding of Korea's economic ascendancy and rapid industrialization is essential for an informed citizen in the globalizing era.

Along with its impressive economic development, Korea is important geographically. In the thirteenth century, Korea was used by Mongols as a base from which to launch an invasion of Japan, a campaign that failed largely on account of the storms which is called the "divine wind" (kamikaze) in Japan. And a little more than a century

ago, Korea was again caught in the middle of a war between Russia and Japan, the Russo-Japanese War (1904-1905), which was waged on Korean soil. During the Korean War, some 33,625 young Americans lost their lives, and the United States gave over $1.3 billion in aid to Korea. Despite intensive contact between the United States and Korea for the past half century, there have been very few experts on Korea in the United States. Even during recent situations, such as North Korea's nuclear weapons testing in October 2006 and later, and ongoing negotiations between Korea and the United States to sign a Free Trade Agreement (FTA) in April 2009, few Western experts on Korea have been available.

Most recently, maritime disputes in East Asia have drawn the world's attention — disputes over Dokdo involving Korea and Japan; Xisha or Paracel Islands involving China, Vietnam, and Taiwan; Diaoyu/Senkaku Islands involving China, Japan, and Taiwan; Spratly Islands involving China, Taiwan, the Philippines, Vietnam, Malaysia, and Brunei; and Kuril Islands involving Russia and Japan. Dokdo is currently controlled by Korea; Xisha or Paracel Islands are effectively controlled by China; Diaoyu/Senkaku Islands are effectively controlled by Japan; Spratly Islands are controlled by China and three other countries; and Kuril Islands are currently controlled by Russia. These disputes originated in imperial powers' decolonization after World War II, during which time they neglected to clarify maritime demarcations for former colonies.

Not many Americans are aware of the fact that the situation became worse when Japan failed to recognize its colonial past. Specifically, at the signing of the San Francisco Peace Treaty in 1951, forty-eight allied countries and Japan, excluding China and Korea, failed to make territorial distinctions for minor islands that imperial Japan had incorporated into its territory. Since the China Sea is believed to cover some 30 billion tons of crude oil, the disputes over islands with Japan present a volatile situation. Japan can no longer be a unilateral actor in East Asia. Again, being located as it is between

China and Japan, Korea is a country that the world needs to pay attention to.

My original desire to write this kind of book arose quite long ago, in 1971, when I was assigned to teach a survey course on East Asia at the University of Tennessee at Martin and was unable to find an adequate textbook on Korea. Colleagues who had similar teaching assignments shared the same difficulty. As representative of Anthropologists for Korean Studies (AKS), an interest group in the American Anthropological Association, I assembled an ad hoc committee to edit a book to meet the need. The committee worked on the project until the mid-1990s, but its members were too overwhelmed by other commitments to complete the volume. I believe that the demand for such a text still exists.

One reason I decided to write this book is the recent popularity of Korean pop culture: *Hallyu*, the Korea wave.* Because of its growing worldwide popularity, the wave has created a great ripple effect. Increasing numbers of foreigners are becoming interested in learning about Korean culture and the Korean language.

Also, demand for an up-to-date informative introduction to Korea comes from overseas Korean descendants—Korean Americans, Korean Canadians, and others—who are eager to learn about their ethnic heritage. This interest has been fueled by *Hallyu*. Additional impetus comes from the nonacademic sectors of business and industry. As overseas direct investment has grown, Korean business and industrial circles have realized the need for a book in English to introduce Korea and its culture to people who work for overseas Korean firms. Korea's commercial presence abroad was in fact the reason why my earlier book on Korea was translated into Arabic and Vietnamese (Kim 2007).

My earlier book, published in 2007, could not describe important

---

* *Hallyu* is the Korean version of the Chinese phrase *hanliu,* and it refers to the widespread popularity of South Korean entertainment and fashions starting in the 1990s.

new trends in contemporary Korea: increasing multiculturalism, the election of a female president in a patriarchal Confucian society, and impressive conservation and environmental protection in a country dedicated to fast economic growth. A new survey of Korean society needs to address these emergent trends against the background of Korean history.

I also have a personal reason for writing this book. I wanted a book to teach my American-born grandchildren about Korea and its culture. Writing with one's own grandchildren in mind, one realizes how important it is to select essential subjects and present them in a balanced view while sustaining reader interest.

Contents of the book

I have organized this book into ten chapters and a brief postscript. Chapter 1 discusses the ethos behind South Korea's rise to world prominence and tries to explain what makes Koreans tick by tracing the origins of the Korean ethos through social and cultural patterns of the country's past. Chapter 2 tell us who Koreans are and where they came from. Chapter 3 describes Korea's faithful endurance and tenacity in facing foreign invasions. Chapter 4 accounts for how Korea was able to initiate various modernization programs under colonial rule and after a devastating war. Chapter 5 describes Korean marriage, family, and the kinship system, and how they have changed.

Chapter 6 discusses the dwindling population and economic decline of Korea's rural villages as a result of rapid urbanization and industrialization, and the new policies meant to slow down urbanization. Chapter 7 describes Korea's religious syncretism and introduces various indigenous belief systems and imported religions. Chapter 8 describes Korea's traditional social stratification and educational system, Koreans' obsession with education, and the importance of education in determining upward mobility in Korea's modern open-class society. Chapter 9 describes Korea's

miraculous economic development, its slowdown at maturity, and its transformation from a foreign aid receiver to a foreign aid donor. Chapter 10 explores four paradoxes of Korean culture: ethnic nationalism versus multiculturalism; inwardness versus outwardness; economic development versus environmental conservation; and Confucian patriarchy versus a female head of state. In the postscript, I make a few personal remarks about my return to Korea, and describe Korea after many years spent living abroad.

Uniqueness of the book: its anthropological lens

This book has some unique characteristics. For one, it maintains a balanced outlook on the various issues related to Korea. While some introductory books on Korea tend to overemphasize its economic success stories, I have made every effort to maintain balance by covering other issues. For another, this book is not merely a synthesis of the existing literature; it draws liberally on my own anthropological fieldwork. At times I punctuate the historical narrative with stories taken from my own life, especially from the Japanese colonial period and the Korean War, both of which I recall firsthand. To some extent, this book tells "my story" in the process of telling Korean "history," but I sought to keep my subjectivity in check by drawing on my dual identity as both cultural insider and outsider. On the one hand, I am an insider to Korea — someone born, raised, and partly educated in Korea for twenty-seven years. On the other hand, I am an outsider to Korea — having lived far from Korea for thirty-six years, raising a family, teaching, and pursuing research in the United States. Over time I acquired a capacity for reflexivity, a sense of distancing from the self. Reflexivity has been an asset to my way of thinking — a mentality acquired and cultivated through my life and work in another culture.

Because my life spans such so much — both chronologically, from premodern to ultramodern Korea, and geographically, from East to West and back East — this book has value because of the

scope of its author's lived experience. The reality is that working scholars who lived through the turbulent twentieth-century years that defined Korea as I did are few. Among contemporary South Korea's 50 million citizens, only 14 percent were born before Korea's liberation from Japan, and only 18 percent were born before the Korean War. Those Koreans who experienced both Japanese colonial rule and the Korean War constitute fewer than 10 percent (about 5 million) of all living Koreans. If those living memories go unrecorded, undescribed, then the living will have only secondhand accounts about Korea's past.

Intended audiences and choices on footnotes, bibliography and Romanization

Although I write as an anthropologist and academic, I wanted this book to be accessible to a wide audience. Accordingly I tried to minimize discipline terminology. The target audience for this book includes scholars and students of East Asian studies, anthropology, sociology, history, regional studies, and ethnic and racial studies. This book was also written for general readers interested in Korea and East Asia, particularly those interested in the Korean wave, *Hallyu*. With these readers in mind, I have avoided scholarly apparatus that might hinder reading. My use of explanatory footnotes is minimal.

While I aimed to write a reader-friendly book, I also wanted to provide sufficient references throughout the book to meet the needs of an academic audience. Where I draw upon, without quoting, other scholars' ideas, explanations, and viewpoints, I cite the author and year of publication. When there is a need to distinguish publications by the same author published in the same year, I add a lowercase letter to the year of publication, e.g., 1977a or 1977b. In the case of two different persons with the same surname who have publications in the same year, I have put the initial of the first name before the surname, such as E. Kim. When I quote directly from a source, I cite author, date of publication, and page number(s). Readers need

only consult the references listed at the end of the book for full bibliographic information.

Throughout, for names and places, I have opted to Romanize in accordance with the new system developed by the National Institute of the Korean Language. The exceptions are the names of a few Koreans, including myself, who have established different Romanizations for themselves (e.g., Rhee Syng-man), along with certain place names (e.g., Seoul). When quoting directly from original sources with the new Romanization, I have acknowledged my own use of the McCune-Reischauer system in parentheses. And when quoting from other scholar's works, I used the new Romanization system wherever possible. Also, following Korean, Chinese, and Japanese usage, when I refer to Koreans, Chinese, and Japanese, I give their surnames (family names) first, before their personal names.

In referring to individuals who are not public figures, in accordance with the ethics of my discipline, I have tried to protect their privacy and defend their dignity, cultural values, and geographical locations. For this reason, I have used pseudonyms for individuals, clans, lineages, and locations, even though Korean custom considers using a fictitious name an intolerable insult. At the same time, in many cases I have used actual names for certain individuals (e.g., colleagues), organizations, and locations whose identities would be difficult to conceal because of the contextual information provided.

The official name of South Korea is the Republic of Korea (ROK) and that of North Korea is the Democratic People's Republic of Korea (DPRK). Throughout this book the informal designation of the ROK as Korea, or South Korea at times, is adopted for easier reading. The DPRK is specified as North Korea to avoid any possible confusion. In adopting these terms, I do not mean to undermine or discredit the integrity of either regime.

1
The Korean Ethos

As an effort to understand why Koreans think, behave, and believe as they do, this book begins with a discussion of the Korean ethos from its very beginnings. According to E. Adamson Hoebel (1958:543), an "ethos expresses a people's qualitative feeling, their emotional and moral sensing of the way things are and ought to be — their ethical system." Others call it "national character," especially psychologically oriented anthropologists writing during and directly after World War II (Benedict 1946; Gorer 1949; Mead 1942, 1951). Still others call it "patterns" (Crane 1978), or even "Koreanness," referring to the Korean ethos (Han 2003: 5-31). Since the term "national character" has other connotations, I prefer the term "ethos," but these terms are often used interchangeably. My intention in this chapter is to delineate what Koreans believe in as an ideal culture and set of values and also how they behave as a practical matter in everyday life. Or, to express the same idea in colloquial language, I am interested in what makes Korea "tick."

The Korean Spirit of *Ppalli ppalli*

"*Ppalli ppalli*" is apparent in daily activities

Ppalli ppalli (meaning "hurry up") was the first Korean phrase that former head coach of the Korean National Soccer team, Dutchman Dick Advocaat, learned in September 2005 to prepare for the 2006

Fédération Internationale de Football Association (FIFA) World Cup in Germany. He learned *ppalli ppalli* first for two reasons: it was the most frequently used phrase reflecting the Korean character, and it was entirely appropriate for the game of soccer. Also, when Alan Cassels was appointed CEO of German-based Dalsey, Hillblom, & Lynn-Korea (DHL-Korea), an international express mail service firm, he declared that it was his business ambition to satisfy fast-paced Koreans accustomed to *ppalli ppalli*.

When I first returned to Korea in 2001 after being absent for a prolonged period since 1965 (except for brief visits on several occasions), I found it curious to see Koreans running up the escalators at most subway stations in Seoul. While it may not be particularly safe to hop up an escalator, many Koreans do (Kim 1995). To accommodate those in a hurry, most escalator stairs are divided down the middle with a white or yellow line partitioning the stairs into standing and climbing sides. And once climbers get into an elevator, they push the "close doors" button repeatedly.

As Paul Crane (1978:54), son of a missionary who dedicated himself to medical missionary work in Korea, and author of a best-selling book on Korea, has noted, "Modern drivers in Seoul seem to practice the same tactics as the famous *Kamikaze* taxi drivers of Tokyo, and have lost all pretense of courtesy on the road." If anyone driving around Seoul slows down to read a road sign, cars behind will honk their impatience. The rules of the road are little respected: drivers change lanes without warning; they tailgate; they speed up when they should slow down. For a good many Korean drivers, a yellow light means "speed up to beat it." If the car ahead does not accelerate as soon as the light turns green, the driver behind is likely to punch the horn and shout, "Hurry up!"

And those who walk the streets of Seoul instead of driving are likely to brush up against swift-walking Seoulites hustling down the city streets. According to Kuk Hŭng-ju[Guk Heung-ju](1986: 117-119), a former newspaper reporter and freelance writer, an average European

walks twenty-five steps per minute, an American twenty-seven steps, a Russian thirty steps, a Japanese pedestrian thirty-eight steps, while the slowest Korean takes forty-five to fifty-five steps on average per minute. Most Koreans, though, walk a fleet seventy steps per minute, which is almost three times faster than the average European.

Two popular native Korean dishes — *bibimbap* and *gukbap* — are food one can eat fast. *Bibimbap* is a mixture of rice, topped with some meat, sautéed and seasoned vegetables, and a variety of sesame seed oil and hot pepper soybean paste, and served in a large bowl. *Gukbap* is rice mixed in a soup. According to a study done by Korean cooking expert Jang Eun-jae, "it takes about 14 minutes to finish when one eats soup and rice separately, whereas eating them together mixed in one bowl, it will take only 11 and a half minutes" (H. Hwang 2010:454). On 12 October, 2012, the *Dong-A Ilbo* reported that, according to a study done by a medical team from Korea University Medical School during 2007-2009 surveying 8,771 Koreans, 52.4 percent of the respondents take less than ten minutes for a meal, and surprisingly 8 percent take less than five minutes. Overall, one out of ten people included in the study takes less than fifteen minutes. Whether it takes ten or five minutes, the average time Koreans usually spend on a meal is very short, while the average time for Western Europeans, especially in France, Belgium, and Switzerland, is protractedly by comparison. After having lived for more than three decades in a rural university town in western Tennessee, I found myself unable to keep up with speedy Koreans.

Korea is a place where one can get many things done presto. Michael Breen (2004:176) tells a story about his experience with Korean hustle:

Car breaks down? No problem. Once I was on the motorway with my family when the accelerator cable snapped. We were spotted by a pickup vehicle that patrolled the roads looking for victims. In no time the driver and his mate had hoisted the car off its front wheels and were

tugging us along the road. We were still in the car of course. Going along a road at about fifty m.p.h[about eighty k.p.h] on your back wheels with no view except the back end of a truck may be exciting for children but is unnerving for adults. We were pulled to a small village where they had a workshop. A lad was dispatched to the nearby town to get the part and we were shown the village restaurant. After some noodles and kimchi, the car was done and we were back on the road.

"Ppalli ppalli" as integral to the Korean ethos

The practice of *ppalli ppalli* is not merely part of daily life for Koreans; expeditiousness is imbedded deeply in their minds as a basic value. Let me illustrate this trait with several cases related to Korea's modernization and industrialization.

The construction of the Seoul-Busan highway is a good case in point. It is the main artery for Korea's transportation, travel, and distribution of goods between the nation's capital and its largest port. The construction of a highway connecting the two cities was pursued with almost religious fervor by President Park Chung-hee[**Bak Jeong-hui**]. The project began in February 1968 and proceeded under a relentless push for completion ahead of schedule. Amazingly, a total of some 416 kilometers (258.5 miles) of road — the longest of all South Korean highways, with 305 bridges and six tunnels — was completed in a mere two and a half years, well ahead of schedule. This same speed and efficiency has been observed in building construction as well. Michael Breen (2004:175) reports, "On construction sites in the Middle East and South-east Asia, they [Korean workers] have impressed governments with their round-the-clock operations and their ability to *beat deadlines*" (emphasis mine).

Although Korea had no prior experience in modern shipbuilding, Chung Ju-yung[**Jeong Ju-yeong**], the founder of the Hyundai conglomerate, built the world's largest shipyard in Ulsan. The first ship was completed in three years rather than the expected five. Chung's shipyard had technical support from the Scott Lithgow

Shipyard in Scotland. A consortium of English banks agreed to finance the procurement of shipbuilding equipment from five European countries. A Greek owner bravely placed an order for the first two "very large crude carriers" almost at the same time in 1971. Since then, it has taken less than thirty years for Korea to become the first and best country in shipbuilding, in both volume and value (S. Hwang 2010).

Steel production started in the mid-1960s in the small fishing town of Pohang, which soon became the site of one of the world's largest steel production plants. The initial installation of the Pohang Iron and Steel Company, Ltd. (POSCO), founded by the Korean government in 1968, became one of the most price-competitive steel makers in the world. It originally started almost entirely on a turnkey basis through Japanese technology. Although over 500 engineers and front-line supervisors had received overseas training prior to the start-up, "when operations commenced in 1973, local engineers reached desired normal iron production level *within eight days, an unprecedented record in the history of the industry*" (L. Kim 1989:125, emphasis mine).

During the financial crisis that followed the depletion of foreign exchange reserves, the Korean government received a $57 billion bailout loan from the International Monetary Fund (IMF) in December 1997. It was shocking to Koreans, but they wasted little time in recovering economically. In response, there was a three-month-long gold collection campaign, which raised $2.17 billion (225 tons of gold) in early 1998. People lined up to donate or sell their gold after experts had announced that an estimated 20 billion dollars' worth was kept in Korean homes. Some three and a half million Koreans participated in this campaign, which helped the country recover faster (*ppalli ppalli*) than other countries in Asia, with growth rates of 10 percent in 1999 and 9 percent in 2000.

Korea's economic development and rapid industrialization in the latter part of the twentieth century was initiated by President Park

Chung-hee (1917-1979). Park's basic goal was to create an economic base for industrialization and self-sustained growth. The first five-year economic plan was designed to attain an annual growth rate of 7.1 percent between 1962 and 1966, but this target rate was exceeded beginning in 1963. Successive five-year plans — the second (1967-1971), third (1972-1976), fourth (1977-1981), and fifth (1982-1986) — contained specific goals and directions, but the fundamental policy behind the particulars was export-oriented industrialization and growth. Notably, all the plans exceeded those that came before (Kim 1992). The passion for *ppalli ppalli* drove the country to this remarkable accomplishment in such a short period of time.

Korea is currently the world's most wired nation with the highest per capita broadband penetration. Korea also ranked first among 192 countries in the UN Global e-Government Survey in 2010. "It can be said that *ppalli ppalli* still has an important role in driving Korea forward in the speedy twenty-first century" (H. Hwang 2010:452). Choi In-Hyuk[Choe In-hyeok] (2010:358), managing director of the Boston Consulting Group (BCG) in Korea, has made a similar observation: "The impatience of the Korean people, shaped by a history of compressed development and captured in the phrase *ppalli ppalli* (hurry, hurry), also had a significant impact. Korea is ten times faster than the U.S. in Internet downloading."

Whether properly called an ethos or not, *ppalli ppalli* is a well-institutionalized behavior that manifests itself in all kinds of activities that Koreans engage in. At times there has been a downside, though, to such a furious work ethic, as evidenced by two major accidents in the 1990s: the collapse of the hurriedly built bridge across the Hangang (Han River) and the collapse of the Sampoong Department Store in Seoul. Despite these regrettable events, the fast-paced work ethic in Korea is widely accepted as an ideal. Most Koreans believe that without it Korea never would have been able to catch up with its neighbors, particularly Japan. Thanks to this culture of hurry, Korea was able to achieve tremendous economic progress

and industrialization in a very short period of time. While Japan took nearly 100 years to become one of the world's top automobile manufacturers, Korea became internationally competitive with Japan in automobile sales in only fifty years (Kim 2007:264).

Origin of the "*ppalli ppalli*" ethos

Some may think that the Korean ethos of quickness is a recent historical development, particularly during the Japanese occupation and high economic growth period, for Korean Confucian gentlemen of the past were measured, methodical, and slow. There is evidence, however, that the hurried Korean culture of today is not a new phenomenon, but has its traditional roots in the Korea of the past. For instance, building and construction in the historic past were also completed ahead of schedule, as evidenced by the construction of Hwaseong in Suwon, Gyeonggi-do (Gyeonggi province), by the twenty-second king of the Joseon dynasty, Jeongjo (1776-1800). This 5.74 kilometers (3.59miles) stone wall with four gates and forty-four other structures, was originally supposed to be built in ten years, but it took only two years and nine months to complete. This happened in a period dominated by Confucianism. No one really knows, then, whether the hurried culture of Korea was established before the introduction of Confucian-oriented *yangban* (noble) culture. It might be that a tendency to rush coexisted with a contrary tendency as a paradox, a pattern in Korean culture.

Kuk Hŭng-ju (1986:117-119) hypothesizes that the urge to hurry comes from Korean ancestors who were horse-riding nomadic northern people (people of the Goguryeo dynasty, 37 BC-AD 668). Koreans became accustomed to making snap decisions on horseback while moving swiftly. Moreover, Koreans had been attacked so often by foreign enemies that they had grown accustomed to finishing everything quickly so they could flee invaders. Perhaps Koreans' preference for eat-on-the-run meals like *bibimbap* and *gukbap* comes from their ancestors' need to always be on the lookout.

Historical Circumstance and the Korean Ethos

The Korean ethos during the Japanese colonial era

A particular historical circumstance can be very influential in the formation of an ethos. This was clearly the case for Korea during the Japanese colonial period. The Japanese colonizers made efforts to describe the Korean ethos in papers such as "The Characteristic Features of the Korean People," issued by the Japanese Governor-General's Office in 1927, and "The Real Nature of the Korean People" and "The Causes of Ills," both written by Choe Nam-seon (1890-1957), a Korean historian and the author of the declaration of the 1919 March First Independent Movement in the 1930s. These works cited an array of supposed characteristics of the Korean people, too numerous to list in all, ranging from "emotional volatility to lack of public-mindedness." All of them are negative (Han 2003:16, 27). Collectively, the inventory of traits is no better than George Kennan's derogatory description of Korea and Koreans.[*]

Yi Kwang-su[Yi Gwang-su] (1892-1950), a well-known writer and cultural nationalist, summarized the Korean ethos (*minjokseong*) in *Gaebyeok* (Creation), a monthly magazine, under the title of "Treatise on the Reconstruction of the Nation (*Minjok Gaejoron*)" (Yi 1922:18-72). In that article, Yi "lashed out at the Korean tradition as an obstacle to progress, became a champion of individualism and free will,

---

[*] Kennan (1905), a well-known writer and intimate friend of President Theodore Roosevelt, is the source of the worst image of Korea presented to the Western world. He blasted Koreans as the "rotten product of a decayed Oriental Civilization" and suggested that Japan's takeover of all Korean affairs would be logical, for as a people Koreans were inferior to the Japanese. Before the Japanese protectorate treaty over Korea was signed on 17 November 1905, the United States, in a secret agreement between Roosevelt and Katsura, endorsed Japanese domination over Korea in exchange for a pledge from Japan not to harbor any aggressive designs on the Philippines. The defeated Russian government after the Russo-Japanese War (1904-1905) recognized Japan's paramount political, military, and economic interest in the Korean peninsula. Later, the Korean people learned that Kennan had been an impetus in the formation of the Taft-Katsura secret agreement on Korea (Choy 1979).

criticized early nationalist reformers for failing to maintain Korean independence, and encouraged capitalistic economic development as the basis for the rise of a middle class leadership" (Robinson 1988:67). Yi thought it was his responsibility as a leading intellectual of that troubling time to identify and condemn the shortcomings of the Korean national character so that it could be rectified, thus leading to national independence. But Yi's call to regain national independence by getting rid of harmful traditional traits was not fully acknowledged or appreciated by all Koreans, especially radical nationalists who advocated social revolution and overt resistance to Japanese colonialism. Condemning Yi's pro-Japanese stance, they criticized his depiction of the Korean ethos because it was made under the extraordinary circumstances of Japanese oppression and exploitation of Koreans as colonial subjects.

Major national crises and their impact on the Korean ethos

During the course of their history, Koreans have experienced major crises that have threatened their existence: Chinese domination, Mongol invasion, Japanese colonial rule, war mobilization on behalf of Japan during World War II, and the fratricidal Korean War. Koreans struggled to survive at these harrowing times, and this in turn influenced the formation of the Korean ethos.

Han Kyung-Koo[Han Gyeong-gu] (2000b) argues that because of their history, Koreans have developed a particular kind of mentality adept at surviving, adapting, and overcoming crises. The resulting modes of behavior include: 1) an emphasis on effectiveness over efficiency: employing any available means to accomplish a goal even if these means areit is improper and inefficient, in order to survive; 2) an attitude of "It's now or never": a belief that if something cannot be attained now, there will be no second chance; 3) a sojourner's mentality: instead of having long-range plans and pursuing a goal methodically, a task is carried out hastily even if it proves less profitable; 4) a belief that it is acceptable to violate existing rules

because employing the correct and legitimate procedure may result in losing out to others who use illegitimate means; 5) the development of factionalism to attract and assemble sympathizers and defeat opponents, which in turn fosters further factionalism. Many traits of the Korean ethos may have resulted from such crisis mindedness.

The liberation of Korea from Japan did not change, for some time, how the Korean ethos was negatively characterized. In the early 1960s, Lee O-young[Yi Eo-ryeong] (1963), a popular Korean writer and intellectual, enumerated a list of mostly negative Korean characteristics, such as feudalism, irrationalism, cowardice, and cruelty. However, in the revised fortieth anniversary edition of the book, published in 2002, "Lee changed many aspects of his position and reinterpreted the same cultural patterns and artifacts in a more positive way, justifying his former statements as well-intended criticisms to help Korean society achieve the goal of modernization and economic growth" (Han 2003:18). Yi Kyu-t'ae[Yi Gyu-tae] (1981) also listed mostly negative traits of the Korean ethos, including an inferiority complex, a disposition to conceal, introversion, fatalism, a tendency toward self-deprecation, and dependency. Lee's intention behind identifying such negative traits seems to have been the same as Yi Kwang-su's in 1922.

Generational character and ethos

A change in the traditional Korean ethos began in the 1980s with Korea's remarkable economic ascent. A new generation of Koreans appeared who had not been influenced by the negative traits that come with coping with crises. These new Koreans are probably best represented by the 386 generation, which is not only great in sheer numbers, but is also composed of people able to free themselves from the influence of old values and to resist old practices in the workplace. As Han Kyung-Koo (2000a: 355) has said, "We could perhaps discuss generational character, instead of national character."

While previous generations of Koreans could not escape the

old values and practices, and tended to perpetuate them, the 386 generation has shown a very different character. As Korea achieved economic affluence, there was some denouncing of young people for their carefree attitude and lifestyle of conspicuous consumption, but positive characteristics also began to emerge: self-confidence and pride, rallied by the slogan "We can do it." This transformation is described in a book by Yi Chang'u [Yi Jang-U] and Yi Min-hwa (2000), who use the metaphor *sinparam* (wind to describe this new attitude of doing things willingly, cheerfully, and going at tasks "like crazy"). Koreans and Japanese use the same Chinese characters to write this word, but it has different phonetic sounds and meanings in the two languages: in Korean, *sinparam* refers to the state of ecstasy that a shaman enters when possessed by a spirit: in Japanese, *kamikaze*, the divine wind, was credited in 1281 with saving Japan from attack by Mongols. Even if *sinparam* could be translated literally as "divine wind," its meaning would be closer to "elation" or "high spirits" in shamanistic *gut*[gut] (or ritual).*

Other aspects of this transformation in attitude have been pointed out by Han Kyung-Koo (2000a: 354): "To be unruly, hasty, disobedient, uncooperative, overly competitive, etc. is no longer considered bad; such qualities are now expected to make Koreans into creative, resourceful, and independent-minded workers suitable for venture industry in the rapidly changing future." When Korea was colonized by Japan in 1910, Confucianism was identified as a major cause of Korea's misfortune and came under heavy attack. Now, however, some native Korean scholars as well as foreign observers are reevaluating the role of Confucianism in the Korean ethos. Koreans' view of Confucianism is indeed confusing, contradictory, and inconsistent at times (Kim 1992).

---

* Daniel Tudor (2012:124) suggests that "*Sinparam* may have a Buddhist underpinning as well as shamanist one."

A new Korean ethos emerging as Korea changes

When I left Korea in the mid-1960s, it was a poor agrarian country with a per capita GDP of about one hundred dollars a year. Because of the poor state of the Korean economy and the low standard of living, during my early years in America I always felt uneasy and uncomfortable and often defensive. But within less than two decades, most Korean students who came to the American university where I taught were confident, self-assured, and even scornful of the poor facilities in a rural Tennessee college town. Most of them were well acquainted with Western manners. As a result, they lacked even a trace of the defensiveness I once felt.

Koreans' pride, their upbeat mood, and self-confidence as manifestations of the new Korean ethos were fully on display during the 2002 World Cup hosted jointly by Japan and Korea. As the Korean team kept defeating several strong European teams, millions of cheering supporters, called *Bulgeun Akma* (Red Devil), followed the team on and off the soccer field chanting "*Daehanminguk*" (the Great Han People's State or Republic of Korea), "*O, Pilseung Korea*" (Oh, victory Korea), and "*Urineun Hana*" (We are one). At the semifinal game, some 200,000 red-shirted cheering young people roared, shouting these slogans, and at least 7 million Koreans poured out into the streets all over the country to cheer for the soccer team. Amazingly, there were practically no mishaps as the multitudes gathered spontaneously to celebrate. After the cheering was over, the participants even picked up the litter, cleaning the streets themselves.

Shin Gi-wook[Shin Gi-wuk] (2006) describes similar rallies held overseas by Koreans in the Staples Center in Los Angeles, in the city center of Paris, and at the Korean embassies in Germany and in the Netherlands. Over 5.6 million overseas Koreans expressed their pride in being ethnic Korean. The fervor over the World Cup, according to Shin, was not simply about soccer, but was an expression of Koreans' pride, identity, and confidence. More recently, most Koreans were not able attend the XXX London Olympic Games. But during

the quarterfinal match between Korea and Great Britain, Koreans cheered in several city squares in Korea. The South Korean team defeated Great Britain's team and went on to win a bronze medal. The character that Koreans displayed during the World Cup and the Olympics does not sound like one that is "hard to move emotionally" (as the Japanese Governor-General's office put it in 1927), nor does it resemble "weak willpower," "lack of confidence," or "lack of pride" (as Choe Nam-seon wrote in 1930), nor, for that matter, does it seem to partake of "inferiority" or "fatalism" (Yi Kyu-t'ae wrote in the 1970s and 1980s).

Clearly, new traits have emerged in the nature of Koreans, replacing or merging with older ones, though some older traits and characterizations still persist today. Each period in history has contributed to the sum total of Korean heritage. In addition to the emergence of the new ethos, some traits have been reinterpreted at different times. Aspects of the Korean ethos can be grouped into three categories: contradictory patterns, diminishing traditional patterns, and faithfully persisting patterns.

Current status of the study of ethos

Ethos was once a popular subject in anthropology in the 1930s, 1940s, and even the early 1950s, mostly taken up by psychologically oriented anthropologists with an interest in national character (Benedict 1946; Gorer 1949; Mead 1951, 1953, 1962; Mead and Metraux 1953). However, the popularity of national character studies faded after the war, and recent anthropology textbooks do not even include the subject in their indices (Hsu 1979:528).

It is difficult to characterize the ethos of a nation like America because its racial, ethnic, and cultural diversity is so great that generalizations do not easily obtain. There is another, more general pitfall in conceptualizing ethos: the tendency to treat characteristics as if they were synchronic without considering their historical origins and alterations over time. Nevertheless, Francis L. K. Hsu (1979:528), a Manchurian-born American anthropologist, interested in

psychological anthropology, recognized "a new urgency for studies of national character," as business and industries become increasingly global. A growing number of multinational corporations have shown a keen interest in contrasting values cross-culturally (Ferraro 1998:88-114; Reeves-Elington 1999:5-13; Serrie 1999:35-41; Young 2000:13-17). In the late 1980s in Korea, a new type of *Hanguginnon* (discourse on the Koreanness of the Koreans) developed as a form of cultural nationalism (Han 2003: 25), marked by an effort to revitalize the national community by creating, maintaining, and strengthening the nation-state's cultural identity (Han 2003; Kim 1998; Yoshino 1992).

The Paradox of the Korean Ethos

Michael Breen (2004:17) has noted that "Koreans have a way of upsetting you and getting into your heart at the same time." He observed that most Koreans credit *jaebeol* (big business conglomerates) with having built the country and with providing employment opportunities for millions. But, at the same time, these companies are resented. "The corrupt collusion with politicians, speculation in real estate, and domination of their local markets create an impression of capitalist greed and murky hands controlling the country" (Breen 2004:147). It appears that Korean patterns of contradictory formal values are often quite acceptable and may even be regarded as praiseworthy.

Values unhurried calmness, yet craves fast results

The prime example of such contradictory currents can be illustrated with *ppalli ppalli*. Paul Crane (1978:13) reports that he had difficulty understanding "what the Koreans really think," adding that, "the Oriental has had a distorted reputation for being inscrutable and impossible for Westerners to understand." I have lived in the American South for as long as Crane has lived in Korea, and just

as Crane had difficulty understanding Koreans, I had difficulty understanding southerners and have come to the conclusion that they are inscrutable (Kim 1977).

If anyone from Mars had visited Korea during the Joseon dynasty and observed a Confucian gentleman and his mannerisms, the Martian would have concluded that Korean behavior was not hasty and never seemed hurried. Instead, the Martian would have seen Koreans as slowly and gracefully moving through life, a polite and gentle people. Crane (1978:16) depicts the unhurried, calm, and quiet behavior of a typical Confucian *yangban* gentleman astutely. He points out that a hurried culture was not only denigrated by Confucians but by traditional scholars and farmers as well. In early childhood, Koreans of my generation—who are now seventy years or older—were instructed repeatedly not to run, dash, or hurry, but to walk as cautiously and slowly as possible. A hurried culture was interpreted as rash, imprudent, and, most damning of all, "un-Confucian." Times have changed, however, and so have Korean patterns of behavior.

An inclusive worldview with exclusive "oneness"

If we define the word "inclusiveness" as "the act of incorporating or attitude of wishing to be incorporated," this trait is prominent in Korean families, kin groups, and other socially defined groups (Hsu 1965:638-661). Koreans extend the family group concept not only to their immediate family but to the entire kin group to which they belong. Loyalty goes first and foremost to the immediate family, then to known blood relatives, and then to lineage and clan (Crane 1978:32). To Koreans, a kinship network based on blood ties (*hyeoryeon*) is of the utmost importance. However, Koreans extend the boundaries of inclusiveness to school ties, modeled on the pattern of kinship ties. The bonds among school classmates and alumni (*haggyeon*) are very intimate and strong. The intimate connections among those who have the same region (*jiyeon*) are equally important and solid.

Classmates and schoolmates are obliged to look after one another when in need. For instance, the 1961 coup d'état led by Major General Park Chung-hee was initially carried out largely by members of the eighth class of the Korean Military Academy. In addition to classmates, the relationships among alumni, especially between seniors (*seonbae*) who graduated ahead of juniors (*hubae*) from the same school, are analogous to kin relationships between older and younger brothers (or sisters), and schoolmates actually address each other using the terms "older" and "younger" brother (or sister). When school and regional ties overlap, this combined bond becomes even stronger than kinship ties, and interpersonal relationships are indeed inclusive. It has been recognized that in the Korean business world, school connections, regional ties, and kinship networks influence not only the formation of power groups at the top but also the formation of informal relations and cliques at all organizational levels (Lee 1989:156-157).

Some people are critical of appointments to elite government positions for "in-group members" with ties of kinship, region, alma mater, or even church membership. As an example, after Lee Myung-bak[**Yi Myeong-bak**] won the 2007 election, and was sworn in as the seventeenth president of Korea in 2008, some criticized him, saying he had filled important government posts with members of the so-called "Ko-So-Young[**Go So-yeong**] (pronounced the same as the name of a famous actress)" group. The "Ko" stands for "Korea (Goryeo) University," Lee's alma mater; "So" is an abbreviation for the Presbyterian Somang Church, where Lee and his family were members and he was an elder; and "Young" is short for Yeongnam, the southeastern region of the Korean peninsula where Lee is from. I am not in any position to prove or disprove this accusation of favoritism, but Koreans sometimes resent the same network connections they respect in other circumstances.

As for Koreans' behavior toward outsiders with whom they do not share some common tie, Lee Kwang-kyu[**Yi Gwang-gyu**] (2003:275),

a Korean cultural anthropologist, observes, "To someone they do not know, members of an intimate circle tend to show attitudes and behaviors that are cold, unkind, unpleasant, and rude." Similarly, British Catholic priest Clifford E. J. Smart (1978:117-123), who has lived in Korea since 1956, says, "Koreans are kind in treating strangers when they visit their homes[within their fence], but outside the fence of their boundary or on the street, their attitude toward strangers is different. They pretend not to know them, and even ignore the strangers." Breen (2004:52) points out that "there is no guilt about behaving unfairly or rudely towards someone who is outside . . . Koreans can be extremely rude towards non-persons[outsiders]. . . The Koreans can also be extremely cruel to non-persons." In short, Koreans can be xenophobic. In the past, before Korea became more multiethnic and multiracial in the 2000s, a xenophobic attitude toward foreigners or outsiders was evident in Korean society's institutionalized discrimination against children of mixed marriages.

While it cannot be condoned, Korean xenophobia is the result of countless foreign invasions and serial domination by hostile neighbors. Korean uneasiness with outsiders and hostility toward strangers and foreigners is an understandable, if not ultimately excusable, byproduct of a long history punctuated by oppression and occupation. Recent Korean attitudes toward foreigners, especially toward foreign brides, have changed. I will comment on this when I discuss multiculturalism later.

Remarkable endurance, explosive impatience
("*naembi*" or "thin-pan" culture)

Crane (1978: 96), for one, has praised Koreans for their endurance: "One of the great virtues of many Koreans is their ability to endure hardship. Korea is the land of those who have learned to endure in order to survive." The geopolitics of the Korean peninsula has long made the country vulnerable to attacks. In addition to invasion and domination by Chinese dynasties over the centuries, including the

Chinese People's Volunteers (CPV) in the Korean War, there have been repeated intrusions by nomadic northern tribes such as the Khitan, Jurchen, and Mongols. Two full-scale Japanese invasions of Korea initiated by Toyotomi Hideyoshi in the late sixteenth century devastated the peninsula and eventually led to Korea's annexation by Japan in 1910.

When Korea lived under Japanese rule from 1910 to 1945, Japan tried to eliminate Korean culture and assimilate Koreans into Japanese culture. Although Koreans adopted some external traits from the Japanese that fit into traditional Korean patterns, they rejected most manners and customs that were distinctly Japanese. Despite the invasions by Chinese, Mongols, and others, "Koreans have remained true to their own culture and patterns of thought as developed through the centuries" (Crane 1978:125).

Not only has Korea as a nation demonstrated endurance, but Koreans as individuals have exhibited remarkable endurance under the tragic circumstances of family division and dispersal before, during, and after the Korean War. Although some separated couples have since remarried others, a great many have not done so for over some sixty years, choosing instead to remain estranged, effectively single, yet hopeful of someday reuniting with their loved ones (Kim 1988a).

Until recently, Koreans tended to accept misfortunes and sufferings as fate. Fate is understood to be a destiny beyond one's own power to control. A few writers view fatalism as a Korean characteristic (Gibson 1978; Hong 1975; T. Kim 1977; Poitras 1978; Ti 1978; Yun 1971). Others find the origins of fatalistic belief in shamanism (I. Kim 1980). In Korea, endurance, if not fatalism or predetermination, has traditionally been considered a virtue; impatience, by contrast, is thought to be "a major sin" (Crane 1978:97). Nevertheless, in a contradictory manner, Koreans display explosive impatience in their rushed and hurried culture.

When it comes to Korean impatience, there is a widely circulated saying that Koreans are like a "thin frying pan" that gets hot easily

and cools off quickly. Koreans can get mad and upset easily, but they usually forget or soon forgive. In my own experience living in the United States, Americans tend to wait in long lines dutifully and patiently without complaining, as long as the line is maintained in an orderly fashion; Koreans, by contrast, tend to grow impatient when having to wait in line, so they make every effort to keep the line short. This sometimes leads to disorderly queues.

According to Breen (2004:27), Koreans are not trained to think in a sufficiently rational and legalistic way; even "Korean negotiators in international forums make themselves look rather silly and end up making emotional appeals rather than reasoned arguments." He sums up Koreans in this way: Koreans are the "Irish of the East. . . . They are as vigorous in their character and the defense of their identity as the Israelis, and as chaotically attractive as the Italians . . . like the Irish, the Koreans are also a lyrical people, inclined to the spiritual, and exhibiting a warmth and hospitality that belies their violent image. They can be unrestrained in their passions, quick to cry and to laugh" (Breen 2004:35). One of the nicest aspects of Koreans is that they are not raised to feel that displays of emotion are a weakness. They push themselves to study and succeed. At the same time, they can be embarrassingly earthy and blunt.

According to Crane, in expressing emotion as well as in interpersonal relationships, *gibun* (feeling or state of mind) is one of the most important factors influencing conduct and relations with others. Crane (1978:25) points out, "This rich word has no true English equivalent. 'Mood' may come close but much more is involved. When the *gibun* is good, one 'feels like a million dollars,' when bad, one 'feels like eating worms.'" One's bodily functions are largely dependent on the state of one's *gibun*. If the *gibun* is good, then one functions smoothly and easily. If the *gibun* is upset, then functions may come to a complete halt. The way Koreans display emotion toward others in interpersonal relationships is governed largely by the state of the *gibun*.

Diminishing Traditional Ethos

Several traits of the traditional Korean ethos, once obvious and dominant, have begun to change or disappear in response to broad changes in Korea. Though now diminished, they deserve mention.

From politeness and humility to the "can do" spirit of self-confidence.
Crane (1978:51), an American southerner himself, who lived in Korea for more than twenty-two years, compared Koreans and American southerners and remarked that, "In the remote mountain village, one will find gracious manners practiced unconsciously. Etiquette is observed in the humblest home as well as in the compounds of the great. The exquisite niceties of a cultured Korean make even an American Southern Gentleman 'seem crude and barbaric.'"

Koreans are known to be polite, kind, and humble to others. There is a Korean proverb about "three unworthy, uncivilized, and uncultured persons (*sambulchul*)": one who brags about himself, one who praises his children in front of others, and one who boasts about his wife. Even if one's accomplishments are outstanding, one has to show humility, which is regarded as a virtue and ideal trait in traditional Korean society. At meals where guests are present, the host sits at the lowliest place at the table, farthest from the place of honor, and always claims to have "prepared nothing" even when the food is the most lavish the host can afford.

Such things are changing, though, as Korea becomes a competitive society. After Korea adopted a democratic electoral system, candidates must now mount a campaign and promote themselves in order to get elected. Since Korea is no longer a society of limited mobility, where everyone knew everyone else living in the same area, someone who today runs for office must introduce him- or herself to the constituency and work to win people's confidence. As a result, some tend to brag about themselves, whether intentionally or not. This new phenomenon is reinforced by the "can do" spirit inspired by President Park Chung-hee and by the remarkable sense of self-confidence that

has come from building a powerhouse economy from the ashes of a civil war.

From inward worldview to outward effort. The first Western anthropologist to conduct anthropological fieldwork in Korea, Cornelius Osgood (1951), observed that Koreans are passive and inner directed. Edward Poitras (1978) goes further by implying that such inner directedness has encouraged Koreans to feel a strong attachment to their home country even after they emigrate, so they remain "aliens" rather than citizens of their new countries. Yi Kyu-t'ae (1981, vol. I: 297-338) agrees with this view that inwardness is at the core of Korean cultural patterns. Such inwardness can even be seen in tool-making. While American-made handsaws cut wood when one pushes outward, Korean-made handsaws cut when one pulls inward toward oneself. Koreans opt to use this metaphor: "The arms naturally bend inward" (*Pareun aneuro gupneunda*).

Because of this inward thinking, Koreans are strongly attached to their hometowns. Until recently, Koreans rushed home during the holidays with the same intensity that American workers rush to the parking lot after five o'clock. Furthermore, people like to be laid to rest in their hometown, even if the buried token is no more than a broken piece of tooth, a lock of hair, or a pair of shoes they once wore.

This characteristic of inwardness is also shared by China and Japan. Korea was forced to broaden its perspective when foreign attacks resulted in a Korean diaspora. Recently, however, Koreans have been expanding their sphere of interaction voluntarily toward the outside world through diplomatic missions, business expatriates, students, overseas missionaries, and by expanding free-trade agreements with forty-five countries, thereby making Korea the third largest territorial sphere for free economic trade. Perhaps Koreans, long characterized by inwardness, are on their way to becoming one of the most outward-looking people in the world.

From a prohibitive norm-oriented pattern to a permissive norm-oriented one. Classic anthropological studies show that in a traditional society, norms are prohibitive or constraining, but in a modern society they are permissive by providing alternatives (Redfield 1947). Some anthropologists consider this dichotomized explanation too simplified (O. Lewis 1966), but such a comparison does seem to hold true when looking at how Korean society has evolved. Many Koreans of the older generation vividly remember being taught under the strict rule of prohibitive norms: "don't do this" and "that is not to be done." Such a child-rearing practice often resulted in blind obedience to parents, seniors, and supervisors. Vincent Brandt (1971:173) has observed that when children are punished, beaten, or slapped, "it is usually for disobedience rather than wrongdoing."

As Brandt reports, Korean children are encouraged to be dependent, obedient, and cooperative, which differs from European and American norms. In America, most families enforce scheduled feeding and a fixed bedtime, but in Korea, until recent times, children tend to stay up as late as they wish at night until they fall asleep from exhaustion. As a step toward becoming self-reliant, North American children sleep alone in separate rooms according to a bedtime schedule. Korean children, however, go to bed with their parents. Such a practice might satisfy the children emotionally, but it promotes great dependency on the parents, the mother in particular, and inhibits the formation of self-reliance. On a social level, Korean children have been brought up to be so obedient that they are reluctant to speak their minds to superiors at work, which discourages feedback.

Recently, however, this prohibitive norm is becoming more permissive. There are many plausible explanations for this change, but a major contributor is improvement in the Korean standard of living. A growing number of urban middle-class people can afford to have a separate room for children, in keeping with Western child-rearing practices. In such cases, while many parents still prefer to

sleep on an *ondol* floor, almost all children sleep on beds. The *ondol* is a unique heating arrangement of flues conducting warm air from the cooking fire through pipes under the floors to heat the house.

Another factor contributing to the development of a permissive pattern is the small number of children in contemporary Korean families. Since Korea is a nation with one of the lowest birth rates in the world, children are considered extremely precious. Parents do not treat children the way the older generation did years ago in the days of overpopulation. Parents' obsessive and slavish concern for their children's welfare has turned them into dedicated "servants" of the children. Nowadays, it appears that Korean parents are less firm in disciplining their children than previous generations, becoming instead excessively protective and indulgent.

Many of today's Korean mothers tend to think that imposing prohibitive norms on their children would discourage their *gi* (exultant spirit). As a consequence, some children quickly learn that they can abuse permissive norms, taking advantage of them for their own self-interest. Contemporary Korean parents seem to be even more permissive than their Western counterparts.

Persisting Patterns

While some traditional Korean patterns have changed, altered, or been replaced with emergent ones, other traditional patterns persist. These remaining Korean norms are an emphasis on education, a burning desire to realize or relieve *han* (unfulfilled wishes and desires), the emotional display of *gibun*, and the pattern of seeking to outdo others (one-upmanship).

Emphasis on education. Although educational opportunities were once limited to certain privileged groups such as aristocratic families and the *yangban*, beginning in the Three Kingdoms period (57 BC-AD 668) Koreans recognized the importance of education as key to improving social and economic standing in society. The

Koreans' respect for education has not simply persisted over time; it has intensified as Korea has increasingly become an international presence and economic power.

A burning desire to overcome "han." Although a perfect translation of the Korean word *han* into English is impossible, "unfulfilled wishes and desire" comes close. Some scholars who are quite competent in both Korean and English have attempted to translate the word *han* into English, but the translations do not come to close to the original nuance of native Korean usage. Laurel Kendall (1988:8) translates it as "unfulfilled desires," Hesung Chun Koh**[Jeon Hye-seong]** (1983:170) suggests it is "a haunting sense of regret," and Carter Eckert (1990:400) offers yet another translation as "catalytic bitterness and anger." Michael Breen (2004:38) elaborates on the meaning of *han* as "a kind of rage and helplessness that is sublimated, and lingers like an inactive resentment."

The burning desire to realize or relieve *han* has served as a major force driving Koreans to accomplish things in a short period of time. To maintain a decent way of life, persistent hunger and poverty have to be eliminated. *Han* with respect to material goods has been relieved for many Koreans by economic gain.

Gibun. An adequate translation of the Korean word *gibun* (feeling, mood, or state of mind) into English may be as difficult as *han*, but *gibun* is of prime importance in influencing conduct and relations with other people. If *gibun* is good, everything goes smoothly and easily, but if *gibun* is bad, even ordinary tasks become impossible. If one damages the *gibun* of others in personal relations, nothing can be accomplished. One American businessman told me that in dealing with the chairman of a large Korean business firm, he did not have to attend the second and third scheduled meetings because the Korean chairman could foresee everything that was going to happen if his *gibun* was good, including the final outcome. When one's *gibun* is

bad, one is "justified in behaving badly, rejecting business proposals, barking at your wife and secretary" (Breen 2004:39).

Most of all, possessing good *gibun* gives one enormous power to drive forward beyond ordinary physical limits. Recent Korean economic prosperity has come so quickly because of Korean haste supported by rising *gibun*. Indeed, according to Crane (1978:25), who is very perceptive about Korean patterns of *gibun*, "In interpersonal relationships, keeping the *gibun* in good order often takes precedence over other consideration."

Injeong or jeong *(abbreviation of injeong).* An accurate translation of the Korean word *jeong* (or *injeong*) into English is as difficult as for *han* and *gibun*, if not harder. If any foreigner can understand the meaning of that word with the same intensity as the natives do, he or she could fully understand Koreans' warmest and kindest feelings toward others. I have made every effort to find a good definition that is close to the original Korean word, but I have not yet been able to find one. Daniel Tudor (2012), who once even taught English to Korean students, instead of offering his own translation, quoted various definitions offered by others: "an invisible hug that brings people together," and "feelings of fondness, caring, bonding, and attachment that develop within interpersonal relationships" (Tudor 2012:93). One foreigner who lived in Korea for many years told me that he has been living in Korea so long because he has been fascinated with the "gluey" Korean *jeong*. Boyé De Mente (2012:151) describes *jeong* as "personal affection and compassion." Nonetheless, such a translation may not be sufficient.

Outdoing one another *(one-upmanship).* Koreans were good at learning Chinese characters before they invented their own written language, *Hangeul,* in 1446. They also adopted Chinese ethical and religious creeds such as Confucianism, Taoism, and Buddhism. Beginning in the late eighteenth century, in willy-nilly fashion Koreans adopted

Christianity and some aspects of Japanese culture, even though it was forced on them.

After liberation, through intensive contact with the United States, Koreans became knowledgeable about American political, academic, economic, business, and military affairs. For instance, Hyundai Construction Company, one of Korea's major conglomerates, became a world-class construction company by learning how to win contracts for U.S. Army barracks construction and airport expansion and bridge-building projects during wartime. Koreans then transferred the skills and knowledge they acquired from these projects to the Middle East and other parts of the world (Jones and Sakong 1980: 356-358).

Not only have Koreans been good students of other cultures; they have also been good teachers, transferring knowledge learned from other cultures to other countries. Japan has been a major beneficiary of Korean teaching on Buddhism and various arts associated with Buddhism and Neo-Confucianism. In early Japanese culture, "Chinese cultural influence had been imported by way of Korea for centuries and the Chinese script used for records from 400 onwards," writes Arthur Cotterell (1993:62). During the reign of Shōtoku (574-622), who laid the foundations for the Japanese state. Cotterell (1993:64) further states, "That something akin to the Korean nobility should exist in early Japan is likely, considering the close relations between them. Nearly a third of the Japanese nobility had ancestors who were originally refugees from Korean states."

Once Koreans learn foreign religions and ideologies, they excel at proliferating the borrowed culture and often outdo its originators. Korean perpetuation and development of Confucianism, Buddhism, Christianity, communism, and capitalism are among the most telling examples. Koreans have shown themselves to be more Confucian than the Chinese in their devotion to Confucianism, particularly Neo-Confucianism (Janelli and Yim 1982:177; Osgood 1951:332: Peterson 1974:28). Korea has enthusiastically embraced Christianity. As for communism, North Korea remains one of a very few countries still

true to communism, along with Cuba, even after the fall of the Soviet Union. And South Korean capitalism can be seen as second to none.

I hope that my effort in this chapter to characterize and historicize the Korean ethos may whet readers' appetite to learn more about Korea's history, ethnic and racial makeup, sociopolitical and economical development, and present popular culture. It is to these subjects that I turn my attention in the chapters to come.

2
Ethnic Origins of Koreans

Every once in a while I was asked by American colleagues at the university where I used to teach whether I could identify the nationality of East Asians—Chinese, Japanese, or Koreans—just by looking at them. In order to spark a lively conversation, I used to say, "Although I might not be able to provide any definite way of discerning them, I think I might be able to tell fairly well when I see an East Asian" (Kim 2007:125-126). This is analogous to an astute remark made by former U.S. Justice Potter Stewart when he was asked to distinguish between "art" and "obscenity." Steward answered, "Although I couldn't rightfully define obscenity, I know it when I see it" (Wallace and Mangan 1996:17). Nevertheless, I have to confess that it is difficult to judge by appearance alone, for some Koreans have features more similar to Chinese than to fellow Koreans. For instance, Francis L. K. Hsu (1909-1999), a Manchurian-born anthropologist and my former mentor, used to comment to me, "You and I look more alike than any other fellow Chinese and I. Your ancestors and my ancestors might have belonged to the same tribe." It was a casual remark, yet it provokes curiosity about the origins of East Asians in general, and Koreans in particular.

In spite of the complexity of determining nationality by appearance, East Asians do seem to belong to different physical groups. Sarah M. Nelson (1993:6) states that "Koreans as a people can be distinguished as a physical type, different from the Japanese and Chinese. Physical comparison of many kinds, including blood types

and fingerprints, show the Koreans to be related to their neighbors, but possessing their own distinctive patterns of gene frequencies." Perhaps the following survey of the prehistory of the Korean peninsula is somewhat anthropological, but it seems the best way to address the origins of the Korean people.

Indeed, any effort to trace the ethnic origins of Koreans on the Korean peninsula—who they were and when they arrived—may not be an easy task. Although Sarah M. Nelson surmises that the Korean peninsula was inhabited by its earliest settlers half a million years ago, whether contemporary Koreans are the descendants of these early inhabitants remains an unanswered question. Nelson (1993:267) states that many of the hypotheses and propositions about Korean ethnic origins sound like "fairy tales."

The matter is more confusing still when one explores ancestry in relation to the modern nation-state. Lothar von Falkenhausen has asked, when we speak of Korea, "What territory do we mean?" (Nelson 1993:1). The prehistoric inhabitants of East Asia did not have the same territorial boundaries that exist today. Their sphere of occupancy stretched from the eastern border of Mongolia via Manchuria, a northern part of China proper, into central Japan. Even the word *Asia* may be irrelevant, for people were in the region long before that designation was introduced (Kim 2011b). Indeed, there are more questions about the earliest inhabitants of the Korean peninsula than there are definitive answers. Furthermore, since I am attempting to trace Korea's prehistory and ethnic roots over half a million years in a single chapter, I have to be ruthlessly selective and parsimoniously brief in my description.

The Early History of Korea

Prehistoric Korea and the origins of Korean ethnicity

Some archaeologists have traced the origins of the inhabitants

of the Korean peninsula to a mass migration from the Lake Baikal region to the north. However, there is no definite and direct evidence to support the single migration theory from the north (Choe 1991; Nelson 1993). Some physical anthropologists and archaeologists, such as Na Se-jin (1963), have studied the physical traits of present-day Koreans, including the cranium index, epicanthic fold, and skin color, for comparison. However, Choe Chong-Pil[Choe Jeong-pil] (1991) indicates that the division of the populations of any species into biological 'races' tends to be arbitrary; thus, particular physical traits cannot delineate the boundaries between ethnic groups. New traits were introduced to the Korean peninsula gradually and proliferated into many strands over thousands of years. From a physical and archaeological standpoint, there is not enough evidence to reach solid conclusions about the origins of Koreans on the peninsula.

Tracing aspects of Korean culture, including the Korean language and traditions, may shed light on Korean ethnicity, although some Chinese cultural influences are prominent and profound, as Lee Hi-seung[Yi Hui-seung] (1963:13-16) has shown. As Sarah M. Nelson (1993:6) indicates, "The Korean language is a prime example of both the distinctiveness of the peninsula from nearby lands and the relative homogeneity within." Korean is spoken as the primary language of the entire population, and dialect differences are minor across the peninsula. The Korean and Chinese languages are entirely different and unrelated, even though Korean vocabulary has been enriched by Chinese loan words. There is, however, an affinity between the Korean and Japanese languages. They are comparable in grammatical structure, but their vocabulary similarities are largely based on Chinese loan words (Befu 1971; Miller 1980).

Other ethnographic evidence sheds additional light on the origins of Korean ethnicity and its continuity. Anthropologists have recently traced a particularly potent symbol of personal and group identity by describing and analyzing certain foods (Wilk 1999:244-255). Some archaeologists use beverages such as beer to denote ethnic identity

(Farnsworth 2000; Wilkie and Farnsworth 1999). *Kimchi*, a traditional Korean dish, is a food that can be used to trace Korean ethnic identity (Kim 2000). There are several other ethnographic clues to Korean identity, all of which have been corroborated by archaeological findings. These include clothing, hairstyles, dwellings, straw sandals, and the *jige*, a device for carrying loads on the back.

This chapter begins by dividing Korean prehistory into the Paleolithic (the Old Stone Age, from 300,000-350,000 BC to 10,000 BC), the Neolithic (the New Stone Age, from 10,000BC to 1,500 BC), the Bronze Age (from the dawn of civilization, i.e., around the 15th century BC), and the early tribal kingdom, with brief discussions of each.

The Paleolithic period or the Old Stone Age
(from 300,000-350,000 BC to 10,000 BC)

Although it is accepted that the Korean peninsula was inhabited by its earliest settlers half a million years ago, the most recent archeological findings in Gyeonggi-do indicate that it was inhabited by Paleolithic people between 300,000 to 350,000 years ago at the earliest (Bae 2002). Findings from Paleolithic sites uncovered since the 1980s have yielded various stone tools used to hunt animals and to process the vegetal resources of deciduous forest. Shelters unearthed indicate that these early inhabitants lived in small foraging groups consisting of extended families. Their largest social unit seems to have been the band.

Although the remains of artifacts made during the Paleolithic period are relatively rich, human remains, except for a few pieces of broken bone, are limited. Human remains from a Paleolithic site in North Korea excavated in 1986 have been dated to about 200,000 years ago and appear to be Mongoloid. However, some other human remains, including a skull, lower jaw, pelvis, humerus, and femur—uncovered at a Paleolithic site in Mandal-ri, near Pyeongyang in North Korea—of an adult estimated to be 25 to 30 years old had the "long skull" characteristic of a Caucasoid (B. Kim 1994:91). This

Paleolithic Stone Tools

archaeological finding suggests that the Korean peninsula was inhabited not only by Mongoloid peoples but by Caucasoid peoples as well. Both racial groups appeared to have lived side by side.

Prior to the 1900s, such an interpretation of archaeological evidence would not have been seriously entertained by native scholars. Only with the rising popularity of multiculturalism beginning in the 2000s would such theorizing gain some credence. Yet, even with more archaeological sites revealing evidence of a Caucasoid population on the peninsula, no one can yet say with certainty that contemporary Koreans can trace an ancestral lineage to a Caucasoid population once inhabiting the Korean peninsula

(Lee 1984). After all, no one knows whether Paleolithic foragers on the peninsula metamorphosed into villagers or whether a new group of pottery producers migrated from the north, bringing with them an advanced foraging technology.

The Neolithic or New Stone Age via the Mesolithic period
(from 10,000 BC to 1,500 BC)

Before the Paleolithic period ended and the Neolithic period began, a relatively short Mesolithic period, known for the advent of "broad spectrum food collecting" occurred in parts of the Old World beginning around 12,000 BC. During this time, humans availed themselves of a wide variety of food sources. In the past, some historians expressed skepticism about the existence of a Mesolithic period in Korea (Eckert et al. 1990:3). However, recent archaeological findings indicate that on the peninsula there had been a Mesolithic culture some 10,000 years ago with a settled village life (Choe and Bale 2002).

As the Mesolithic turned into the Neolithic, the settled village (sedentary life) appeared around 6000-2000 BC. It was characterized by *Jeulmun* or "combware," a type of incised pottery whose exterior is decorated with geometric patterns. The term is used generally to describe the first 4,000 years or so of settled villages in Korea, analogous to the Jōmon in Japan's chronology. According to Kim Byung-mo[Gim Byeong-mo] (1994:92), inhabitants of the Korean peninsula during this period might be ancestors of modern Koreans; these Paleoasians had both Mongoloid and Caucasoid characteristics. The Ainu of the northern tip of Japan, the natives of Sakhalin, and the Eskimos of the eastern coast of Siberia are all descendants of these Paleoasian tribes.

The combined data on flora and fauna, artifacts (including stone hoes, stone sickles, and pottery), and dwellings indicate that the Neolithic inhabitants practiced horticulture, had stable residences, and possessed the ability to store food. There are some speculations regarding their

social organization and belief systems, but no archaeological findings substantiate any of these conjectures. According to Choe Chong-Pil and Martin Bale (2002:96), "The stone-bronze-iron age sequence was created for European prehistory, where pottery, ground stone tool-making technology, sedentism, and agriculture are elements of the Neolithic cultural complex." During the Neolithic period, networks of trade and other interactions were probably limited to the region.

The Bronze Age as the dawn of civilization
(beginning in the fifteenth century BC)

The Bronze Age, synonymous with "civilization" on the Korean peninsula, was believed to begin around the fifteenth century BC, although some historians such as Carter J. Eckert and his associates (1990) consider the date to be later. Cultural achievements of Korea in the Bronze Age were not as sophisticated as those of the Xia and Shang dynasties of China. However, the essential characteristics of Bronze Age culture were well displayed. Most notably, the era was marked by intensive agriculture, possibly rice cultivation. In older archaeological accounts, rice cultivation in Korea was dated to around 1200 BC (W. Kim 1982), but now the dates are assumed to be earlier, around 2400 or 2100 BC (Choe 1991). Some archaeologists believe that rice was probably brought from south China across the Yellow Sea to southern Korea (Nelson 1993); others, such as Kim Byung-mo (2008), contend that it was introduced from the south, most likely from Southeast Asia. Kim hypothesizes that it was people from South and/or Southeast Asia who came to Korea and introduced the necessary techniques for cultivating rice.

While some archaeologists, such as Nelson (1993:163), are skeptical about a southern route for the introduction of rice, owing to inconclusive archaeological evidence, Kim Byung-mo (2006, vol.1:50-53; 2008:44) points to linguistic evidence of a possible South Asian connection: identical phonemes in certain words related to rice cultivation in the Korean language and India's Dravidian language,

spoken by over 220 million people—the majority of whom are from southern India and parts of eastern and central India as well as northeastern Sri Lanka. For example, the Korean words *byeo*, raw rice still bearing husks, *ssal*, rice without husks, *ssi*, meaning "seed," and *garae*, referring to a tool for tilling soil have parallels in the Dravidian words. Kim has listed about four hundred likely cognates between the two languages.

Another possible sign of an influx of Southeast Asians can be seen in the distribution of dolmens, a cultural characteristic of southern, not northern, peoples. It seems certain that some southern people came as a large group to the Korean peninsula and established contact with Korean and southern and southeastern peoples of Asia. Also, the remains of dolmens suggest that Caucasians once lived on the Korean peninsula.

According to Kim Byung-mo (2006, vol.I:22-25), in 1965, when archaeologists excavated skeletal remains under a dolmen at a site in Chungcheongbuk-do, the remains were first identified as belonging to a forty-year-old male with a "long skull" with a cephalic index of 66.3 (in contrast with the Korean average of 81.5). It was speculated that this person lived around 410 BC. Despite the fact that the skull bore Caucasoid characteristics, the prevailing belief in the academy at the time was a single-ethnic nationalism, and the excavation team was reluctant to contradict the conventional view that the Korean peninsula was never home to Caucasians. So, researchers simply labeled the remains Hwangseok-ri Man (*Hwangseok-ri in*), after the site where they were found. Recently, however, anatomist Cho Yong-jin[Jo Yong-jin], professor at Seoul National University of Education(Seoul Gyodae), reconstructed the skull using digital technology. He concluded that Hwangseok-ri Man was Caucasian. Also, Cho recognized that contemporary inhabitants living in the same area have skulls similar to Hwangseok-ri Man (Kim 2011b:5).

Recently, a mitochondrial DNA (mtDNA) study of forty-five individuals from seven ethnic groups in East Asia showed that

Koreans appear to be more closely related overall to Korean-Chinese and Manchurians than to Han Chinese (Kim & Kim 2005). In 2009, some ninety scientists from ten countries, including Mahmood Ameen Abdulla, at the Singapore-based Human Genome Organization (HUGO) Pan Asian SNP Consortium, published the results of their research on human genetic diversity in *Science* (2009:1541-1545), focusing on Southeast Asian and East Asian populations. The results of the study showed that genetic ancestry strongly correlates with linguistic affiliations and geography. More than 90 percent of East Asian haplotypes could be found in either Southeast Asian or Central Asian populations and show a clinal structure with haplotype diversity decreasing from south to north. This study provides another piece of scientific evidence supporting the idea that some Korean ancestral lines may have originated in the south.

From the standpoint of physical anthropology and archaeology, there is not enough evidence to reach solid conclusions about the origins of Koreans on the peninsula. Nevertheless, it seems probable that a major population influx occurred during the Neolithic period from the north around Lake Baikal, while newly uncovered evidence suggests the possibility that some Korean ancestral lines originated in the south.

The Early States and the Iron Age

In reconstructing the prehistory of Korea, one encounters notable differences in orientation and interpretation between historians and anthropologists, including archaeologists. Also evident are biases resulting from disciplinary and nationalistic sentiments linking China and Korea. Descriptions, for instance, of Bronze Age peninsular inhabitants who established the prototype of state structure called the "Early state" were based on written documents such as *Samguk sagi* (History of the Three Kingdoms) by Kim Bu-sik (1075-1151) and *Samguk yusa* (Memorabilia of the Three Kingdoms) by the monk Iryeon (1206-1289). These two history books have been very important sources

for reconstructing Korea's past. Despite their exalted stature, these written documents from long ago carry intentional and unintentional biases. Some of these biases come from the Confucian and Buddhist beliefs of their authors: Kim Bu-sik was an advocate of Confucianism and Iryeon was a Buddhist monk. Moreover, as Sarah Nelson (1993:206) has pointed out, "they were written many centuries after the events they record, and each has a point of view which guided the selection of topics to be included."

Prior to the historical period on the Korea peninsula, the state of Buyeo arose in the Songhua River basin as a Early state north of the peninsula. Yemaek developed along the middle reaches of the Yalu River (Amnnokgang), and Gojoseon (Old Joseon) arose in the basin between the Liao and Daedonggang (Liao and Daedong River). The most advanced of these states was Gojoseon, a confederate kingdom whose founding is the subject of the Dangun (Dangun Wanggeom) legend. A common version of the story begins with a female bear and a tigress both aspired to become human. "Hwanung, the son of Hwanin the chief god, gave them mugwort [ssuk in Korean] and garlic to eat, and instructed them to stay in the dark and not see the sun for 100 days. The tigress became restless and failed at the task, but the she-bear persevered in the cave and became human, married Hwanung, and bore a son named Dangun Wanggeom" (Nelson 1993:155). Dangun set up a kingdom in Pyeongyang and named the country Joseon, meaning "morning calm and freshness."

Legend has it that Koreans are descendants of Dangun. Traditional Koreans during the Goryeo and Joseon dynasties did not believe that they shared a common biological ancestor but considered Dangun to be the first king of Korea, not the progenitor of the Korean people. While some were the descendants of Dangun, others were the descendants of naturalized immigrants from elsewhere. As the Dangun mythology was growing stronger, and ethnic nationalism was rising during and after Japanese colonization, most mainstream Korean historians challenged the historical status of Gija (Jizi in Chinese). Gija is a

nephew of the last king of the Shang dynasty of China (ca. 1600-1046 BC). According to tradition, Gija departed with a retinue of 5,000 people and went into exile in Korea, where he founded a state called Gija Joseon. Until recently, however, most conventional Korean historians rejected the idea that the Daedonggang basin was dominated by the Gija Joseon and believed that it was indigenous rather than colonial (Lee 1984:15-16). Archaeologists such as Sarah M. Nelson (1993:156-157) have been unable to find any conclusive evidence to prove the legend.

In a reinterpretation of Korean history, however, Pai Hyung Il[Bae Hyeong-il] (2000:60), an anthropologist as well as East Asian archaeologist, offers her own perspective on Gija and Wiman Joseon: "The elevation of Dangun to historical status is a direct challenge to Gija, a Shang aristocrat enfeoffed in Joseon at the time of the fall of the Shang dynasty (ca. 1000 BC). Gija was later followed by Wiman, a general from the state of Yan who arrived around 195-194 BC to set up Wiman Joseon and whose descendants later contested Han emperor Wu's invasion in 108 BC. Thus, the traditionally accepted dynastic state sequence of the Three Joseons of Gojoseon, Gija Joseon, and Wiman Joseon has been overturned in the revised Korean ancestral state lineage." In such a social and academic milieu, Korean history books have been largely silent on contributions made by foreign immigrants, such as Yi Ji-ran (1331-1402), a Jurchen immigrant and intimate friend of Yi Seong-gye (Taejo), founding father of the Joseon dynasty—the reason being that such figures do not fit neatly into a story of ethnic nationalism.

Korea is not the only country with historiographical biases stemming from nationalistic sentiments. Korea's nearest neighbors have self-aggrandizing slants of their own. According to Sarah M. Nelson (1993:9), "Japanese sources, more nearly contemporaneous with the Three Kingdoms, tend to ascribe a secondary status to Korea, a stance which may have arisen from motives other than historical accuracy." She offers a similar caveat regarding Chinese sources: "Chinese[historical] documents should be treated with

caution for many reasons. Errors in transcription or translation have probably crept in; embroidering on facts by the Chinese for their own purposes (to point a moral, for example) may have occurred; and the original observers of the 'barbarians' might have misunderstood what they saw" (Nelson 1993:165).

Perhaps the most significant recent Chinese influence on Korean historiography comes from the Northeast Asia Project (*Dongbuk gongjeong* in Korean). Since 2002, the Chinese government has launched a major campaign to make the history of Goguryeo (37 BC-AD 668) and Balhae (698-926) part of China's regional history. This line of interpretation holds that Goguryeo was a local ethnic government under Chinese control in the northeastern region. In support of this proposition, the Chinese government has sponsored various research projects on the subject.

In response to the Chinese Northeast Asia Project, on 1 March 2004, a group of Korean historians established the Goguryeo Research Foundation with the support of the Ministry of Education and Human Resources Development (now the Ministry of Education). In September 2006, the foundation merged with the Northeast Asian History Foundation. Many Koreans have expressed concern about the ulterior motives of the Chinese Northeast Asia Project, which they see as distorting the early history of Korea, the Three Kingdoms period in general, and the history of Goguryeo in particular, since it was located in the northernmost part of the Korean peninsula.

The Three Kingdoms Period

Traditionally, Koreans tended to focus on the histories of more recent dynasties, either Goryeo (918-1392) or the Joseon (1392-1910). Interestingly enough, since 2006, Koreans have shown considerable interest in the history of the Three Kingdoms, Goguryeo (37 BC-AD 668), Baekje (18 BC-AD 660), and Silla (57 BC-AD 935). As evidence of the

shifting interest of Koreans, for instance, from 2001 to 2005, only one TV drama out of fifteen series telecast by the three major Korean TV networks (KBS, MBC, and SBS) dealt with the Silla dynasty, the rest being set in either the Joseon or the Goryeo. Suddenly, beginning in 2006, all but one TV series of the three major networks focused on the Goguryeo and Balhae dynasties, indicating a rising interest in the Three Kingdoms.

I can only speculate about Koreans' fascination with the Three Kingdoms based on the following factors (Kim 2007:25-26). First, China's Northeast Asia Project, especially the fear that it might misrepresent the early history of Korea, has generated much interest in Goguryeo. Conjuring an image of mounted warriors confronting nomadic northern tribes and the powerful Chinese Sui and Tang dynasties, Goguryeo symbolizes bravery and has become a source of national pride for Koreans, as it represents the triumph of the underdog. Second, contemporary Koreans see a striking resemblance between the time of the Three Kingdoms, when the peninsula was divided into three regions, and present-day Korea, which is divided into north and south. Third, some essential aspects of contemporary Korean culture appear to have their roots in the Three Kingdoms period. The male-dominated system of family relations, deeply influenced by Confucianism, and now evolving, though at a snail's pace, is a case in point. In fact, before Korea was deeply influenced by Chinese Confucianism in the Joseon dynasty in particular, Korean society during the Three Kingdoms appeared to be a society of relative gender equality. Indeed during the Silla dynasty there were three queens. Korea's election of a woman president for the first time in East Asia may not be accidental, but may reflect the cultural heritage of the Three Kingdoms, Silla in particular.

Before the formation of the Three Kingdoms, the southern part of the Korean peninsula was inhabited by a number of distinct yet related tribes: to the south of the Hangang were three Early States with a widely disseminated iron culture—Jinhan, Mahan, and

Byeonhan, known collectively as Samhan (or Three Hans). Mahan was located in the region of the modern provinces of Gyeonggi, Chungcheong, and Jeolla; Jinhan was east of the Nakdonggang (Nakdong River) in the province of Gyeongsang; and Byeonhan was in the province of Gyeongsang west of the Nakdonggang.

In addition to these, small polities known collectively as Gaya existed alongside the Three Kingdoms. However, Gaya never joined the big three to become a true state. Gaya was caught between Silla and Baekje, and the struggle between those two kingdoms rendered it difficult for Gaya to achieve full political and societal development. Parenthetically, according to *Samguk yusa*, Kim Su-ro, the king of Gaya, married Heo Hwang-ok, the princess of Ayodhya, India, in AD 48. This may well have been the first international, interethnic, and interracial royal marriage. Some eight million contemporary Koreans whose clan seat surnames include Gimhae Kim[Gim], Gimhae Heo, and Incheon Lee[Yi] claim to be descended from King Kim Su-ro and Queen Heo Hwang-ok (Kim 2011b). This alone supports the notion that Koreans are not descendants of a single ethnic and racial group.

Goguryeo

Goguryeo, located in the far north, was the first of the three kingdoms to organize. It was founded in 37 BC by Jumong, who was said to be from Buyeo, a Early State in the Songhua River basin. The people of Goguryeo were engaged in agriculture, but their land was not fertile enough for intensive farming.

Goguryeo was under constant threat from invading Chinese forces and nomadic tribes in the northern frontier. In response, the Goguryeo people became warrior horsemen and established military dominance over Baekje and Silla in the early years. The height of Goguryeo's power came under Gwanggaeto Daewang (King Gwanggaeto, Gwanggaeto the Great)(391-413), whose impressive military record is carved in the memorial stele at his tomb in modern Tonggou on the

northern frontier. Goguryeo was strong enough to defend itself from attacks by the Sui dynasty in 598 and 612 and Tang expeditions in 645 and 647.

Archaeological findings from Goguryeo include stone tombs with wall paintings as well as cities and forts surrounded by stone walls. Written documents indicate that Goguryeo was a stratified society with wealthy and powerful elite capable of mobilizing a large labor force to build tombs for the upper class and other public works projects. Scenes from tomb murals show brightly colored hunting scenes, and other murals show husbands and wives together, implying that women enjoyed considerable equality. Dress and house styles from this time show some continuity with those of historic Korea.

The only writing system at the time employed Chinese characters, which the elite learned in order to function effectively. In 372, Goguryeo established a National Confucian Academy, or "university." The Goguryeo elite emulated the Chinese model while maintaining their native Korean culture and tradition (Nelson 1993). Buddhism was introduced to Goguryeo from northern China and was officially recognized in 372. Nevertheless, native shamanistic religious practices continued to coexist with Buddhism.

For a northern frontier state, Goguryeo cultural accomplishments were considerable. Contemporary Koreans, however, tend to think of Goguryeo mainly as a strong kingdom whose military might halted Chinese aggression and even led it to expand its territory toward China. Goguryeo did in fact conquer a total of sixty-four fortresses, including 1,400 villages in China, extending its domain to include most of China's Manchuria (Lee 1984). For having faced down a bigger aggressor, Goguryeo has become a symbol of Korean pride.

Baekje

Baekje was founded in 18 BC, when Onjo and his brother, sons of Jumong, the founder of Goguryeo, moved south. Onjo built his

Goguryeo at the Height of Its Expansion in the Fifth Century

headquarters on the Hangang, southeast of Seoul. Since Baekje was founded in one of Korea's most productive rice-growing areas, its economy was mainly agrarian.

Cultural artifacts from early Baekje have been poorly preserved, and little has been recorded. Not much remained after the armies of Tang and Silla plundered and burned the state. Tombs were looted and abandoned, cities razed, and temples destroyed. What is left are temple foundations and pagodas near Buyeo, Baekje's last capital, and Gongju, farther north of the capital.

Recently, however, some sites have revealed new information about this era. Surprisingly, most surviving examples of Baekje art and architecture are to be found in Japan as carefully preserved sacred relics. The temple foundations near Buyeo in Korea show that the layout was the same as that of early temples in Japan, a plan apparently duplicated by Baekje architects. The Baekje court was literate in Chinese at least by the fourth century, and probably earlier. Buddhism was introduced to Baekje in 384. The tomb of Muryeongwang (King Muryeong) (501-523) shows the king and queen wearing gold crowns and bronze shoes, evidence of a luxurious lifestyle for the Baekje elite.

Baekje dwellings were heated by the *ondol* system — in which warm flues from the kitchen run under the stone floors to all areas of the house — still widely used in Korea today. Bruce Cumings (1997:35) reports that "Ice may form in a water jug on the table, while a person sleeps comfortably on a toasty warm *ondol*." The *ondol* may explain a Korean preference for stiff-backed chairs and high tables; it may also have encouraged Koreans to be closer to nature, to the earth.

Baekje could be characterized as one of the most "internationalized" kingdoms in Korea because of its relations with southern China and western Japan. Baekje imported Buddhism, literacy, and many art forms from China, incorporating them into its own unique culture and then exporting them to Japan. Baekje art became the basis for the art of the Asuka period (552-645) of Japan (Hatada 1969; Cumings 1997).

After Baekje became literate in Chinese in the fourth century, Baekje scholars were sent to the Yamato court in Japan to teach the Chinese classics (Nelson 1993). The crown prince of Baekje was sent to Japan in 397, thereby cementing relations with that country. Contents of the Fujinoki tomb near Nara, Japan demonstrate close stylistic ties with Baekje and are evidence of cultural bonds between Baekje and Japan (Nelson 1993).

Contrary to its friendly relationship with both China and Japan, Baekje had difficulties in its relation with Goguryeo. Silla, which had not been a party in the early armed struggles between Goguryeo and Baekje, was invited by Baekje as an ally against war with Goguryeo; in 551 Baekje could, with the help of silla, drive of Goguryeo forces from the Hangang area. However, two years later, Silla drove out Baekje and took exclusive possession of the area. As result Silla became Baekje's mortal enemy.

Silla

In 57 BC, at the council meeting of the six villages of Saro, or Seorabeol, in the Gyeongju plain, one leader was chosen from the Park[Bak], Seok, and Kim[Gim] clans that ruled the kingdom on a rotating basis. From the fourth century onward, kingship became hereditary within the Kim clan. In the third century, Silla was invaded once by a Goguryeo tribe, but from the fourth century on, Silla was able to control the area around the Nakdonggang and even conquered the Gaya kingdom. Silla's expansion was possible largely due to its geographic location, which was at a relatively safe distance from the Chinese border. Silla had an elaborate social stratification system based on the "quality of bone" (golpum): the "holy bone" (seonggol) being the highest group and "jingol," the next highest group, followed by three lesser ranks.

Silla left rich archaeological remains, including forts, shrines, Buddhist temples, pagodas, a palace, and even an astronomical observatory (Cheomseongdae). Silla was also equipped with high-quality

Silla's Golden Crown

iron weapons. Silla was famous for its youthful warrior society, *hwarang* (Flower of Youth). It had five secular injunctions: loyalty to the king, filial love toward one's parents, fidelity in friendship, bravery in battle, and chivalry in warfare. These values reflect a mixture of Buddhism and Confucianism.

Silla culture was best preserved in elite tombs in the capital of Gyeongju. Burial goods include gold crowns, gold earrings, belts with dangling pendants, gold bracelets, and gold rings, which were found on every finger of one ruler. In fact, Silla was referred to as the "gold-glittering nation" in the ninth century, known to the Arabs as "el Sila" (McCune 1976:3).

Chinese thought and custom began to influence Silla a century before Buddhism was introduced and accepted. Some stone monuments with Chinese inscriptions are clear evidence that Silla was literate in the fifth century. Bunhwangsa Pagoda (Bunhwangsa Mojeon Seoktap), a truncated brick pagoda only three stories high resembles the Giant Wild Goose Pagoda in Xian, capital of the Tang dynasty. The capital of Silla was laid out in imitation of Xian, as was Nara in Japan. The largest and most important of the Silla temples was Hwangryongsa (Hwangryong temple), erected in 553, which lasted until the Mongolian invasion of 1238. The famous temple, Bulguksa remains intact even today.

Interrelations among the Three Kingdoms and their cultural legacy

The Three Kingdoms did not have a symbiotic coexistence but instead attacked each other frequently, alone or in alliance with one another. Finally, allying itself with Tang China, Silla conquered the lower Hangang basin, by the Yellow Sea. Silla then defeated Baekje in 660 and Goguryeo in 668, finally becoming the sole ruler of the peninsula as United Silla.

After the defeat of Baekje and Goguryeo, the Chinese tried to establish an administration to govern the peninsula, including Silla. Silla responded to this aggression by helping Goguryeo's resistance movement in the north and by moving against Tang troops in the south. By 671, Silla had taken the old Baekje capital, and in 676, Silla expanded to the Daedonggang. The Tang Chinese invaders had to withdraw to Manchuria. At last, in 735, they were forced to recognize Silla's domination over the area south of the Daedonggang. Among its many accomplishments, Silla can be credited with unifying the Three Kingdoms through diplomatic shrewdness in allowing the Tang to aid its conquest of Baekje and Goguryeo. Although Silla was unable to control all the former territory of Goguryeo, which extended to much of Manchuria, the peninsula has

been governed by a single kingdom since the seventh century.

In the meantime, after the fall of Goguryeo, Dae Jo-yeong, a former Goguryeo general, founded Balhae (698-926) with most of the remaining Goguryeo people. Its territory extended from the Songhua River and Heillong River in northern Manchuria to the northern provinces of modern Korea. Balhae gained control of most of the former Goguryeo territory and then confronted Silla. However, later in 926, Balhae was conquered by Khitans.

In terms of cultural legacy, before the Three Kingdoms unified into Silla, each had its own unique and distinctive political, social, and cultural customs, yet all three shared several characteristics that have had a long-lasting impact on Korea history. The cultural legacy of the Three Kingdoms period persists in contemporary Korean life. In terms of foreign relations and diplomacy, Silla and Baekje sought Chinese power to beset Goguryeo, which inaugurated a tradition of involving foreign powers in Korean internal disputes (Cumings 1997). Such a move was repeated toward the end of the Joseon dynasty in the nineteenth century. After World War II, the peninsula was again divided by world politics and remains so today.

There is ample evidence that the Three Kingdoms had a tradition of gender equality. The Goguryeo tomb mural shows a group of noblewomen wearing pleated skirts as well as an armed female warrior riding an armored horse. Three Silla rulers, the twenty-seventh, Seondeok yeowang (Queen Seondeok) (632-647); twenty-eighth, Jindeok yeowang (Queen Jindeok) (647-654); and fifty-first, Jinseong yeowang (Queen Jinseong) (887-897), were queens. There was no cultural tradition of patriarchy in the Three Kingdoms period. The gender equality of the era is one reason why a new generation of Koreans prefers the Three Kingdoms period to any other.

The Goryeo Dynasty (918-1392)

With unification, Silla reached its peak of power and prosperity. Beginning in the middle of the eighth century, however, Silla was torn to pieces by rebel leaders: Gyeon Hwon, who founded the Later Baekje state in Jeonju; former Silla prince Gung Ye, who established the Later Goguryeo state; and Wang Geon, a former minister of Gung Ye's from a gentry family in Gaeseong,* who overthrew Gung Ye in 918. Wang Geon's power grew over the next two decades; he raided the Later Baekje, and his posthumous title is King Taejo (918-943). Eventually, Silla yielded its power to Wang Geon, who united the peninsula again and established the new state of Goryeo, whose name was derived from Goguryeo. Wang Geon adopted a policy of leniency toward the Silla aristocracy and even married a woman of the Silla royal clan. He remained alert to a possible conflict between his state and the northern nomadic states in the former Goguryeo territory. He also advised that Buddhist temples could not be interfered with and warned against usurpation and internal conflicts among the royal clans. He tried to justify his rule by claiming moral superiority.

Goryeo's culture was rich, colorful, and sophisticated. Goryeo's celadon ware was the dynasty's most celebrated artistic achievement. Song porcelain was the inspiration for this fine celadon ware, and its

---

* Gaeseong (with nicknames of Songdo and Gaegyeong), a city of southern North Korea near the border with South Korea, was the capital of the Goryeo dynasty for over four centuries. On 19 June 2013, because of its rich historical monuments and sites, Gaeseong was added to the World Heritage List of the United Nations Education, Scientific and Cultural Organization (UNESCO). Recently, its most notable feature is the Gaeseong Industrial Park located about six miles north of the Korean Demilitarized Zone (DMZ), operated as a collaborative economic development with South Korea. As of April 2013, over 100 South Korean light industrial companies were employing over 50,000 North Korean workers. However, on 3 April 2013 when tension between North and South Korea reached its height, the North Korean government removed all North Korean workers from the Gaeseong Industrial Park, which effectively shut down all business activities. Then, after weeks of often spiky negotiations aimed at easing inter-Korean tensions, the inter-Korean industrial zone reopened in September 2013.

delicate jade-green color and remarkable decorations reflect Taoist simplicity and Buddhist tranquility. As Bruce Cumings (1997:40) recognizes, "The Goryeo dynasty ruled for just short of half a millennium, but in its heyday the dynasty ranked among the most advanced civilizations in the world."

Goryeo science and technology were also highly advanced. The Goryeo woodblock-printing technique allowed for the publication of a wide variety of books, and advanced cast-metal type printing was devised, thus pushing back the date for the first movable metal type to 1234, some 200 years before the Germans "invented" it (Steers et al. 1989). Gunpowder was also manufactured for the first time in Korean history, and, by 1377, was utilized in the production of weapons.

Buddhism flourished in the Three Kingdoms period under royal patronage, especially in Silla, but the Goryeo dynasty created a Buddhist state. Priests became politicians, and several princes became Buddhist monks. The impact of Buddhism in Goryeo was of greater significance than just the development of religious belief. The founder of the dynasty, Taejo (918-943), built many temples, and for him, these founding temples might have had more than religious meaning. According to Lee Ki-baik[Yi Gi-baek] (1984:132), "the founding of temples had not simply a religious meaning. The Heungwangsa, extending over 2,800 *gan* (as a modern measure of area about 9,270 square meters) of floor space and completed after twelve years of construction in 1067, is perhaps the most notable example of a temple built with the objective of ensuring dynastic well-being. The proliferation of temples in Goryeo—there were as many as seventy in Gaeseong alone—itself conveys a clear picture of Goryeo as thoroughly Buddhist state."

Further evidence of Goryeo's preoccupation with Buddhism as more than religion can be seen in the *Tripitaka*.* The woodblock

---

* The original woodblocks were destroyed in the thirteenth-century Mongolian invasions, and the *Goryeo Tripitaka* that remains today at Haeinsa represents a new edition begun on Ganghwado (Ganghwa Island) where the Goryeo court had taken

painting of the first *Tripitaka*, the Buddhist canon in Chinese translation, was completed in 1087. *Tripitaka* is a Sanskrit word made up of *tri*, "three," and *pitaka*, "baskets," which refers to the *gyeong, yul*, and *non*, meaning discourses with the Buddha, the Buddhist laws of ascetic life, and commentaries on the sutras by eminent monks and scholars. Geomancy based on the ideas of Buddhism and Taoism was also popular among the Goryeo people.

Confucianism had begun to influence Goryeo from the reign of the sixth king, Seongjong (981-997), after the failure of the reforms of the fourth king, Gwangjong (949-975). One impact of the principle of rule by civil officials in accordance with Confucian political ideology was the rejection of the Buddhist doctrine of reward for good work. Nevertheless, "Goryeo Confucians by no means completely rejected Buddhism; instead, regarding it as the doctrine for achieving spiritual tranquility and otherworldly salvation, they felt that it could exist side by side with Confucianism. Accordingly, many men were versed in both, and in this respect they differed from the Confucian scholars of late Goryeo and the Yi dynasty[Joseon dynasty]." (Lee 1984:130).

Goryeo's political ideology was based on Confucianism. In 992, in order to enhance Confucian ideology, Seongjong established a national university consisting of six colleges. Buddhism still flourished alongside Confucianism.

From the beginning, after unifying the later Three Kingdoms, Goryeo was ambitious to establish a great dynasty modeled on the cultural and political system of the Song dynasty (960-1279) of China. To accomplish its goal, Goryeo engaged in trade with Song China. In the early dynastic period, Goryeo recruited talented human resources by adopting an open immigration policy, welcoming men of letters, medicine men, musicians, translators, merchants, monks, and even fortune-tellers. Goryeo also embraced northern tribes, including Jurchens and Khitans, and refugees from Balhae. They

---

refuge from the Mongolian invasion, and was completed in 1251.

were welcomed into the country for the defense of the northern border and for their skills and knowledge as workmen and artisans (O. Park 1996).

After the eleventh century, Goryeo suffered a great deal from internal strife between civil and military officials. A military coup challenging favoritism in the royal court of King Uijong (1146-1170) took place in 1170. Military officials rose up against civil officials, many of whom were killed. The second major purge took place three years later, and eventually political power passed from civil officials into the hands of the military, and then returned to the civil aristocracy, mainly scholar-bureaucrats. Such internal conflicts weakened the dynasty. Also, beginning in the eleventh century, Goryeo suffered invasions from Khitan, Liao, and Jurchen. The most devastating blow came from the Mongols in the thirteenth century after they invaded China in 1206. Having conquering China, in 1231 the Mongols, equipped with new weapons, chased diehard Liao refugees and attacked Goryeo itself. During the Mongol invasion, Goryeo moved its capital to Ganghwado .

Over the course of the war (1231-1270), Mongols took with them more than 200,000 Goryeo captives when they returned home, leaving behind much death and destruction. The number of captives constituted almost one-tenth of the total Goryeo population of two million total at the time. The invaders burned property and destroyed numerous cultural treasures and relics, including the original of the *Tripitaka*. In 1271, the Mongolians established the Yuan dynasty and demanded that Goryeo join with them in subjugating Japan in 1274, and again in 1281. Goryeo was responsible for the construction of warships and the provision of supplies for both invasion attempts. These campaigns ended in failure due largely to the sudden storm which the Japanese named "Divine Wind (*kamikaze*)."

Also, the Mongols occupied Jejudo, where they had dispatched their mighty army. Recognizing that the island had ideal conditions for breeding horses, beginning in 1276, the Mongols made Jejudo a

center for horse breeding. They occupied the island for one hundred years, a century that saw many social, cultural, and linguistic changes for the Jejudo people (Kim 2002).

Because of Yuan's military domination, a succession of Goryeo kings was required to take princesses of the Yuan imperial house as wives. These international marriages between two royal families of Yuan and Goryeo were initiated by Goryeo to strengthen the royal authority within Goryeo and to bring reconciliation with the Yuan. With permission from the Yuan emperor, Goryeo's King Wonjong (1259-1274) arranged for his son (who later became Chungyeolwang, King Chungyeol) (1274-1298, 1298-1308) to wed a Yuan princess, a daughter of the Yuan emperor Shizu (Kublai Khan). She later became King Chungyeol's queen. Thereafter a succession of four Goryeo kings—Chungseon (1298, 1308-1313), Chungsuk (1313-1330, 1332-1339), Chunghye (1330-1332, 1339-1344), and Gongmin (1351-1374)—had princesses of the Yuan imperial house as their primary consorts, while sons born to these queens typically succeeded to the throne. Such arranged marriages continued for a century.

Besides maintaining relations with the Yuan, Goryeo had to deal with Japanese pirates, or *waegu*, a derogatory term referring to those pirates who landed along the Goryeo coast and plundered farming villages. For a century, when Yuan princesses came to Goryeo, they were accompanied by a host of chamberlains and aides-de-camp. Many of these attendants remained in Korea and eventually became naturalized Koreans. Kim Chŏng-ho[Gim Jeong-ho] (2003:226) estimates that they account for twenty *seong* (surnames) and forty *bon* (names of clan seats) and their descendants amount to 429,012 contemporary Koreans out of a population of 50 million South Koreans.

Goryeo would not be free from Yuan influence until the Yuan were driven northward by the rise of the Ming dynasty (1368-1644) of China. Goryeo then had little choice but to adopt a pro-Ming stance. In 1388, the newly established Ming dynasty proclaimed its intention to claim Goryeo's northern territory. Outraged at this move, Goryeo

commander-in-chief Choe Yeong was determined to strike Ming's forces and mobilized troops, but his deputy commander, Yi Seong-gye, opposed the expedition. Leading his army back from Wihwado at the mouth of the Amnokgang, Yi Seong-gye deposed the king and seized political control for himself in a bloodless coup.

The Joseon (Yi) Dynasty (1392-1910)

In 1392, Yi Seong-gye overthrew Goryeo's king and usurped the throne to become King Taejo (1392-1398), founder of his own dynasty, the Joseon. Afterwards, the throne of the Joseon dynasty was either inherited, or, if there was no apparent heir, a ruler was chosen from among members of the royal family of the Jeonju Yi clan. Because of this monopoly by Yi clan members, the Joseon dynasty has also been called the Yi dynasty at times.

The new kingdom maintained a close relationship with the Ming of China because of Yi Seong-gye's ties to it. Yi also embraced Neo-Confucian doctrines, which gave the traditional ethico-political cult a metaphysical interpretation. The reformers surrounding Taejo intensified their drive to impose Confucian norms on people's lives, which in turn spelled the decline of Buddhism. By confiscating land and forcing many temples to close, the new dynasty weakened Buddhism to a subservient position.

The changing status of Buddhism in Joseon society brought about many changes. Korean burial rituals, which had thus far been an amalgam of indigenous customs and Buddhist traditions, were replaced by Confucian customs. The Buddhist ritual of cremation, for instance, was thrust aside in favor of Confucian ancestor worship and its related rituals. Before the Joseon dynasty, endogamous marriage (marrying within one's kin group), polygamy, and remarriage of widows were permitted. However, Joseon society expanded the range of kin with whom marriage was prohibited, forbade the practice of

giving equal status to multiple wives, and discouraged remarriage.

In the end, Taejo became more of a figurehead than a ruler, but the third king, Taejong (1400-1418), who ascended the throne after killing his brother, the heir-apparent, strengthened the monarchy. King Sejong (1418-1450), Taejong's successor, who was known to be intelligent and scholarly, was regarded as one of the greatest kings, if not the greatest, in the dynastic history of Korea. His rule in the mid-fifteenth century was marked by progressive ideas in administration, economics, science, music, medicine, and humanities. Sejong ordered the development of a rain gauge in 1442 that preceded Castelli's 1639 "invention" of the pluviometer by almost two hundred years. Sejong's interest in astronomical science was all-encompassing: sundials, water clocks, orreries of the solar system, celestial globes, astronomical maps, and atlases of seven planets were the creative results of Sejong's encouragement (Kim 2007).

Sejong also established the Jiphyeonjeon (Hall of Worthies) to promote research into institutional traditions and political economy. He then directed scholars of the Jiphyeonjeon to devise an alphabet for the Korean language called *Hangeul*, his most celebrated achievement. *Hangeul* consists of eleven vowels and seventeen consonants and is so simple and well conceived that a literate person can learn it in a matter of hours. Despite strong opposition from Confucian scholars, whose mastery of Chinese characters guaranteed their elite positions, the king persisted in promoting *Hangeul* for the benefit of the masses and distributed the first Korean written language in alphabetic form to the people in 1446. The *Hangeul* project was described in 1445 in as document entitled as *Hunmin jeongeum.** In the meantime, though, the official written language

---

* *Hangeul* is known to be unique, and world's most intuitive writing system. During his visit to Korea in fall 2013, Eric Schmidt, the top executive of Google, has traced Korea's success in the digital world to the creation of *Hangeul* , because it is simplified and easy-to-learn alphabet that facilitates information exchanges among people. Now, Google has come forward to the propagation of *Hangeul* (see the detailed report

continued to be Chinese, just as Latin was in Europe at the time.

The seventh king, Sejo (1455-1468), implemented a radical policy by defying Confucian orthodoxy in support of Taoism and Buddhism. Sejo assumed direct control, intimidated his critics with purges and executions, instituted the banishment of officials, and seized property. However, the ninth king, Seongjong (1469-1494), reinstated traditional ideas in the form of Neo-Confucianism. State support of Buddhism gradually diminished, and Confucianism once again assumed its place in the royal administration (Kim 2007).

Development of the "*yangban*" legacy in Joseon

In establishing Joseon, the role and strength of the military was essential for the success of Yi Seong-gye's coup. However, without strong support from the literati, his coup d'état would not have been successful. Because they provided crucial support, the literati began to attract the attention of Joseon kings, and their role in government became quite significant. It was the powerful literati who set about codifying a corpus of administrative law that informed the political modus operandi of the Joseon dynasty (Kim 2007).

The dominant social class of the Joseon dynasty was the *yangban*, meaning two orders of officials, civil and military. The *yangban* class directed the government, economy, and culture of Joseon. Therefore, Joseon has been aptly characterized as a *yangban* society. The *yangban* was more broadly rooted than the ruling class of Goryeo or earlier kingdoms. Its size as a class increased by the state examination system used to recruit officials, while "protected appointments" severely limited the dynasty's policies.

The basic marriage pattern of the *yangban* was exogamous (that

by *The Korea Herald*, 31 October, and 1 November 2014). Coupled with the popularity of the Korean Wave(*Hallyu*), a growing number of people throughout the world is interested in learning the *Hangeul*. In response to such an interest, The Cyber University of Korea(CUK) offers to a free on-line education program for learning the Korean language(see: http://korean.cuk.edu).

is, outside one's own[patrilineal kin] group), but the selection of marriage partners was "endogamous" with respect to class to preserve hereditary status. The *yangban* created a district residential pattern. While *samurai* warriors in Tokugawa Japan (1603-1868) were not allowed to live in the countryside, many *yangban* families resided in the countryside of Joseon, making school, party, and lineage ties much more important than communal solidarity based on common residence (Han 2003). Even in the capital of Seoul, the *yangban* resided as a group in certain sections.

In order to protect their status, the *yangban* sent their youths to private tutorial schools, called seodang, where they learned basic Chinese characters and practiced writing Chinese. They could then move on to advanced schools in Seoul or in their local counties. Seoul was home to the National Confucian Academy (Seonggyungwan). Certain limitations applied to the descendants of secondary wives of the *yangban*. There was also regional discrimination against the residents of the northern provinces. As the power base of the *yangban* expanded, particularly as the *sarim* (rural Neo-Confucian literati) emerged into political prominence through the civil service examination process, the majority of *yangban* literati had to compete among themselves, and many power struggles ensued. As a result, there were four major purges: in 1498 (*Muo sahwa*), 1504 (*Gapja sahwa*), 1519 (*Gimyo sahwa*), and 1545 (*Eulsa sahwa*). Although the extent of violence varied, these purges signified the start of fierce struggles among political cliques vying for political power.

Foreign policy and Japanese invasions

As might be expected, Yi Seong-gye adopted a pro-Ming stance, but he went further by dispatching diplomatic envoys to Ming China each year to offer New Year's felicitations, to congratulate the Ming emperor on his birthday, to honor the birthday of the imperial crown prince, and to mark the passing of the winter solstice. All these missions were political in nature, intended to secure the safety

of the new dynasty. Even though it was a strategic maneuver, such a policy was described as *sadae*, meaning to serve the great or big. Since then, the word *sadae* has had a negative connotation and is used to describe Korea's submissive foreign policy in dealing with countries bigger and stronger than itself.

Joseon also had to protect itself from Japanese marauders from Tsushima. In 1419, Sejong sent a strong military force to wipe out the Japanese bases. Through negotiations, Joseon's three ports were opened to Tsushima and limited trade began. Larger, better-organized Japanese invasions took place under Toyotomi Hideyoshi in the sixteenth century. A military general, Hideyoshi emerged as a strongman after his military victories resulted in a unified Japan. His ambition was to conquer the Ming empire by way of invading Korea. Even before the Hideyoshi invasions, Korea had been troubled by sporadic attacks on its coasts by the Japanese in the mid-sixteenth century. The *yangban* bureaucrats were content to take temporary measures, fearing that a permanent peace could not be easily attained.

In April 1592, Japanese forces landed at Busan with an overwhelming number of soldiers, and their northward attack was swift. The fourteenth king, Seonjo (1567-1608), and his court fled toward the far northern town of Uiju on the Amnokgang. During the invasion, Korean ground forces, inexperienced and inept, proved ineffectual against the well-trained Japanese forces. However, naval hero Admiral Yi Sun-sin (1545-1598) fought effectively against the Japanese navy by devising the "turtle ship" (*Geobukseon*), which is believed to be the world's first ironclad ship. The heroic role of Admiral Yi, an increase in the "righteous armies" known as *uibyeong* (guerrilla forces), and Ming military assistance forced the Japanese to pull back. Through negotiations, a settlement was finally reached. However, in January 1597, the Japanese renewed their war efforts, bringing in 100,000 soldiers. This time the Japanese faced stiffer resistance from Koreans and the Chinese garrison, and the invasion was limited to the southern provinces. Nevertheless, Admiral Yi was killed by a Japanese bullet

while standing in the bow of his flagship in 1598. In the same year, the death of Hideyoshi prompted the Japanese to bring the war to an end.

Hideyoshi's invasion resulted in a massive number of Korean casualties, and Japan benefited from the abduction of skilled Korean prisoners of war: artisans such as weavers and porcelain manufacturers, priests, and Confucian scholars. These Korean artisans were instrumental in a great advancement of Japanese ceramic arts. The story of captive Korean artisan Sim Dang-gil and his family, who were forcibly taken to Kagoshima, Japan, during the Hideyoshi invasion, is a poignant saga (Kim 1988a). The numerous books seized by the Japanese in Korea contributed to the development of learning in Japan, especially the study of Neo-Confucianism.

After the Japanese invasions, Joseon was once again subject to the depredations of its northern neighbor. In Manchuria, the Jurchen tribes had united under the leadership of Hong Taiji (Qing Taizong) and began sporadic attacks along the northeastern border. The fifteenth King, Gwanghaegun (1608-1623), his realpolitik approach and skillful diplomatic efforts worked for a while to preserve precarious peace in Northeast Asia where balance of power was changing rapidly in favor of Manchu. The new court of King Injo, who deposed Gwanghaegun, tended to take a moralistic approach to international relations and emphasized moral obligations to Ming. This resulted in two "successful" invasions by Manchu in 1627 (Jeongmyo horan) and 1636 (Byeongja horan). As result of military disasters and capitulation, Manchu was able to exert its power over Joseon and establish a tributary relationship, forcing Joseon to sever ties with the Ming court and securing two Joseon princes as hostages. The Manchu went on to conquer Ming China and ruled China as the Qing dynasty (1644-1912). After that, Joseon was unable to escape the influence of Qing until the latter was defeated by the Japanese in the Sino-Japanese War in 1894.

In the seventeenth century, Joseon began to understand the West, mainly through Catholicism, which was called Western Learning

(Seohak). "Practical Learning" (Silhak), a pragmatic form of scholarship of the seventeenth and eighteenth centuries, took a broad and varied approach to reforming Joseon dynasty institutions and led to "Enlightenment Thought" (*Gaehwa sasang*). Since enlightenment would serve as a guiding metaphor for future modernization (accompanied by increasing mercantile activities that accelerated commercial farming and the transformation of rural life), some critics see the eighteenth century as the earliest burgeoning of indigenous capitalism and the beginning of Korean modernization. However, some Western scholars argue that this was not the case, asserting that Korean modernization started in the late nineteenth or early twentieth century (Eckert 1991; Deuchler 1977a).

Koreans are not a single ethnic or racial group

Despite the traditionalist view in Korea, evidence from Korean prehistory and history suggests that the conventional view of Korea as a racially and culturally homogeneous society has no real foundation in fact. According to newly revealed archaeological evidence, during the prehistoric Paleolithic period through the Neolithic era and into the Bronze Age, the Korean peninsula was inhabited by two major racial groups, Caucasoid and Mongoloid, who appear to have lived side by side.

Also, during the historical periods, various groups of foreigners — the Han Chinese, Mongolians, Manchurians, Vietnamese, Jurchens, Khitans, Yen, Japanese, Arabs, and various groups of foreigners — immigrated to the Korean peninsula and were naturalized. The descendants of these foreign immigrants have been identified and represent almost twelve million of South Korea's total population. This figure alone is a strong refutation of South Korea's description as monoethnic. Sarah Nelson (1993:163) sums it up well: "There is no evidence that a single ethnic group swept into Korea. . . . It seems much more consonant with the evidence at hand to postulate that over the course of 2,000 years various groups entered the peninsula and found a niche in the mosaic of a developing complex society."

3

Foreign Invasions
and Korean Endurance

Korea has a history interspersed with a series of attacks, dominations, and invasions by neighbors because of its geopolitical location in the middle of the Far East. To the north, the Korean peninsula connects with the vast land of Manchurian China and Siberian Russia, with which Korea shares some 17.5 kilometers (about 11 miles), and across the East Sea from Korea sits the island nation of Japan. The channel between Japan and Korea is so narrow that on a clear day Japan's Tsushima Island can be seen from Busan at the southeastern tip of Korea.

Considering the adverse geopolitical location of Korea, I have had the idle fancy that if the Korean peninsula had drifted away from the Manchurian landmass along the river lines of the Amnokgang and Dumangang, it would have gained a natural buffer like Britain's English Channel, and Korea could have enjoyed the water defense that Britain has in modern times. While the English Channel has halted invading armies, Britain's proximity to the North Sea has allowed it to blockade the continent. In fact, the most significant failed invasion threats came when Dutch and Belgian ports were held by a major continental power, Napoleon during the Napoleonic Wars, and later Nazi Germany during World War II. Such a geographic fantasy for Korea is only just that, of course.

Even if the Korean peninsula had detached from the Asian continent and become an island, it would not have been exempt

from the ravening of the "Japanese pirates" (wōkòu in Chinese; wakō in Japanese; and waegu in Korean) unless the "fantasy island" of Korea were located far from Japan. Japanese pirates raided the coastlines of China and Korea from the thirteenth century onwards. However, if Korea were distanced from China as Japan is, it would not have been the beneficiary of Chinese cultural diffusion beginning in the Three Kingdoms period. Chinese cultural influences spreading to Korea have been numerous and profound—including Chinese script (until Korea invented its own written language in the fifteenth century), Confucianism, surname patterning, bureaucratic systems, and even an examination system. Also coming to Korea by way of China were cultural influences originating west of China, such as Buddhism and Catholicism.

Is Korea located in just about the "right" place to be "wrong" geopolitically? Weighing the advantages and disadvantages of Korea's location in the Far East, many nowadays tend to privilege the advantages:

Korea's vulnerability to foreign intrusion and invasion used to be blamed on its geopolitical location between China and Japan. However, Korean has been successful in capitalizing on the worst situation to turn it to advantage. Among all the Asian countries, Korea is situated closest to the three economic giants, Japan, China, and the United States. This is convenient for trade and commerce. Seoul, the capital of Korea, can easily serve as the dispersal point for other major Asian countries: Tokyo, Beijing, Osaka, Hong Kong, Singapore, and Shanghai. By air, only a few hours separate Seoul from these cities. Seoul also has great potential to service as a center for commerce, transportation, and as an international money market for the Pacific Rim countries. If I may add, Korea may have the largest number of English-speaking natives, with the exception of the two city-states of Hong Kong and Singapore, and the Philippines. Korea's selection as host of the G-20 Economic Summit in Seoul, Korea, in November 2010 is no accident (Kim 2011a:114-115).

Intrusions and Invasions by Hostile Neighbors

At times, the greedy ambition of certain Chinese dynasties to invade and subjugate Korea brought about their own collapse. For instance, the Sui dynasty (581-618) of China launched unsuccessful attacks against Goguryeo in 598 and 612, and the consequent failure of these military raids contributed to the collapse of the Sui in 618, facilitating the rise of the Tang dynasty (618-907). The Tang sent expeditions against Goguryeo in 645 and 647, but it also failed. Since border skirmishes by nomadic northern tribes and full-scale attacks and invasions by neighboring states have been so numerous in Korean history, it is impossible to describe them all in the limited space of this chapter. Therefore I concentrate on large-scale events with big impacts.

Mongol invasions of the Goryeo dynasty (1231-1259)

In the early period of the Goryeo dynasty, before internal political strife had begun in 1170 between civil and military officials, and before external intrusions by nomadic northern tribes, particularly the Mongols (1231-1259), Goryeo was known to be one of the most advanced civilizations in the world, according to Bruce Cumings (1997, 2005). The dynasty was equipped with sophisticated artistic and scientific skill and knowledge. Goryeo was tolerant enough to adopt foreign religions and ideologies such as Confucianism and Buddhism. In order to recruit talented human resources, Goryeo adopted a liberal policy in accepting foreign immigrants regardless of their ethnic and national origins.

In 1231, when the first of six Mongol invasions occurred, the invaders crossed the Amnokgang, quickly securing the surrender of the border town, and soon took the capital at Gaeseong. During the battles, while the peasantry and lowborn classes joined in fighting against the Mongol enemy to defend the homeland, the aristocratic officials all fled. Lee Ki-baik (1984:149) sums up the devastating impact

of the Mongol invasions:

> While moving the capital to Ganghwado the military regime had
> instructed the peasantry to take refuge in mountain fortresses and on
> islands off the coast. These areas thus became the base points for the
> struggle against the Mongols. Unable to overcome the stout resistance
> of these redoubts, the Mongols adopted the tactic of laying waste by
> [setting] fire to the ripened grain fields. . . . The most severe suffering
> and destruction resulted from the invasion led by Jalairtai in 1254. On
> this occasion it is said that the number of captives the Mongols took
> back with them reached more than 200,000, while the corpses of the
> dead were too many to be counted and the entire region through which
> the Mongols passed was reduced to ashes. The population thus declined
> and whole villages fell into ruin.

Some 200,000 Goryeo captives represented a significant portion
of the overall Goryeo population, which is estimated to have been a
little over 2 million; thus the captives amounted to one-tenth of the
whole. Goryeo consequently faced a serious labor shortage. To make
up for it, Goryeo made every effort to take in foreign immigrants
and fugitives (M. Park 1996).

As a personal aside, I have at times wondered what became of
the descendants of the Goryeo dynasty who were captured and taken
to Mongolia. Such a thought came to me in 2007 while attending
an Internet training session for The Cyber University of Korea's
e-Learning Campaign to teach the Korean language and culture to
foreign brides.* Upon meeting a Mongolian-born woman enrolled
in the program, I would wonder whether she just might be one of
the remote descendants of the 200,000 Goryeo people captured in

---

* This campaign was designed to teach the Korean language and culture to foreign
brides who married Korean men via the Internet. Financial support for the campaign
came from POSCO and Goldman Sachs. Administrative assistance for the project came
from central, provincial, municipal, and local governments.

1254. Considering such a possibility, I have made an effort to locate Mongolian brides with Korean maiden names such as "Kim[Gim]," "Lee[Yi]," "Park[Bak]," and others. I have asked Mongolian brides to tell me if they know of anyone who claims to descend from a remote Korean ancestor. So far, out of the total 2,806 brides from Mongolia who have enrolled in CUK's program, I have yet to meet anyone claiming to know such a person (Kim 2011b).

Besides the human casualties, during the Mongolian invasions many irreplaceable cultural treasures were lost, among them, the nine-story wooden pagoda at Hwangryongsa in Gyeongju, the capital of Silla, and woodblocks for the *Tripitaka* that were mentioned in the previous chapter. By the way, the depositories of *Tripitaka* at Haeinsa were designated as National Treasure No. 52 and registered on the UNESCO World Cultural Heritage List in December 1995.

Above all, as a result of the Mongolian invasions, beginning with Wonjong (1259-1274) and for approximately eighty years until Yuan was replaced by the Ming dynasty (1368-1644) of China, Goryeo was a vassal state and compulsory ally of the Mongol Yuan dynasty. In consequence, Mongols and Goryeo rulers were bound by marriages, as Mongol royalty and aristocrats married their Korean counterparts; by these bonds, Goryeo's subordinate relationship to Yuan was cemented. As Lee Ki-baik (1984:155-156) has reported, "Thus Goryeo became a 'son-in-law nation' to Yuan, in a sense an appanage under the Mongol imperial house. Subsequently it became the practice for Goryeo crown princes to reside in Peking as hostage. Even after their accession they would visit Peking frequently, leaving the throne in Gaeseong empty. During the Mongol period the Goryeo kings came to take Mongol names, wear their hair in Mongol style, wear Mongol dress, and use the Mongol language. The royal houses of the two nations had become a single family."

Foreign Invasions and Korean Endurance

Japanese invasions led by Toyotomi Hideyoshi (1592-1598)

Although the Japanese pirates were troublesome, particularly during the thirteenth and fourteenth centuries, the Japanese attacks on the Joseon dynasty from 1590 to 1598 led by Toyotomi Hideyoshi were devastating. Unlike the pirates' plundering of Korean coastlines, Hideyoshi's attacks were a full-blown invasion aimed at conquering Joseon, the Jurchens, and eventually the Ming dynasty of China. Koreans call these invasions the *Imjin waeran*, meaning, literally, the "Japanese disturbance" that started in the year of *Imjin* (1592) in the sexagenary cycle.

From the beginning of the war, Japanese forces were overwhelmingly successful in most land battles because Hideyoshi had half a million battle-hardened soldiers at his disposal to form a remarkable professional army. Hideyoshi's forces were also equipped with innovative weapons such as muskets introduced by traders from Portugal. By comparison, the Joseon soldiers were ill trained, ill equipped, and too disorganized to mount a successful challenge to Hideyoshi's well-prepared forces. The only good thing Joseon had going was the technologically advanced Korean navy led by Admiral Yi Sun-sin and his innovative vessels called *Geobukseon,* or "turtle ship," which had a protective armor thought to have been made of iron plate. The ships were also armed with cannon around their entire circumference. With these ships, Admiral Yi destroyed the Japanese fleet in whatever waters the two enemies happened to meet. Lee Ki-baik (1984:212) has described the effect of Admiral Yi's victories: "Admiral Yi's successes gave complete control of the sea lanes to the Korean forces, with the result that the Japanese efforts to move north by sea and effect a link with their land armies were crushed. Moreover, the fact that the grain-rich region of Jeolla-do remained safely in Korea's hands also was owing to Admiral Yi's achievements. Not only this, but his operations imperiled Japanese supply routes, hampering their freedom to launch fresh attacks." By the way, on 19 June 2013, the war diary of Admiral Yi, called *Nanjung ilgi*, was listed in UNESCO's Memory of the World Register.

No matter how great Admiral Yi's accomplishments, in the end ground forces proved decisive. Hideyoshi's superior land forces occupied garrison after garrison, and town after town. Finally, they occupied almost the entire peninsula. Eventually King Seonjo fled toward Uiju, the peninsula's northwestern corner on the Amnokgang. Distrusting the disorganized regular army of the Joseon dynasty, guerrilla forces sprang up all over the country, including *yangban,* who had been exempt from military service, Neo-Confucian literati, Buddhist monks, peasants, and even slaves. Their strength grew in proportion to their numbers and their expansion of operations. Moreover, a Ming Chinese relief army of some 50,000 strong pushed Hideyoshi's forces southward. This circumstance led to the opening of truce talks between Ming and Hideyoshi. Even though the talks did not go successfully, the first phase of invasion from 1592 to 1596 was brought to an eventual stalemate. In 1597, Hideyoshi invaded Joseon a second time. This time, however, things did not go as smoothly as the Japanese army had planned, for the Koreans were now better equipped and ready, and the Ming army moved swiftly into action. The Japanese land forces could achieve no more than limited success and confined themselves to Gyeongsang-do. At this point in mid-1598 Hideyoshi died, and his death led the Japanese to withdraw completely from the peninsula.

In the course of the seven-year struggle, the whole of Korea's eight provinces became an arena of Japanese pillage and slaughter, but Gyeongsang-do suffered the most, particularly during the second phase. The loss of cultural treasures and relics was substantial. The wooden structures at Bulguksa in Gyeongju and Gyeongbokgung (Gyeongbok Palace), along with the volumes stored in three of the four History Archives (Sago), were reduced to ashes. The human casualties for the Joseon military were estimated to be 260,000, 170,000 for the Japanese and 30,000 for the Ming. Because of such high Joseon mortality, depopulation led to some villages being laid waste.

The "Mound of Ears," or *Mimizuka,* often translated as "Ear

79

Tomb," located near Kyoto, Japan, is a reminder of the cruelties of the Hideyoshi invasions. Traditionally, Japanese warriors would bring back the heads of enemies slain on the battlefield as proof of their deeds. During Hideyoshi's second invasion of Korea, however, the Japanese thought that it would be far easier to bring back just noses or ears instead of whole heads. The Hideyoshi forces meticulously counted, recorded, salted, and packed noses bound for Japan — noses from slain Korean soldiers and civilians as well as Ming troops. The monument enshrines the mutilated noses and ears of at least 38,000 Koreans killed during the invasions. To call it a mound of ears is a shade less brutal than a mound of noses.

Unlike Joseon, Japan benefited from the invasions. The numerous Korean books seized by the Japanese contributed to the development of learning in Japan, particularly the study of Neo-Confucianism. The Japanese forces abducted skilled Korean potters as prisoners of war; these artisans later became the instruments of great advances in the ceramic arts of Japan (Lee 1984).

Among the abducted skilled potters, the Sims are well known. Sim Su-gwan, for example, is a contemporary descendant of one of these abducted artisans. A fourteenth-generation descendant of a captive Korean artisan, Su-gwan's ancestor was Sim Dang-gil, a skilled worker in porcelain. Dang-gil was captured by Hideyoshi's forces in 1597 during the second invasion and was forcibly taken to Japan. He settled in Naeshirogawa, a village in Kagoshima in southern Japan, and worked as a manufacturer of porcelain. Nearly four centuries later his descendant Su-gwan began searching for his identity. In 1964, Su-gwan was able to trace Dang-gil back to Namwon in Jeollanam-do in South Korea, the site of his capture. Finally, Su-gwan found the original village of his ancestors. He often visits his ancestral land and has shared his kinship with his clan members (Kim 1988a). On 13 January 2005, when I visited Sim's porcelain manufacturing plant in Kagoshima, among the many keepsakes Sim displayed in a shadowbox, I was struck by a handmade

Korean dictionary, a sign that the descendants of Sim in Japan had not wanted to forget the Korean language.

The Manchu invasion of 1636 (*Byeongja horan*)

After the Hideyoshi invasions, Manchu's first major invasion of Korea took place in 1627 (*Jeongmyo horan*). After the invasion, Joseon was granted peace in exchange for its pledge to play the role of "younger brother" to Manchu's "elder brother." Because of this pledge, the Manchu subsequently withdrew their army from the peninsula. Before long, however, Manchu (Emperor Taizong) of the Later Jin changed the name of the state to Qing and demanded an annual tribute (suzerainty) from Joseon. In response to Joseon's refusal to comply with this demand, the Qing emperor himself led a second invasion in 1636 (*Byeongja horan*). During this invasion, the sixteenth king, Injo (1623-1649) sent his court, including his sons and their wives, and his ministers to seek refuge on Ganghwado, while he took refuge in Namhansanseong (South Han Mountain Fortress). But his sons and ministers were captured, along with 200 other hostages. In order to humiliate Injo, the Qing emperor set up a platform in Samjeondo, on the upper reaches of the Hangang. At the top of the platform the Qing emperor accepted King Injo's submission and allegedly forced him to repeat the humiliating ritual many times.

Consequently, Qing was able to exert power over Joseon to establish a tributary relationship, forcing Joseon to sever ties with the Ming court and securing two Joseon princes as hostages. The Manchu went on to conquer Ming China and rule China as the Qing dynasty from 1644 to 1912. After that, Joseon was unable to escape the influence of Qing until the latter was defeated by the Japanese in the Sino-Japanese War in 1894.

In comparison with the Hideyoshi invasions, the Qing invasions of Joseon in the seventeenth century were short in duration, the region of impact limited, and the damage much less severe. Nonetheless, once again Joseon Korea became subject to the depredations of

its northern neighbor, and it was perhaps the most, humiliating experience any Korean king has ever encountered through all the dynasties of Korea.

Threat from the West and Japanese Colonization

Pressure to open Korean ports and the Treaty of Ganghwado (1876)

Beginning in the early nineteenth century, when the nascent Korean modernization movement was about to emerge, Joseon had to deal with yet another threat from the West. This time it was a non-military threat, yet it was as formidable as any military one. Even when Lee Ha-eung (1820-1898), better known as Heungseon Daewongun, father of King Gojong, adopted a policy of isolationism, he was aware of challenges from the West, as well as the Japanese, and of the potential impact of foreign influence on the peninsula.

At last, in the name of modernization, Korea was forced to sign the Treaty of Ganghwado with Japan in 1876. The most important feature of this treaty was the provision for opening Korean ports to the outside world. Although the treaty was unfair, it brought Korea for the first time onto the international stage. Beginning in the mid-nineteenth century, foreigners competing for Korean trade clashed on Korean soil, leading to the Russo-Japanese War of 1904-1905.

When the Russo-Japanese War came to an end and Russia was ready to make a peace agreement, American president Theodore Roosevelt attempted to mediate the terms of the treaty. Despite the recommendation of the U.S. minister of legation in Seoul, Horace N. Allen, that the U.S. government should intervene in the Korean situation to counteract Japanese aggression, Roosevelt felt that "it was necessary to acquiesce in Japanese domination of Korea as a *quid pro quo* for Japan's recognition of U.S. hegemony over the Philippines" (Lee 1984:309). The deal between the U.S. and Japan was

known as the secret Taft-Katsura Agreement because it was signed by William H. Taft, U.S. secretary of war, and Katsura, prime minister of Japan, in July 1905. As described in Chapter 1, in this agreement Japan promised not to interfere with American domination of the Philippines in exchange for complete freedom of action in Korea.

As a result of its victory in the Russo-Japanese War, and with the blessing of the U.S., Japan acquired a firm base in Korea for eventually taking some control of the peninsula. Japan moved immediately to establish a protectorate over Korea, forcing the Ministry of Foreign Affairs to sign the Protectorate Treaty in 1905, a treaty so humiliating that Koreans call it "*Eulsa neukyak*," meaning literally "a humiliating treaty signed under coercion in the year of *Eulsa*," a reference to the Korean sexagenarian cycle of time. Five years later, Japan annexed Korea and maintained it as a colony until 1945.

In its nascent efforts to modernize, Korea faced two major challenges: dealing with the immediate threat of foreign forces, particularly Japan, and bringing about domestic reform and modernization in order to retain its sovereignty. From the collapse of the Joseon dynasty to the Treaty of Ganghwado to Japanese annexation, various reform movements emerged under the influence of Enlightenment Thought (Gaehwa sasang), which germinated from Practical Learning (Silhak) in the seventeenth and eighteenth centuries. Enlightenment Thought served as a guiding metaphor for Korea's future modernization. Efforts were made to find solutions to the pressing problems of nineteenth-century Korea by taking new directions. Enlightenment Thought stressed national self-strengthening through education and the development of Korean commerce and industry.

Nevertheless, the ambitious effort to copy Japan's Meiji Restoration and to make Korea an independent nation failed because of factional strife within the reform movement, the interference of Chinese troops, and the unrealistic goal of winning Japanese support for

progressive plans. When the coup d'état of 1884 (*Gapsin jeongbyeon*) led by progressives failed, all these aspirations came to an end. However, various reforms, revolts, and rebellious movements continued to appear, one after the other, among them the Reform of 1894 (*Gabo gaehyeok*), the peasant revolution (*Donghak nongmin undong*) of 1894, and the righteous armies (*uibyeong*) and Independence Club (*Dongnip Hyeopwe*) movements of 1896. These actions were all aimed at retaining Korea's sovereignty, resisting foreign threats, and curing the domestic ills that resulted from a class system incompatible with reform, a subsistence-level economy, and an inept government unable to deal with domestic problems.

The Reform of 1894 was a sweeping one, affecting virtually every aspect of the administration, economy, and sociocultural activities. There was an effort to eliminate class distinctions between *yangban* and commoners and to introduce the concept of equality and dignity for all. The reform package was so broad and extensive that it included new standardization of weights and measures, a new calendar, and an order to cut the Korean male's topknot (*sangtu*). Since the reform introduced some modern features, some Western scholars such as Martina Deuchler (1977a) believe that it was the starting point of Korea's modernization. The reform package, however, did not include strengthening the military, which was essential to the security of a state confronting foreign threats, and some of the reform programs, such as ordering the cutting of the topknot, provoked furious opposition from conservative Koreans. Moreover, an unintended consequence of the reforms, planned as they were during Japanese domination, was an acceleration of Korea's penetration by Japan's developing capitalist economy. Despite these failings, the reforms as a whole significantly advanced Korea's modernization, even if they fell short of guaranteeing Korea's sovereignty.

In direct response to Japanese domination, in 1895 *yangban* officialdom and the Confucian literati mobilized the peasantry and formed guerrilla bands of righteous armies throughout the country.

Some bands included hundreds or thousands of fighters, but until they absorbed the government soldiers disbanded by the Japanese in 1907, they possessed neither military training nor military discipline. The bands were for the most part equipped only with the spirit to fight the Japanese. Using guerrilla tactics, some bands were successful in attacking Japanese garrisons. In 1907, around 10,000 mobilized guerrilla forces from all over the country attacked the Residency-General headquarters and Seoul's East Gate (Dongdaemun). Despite the large number of fighters, they were too weak in manpower and weaponry to defeat the Japanese forces in Korea. The activities of the righteous armies reached a peak in 1908 and declined thereafter, and after annexation their soldiers became independence fighters.

Unlike the righteous armies, the peasant rebellion undertook two major tasks: domestic reform and fighting against Japan to retain sovereignty. After the execution of its founder Choe Je-u, in 1864, the peasant rebellion went underground, but by then it had expanded and was well enough organized to express the peasantry's deep hostility toward the *yangban* class. The rebels led a resistance movement against the inroads of foreign powers, hoisting banners and calling for a crusade to expel the Japanese and Westerners. The peasant rebellion erupted into a revolutionary peasant struggle, employing large-scale military operations.

From the beginning, in Gobu-gun (Gobu county) of Jeolla-do, the peasant rebellion fought against the country magistrate's abuse of power and corruption. Peasants from all the surrounding areas joined forces with the righteous armies, swelling their ranks to over 10,000 men who eventually controlled parts of Jeolla-do and Chungcheong-do after crushing government troops. Eventually, the movement spread to other provinces. When Japan intervened militarily, the righteous armies fought the Japanese toe to toe. However, professional Japanese troops, armed with superior weapons and better training, defeated the ill-equipped peasant army. Nevertheless, the aim of the righteous armies reflected a recurrent demand in Korean history (Lee 1984).

The founding of the Independence Club in 1896 by Seo Jae-pil (Philip Jaisohn), a self-exile to the U.S., and by other new intelligentsia influenced by Western thought, heralded the arrival of the Westernization movement. The Club's activities were focused on three goals: first, to safeguard the nation's independence in the face of external aggression; second, to bring about wider participation in the political process by means of a popular-rights movement; and third, to promote national self-strengthening. Unlike earlier programs and movements, the Club not only dealt with both the nation's independence and domestic reforms; it also pursued the rights of individuals and civil liberty. The goals of the Club "were to establish schools in each village to provide a new-style of education; to build textile and paper mills and ironworks, thus furthering the country's commercialization and industrialization; and to ensure the nation's security by developing a modern national defense capacity" (Lee 1984:304).

In 1896, to express the views of Independence Club members, Seo founded the *Dongnip Sinmun* (The Independent), a thrice-weekly newspaper that eventually evolved into a daily. It was the first genuinely modern newspaper written in the Korean *Hangeul* alphabet. As the activities and goals of the Independence Club gained popularity among the general public, those in power feared that the Club's hidden goal was to abolish the monarchy. They threatened to destroy the Club and drove Seo back to the United States. Eventually the ailing dynasty arrested the leaders of the Club and then called in troops to clear the street of demonstrators protesting the arrest of their leaders. The Club came abruptly to an end.

Japanese Colonization and the Independence Movement

Independence movement

The first phase of Japanese rule began on 22 August 1910 with the appointment of Terauchi Masatake (1910-1916) as the first Governor-General, and was known as the "dark period" (*amheukki*) because of the extensive repression of Korean political and cultural life that took place during this time (Eckert et al. 1990). The Japanese banned political organizations, and it became illegal to assemble for almost any purpose without police permission. In the cities, the police watched intellectuals, religious leaders, and nationalist politicians and made arrests for all crimes (Eckert et al. 1990).

A plot to assassinate Governor-General Terauchi by An Myeong-geun, cousin of An Jung-geun who had assassinated Itō Hirobumi in 1909, resulted in an intensive round-up of nationalists in December 1910. Itō Hirobumi, former prime minister of Japan, was known to Koreans as the principal instrument of Japanese aggression against Korea; he was killed in 1909, one year before the formal annexation of Korea, by a bullet fired by An Jung-geun. The police arrested over 600 Koreans. The long list of those indicted included many leading Korean nationalists. Japanese officials, by dealing harshly with Koreans, hoped to strike a decisive early blow against the nationalist movement.

In order to exploit the colonial economic system, the Japanese mustered their administrative resources and personnel, mobilizing both military and civilian police forces. The colonial government initiated a land survey to lay the foundation for Japan's expropriation of the Korean nation and established the Oriental Development Company as its mechanism. Consequently, the company was able to expand its ownership of land to 154,221 hectares. The number of tenant farmers deprived of their land by the company exceeded 300,000. In the meantime, some 98,000 Japanese landowning families settled in Korea by 1918. David Steinberg (1989) offers a detailed

analysis of the Japanese exploitation of Korean landownership.

Even though Japanese colonial policy was brutal, Koreans continued to fight for their sovereignty. Between 1907 and 1910, some 150,000 Koreans demonstrated and fought against the Japanese. Although the Japanese claimed that resistance ended by 1912, it may have continued sporadically until 1915 (Steinberg 1989). Members of the Korean resistance fled to Manchuria, the Maritime Province, Hawaii, and elsewhere. This contributed to the Korean dispersal and diaspora. Consequently, as of 2012, Korea has a larger proportion of ethnic Koreans living overseas (13.6 percent of the total South Korean population of 50 million) than China has ethnic Chinese (3.8 percent out of 1.3 billion) or Japan has ethnic Japanese (2.0 percent of 128 million).

Although the Korean nationalist movement was united in the single goal of regaining Korean independence, internal strife hampered its attempts to harness nationalist energies into a unified drive to unseat the Japanese. Instead, Korean nationalists were sharply divided into two factions: radical nationalists who advocated social revolution and resistance to Japanese imperialism, and moderate nationalists who advocated gradual solutions to the problem of independence. The latter, who have been labeled cultural nationalists, advocated for education and enlightenment to nurture new values and skills while shaping mass national sentiment to lay the foundation for Korea's future independence (Kim 1988a; Robinson 1988, 2007; Suh 1967). The cultural nationalists considered their objective not simply the immediate goal of throwing out the Japanese at any cost, but of transforming the nation by developing fundamental strengths based on the Western model (Kim 1988a).

The cultural nationalist movement faced a serious challenge from radical nationalism, which attacked its fundamental premise. Michael Robinson (1988:100), an American historian of modern Korean history, sums up the sentiment of the radical nationalists: "Heavily influenced by their study of Marx and other Socialist writers, radicals attacked the fundamental precepts of the cultural nationalist program.

They questioned the utility of national reform within the colonial system, arguing that without political independence talk of national development was meaningless." Most of all, because the cultural nationalists had to work within the limits of colonial rule and deal with the Japanese authorities, their tactics required conciliatory gestures toward the Japanese at times, leaving them vulnerable to the charge of collaboration even to this day. Such factional divisions and disputes were precisely what the Japanese hoped to foment with their strategy of "divided and conquer."

March First Movement and Japanese policy

When Japanese colonial rule intensified, many Koreans participated in a nationwide anti-Japanese demonstration on 1 March 1919. Known as the "March First Movement or March First Uprising" (*Samil undong*), it declared Korean independence from Japan. As Michael Robinson (2007:47) states, the March First Uprising "marks a shining moment of national unity during the long dark night of Japanese rule." The doctrine of self-determinism put forward by American President Woodrow Wilson as an integral part of the post-World War I peace settlement provided an indirect impetus for the protest. The movement was initially sparked by overseas Korean independence fighters in Shanghai, Japan, Manchuria, and Siberia, but it was coordinated through various religious organizations, including Cheondogyo (Religion of the Heavenly Way), Christians, and Buddhists, among others.

Thirty-three representatives of the movement met at the Taehwagwan restaurant in Seoul and formally promulgated a Declaration of Independence proclaiming that Korea had become an independent nation. The opening line of the declaration read, "We herewith proclaim the independence of Korea and the liberty of the Korean people." Students and citizens gathered in Pagoda Park in Seoul and marched through the streets. Passions spread quickly through the city, and the declaration soon led to a nationwide movement, involving at least two

million participants throughout the entire peninsula.

In the brutal military response known as the *Mudan tongchi*, the Japanese authorities mobilized a 5,402-man police force at 751 stations along with several thousand military police. They reinforced these forces with an additional six infantry battalions and 400 military police in their suppression campaign. These combined forces killed 7,509 Koreans. Additionally 15,961 were wounded, and 47,000 were arrested (Steinberg 1989). Defining any Korean taking part in the independence resistance as a criminal, the Japanese decided to cope with subsequent demonstrations by a policy of mass killing. The worst atrocity up to that point took place on 15 April 1919 in the village of Jeam-ri, Suwon, Gyeonggi-do. Lee Chang-soo and George De Vos (1981:29) describe what happened:

> A nearby Japanese garrison had come to the village. Some of the soldiers had roughed up several male inhabitants believed to have joined in the general active protest. The protesters had been part of the Christian community of this village. Two days after this unpleasant episode, some troops returned. They told all the villagers present to assemble in the Church. The villagers did so, thinking they were to hear some word of apology for the brutal behavior of the Japanese soldiers. Once they were all inside, the troops barred the doors, nailed them shut, and poured gasoline about the wooden structure, setting it on fire. Everyone inside was incinerated.

While the church burned, the Japanese soldiers directed a barrage of gunfire at the civilians, killing all of them, including women and infants. The Japanese burned thirty-one houses in the village and set fire to another 317 houses in fifteen villages in the vicinity of Jeam-ri (Han 1981:476).

Despite such horrible burnings and mass murder, Korean independence fighting and demonstrations never flagged, including the "June Tenth Anti-Japanese Movement" (*Yuksip manse undong*), in

1926, and student uprising in Gwangju in 1929. Although the March First Movement and other anti-Japanese independence movements failed to achieve their ultimate goal, they did accomplish several things. Despite the enormous number of casualties, the movements demonstrated national pride, highlighted the inhumane treatment of Koreans by the Japanese occupiers, and demonstrated the potential power of Koreans against their aggressors. The Korean people's political consciousness reached a new stage of awareness. The demonstrations showed that nationalist passions among Koreans at every level could be mobilized for anti-Japanese activities.

The establishment of the Korean Provisional Government (*Daehanminguk Imsi Jeongbu*) in Shanghai in April 1919 was a by-product of the March First Movement. The independence fighters in Manchuria and the Russian Maritime Territory regrouped under the banner of the General Headquarters of the Restoration Army (*Gwangbokgun Chongyeong*) in Antung prefecture in Manchuria. The provisional government was able not only to dispatch its envoys to international conferences and to put out its principal publication, the *Dongnip Sinmun*, but also to continue providing information for the independence movement both within Korea and in the outside world.

Obvious changes occurred in Japan's colonial policy, which was now carried out by the so-called enlightened administration (*Munhwa tongchi*). In a conciliatory move, Japan announced that it was abandoning reliance on its gendarmerie to maintain control in Korea in favor of an enlightened administration. Japan even abolished the wearing of uniforms and swords by civilian officials, although all these moves remained gestures at best. Admiral Saitō Makoto was appointed the new Governor-General. Eventually, Saitō was proclaimed leader of the enlightened administration.

After experiencing Japanese brutality and accepting the harsh political reality, after the March First Movement, that Korea's political independence was for the time being unobtainable, many

Korean nationalists, particularly cultural nationalists, adopted a secondary goal. They advocated for education and enlightenment to nurture new values and skills while cultivating mass nationalist sentiment to lay the basis for future independence. They established schools and industries as well as Korean newspapers in the Korean language, including the *Dong-A Ilbo*, the *Chosun Ilbo*, and the *Sidae Ilbo* (Kim 1998).

Admiral Saitō Makoto replaced the naked coercion of Japan's earlier colonial policy with softer but more effective policies of coercion known as "harmony between Japan and Korea" (*Naeseon yunghwa*). The later period of Japanese colonization was economically and emotionally harsher than the earlier one characterized by overt brutality. Throughout the 1930s, when Japan moved closer to its 1931 occupation of Manchuria and before and after the Sino-Japanese War in 1937, Korea was economically developed and exploited for the Japanese realm. Huge quantities of Korean rice had to be shipped to Japan to overcome a severe shortage there. According to one estimate, about half of the rice produced in Korea was exported to Japan (Steinberg 1989). Korea became a market for the output of Japanese industry, particularly clothing, yarn, and thread—all in all a classic colonial economy. Even the development of Korean hydroelectric facilities, together with various industries that relied on that power, was logistically important to the Japanese to further continental aggression.

"Development without development": Economic exploitation

According to statistics provided by Edward Mason (1980:75-82) and his colleagues, economic growth in Korea between 1910 and 1940, both in manufacturing, with an annual growth rate of over 10 percent, and in agriculture, with a 2 percent annual growth rate, appeared to be substantial. Korean annual economic growth between 1911 and 1938, for instance, averaged 3.5 percent, compared to 3.4

percent in Japan. Mason (1980:76-77) and his associates provide the following explanation for such economic growth:

> In 1940, the Japanese accounted for 94 percent of the authorized capital of manufacturing establishments in Korea, and such key sectors as metals, chemicals, and gas and electrical appliances were almost wholly Japanese. Korean firms, where they existed, were much smaller and financially weaker than those of the Japanese. There were over 1,600 Korean technicians in these industries [in 1944], but this number was only 19 percent of all technicians in Korean manufacturing and construction. The other 81 percent were Japanese, and this percentage rose to 89 percent in such high technology industries as metals and chemicals.

The size of Japanese investment in Korea and Japanese transfer of their technology sound impressive, considering the inventory of the Korean economy at the time. According to a calculation made by Huh Soo Youl[Heo Su-yeol] (2005:314-317), the total values of Japanese assets in Korea by August 1945 were only one seventh of the accumulated amounts of U.S. foreign aid given to Korea up to 1960.

In an effort to counteract, if not eliminate, this misinterpretation of Japan's role in modernizing Korea during the colonization period, Huh Soo Youl (2005) published a comprehensive book with detailed statistics in which he states that economic indicators definitely show that economic growth took place in Korea during the colonial period. Nevertheless, Huh methodically and persuasively asserts that Korean economic growth at that time did not benefit Koreans and had nothing to do with the subsequent expansion of Korean economic growth and industrialization since the mid-1960s. Huh terms it "development without development" (gaebal eopneun gaebal) for Koreans, as he astutely titles his book. For example, despite economic growth during the Japanese occupation, Korean farms suffered great economic privation at the hands of the Japanese.

According to David Steinberg (1989:46), "By 1930, 75 percent of farmers were in debt, and three-quarters of that debt was to Japanese financial institutions. Tenancy and partial tenancy became the norm: some 12 million people (2.3 million families) were tenants, paying exorbitant rents. There was migration out of rural areas: in 1925, 2.8 percent of such migrants went to Manchuria and Siberia, 16.9 percent to Japan, and 46.4 percent to Korean urban areas, where living standards were also low."

Even if the Japanese created the infrastructure for economic growth and industrialization in the peninsula, the ultimate question remains, in the words of Steinberg (1989:40), "For whom . . . was this infrastructure built and the Koreans trained?" The answer, as Koreans argue, is "that it was for the Japanese, to serve their expansionist and military interests. The welfare of the Korean people was not a primary, not even a secondary concern." As evidence, the Japanese focused on constructing industrial plants in northern China proper.

The Japanese plan for Korean cultural genocide

While Korea was exploited by the Japanese economically, Japan instituted policies of deliberate Korean cultural genocide under the slogan of *Naeseon Ilche* (*Nai-sen Ittai* in Japanese), meaning Japan and Korea are one entity. This movement aimed to eradicate Korean national identity by eliminating traditional Korean culture and transforming the Korean people into Japanese imperial subjects (*Hwangguk Sinminhwa*). The overarching aim of *Naeseon Ilche* policy was to eradicate Korean national identity. Japanese authorities pressed Koreans to adopt Japanese customs and habits, including clothing, food, housing, and all aspects of daily life. The policy included promoting Shintōism and the imperial cult; strictly enforcing use of the Japanese language after 1938 in educational institutions, public, and quasi-public places as well as in homes; and forcing Koreans to adopt Japanese names (*Changssi gaemyeong* or creation of family names and change of personal names), beginning in 1940.

I myself was subjected to this cultural genocide. When I was a first grader in a Japanese-run elementary school, together with other pupils I had to go to the Shintō shrine in the morning and recite the imperial oath, pledging, "I am an Imperial subject of the Great Japanese Empire." Not only was I too young to have any opinion regarding the divine origin of the emperor, but I was also physically unable to participate every day in the morning ritual, for the shrine was located atop a steep mountain and I was too weak and sick most of the time to climb it. Because of *Changssi*, I had difficulty adjusting to a strange name, my supposed new "Japanese name." Most of the time, I could not respond promptly when my homeroom teacher, who was Japanese, called the Japanese version of my name.

In addition to *Changssi*, we schoolchildren were put to work collecting all sorts of material to support the war. After a couple of hours of lessons, we had to go out to gather rubber, copper, and brass items, including shoe soles, dishes, brass chopsticks, candlesticks— even utensils used in Korean ancestor worship. We had to gather turpentine (pine resin) from pine trees. It was hard for me to climb up the steep mountains, and then it was hard to empty the collecting cans hanging from the trees. None of this was easy for a weak child like me. Tired of the manual work at school, I played hooky with my friend. As we did not attend school for months, finally I was expelled from school. Eventually, I reentered the school on 1 September 1946, almost one year after Korea became independent from Japan on 15 August 1945. If Korea had not become independent, I would never have had a chance to finish even elementary school.

The Japanese authorities pretended that the policy of *Changssi* was voluntary, but in reality it was mandatory. In my case, if I did not change my name to the Japanese style, I could not enroll in public school. Often police were used to enforce the policy. Those who did not conform to the policy were thought to be anti-imperial and were discriminated against in employment. Despite some vehement opposition, less than four months after the announcement

of the policy, over 300,000 Korean households (about 87 percent of the total) had changed their names (Kim 1988a).

The Japanese authorities thought that the major hindrances to their cultural-eradication movement were the Korean newspapers and other *Hangeul* publications. Therefore, the Korean Language Society (*Hangeul Hakoe*) became another Japanese target. In October 1942, the leaders of the Korean Language Society were arrested, and some such as Lee Yun-jae died in prison. In 1938, Korean-language teaching was banned from secondary school curricula; beginning in 1943 the Korean language was no longer taught in primary schools. Japanese control of writing, speech, books, films, and music was thorough, and anything that obstructed or hindered the implementation of *Naeseon Ilche* was a target for eradication.

Facilitating opportunities for higher education was the top priority of Korean cultural nationalists since there were very limited educational opportunities in the colony beyond middle school. Increasing numbers of college-bound Koreans went to Japan. To counteract the undesirable social effects inherent in such a system, nationalists mounted a drive to establish a Korean university (Eckert et al. 1990). The cultural nationalists formed the Society for the Establishment of a Korean People's University in November 1922, with the help of 1,170 supporters. The goal was noble, hopes were high, and expectations great, but the movement came to naught because of "Mismanagement of donations, infighting between chapters, vitriolic criticism from more radical nationalists, including the withdrawal of support from the important All Korean Youth League" (Eckert et al. 1990:291). In addition, the Japanese pushed the movement toward failure, employing the tactics of "divide and conquer" against cultural nationalists and radical leftists.

In 1926, the Korean nationalists' drive to establish their own university further diminished public interest in a Korean people's university. The dream of a Korean people's university, however, never died for some cultural nationalists. Kim Sungsoo[**Gim Seong-**

su], for one, made a faithful attempt to build a national university. Kim's drive materialized in 1932, when he took over Boseong Junior College and eventually expanded it to Korea University after Korea became independent from Japan following World War II (Kim 1998).

Japanese mobilization of Koreans

The greatest Korean suffering during the Japanese colonial period took place when Japan began to mobilize Korean manpower to serve its war machine. This process steadily escalated after 7 July 1937, when Japan launched its full-scale assault on China. In February 1938, as combat grew more intense, the Japanese announced the Special Volunteer Army Act, and some Koreans were mobilized in June of that year. In 1939, the Japanese proclaimed the National Manpower Mobilization Act, under which Korean laborers and military draftees were involuntarily brought to Japan to compensate for the manpower shortage created by the expansion of the war to Southeast Asia. These mobilized laborers were forced to work in munitions plants and coal mines, and to perform various other forms of physical labor to support the war. According to South Korean government statistics, between 1939 and 1945 over four million Koreans were drafted into Japanese work programs in Korea, while more than 1.2 million were forced to work in Japan. Many Koreans were sent to coal mines in Japan, Sakhalin (formerly a Russian island until it was divided after the Russo-Japanese War), and elsewhere, which became one of the major contributors to the Korean diaspora.

As Japan escalated its war effort, the National Mobilization Law of 1942 entrapped increasing numbers of Koreans. Following the Japanese attack on Pearl Harbor, Koreans were subject to the Japanese military draft. The number of Koreans drafted into the Japanese military totaled 360,000 by the end of World War II. These conscripted soldiers were sent to the South Pacific, Southeast Asia, and China. Almost half of them died or were missing in action. The aggregate number of Koreans mobilized throughout the war by the

Japanese government in both Korea and Japan reached almost 6 million (Kim 1988a, 1998).

The Japanese military draft hit my own family. My oldest brother was drafted in July 1944 when I was seven years old. My parents and relatives were terribly worried; causalities were so high that draftees had small hope of returning home after the war. Eventually, my brother was sent to a battlefield in the Shandong peninsula in China. He later escaped and joined the army of the Korean Provisional Government in Shanghai, *Gwangbokgun*. He and his comrades fought with the Chinese army against the Japanese. Because he did not come home immediately after the war, we thought he had died on the battlefield. He came home several months after the liberation when the provisional government returned from China.

Mobilization of Korean women for sexual slavery for Japanese soldiers

The Japanese mobilization included females, ranging from twelve to forty years of age, who served under the designation of the Women's Volunteer Workers Corps. The mobilized females were forced to engage in harsh manual labor, and a good many of them were sent to the war zone to work in brothels for Japanese soldiers. The Japanese authorities even picked up pregnant women to meet their assigned quotas despite instructions that they draft only single females between the ages of eighteen and twenty-nine. I have revealed the story of this poignant ordeal of the so-called comfort women in my book *Faithful Endurance* (1988a) for English-speaking readers. Informing the book was an interview with Yoshida Seiji that aired on South Korean MBC-TV on 3 June 1984. Yoshida, who was involved in "women-hunting" and in charge of drafting Koreans in Gyeonggi-do, Jeolla-do, and Jejudo, confessed his role in the events at a level of detail that Japanese authorities are reluctant to admit. A

complete transcript of the Yoshida interview with Mun Sun-tae was published in Korea (*Yeoseong Dong-A* 246 [June 1984]:393-397), followed by Yoshida's (1983) book in Japanese.

When I published the story in 1988, it went largely unnoticed. But more recently stories are emerging as victims begin to speak out. Sympathetic demonstrations occur daily in front of the Japanese Embassy in Seoul, and a growing number of scholars and intellectuals have written about this tragedy in English (Cumings 2005; Hicks 1995; Kim 1988a; Soh 1996, 2008). The exact number of victims is yet unknown, but Bruce Cumings (2005) estimates there were somewhere between 100,000 and 200,000. Chunghee Sarah Soh (2008:xii) elaborates: "Estimates of the total numbers of Japan's comfort women range between 50,000 and 200,000. Though these included small numbers of Japanese, Korean women constituted the great majority. It is believed that large numbers of Chinese women were also victimized. The Japanese military also used women in Southeast Asia and the Pacific Islands, including the Philippines, Indonesia, Indochina, and Burma—then American, Dutch, French, and British colonies, respectively—which Japan occupied in the early 1940s."

Now that the tragic story of the comfort women has become widely known seven decades later, most Koreans demand that Japan make some formal apology and compensate the sixty known survivors still living today. The Japanese response has been consistent in saying that the issue was settled in a 1965 normalization treaty in which Japan provided South Korea with $800 million in grants and soft loans. Such are the positions, for instance, of Japan's former and current prime ministers. Other right-wing politicos in Japan have been more dismissive of the claims made about the comfort women. Hashimoto Tōru, the mayor of Osaka, for one, said in a press conference there is no evidence that the women were forcefully dragged off with violence, threats, or kidnapping.

In Spring 2013, Japanese nationalist politicians' remarks and behavior underlining their unwillingness to atone for the country's

wartime crimes are drawing the ire of Korea and China, and posing hurdles to the strategic refocus of the U.S. on the Asia-Pacific region. Informed Koreans are concerned that Japan's rightward shift could hamper efforts to ease the confrontational mood stemming from historical and territorial disputes, and multilateral practical cooperation in security, the economy and other areas. Particularly, Japanese Prime Minister Abe Shinzō infuriated the two neighboring states once again after he posed for a photo in the cockpit of a warplane with the number 731 written on its fuselage at an Air Self-Defense Forces unit on 12 May 2013. The figure evokes Unit 731, a notorious covert chemical and biological research unit of the Japanese Army that carried out lethal human experiments during the Second Sino-Japanese War and World War II.

Unsatisfied by this response, Koreans have been pushing Japan to apologize officially by staging demonstrations every Wednesday. By 14 December 2011, the 1,000th demonstration had taken place. As a symbolic gesture, on 14 December 2011 a South Korean civic group erected a bronze statue of a comfort woman in front of the Japanese embassy in Seoul. The statue sits directly across the street from the embassy gate. There is an empty chair beside it, allowing tourists to have their picture taken with the comfort woman.

Balancing out the right-wing politicians in Japan is Kono Yohei, the former Japanese chief cabinet secretary, who issued a formal statement back in 1993 admitting that his country forced Korean women into sexual slavery during World War II. He maintained that Japan must go on record admitting its misdeeds. Recently, Kono said in an interview with the *Yomiuri Shimbun* on 8 October 2012 that "If [Japan] denies the comfort women issue, it will not only lose national credibility from countries in Asia but also the United States and Europe as they will doubt Japan's awareness of human rights matters."

Japan's international reputation has in fact already been tarnished. In February 2007, several U.S. congressmen led by Michael Honda,

who is of Japanese descent, submitted a resolution that in strong words holds Japan responsible for the sexual enslavement of women during its colonial occupation of Asia, including Korea, in the past century and demands its apology. On 26 June 2007, by an overwhelming thirty-nine votes to two, the House Foreign Affairs Committee passed a resolution calling on Japan to formally acknowledge and apologize for the mass coercion of comfort women into army brothels. Eventually, on 30 July 2007, the U.S. House of Representatives unanimously passed a resolution calling for Japan to acknowledge its inhumane deeds fully, not to redirect or deny history by blaming the victims.

In 2013 and 2014, as Abe Shinzō and his right-wing nationalist government, refused to acknowledge that imperialist Japan forcibly took Korean and other Asian women during World War II into its military brothels. In response to such a refusal, on 15 January 2014, the U.S. House of Representatives attached to its spending bill a document that urges the U.S. Secretary of State to "encourage" the Japanese government to address issues raised into its 2007 resolution on "comfort women," a euphemism for those forced into sexual slavery for the Japanese military during World War II. Promptly, on 17 January 2014, President Barack Obama signed the bill.

Also, it was reported in July 2012 by several Korean newspapers that U.S. Secretary of State Hillary Clinton supposedly said that all the State Department reports on the issue must use the term "enforced sex slave" instead of comfort women, although the *Korea Herald* has reported that Clinton's department has neither confirmed nor denied the report (*Dong-A Ilbo*, 7 July 2012; *Korea Herald* 12 July 2012; *Segye Ilbo*, 17 July 2012).

All in all, it appears that although the war ended nearly seven decades ago, postwar problems are still awaiting final resolution even at this date. Besides the issue of comfort women, there are the countless Koreans sent overseas by the Japanese during war mobilization. However, all of them lost their Japanese citizenship when Japan notified them en bloc that they were no longer Japanese

citizens after Japan's surrender to the U.S. Ironically, by then, the Korean peninsula was divided, and both Koreas did not have normal diplomatic relationships with Japan. Thus, these formerly conscripted workers became stateless people. Even at present, some 600,000 ethnic Koreans and their descendants in Japan lack Japanese citizenship. Their legal status in Japan is precarious at best. In Sakhalin, there were roughly 43,000 Koreans when World War II ended, of whom an estimated 1,500 still survive. Recently, a Russian source suggested that several thousand mobilized Koreans in Sakhalin might have been executed by the Japanese as the war ended (*Maeil Business Newspaper* 15 August 2012). Such victims are the bitter legacy of Japanese mobilization during World War II.

Historical adversities as the source of Korea's endurance

Because of its unique geopolitical location, Korea has had to endure many foreign threats, invasions, and occupations. As we have seen, while some of these struggles lasted only a short time, others lasted much longer. In order to survive these ordeals, Koreans developed an ethos of endurance. As Paul Crane (1978:96) has said, "One of the great virtues of many Koreans is their ability to endure hardship. Korea is the land of those who have learned to endure in order to survive." Foreign threat, domination, and intrusion have firmed Koreans' resolve to retain their identity and continuity and overcome hardships. While struggling to sustain life itself, Koreans gained the wisdom and courage to cope with a bad situation and at times were able to turn their worst situations to their advantage. An assessment of Korea made by Gregory Henderson (1968:13) is very perceptive: "Smallness of dimension, stability of boundaries, ethic and religious homogeneity, and *exceptional historical continuity mark Korea*" (emphasis mine). Indeed, despite suffering a long history of foreign intrusion, Koreans have never lost their native culture and language. While the Korea language did pick up some loan words from using Chinese characters (prior to the invention of *Hangeul* in the fifteenth

century) and a few Japanese words during the years of occupation, these words constitute much less than the proportional stock of loan words in English.

It must be said, however, that Japanese colonization for thirty-six years did much to determine postwar Korea's fate. Japanese colonization put into place the preconditions for Korea to be divided into north and south, which then led to war. Had there been no period of Japanese occupation, the Korean peninsula would not have become the site of a Cold War "hot" conflict. Had there been no Japanese colonization, Korea would not have gone through political chaos after liberation in 1945. Had there been no colonization, Koreans could have begun their modernization, economic development, and rapid industrialization much sooner than the mid-1960s. Korea's nascent modernization had been germinated in the seventeenth and eighteenth centuries (Deuchler 1977a: xii; Eckert 1991:5). Korea lagged behind Japan for some twenty years, a lag time one must measure against the duration of Japanese imperialism in Korea.

4
A Long Road Toward Democracy

In its extensive exposure to wars and killing, my generation is one of the most unfortunate generations of Koreans, for it has weathered so much socioeconomic and political turmoil and endured devastating wars. I was born one year after the Japanese assaulted China. Historians do not agree on the exact date World War II started. Some scholars believe that it started when the Japanese launched a full-scale assault on China in 1937, using the Marco Polo Bridge Incident outside Beijing as a pretext (Hsu 1970:60). Others date it from the German invasion of Poland on 1 September 1939. Regardless of this disagreement, I was born at the start of World War II, and the war dragged on until I was seven years old. In writing this chapter I feel as if I am ruminating on my own life history (Kim 2002).

Emotional Burden of the Memories on Post-WW II Atrocities and the Korean War

My eyewitness account of Korea's twentieth-century history of war and related atrocities dates back almost seven decades, yet my memories of that time are vivid. I still remember hurrying into a tunnel-like underground shelter (banggongho) when I heard a warning siren. Every public building as well as every private dwelling had shelters against possible American air raids. Even now, when I ponder my memories of going into these shelters, I am still unable

to understand why American war planes would come to our region of Korea—remote, isolated, mountainous—where there were no military installations, nothing of strategic value, and no Japanese soldiers. However, every once in a while, I was able to spot several tiny silver objects in the sky, which I was told were American warplanes called B-29s.

Although I was unable to comprehend what Japanese Emperor Hirohito's unconditional surrender on 15 August 1945 would do to us, I was old enough then to remember a big celebration in the town square. My parents hoped that my brother, who had been drafted by the Japanese army and sent off to battle somewhere in China, would return home soon. My brother was sent to a battlefield in the Shandong peninsula, but he escaped from the Japanese army and joined the army of the Korean Provisional Government (KPG) in Shanghai. Despite the high casualty rate of the Korean military draftees, my brother miraculously survived. Eventually he returned home, several months later, after Korea's liberation from Japanese occupation, when the KPG returned from China.

Most Koreans born after the Korean War assume that fighting and killing in the Korean peninsula took place during the Korean War (1950-1953), but many brutal and gruesome killings actually took place right after liberation. Communist guerrillas attacked right-wing anti-Communists, and police retaliated against the Communists and their sympathizers. Often killings happened in remote regions where police forces could not intervene. Since my hometown is located at the extreme northeastern tip of Gyeongsangbuk-do, near Taebaeksan (Mt. Taebaek), the second-tallest and most rugged mountain in South Korea, it was a natural sanctuary for Communist guerrillas, and killings were common. In fact, it looked as if we lived in two distinct political systems: by day, we inhabited the capitalistic, democratic, and right-wing-led Republic of Korea; and by night, because the South Korean police force could not protect us, we lived in a *de facto* Communist state.

Very little has been written about the political disarray of this

particular period. According to my experience, the Communist guerrillas used all kinds of tactics to gain control of the region at nighttime. Often I was awakened in the middle of the night and had to leave my house when militiamen who patrolled the village blew a whistle, warning us that Communist guerrillas had infiltrated the village. When daylight came, police came by to search for those villagers who had given food and other supplies to the guerrillas under the imminent threat of death. As soon as these villagers were found, they were dragged to the police station and tortured. Some of them were executed after going through a quick trial. Accidentally, I once witnessed the execution of guerrillas whose faces had been covered with white towels before they were shot. I closed my eyes so as not to see, but I could not close my ears. Such scenes were not uncommon throughout remote regions of the country. In my village, liberation from Japanese rule (haebang) certainly did not bring freedom from fear and pain (Kim 2002).

While a guerrilla war was being waged continuously in my region, a truly full-scale war began on 25 June 1950, when I was a sixth grader in elementary school. In less than one month, the North Korean People's Army (Inmingun) reached our corner of South Korea. Eventually, the North Korean authorities came to our house, evicted us, and made our house the regional headquarters of the northern forces. We were relocated to a hut with a thatched roof. Meanwhile, our life in this miserable shack continued until General Douglas MacArthur's forces made a spectacular amphibious landing at Incheon on 15 September 1950. Since our village is located in the heart of the Baekdudaegan (Great Baekdu Mountain Range), which runs all the way to the northeastern side of the peninsula, many retreating North Korean troops passed through our village and its vicinity. Eventually, the front line of the war moved north of our region, and finally a ceasefire was declared in 1953.

During my college years in Seoul, as the post-Korean War government, led by Rhee Syng-man[Yi Seung-man] and his Liberal

Party (*Jayudang*), was tilting increasingly toward autocratic rule, I was an active participant in the "April 19 Student Revolution" in 1960, which brought down the First Republic. Immediately, the Second Republic was born, but it was brought down by a military coup on 16 May 1961. The country was in disarray, and for the next three decades, it was ruled by the military. I escaped this oppression by going to America for advanced study, and stayed there for the next thirty-six years.

As a professional anthropologist living in America, in the early 1980s I conducted fieldwork on dispersed Korean family members in Korea, fieldwork that brought back my childhood memories of the war. While I was engaged in this study, in 1983 the Korean Broadcasting System (KBS) telecast scenes of reunited families via a reunion telethon that attracted the world's attention. Watching these scenes I spent many nights weeping along with the participants as I heard their tragic stories of separation and witnessed the joy and emotion of their reunions. It has been difficult for me to write about myself and my own people and yet remain objective. I have documented Koreans' endurance in awaiting reunion with loved ones in the book, *Faithful Endurance* (1988a).

To maintain a balance between the compassion I feel as a native anthropologist doing fieldwork with my fellow Koreans and the detachment I need to muster as a scientist, I have decided to set aside, by and large, my personal feelings in recounting Korea's mid-twentieth-century history. In the survey of modern Korean political history to follow, I will occasionally refer to my own experiences when they seem appropriate.

The Post-War Power Vacuum

The dramatic conclusion to World War II on 15 August 1945 came after atomic bombs fell on two Japanese cities. The bombs

that fell on Hiroshima on August 6 and Nagasaki on August 9 claimed over 132,000 victims either dead or missing. Among the victims, at least 10,000 Koreans, most of them dragooned laborers in Japanese war industries, were annihilated (Cumings 2005). Japan's drastic unconditional surrender left Koreans unprepared to organize their own government.

Political chaos after the liberation

Five days before Emperor Hirohito officially announced Japan's unconditional surrender, a middle-rank Japanese (who remains unidentified) from the Bureau of Political Police, sensing that Japanese surrender was imminent, visited Song Jin-woo[Song Jin-u], a journalist and moderate cultural nationalist, in the early morning of 10 August and proposed that Song lead an interim administration to preserve law and order as the Japanese left Korea. Song refused this offer and instead demanded freedom of the press, the release of all political prisoners, and distribution of food to starving Koreans. Song also called for a halt to the Japanese surveillance of his residence. The following day, a Korean attorney named Kang Byeong-sun[Gang Byeong-sun] reassured Song that the Japanese surrender would come within the next few days (Kim 1998).

On 11 August 1945, four Japanese high officials invited Song to an unidentified Japanese home to induce him to head up an interim administration to preserve the peace. Song refused once again, but the Japanese importuned him persistently until the eve of the day of liberation. As an excuse, Song told the Japanese authorities that he was too ill to accept such a responsibility. Bruce Cumings (1981:70) reports that Song "refused the Japanese efforts because (1) he realized that any Korean administration would have to wait for the sanction of the incoming Allied forces; and (2) he believed that the Korean Provisional Government (KPG, established in Shanghai in 1919 and currently in Chungking[Chongqing]) was the legitimate government of Korea. . . Song did not want to give the Japanese the benefit of cooperation in their

time of need." At the final meeting with the governor of Gyeonggi-do at his office on 14 August, Song again refused the Japanese request.

The Japanese were becoming desperate to create an interim administration run by an influential Korean, so they turned to Lyuh Woon-hyung[Yeo Un-hyeong], whose views were a mixture of socialism, Christianity, and Wilsonian democracy. Lyuh had always been willing to work with Communists, and he embraced Marxism as a "good idea" (Cumings 1981:474-475 n.114). Eventually, Lyuh met with Endō Ryūsaku, the Governor-General's secretary for political affairs, in the early morning hours on 15 August and accepted the Japanese offer. Lyuh in turn demanded the following of Japan: "(1) Release all political and economic prisoners immediately throughout the nation; (2) Guarantee food provisions for the next three months; (3) Absolutely no interference with the maintenance of peace or with Korean activities for the sake of independence; (4) Absolutely no interference with the training of students and youths; (5) Absolutely no interference with the training of workers and peasants" (Cumings 1981:71).

Lyuh did not waste any time. He gathered his followers at his home and began to create an organization that would serve as an administrative body for a political movement above and beyond the interim peacekeeping administration. Mobilizing for this purpose his existing underground political organization, the Korean Independence League (*Joseon Geonguk Dongmaeng* or *Geonmaeng* in abbreviation), Lyuh and his followers formed the Committee for the Preparation of Korean Independence (*Joseon Geonguk Junbi Wiwonhoe* or CPKI). The launch of the CPKI did not go smoothly, because the Japanese authorities thought it went too far beyond its original mission of peacekeeping. On or about 18 August, the Japanese demanded that Lyuh scale back the CPKI's functions to the original mission (Kim 1998).

Partition of the peninsula and ideological divisions

Although the official announcement of the division of the Korean peninsula along the thirty-eighth parallel was made on 2 September 1945, the United States had actually planned this division four days before the end of the war. The initial decision to draw a line and divide Korea was made on 10-11 August 1945 in an all-night session of the U.S. State-War-Navy Coordinating Committee (SWNCC). According to Bruce Cumings (1981:120; 1997:186-187), John J. McCloy of the SWNCC directed Colonel Charles H. Bonesteel and Major Dean Rusk, both of whom knew very little about Korea, to come up with a plan to define the zones to be occupied by American and Russian forces (Collins 1969). Preoccupied with dividing the peninsula evenly, they were unaware that Korea would suffer economically if the industrialized north and agricultural south were separated, not to mention that the division could potentially lead to war between the two Koreas. The U.S. officials who made this hasty decision were satisfied because the Soviet Union had no objections and would agree to the placement of the capital city of Seoul in the American-controlled zone.

On 20 August, while Lyuh was mobilizing his CPKI, an American B-29 dropped leaflets signed by General Albert Wedemeyer announcing that the U.S. military would soon arrive and that, until then, the Japanese authorities should maintain law and order. The Japanese promptly ordered the dismantling of all Korean law-and-order and political organizations. The leaflets clearly announced that the troops entering Seoul would be American.

American forces arrived a full month later than Soviet forces. However, U.S. Major General Archibald V. Arnold replaced Abe Nobuyuki as Governor-General. Two days later, Endō Ryūsaku and all Japanese bureau chiefs were removed from office, and the administration changed over to the United States Army Military Government in Korea (USAMGIK, hereafter the U.S. Military Government). Having lost its vital mission, Lyuh's CPKI gradually shifted toward

organizing Communists. In the meantime, right-wingers, encouraged by the fact that Seoul and the south would be ruled by Americans, began to mobilize.

Koreans were sharply divided along ideological lines into right and left. Commanding General of the United States Armed Forces in Korea (USAFIK) John Reed Hodge handled Korean affairs poorly; he and his officials were clearly ill prepared to rule over fifteen million Koreans because they had no experience with Korea and its culture. Hodge was also ill informed about the purpose of the partition of the peninsula (Cumings 1981:126; Henderson 1968:21). Native Korean Baek Nak-jun (George Paik), who served as an advisor to Hodge's military government, observed that "The American military forces drifted away from the mission due to a lack of a clear policy and goal" (Baek 1982).

Meanwhile, as a result of sharp ideological divisions among Koreans, South Korea was bustling with many small political parties and organizations. The most visible activity was organized by Lyuh Woon-hyung, who used the CPKI as a basis for forming the Korean People's Republic, or KPR (*Joseon Inmin Gonghwaguk*). In early September, Lyuh published a list of its officers and cabinet members and their departments, including Rhee Syng-man as chairman, Lyuh himself as vice chairman, and Kim Sungsoo as the minister of education (Lee 1946). He had made an effort to include both left- and right-wing adherents, and cabinet members were chosen according to their various specialists.

While Lyuh's CPKI became active, the rightists led by Song Jin-woo, using the organizational backbone of the Preparatory Committee for National Congress (*Gukmin Daehoe Junbihoe*) together with the other four right-wing factions, formed a political party, the Korean Democratic Party, or KDP (*Hanguk Minjudang*), that was anti-Communist, conservative, and politically right-wing. Some critics such as Bruce Cumings (1981:96) point out that "unlike the KPR, the KDP never tried to reach across Korea's political divisions and

include Koreans on the Left." Relations between Lyuh's KPR and the U.S. Military Government were becoming strained, and the KDP began to receive full support from the U.S. Military Government, a manifestation of the "American-KDP camaraderie" (Cumings 1981:150).

Trusteeship Versus Anti-trusteeship

Because of this rapport between the U.S. Military Government and the KDP, the U.S. Military Government supported the latter's request for the return of Rhee Syng-man and KPG leaders. Subsequently, Rhee returned on 16 October, and Kim Koo[Gim Gu] and twenty other KPG leaders returned on 23 November. Their return, however, exacerbated the existing factional strife in Korean politics.

Although the KPR was instrumental in the return of the KPG leaders, those leaders were critical of the KDP, accusing KDP leaders of being Japanese collaborators, and the KDP and KPG quickly became estranged. If KPG leaders were to exercise political hegemony, they knew they would have to eliminate the KDP leaders; in response, the KDP supported Rhee Syng-man instead of the KPG leaders. In the meantime, Hodge and his advisors were clearly less trusting of Kim Koo, former president of the KPG in Shanghai, than of Rhee Syng-man (Kim 1998).

While all of this political maneuvering was going on, at a conference in Moscow in December 1945, the foreign ministers of the United States, Great Britain, and the Soviet Union adopted a trusteeship plan for five years under the assumption that Koreans were not yet prepared to govern themselves. The announcement of the trusteeship triggered public outrage and violent opposition from Koreans. Although at first the Communists and leftists joined in the anti-trusteeship movement, on 2 January 1946 the Communist groups in Korea, doubtless on Russian instruction, suddenly changed their attitude and came out in favor of trusteeship. Well-rehearsed demonstrations in favor of trusteeship were held in North Korea and

by leftist groups in the south.

On 28 December, Song Jin-woo attended a strategy session against the trusteeship at Kim Koo's residence. While Song urged the avoidance of direct confrontation with the U.S. Military Government, Kim Koo and his KPG leaders not only insisted on using radical and violent means if necessary, but also on clashing head-on with the U.S. Military Government. The argument between Song and the KPG continued until four o'clock in the morning on 29 December. At 6:15 a.m. on 30 December, Song Jin-woo, aged fifty-six years, was assassinated at his home (Cumings 1981:219).

At this point, Kim Sungsoo took over leadership of the KDP. With his involvement in party politics, the anti-trusteeship movement became an anti-Communist movement: when the Communists shifted their position from anti-trusteeship to pro-trusteeship on 3 January 1946, the anti-trusteeship movement became the anti-Communist movement. As the leader of the KDP, Kim Sungsoo made it clear that the KDP absolutely opposed the trusteeship. At the same time, Kim made it clear that he and the KDP supported the KPG leaders, and persisted in trying to bring about cooperation between Rhee Syng-man and Kim Koo (Lee 1991).

In the meantime, Rhee Syng-man organized the National Headquarters for Unification (*Minjok Tongil Chongbonbu*) to establish an autonomous Korean government. Kim Koo and others from the Korean Independent Party (*Hanguk Dongnipdang,* or *Handokdang*) also formed a National Assembly (*Gukmin Hoeui*) to succeed the Extraordinary People's Assembly in launching an anti-trusteeship movement and bringing about national unification between the leftists and rightists. The left-wing political parties formed the Democratic National Front (*Minjujuui Minjokjeonseon*) and carried on a unified pro-trusteeship campaign. The left-wing hoped that by giving their positive support to the work of the Joint Commission they might in turn create support for the trusteeship concept. Nevertheless, "when the police found evidence of large-scale currency

counterfeiting at a press used by the Korean Communist Party (May 1946), the U.S. authorities put out an order for the arrest of its leaders, whereupon the Communists went underground" in willy-nilly fashion (Lee 1984:377).

The General Election and the Birth of the Republic of Korea

When the U.S.-Soviet Joint Commission reconvened in May 1947, the United States proposed deferring the Korean issue for further discussion at a conference of the foreign ministers of the four powers. When the Soviet Union rejected this proposal, the United States submitted the question of Korea's independence to United Nations supervision. As a result, a U.N. Temporary Commission on Korea was created to oversee and facilitate the implementation of Korean independence. However, the U.N. Commission was unable to enter North Korea because of Soviet opposition. On the basis of the Commission's report in February 1948, the Interim Committee of the United Nations General Assembly authorized elections to be held in those areas of Korea open to the supervision of the Commission, which meant only the southern half of the country. This effectively nullified the trusteeship issue.

While Rhee Syng-man welcomed the U.N. decision, Kim Koo wanted to leave room for North Korea to participate in the election after the Soviet Union's interference had been removed. At this juncture, it appeared that a coalition among the nationalists, especially Rhee Syng-man and Kim Koo, could be accomplished. However, the effort to unite Korean leaders on the issue of elections ultimately failed. While Rhee Syng-man and Kim Sungsoo insisted that elections be held exclusively in the south, Kim Koo and his followers urged dialogue between the north and south. The first general election in the history of Korea was carried out only in the south on 10 May 1948. One hundred seats were allocated to the

Rhee Syng-man's Inauguration Address

North Korean provinces, and 200 representatives were chosen by South Korean voters. During the election, Communist disturbances were not minor: 846 people were killed, and 1,040 Communist terrorist acts and assaults were reported. The general election results indicated that Rhee Syng-man's National Society for Rapid Realization of Korean Independence (NSRRKI) had fifty-five seats, while Kim Sungsoo KDP had only twenty-nine seats (Kim 1998).

Lee's shrewd initial political maneuver after the election was to adopt the first Korean constitution. In the summer of 1947, Yu Chin-O[Yu Jin-o], a constitutional scholar and professor at Korea University, had been asked by the U.S. Military Government and Kim Sungsoo to draft a constitution. Yu's original draft included a parliamentary system, but Rhee Syng-man manipulated it into a presidential system. The revised version of the constitution

A Long Road Toward Democracy

was passed by the General Assembly on 12 July, and formally promulgated on 17 July 1948. The National Assembly held a presidential election on 20 July and elected Rhee Syng-man, who took the helm of the government and inaugurated the Republic of Korea (ROK) on 15 August 1948. In the meantime, the Provisional People's Committee for North Korea, led by Kim Il-sung[Gim Il-seong], was formed in February 1946, serving as a virtual government in the north. The Democratic People's Republic of Korea (DPRK) was formally established on 9 September 1948.

Kim Il-sung was officially the supreme leader of North Korea from 9 September 1948 until his death in 1994, having various titles such as prime minister (1948-1972), leader of the Workers' Party (*Joseon rodongdang*) (1946-1994), and president (1972-1994). Following the elder Kim's death in 1994, he was succeeded by his first and eldest son Kim Jong-il[Gim Jeong-il], who was the general secretary of the Workers' Party of Korea, Chairman of the National Defense Commission, and Supreme Commander of the Korean People's Army. Upon the death of Kim Jong-il on 17 December 2011, his third and youngest son, Kim Jong-un[Gim Jeong-eun], only 28 at the time, became the supreme leader of North Korea as his grandfather and father had been. In such a short period of time, the young Kim has held the titles of the First Secretary of the Workers' Party, Chairman of the Central Military Commission, First Chairman of the National Defense Commission of North Korea, and Supreme Commander of the Korean People's Army. In North Korea, leadership succession by three generations of the Kim's family has taken place.

The Korean War (1950-1953)

Outbreak of the Korean War

Rhee Syng-man continued to be plagued by ideological confrontation between left and right. There were many clashes and confrontations

between the two factions. There had also been several major pro-Communist military rebellions in the southwestern region of South Korea, including Yeosu and Suncheon in October 1948. Because of such turmoil, Rhee's government hardened its anti-Communist policies.

While the Rhee government was busy strengthening its anti-Communist stance, at dawn on Sunday, 25 June 1950, North Korea attacked South Korea along the thirty-eighth parallel. The South Korean army was caught completely off guard. Some scholars writing not long after the war speculated that the South provoked the war (Stone 1952:44), but documents relating to the origins of the Korean War that have come to light from Russian sources confirm that the North attacked the South, putting such former speculation to rest. Park Myung-Lim[Bak Myeong-lim] (1996), a Korean political scientist, addresses this issue well in his comprehensive and voluminous book on the Korean War, supporting the conventional view that North Korea was the aggressor.

On the second day of the war, the South Korean army had to give up Uijeongbu, the gateway to Seoul. North Korean tanks reached Seoul on 28 June, the third day of the war. While President Rhee Syng-man assured frightened citizens over the radio that he would make every effort to secure the capital city, the South Korean army blew up the Hangang Bridge, cutting off the major route leading south. Over one and a half million Seoulites were isolated and trapped, panic-stricken and unable to flee. This thwarted retreat separated many family members.

On 25 June, at the request of the United States, the U.N. Security Council passed a resolution calling for the immediate cessation of hostilities and the withdrawal of North Korean armed forces to the thirty-eighth parallel. The Security Council also called upon all United Nations member countries to render assistance in the execution of the resolution. Concurring were sixteen countries, including the United States, Britain, France, Canada, Australia, New

Zealand, the Netherlands, the Philippines, Turkey, and seven other countries. These sixteen nations constituted the U.N. forces.*

On 29 June, 300 planes under U.N. command entered the Korean peninsula, followed by the arrival of U.N. forces in Busan on 1 July. The Security Council authorized the United States to designate a commander of the united forces. Thus, President Harry S. Truman named General Douglas MacArthur commander-in-chief of the United Nations Forces. Nevertheless, the tide of the war was not easily reversed. The U.N. forces continued to retreat. By the end of July, North Korean troops occupied most of the southern peninsula. These forces ferreted out reactionary elements, including members of the South Korean armed forces, police, anti-Communist rightists, and many others who became subject to arrest, imprisonment, abduction, and persecution. There were innumerable massacres by the Communist occupation authorities. The North Korean authorities forced the residents of the occupied area to collaborate with the People's Army of the north. Many South Korean political leaders, scholars, intellectuals, and prominent writers who were unable to escape Seoul were kidnapped and forcibly taken to the north.

While most of South Korea had fallen under northern control, on 15 September 1950, MacArthur's forces made an amphibious landing at Incheon, and the tide of the war turned abruptly in favor of the United Nations. Seoul was recaptured, and the U.N. forces broke out of the Busan perimeter. As the North Korean army retreated northward, the U.N. forces crossed the thirty-eighth parallel and marched north, securing the area to the Amnokgang.

The war then took a complicating twist as CPV appeared

---

* A complete list of the nations that constituted the UN forces (the total numbers of troop each country sent to Korea are written in the parentheses) include: U.S.(40,677); the Great Britain(1,257); Australia(342); the Netherlands(120); Canada(313); New Zealand(241); France(269); the Philippines(128); Turkey(904); Thailand(134); Greece(192); South Africa(34); Belgium(103); Luxemburg(2); Colombia(163); and Ethiopia(121).

at the front in October and November. China had mobilized a massive number of "volunteer soldiers" who swept over the area in continuous waves, without concern for high casualty rates, in a military maneuver that came to be known as "human-wave tactics" (Whiting 1960:118). As to the magnitude of the human wave, "The U.N. command estimated that about 486,000 enemy troops, or twenty-one Chinese and twelve North Korean divisions, were committed to the Korean front and that reserves totaling over one million men were stationed near the Amnokgang, in Manchuria, or on the way to Manchuria" (Miller et al. 1956:4).

The CPV and North Korean troops were able to halt the advance of U.N. and South Korean troops, forcing them to withdraw from the area they had occupied in North Korea and relinquish Pyeongyang on 4 December 1950. During this retreat, the largest number of North Koreans to flee at one time also moved south. Koreans refer to this winter retreat as the "January Fourth Retreat" (*Ilsa hutoe*). However, the retreat actually took place in late November and early December of 1950, not on 4 January 1951, which was when Seoul was taken by the CPV. The military decision to abandon Pyeongyang and the subsequent flight of Pyeongyang citizens across the Daedonggang resulted in bedlam. The damaged iron bridge over the river had not yet been fully repaired, and many desperate refugees made dangerous maneuvers on the broken, crooked railings as they tried to cross the river. Some fell to their deaths in the waters below; others were severely injured. The retreat was equally dramatic from the area of the Heungnam pier located on the northeastern part of North Korea.

When Chinese troops crossed the thirty-eighth parallel and entered Seoul on 4 January 1951, the South Korean government and the U.N. troops pulled out of the city and abandoned the port of Incheon. Once again, they had to deal with the evacuation of refugees. The war during the winter months of 1951 consisted of attacks and counterattacks to the south of Seoul, and in early March,

U.N. troops began to make substantial gains and move steadily forward. Then, on the nights of 14 and 15 March, U.N. troops moved once more into Seoul, which by now had changed hands four times. The U.N. forces fought their way to the thirty-eighth parallel, and on 4 April they broke through that line, opening the door once again for a northward march. However, on 11 April, Truman relieved MacArthur of his command and replaced him with General Matthew Ridgway.

When the tide of the war turned in favor of the United Nations under Ridgway's command, after U.N. troops and South Korean forces had successfully pushed the invading forces north of the thirty-eighth parallel, the Soviet Union proposed cease-fire discussions among the participants in the war. The Truman administration was eager to end the fighting, now that it was possible to establish a division of Korea near the thirty-eighth parallel. When the rulers of China indicated their interest in a truce, Truman authorized Ridgway to begin negotiating with enemy generals. The talks opened on 10 July 1951 at Gaeseong, and on 27 July 1953 at Panmunjom[Panmunjeom] an agreement was reached on terms for an armistice.

Throughout the war, casualties were enormous. "The modest estimates cite 1.3 million South Korean civilian and military casualties; the number for North Korea is 1.5 million out of a population one-third the size of the South's." And, "a total of 33,625 Americans, hundreds of thousands of Chinese and Korean (North and South) soldiers, and millions of civilians died in this brutal 'police action'" (Robinson 2007:114, 194 n.6). Nevertheless, a large number of contemporary South Koreans do not know when the Korean War broke out, reflecting the overall lack of interest about the war that defines inter-Korean relations to this day. According to the results of a nationwide survey conducted by Research & Research, Inc. at the request of the Ministry of Security and Public Administration from May 25 through June 6, 2013 on the basis of a sample of 1,000 adults and 1,000 teenagers,

36.5 percent of adults and 52.7 percent of youths in middle and high schools did not know the year the war broke out. Time has begun to erase the wretched memories of the fratricidal war from the minds of many Koreans.

Family dispersal

Although the literature on the Korean War is relatively rich, accounts of the suffering of civilians, particularly those separated from their family members, have been scarce. To fill the vacuum, I wrote narratives of those who suffered the tragedy of family dispersal during the war in *Faithful Endurance* (Kim 1988a). This book supplements an existing literature that tends to focus on politics, warfare, and weaponry.

Korean family dispersal stemming from the partition of the peninsula along the thirty-eighth parallel has been the most devastating long-term outcome of the Korean War. Although a cease-fire went into effect more than a half century ago, the splitting and splintering of families persists to this day. Once it was estimated that 10 million Koreans (5 million from each side) were separated from their family members. While 10 million may be an exaggeration, no one can be certain. Today, South Korean authorities estimate that the figure is between 750,000 and 1.23 million first-generation displaced family members (Kim 2002:158).

The physical displacement of such a large number of people was painful for the nation, but adding to that pain was the fact that family members who were dispersed to the north and the south found it virtually impossible to communicate for more than a half a century. Despite the fact that millions of Koreans have suffered from this extended diaspora, their misery was poorly publicized until the summer of 1983, when the KBS aired its reunion telethon. The telethon came about almost by accident. On 30 June 1983, while I was conducting anthropological fieldwork on the subject, KBS broadcast a television special on families separated during the war.

A Scene of KBS Telethon

Originally it had been scheduled to air for only ninety-five minutes, but the program was so successful that KBS found it difficult to end it at the scheduled time. Thousands and thousands of people rushed to the studio to register for an appearance on camera. In the end, the program lasted four and a half months, from 30 June to 14 November 1983, claiming 450 hours of airtime and reuniting more than 10,000 persons with lost family members. With the permission of the Korean Red Cross, which was monitoring the reunion for KBS, I was able to gain access to Yeouido Square (later named Reunion Plaza), where the KBS building is located.

Following the telethon, the thirty-ninth North-South dialogue produced the first North-South exchange of hometown visitors and art troupes. Originally, negotiations between North and South Korea for the repatriation of civilians, kidnapped by the North during the war, had begun under the auspices of the United Nations on 10 July 1951, and later resumed in 1953. The negotiations continued through the 1960s, 1970s, 1980s, and 1990s. At last, on 20 September 1985, some 151 visitors, headed by their respective Red Cross presidents, arrived in Seoul and Pyeongyang by way of

Panmunjeom for a four-day visit. Excluding the art troupes, fifty members from each Korea were chosen for reunions with family members, close relatives, and friends.

When Kim Dae-jung[Gim Dae-jung] became president of South Korea in February 1998, he implemented a policy of détente, and later, on his visit to North Korea in June 2000, he facilitated an exchange of visits for dispersed families. One hundred people from each Korea would make visits to Seoul and Pyeongyang to reunite with family members separated for more than half a century. Since then, there have been numerous exchanges, involving a total of 9,977 persons from both sides.

Unfortunately, since the number is limited to 100 persons per side for each reunion, it will take a very long time for all those separated to be reunited. For people who had long anticipated such reunions, the process is moving very slowly. The eighty-one-year old president of the association of Pyeongannam-do noted that if reunion meetings continue at their current pace, it will take twelve and a half years to accommodate the next 150,000 registrants. If he were placed in the last group, he would be ninety-three years old before it happened. Since time is growing short for elderly first-generation dispersed Koreans, to speed up the process the South Korean national Red Cross plans to establish a permanent meeting place where dispersed Korean family members can meet their loved ones anytime they wish. The South Korean Red Cross also facilitates family reunions via on-line video meetings, utilizing fifteen stations throughout South Korea, including the Red Cross headquarters in Seoul. As of July 2006, there had been fourteen meetings and four on-line video meetings among separated family members. However, since 2008, on-line video meetings have been halted, perhaps owing to difficulties in selecting and scheduling participants. I have been informally told by some that technological problems have been a cause of disruption.

Construction of a permanent center to accommodate family

reunions was originally scheduled for completion by 30 August 2005. However, on 19 July 2006, North Korea made a shocking announcement: it was calling off all family reunions in retaliation for South Korea's refusal to provide rice and fertilizer to North Korea following its announcement of a missile test. On 11 March 2007, however, the two Koreas agreed to restart the construction of the reunion center, and visits between dispersed families resumed. Finally, the center was completed on 12 July 2008 in the vicinity of Geumgangsan (Mt. Geumgang) in North Korean territory. The center did not stay open for long, however. One South Korean tourist was shot and killed when she entered a military area demarcated by the North Korean government; tension arose between the two Koreas, and tourism to Geumgangsan stopped and the center closed. North Korea took over the facility, even though South Korea was responsible for building it. The center has not been used since.

Parenthetically, South Korea has made an incessant effort to accommodate family reunion for those separated families between north and south. At last, however, as a response to South Korea's tenacious effort, both Koreas agreed to have a reunion meeting for five days from 20 February to 25 February 2014 at the Geumgang san. At the meeting, 170 families with 813 members from both Koreas have participated. It was the nineteenth reunion since September 1985, and took over three years since the last one in October 2010. Such a prolong interval between such reunions becomes distressful to the sundered family members, knowing many surviving members die as time goes by. In fact, only 72,882 of the 128,842 remain alive as of 31 July 2013, meaning that some 2,000 have died each year. Of the survivors, 9.3 percent were aged over 90, 40.5 percent were in their 80s, 30.6 per cent in their 70s, and 11.4 per cent in their 60s. Time is growing short for the aged Koreans who are long for their loved ones.

The Struggle for Democracy

The Rhee Syng-man government and student revolution

After Rhee Syng-man became president, he exerted complete control over Korean politics. Because his presidency was a long one, Rhee's autocratic ideas had time to take root and grow stronger. His skilled political manipulation, enhanced by fierce anti-Communist slogans and aided by sycophantic subordinates, allowed him to wield enormous power during and after the Korean War. Favoritism and corruption in the temporary wartime capital of Busan were widespread in the government and in the upper ranks of the military. Rhee's arbitrariness and self-righteousness threatened to dissolve the National Assembly. He built up his power base by devising a new, more subtle tool for controlling that body. In late 1951, Rhee formed the Liberal Party, which was composed of a motley assortment of opportunists who employed police surveillance, armed thugs, and gangs to preclude any public criticism of Rhee's regime. In 1952, when Rhee was up for reelection, he proposed the same constitutional amendments that the National Assembly had refused to approve in 1951, which were election of the president, vice president, and a bicameral legislation by popular vote. Rhee then declared martial law and arrested several dozen assemblymen (Kim 1998).

By 1954, employing various immoral, unethical, and illegal tactics, Rhee's Liberal Party had achieved a clear majority in the Assembly. In order to amend the constitution and make himself president for life, Rhee and his party employed every available means to bribe, banish, or threaten independents in the Assembly. The vote for the constitutional amendments on 27 November 1954 resulted in 135 in favor, sixty against, one invalid, and six abstentions. The vote fell one short of the 136 required for passage. The next day, Rhee's Liberal Party made the mathematical argument that two-thirds of 203 was 135.33, so 0.33 should really be rounded down, thereby making the required number of votes 135, not 136. This idea came

19 April 1960 Student Revolution

from a strategy session of the Liberal Party following the shy-by-one vote. Based on the mathematical principle of rounding down, the amendment was considered passed, and Rhee returned to office for a third term (Kim 1998).

The 1960 election was marred by fraud so blatant that it could not be ignored. In March and April 1960, massive student demonstrations broke out in Seoul and other cities throughout South Korea. On 19 April 1960, some 300,000 university and high school students marched toward the presidential mansion, where they were fired upon by police. About 130 students were killed and 1,000 wounded. The occurrence is now known as the April 19 Student Revolution. As a senior at college, I myself was one of the participants, and I still vividly remember the battlefield-like scene of bloody streets as we marched toward the president's official residence in Seoul, then called Gyeongmudae, now renamed Cheongwadae, or Blue House. Gazing at the photo of "19 April 1960" (reproduced above) brings back unforgettable memories of over half a century ago. Despite the bloodshed, the march was not in vain. Because of

the demonstration, Rhee finally resigned on 26 April, and the First Republic came to an end.

The collapse of Rhee's government was followed by a brief interim administration, and the constitutional government was changed to a bicameral parliament consisting of a lower and upper house. Yun Po-sun[**Yun Bo-seon**] assumed the figurehead position of president, and Chang Myon[**Jang Myeon (John M. Chang)**] took on the role of prime minister to lead the new government. However, the tasks proved too daunting for a weak government to handle largely because of incessant political wrangling within the ruling Democratic Party (*Minjudang*) and the social instability brought about by the never-ending street demonstrations after the student revolution. The short-lived (15 August to 16 May 1961) Second Republic fell when a military junta led by Major General Park Chung-hee seized power.

The coup d'état of 1961

Using social and political unrest as a pretext, forty-three-year-old Park Chung-hee took power in a coup on 16 May 1961. Park suspended the constitution, formed a military junta to impose an absolute military dictatorship, and created the Supreme Council for National Reconstruction. Park emerged as its chairman and ruled the country until 1963. With presidential elections scheduled for mid-October of that year, Park retired from the army, ran as the presidential candidate of the Democratic Republican Party (DRP), defeated Yun Po-sun, former president of the Second Republic, and became president of the Third Republic.

In 1967, Park won reelection and two years later secured a constitutional amendment to open the way for a third term. He was elected again in 1971. In an attempt to ensure his unchallenged command of Korean affairs, Park declared martial law on 17 October 1972, and called for a program of "revitalizing reform" (*Yusin*[Yushin]), modeled on the Japanese Meiji Restoration in late 1868. The *Yusin* Constitution was approved by an intimidated populace through

Maj. Gen. Park Chung-hee at the Coup d'état

a public referendum in November 1972, and this effectively transformed the presidency into a legal dictatorship. Under the terms of the new constitution, the president was to be chosen indirectly by members of the National Council for Unification, which was headed by the president himself. Moreover, the president was empowered to appoint one-third of the National Assembly members.

Park's eighteen-year rule saw the degradation of the movement for Korean democracy, but his government revolutionized Korean economic growth and industrialization, employing effective economic development plans with the help of a new and studious apolitical group of technocrats and a well-educated, disciplined, and dedicated workforce.

In contrast with Rhee Syng-man, who maintained strong anti-Japanese sentiments, Park normalized diplomatic relations with Japan by signing a bilateral pact in 1965. Facing vehement opposition, especially from student groups, against such a normalization agreement, Park tried to persuade the public that any compensation resulting from the normalization agreement with Japan could

be used as seed money for Korean economic development and industrialization.

Whatever his ambitions, goals, and accomplishments, Park's rule was brought to an abrupt end on 26 October 1979, when he was assassinated by his close aide and confidant Kim Chae Kyu[Kim Jae-gyu], director of Park's own Korean Central Intelligence Agency (KCIA). Parenthetically, Park's regime presents us with an irony. During his authoritarian rule, when he exerted tight control over Korean politics in what amounted to a dictatorship, many Koreans demanded a liberal democracy, rejecting his system and strongly resisting it. However, polls conducted in May 2005 by the Committee for Evaluating Korean presidents rated Park favorably—as most desirable CEO, 59.2 percent; most likeable president, 51.4 percent; most respectable person throughout all of Korean history, 20.1 percent (a category in which he beat out King Sejong, 16 percent; Admiral Yi Sun-sin, 15.3 percent; and Kim koo, 7.9 percent); and best president, 63.5 percent, in five separate categories.

The period of transition immediately after Park's assassination was characterized by uncertainty, confusion, and contention. Under the 1972 constitution, the prime minister, Choi Kyu-hah[Choe gyu-ha], became acting president and was supposed to serve out the remainder of Park's term. However, a new military force emerged and staged yet another coup on 12 December 1979 to fill the power vacuum in the aftermath of Park's death. The new military group was led by Major General Chun Doo-hwan[Jeon Du-hwan], head of the Defense Security Command, the agency responsible for investigating Park's murder. He was promoted to three-star and, soon after, four-star general within a year and retired from the military in 1980 to devote himself to politics. In late August, Chun was named president by indirect elections in accordance with the *Yusin* Constitution and was inaugurated on 1 September 1980.

With Park's death, Kim Dae-jung, whom Park had sentenced to death, and Kim Young-sam[Gim Yeong-sam], another opposition

A Long Road Toward Democracy

leader, regained prominence. At the same time, demonstrations against the new military leader spread. The most furious and brutally repressed demonstration took place in May 1980 in Gwangju, the most populous city in the provincial capital of Jeollanam-do. Many civilians and students were killed. While the government claimed the deaths amounted to 200 people, the opposition estimated the number to be 2,000. The Gwangju Democratization Movement may have started in response to specific government abuses and to a general sense that the Jeolla-do region had suffered repeated discrimination under all the governments of the previous twenty-five years. Many Koreans blamed the United States for not interfering when brutal mass killings took place during the Gwangju uprising. David Steinberg (1989:60) relates the sentiments of many Koreans who "expected the United States to intervene and force negotiations and were astonished when it did not do so, further attributing U.S. inaction to support for the Chun government."

Despite the demonstrations, commotions, and social unrest, Chun adopted a new constitution that established indirect election of the president, who would serve a single seven-year term. By doing so, Chun was able to assume the presidency in early 1981. After Chun's inauguration in January as president of the Fifth Republic, U.S. President Ronald Reagan invited Chun to be his first official foreign guest. Reagan hoped to improve relations with Korea that had cooled during Jimmy Carter's administration when Carter pressed human rights issues. As part of his campaign platform in 1976, Carter also promised to withdraw U.S. troops from Korea. According to Steinberg (1989), President Reagan's invitation to President Chun actually saved the life of Kim Dae-jung, who was under a death sentence for allegedly inciting the riots that led to the Gwangju incident. Nevertheless, I speculate that for many Koreans, Reagan's invitation to Chun might have been interpreted as the United States' endorsement of the legitimacy of the Chun government. From that time onward, anti-U.S. sentiment began to rise among Korean

youth (Steinberg 1989). Demonstrations by students and labor unions became frequent. In 1985, for instance, there were 3,877 on-campus demonstrations. As massive protests against the Chun government escalated in June 1987, the government was forced to accept the people's demands for a set of democracy measures on 29 June. The constitution was revised again, reintroducing direct popular election for the president with a single-five-year term.

At the ruling Democratic Justice Party (DJP) convention on 10 June 1987, Chun designated Roh Tae-woo[No Tae-u], a former general who had played a central role in the success of Chun's coup, as the party's candidate for president. As the DJP candidate for president, Roh announced a sweeping liberalization program, maintaining a cautious distance between himself and the increasingly unpopular Chun. Roh won the presidential decision, and his government was able to institute some positive foreign policies toward the Communist bloc, including establishing diplomatic ties with Eastern European countries, the Soviet Union, and China. Also, Roh was credited with diplomatic initiatives that enabled both North and South Korea to join the United Nations simultaneously. Roh's administration allowed for rapid liberalization on the labor front, but furious labor strife and student demonstrations were still prevalent. He limited his term to five years as specified in the constitution.

Democratic Development

End of military rule. As Roh's government came to an end, so did military rule. Finally, a civilian government was restored when one of the opposition leaders, Kim Young-sam, became president in 1993. Kim's government had the distinction of eradicating corruption in the bureaucracy by legislating a property registration system for public officials and the practice of using real names in financial transactions. He also restored autonomous local governance (*jibang jachi*), which had been suspended since the 16 May 1961 military coup. Despite all these moves, Kim's government suffered severely,

and the country faced financial exigencies when the foreign currency crisis swept across Asia during 1997-1998. Kim's government failed to defend the national financial system and eventually asked for the IMF for a bail out.

When Kim Young-sam's five-year term as president ended in February 1998, another opposition party leader, Kim Dae-jung, was inaugurated as the new president. Kim's biggest single accomplishment was the first-ever inter-Korean summit with North Korean leader Kim Jong-il. Kim's détente policy even resulted in the North and South Korean teams forming a single group when they entered the Olympic stadium at the opening ceremony of the Sydney Olympics in 2000.

In the December 2002 presidential elections, Roh Moo-hyun[No Mu-hyeon], a straight-talking and self-educated former human rights lawyer from the ruling Millennium Democratic Party (Saecheonnyeon Minjudang), the same party to which Roh's predecessor Kim Dae-jung belonged, won by a narrow margin over the opposition party leader. After he became president, Roh left the Millennium Party on 11 November 2003 to create his own party, the Uri Party (Yeollin Uridang) with forty-seven members of the National Assembly. In the seventeenth general election on 15 April 2004 the Uri Party won a landslide victory. However, Roh's naïve manner and straight talk have often been interpreted as imprudent by his critics. His "sunshine policy" inherited from Kim Dae-jung, together with his generosity in aiding North Korea, has been criticized, especially after North Korea's push for its nuclear programs.

During the tenure of Roh's presidency, following Kim Dae-jung's presidency, the general and ideological division between Koreans became clearly manifest. Younger and more liberal forces were supportive of the Roh government, but older people and conservatives tended to be resentful. The conservative Grand National Party (Hannaradang) and media accused Roh of incompetence. To overcome such criticism, the major task of the Roh government was to negotiate this division while still pushing Korea's economy

forward. Despite his effort, Roh's party began to lose its popularity as evidenced by a miserable defeat in various local, regional, and national elections. As the presidential election drew closer, a growing number of the National Assembly members wished to disassociate themselves from an unpopular president.

Parenthetically, after leaving office when his tenure ended, Roh returned to his hometown village. Fourteen months later, Roh was suspected of bribery by prosecutors, and the subsequent investigation attracted public attention. At last, on 23 May 2009, Roh committed suicide by jumping from a mountain cliff, after leaving a suicide note on his personal computer. In the 19 December 2007 presidential election, Roh's designated successor, Chung Dong-young[**Jeong Dong-yeong**], was defeated by Lee Myung-bak of the Grand National Party nominee with a wide margin of five million votes. Unlike Roh, Lee, a graduate of Korea University, had a rather colorful and successful career as the former CEO of Hyundai Engineering and Construction before entering politics. Later, as the mayor of Seoul, he helped promote Korea's visibility and influence in the region and around the world; in 2010, for example, Seoul hosted the G-20 summit. Despite his political success, there was some criticism of Lee's policies, including his hawkish attitude toward North Korea and bribery scandals involving his close political associates and even his own brother. In fact, the former Grand National Party changed its name to the Saenuridang (*New World Party*).

In sum, after 1993, when Kim Young-sam was elected the country's first civilian president after three decades of military rule, Korean political power was peacefully transferred by the people's choice. Perhaps the single most significant accomplishment of all presidents after Roh Tae-woo will be the peaceful transfer of power to the succeeding president, regardless of party affiliation. To pass the mantle of presidential power across party lines, similar to party oscillations attending the election of successive American presidents, is a remarkable accomplishment for Koreans, who have fought for

this goal for seven decades.

Structure and organization of the current Korean government. Since the Republic of Korea was born in 1948, the Korean constitution has been amended nine times. Nevertheless, except for the months between August 1960 and July 1961, Korea's constitution has called for a presidential system in which the president is both head of state and chief executive. Under the current constitution, the government has three branches: legislative, judicial, and executive. In addition, there are two other constitutionally based institutions, the Constitutional Court and the National Election Commission.

As of November 2012, the legislative branch consists of a single house, the National Assembly, whose 299 members serve a four-year term. Of the total, 243 were elected from single-member electoral districts and fifty-six were shared by their parties in proportional representation. In addition to deliberating bills for legislation, examining government budgets, and ratifying international treaties, the National Assembly is in charge of inspecting and auditing the administration, and approving the appointments of the prime minister and the director of the Board of Auditing and Inspection. The National Assembly can impeach public officials and may recommend to the president the removal of executive officials, including the prime minister.

The judiciary consists of three tiers of courts: the Supreme Court, which consists of thirteen justices and a chief justice; appellate courts, which are established in five large cities; and district courts, which are located in Seoul and twelve other provincial cities. The judiciary also operates a family court, an administrative court, and a patent court.

The executive branch, headed by the president, consists of the prime minister, the State Council, seventeen executive ministries, twenty-four independent agencies, the Board of Auditing and Inspection, and the National Intelligence Service. The president is elected by popular vote for a single five-year term, and the prime

minister is appointed by the president, subject to the approval of the National Assembly.

Also, self-governing powers are given to sixteen higher-level (provincial) governments and 234 lower-level (municipal) governments, including seventy-five cities (*si*), eighty-six counties (*gun*), and sixty-nine districts (*gu*) within metropolitan cities. The local chief executives are elected by district popular vote.

Secure democratic political system. Throughout history Koreans have been good students in adopting foreign ideas, ideologies, religions, and philosophies such as Confucianism, Taoism, Christianity, Buddhism, democracy, Communism, capitalism, and others. Korea started experimenting with democracy when it became an independent country following liberation from Japanese rule. Koreans experimented with democracy before fully realizing its meaning decades later. This is evident in Korea's republican governance. Korea instituted its first republican government after World War II: the constitution of 1948 was based on the principle of democracy. Korea then experienced the strong authoritarian rule of Rhee Syng-man for twelve years and then military rule for thirty-two years thereafter. Finally, as of 1993, Koreans enjoyed a genuine democratic society. After first encountering the idea of democracy, it took nearly seven decades for Koreans to adapt to the democratic principle in both word and deed.

If Koreans had not experienced various political ideologies and systems — such as harsh dynastic rule, colonial subjugation, autocratic dictatorship, and inhumane military juntas — they might not value the democratic system as dearly as they do. Again, perhaps having had a history of adversities and having *han* as an ethos has turned contemporary Koreans into guardians of democracy. In Korea, democracy has been achieved through political evolution, devolution, and revolution, taking nearly a half century, from 1945 to 1993, to become established.

5
Marriage, Family and Kinship

Because I was trained in cultural anthropology with a cross-cultural emphasis, one of my first teaching assignments at The University of Tennessee at Martin in 1971 was on comparative family systems. I thought it would be a good opportunity for me to introduce students to the native Korean family system in a cross-cultural perspective. Students seemed to be interested in my presentation of the subject because I was relating my own stories. The focus of my class was on the future direction of family systems in general and the Korean system in particular. Now, four decades later, some of my predictions about families have turned out to be correct while others were far off the mark.

Among my faulty forecasts I did not foresee that many Koreans today, especially females of marriageable age, would choose not to marry, preferring instead to remain single. In 2012, one-person households comprised 25 percent (4,538,642) of all Korean households (17,950,675). Such a significant percentage might suggest that the "family is finished" (Nimkoff 1965:357) — or as extremist Barrington Moore put it five decades ago: not only is the family not functionally necessary; it is dysfunctional in modern industrial society (Moore 1958). In this view, according to Nimkoff (1965:357), "the current theories of the survival of the family are projections of middle-class hopes." When I was teaching in the early 1970s, I thought such an eventuality might someday occur in the Western world, but I never imagined it could happen in Korea.

Wild geese Fathers, Penguin Fathers, and Eagle Fathers

In addition to that, since returning to Korea I have learned several neologisms related to the family such as "wild geese fathers" (*gireogi appa*), "penguin fathers" (*penguin appa*), and "eagle fathers" (*doksuri appa*). In the early 2000s, there was a dramatic increase in Korean students studying abroad, especially at English-speaking schools, and many Korean mothers accompanied their children overseas while the fathers stayed in Korea and earned money to support their wives and children. To describe this situation, the term "wild geese fathers" was introduced. Geese are migratory birds that fly north to Siberia in the summer and south to Korea in the winter. Like geese, some fathers visit their distant families seasonally or occasionally. However, some fathers cannot afford to do so, and for them there is another neologism: "penguin fathers." Penguins of course cannot fly, nor can they cross into warm ocean water from the cold Antarctic. There is yet another group of fathers called "eagle fathers" who visit their wives and children overseas whenever they wish because they can afford it. This term was probably coined because the eagle is a large and powerful bird that symbolizes freedom.

To support the expense of early overseas study, parents not only have to make financial sacrifices but also disrupt normal family life. This situation divides a family by an ocean, a phenomenon in Korea so common and widespread, and at times heartrending, that the *Washington Post* ran a detailed story entitled "A Wrenching Choice" by Phuong Ly on 9 January 2005. In 2005, educational expenses for supporting students studying abroad at an early age were estimated to be $3.5 billion. If expenses for accompanying family members were added to this, the total expenses that year amounted to around $10 billion.

The separation of Korean couples is not driven solely by overseas study, yet the number of couples living apart continues to grow. According to demographic data, over the fifteen years leading up to 2010, one in ten married couples in Seoul did not live together, due

mainly to work and the education of their children. The number of married Seoulites living apart jumped by 61 percent, up to 210,000 households, from 1995 to 2010. Such couples accounted for 9.5 percent of all households in 2010, up from 5.8 percent in 1995. Meanwhile, households composed of married couples fell, as a proportion of the whole, from 77 percent to 63 percent during the same period. This was due to an avoidance of marriage by members of the younger generation and to an increasing number of divorces among middle-aged couples.

Also, in terms of anticipated family transformations, in the early 1970s I concurred with the prediction that there would be fewer arranged marriages in the future. Contrary to this view, however, there has been a revival of arranged marriages of a sort in Korea coincident with rapid urbanization and industrialization. In this revival the arrangers of marriages are often professional matchmakers who make a business out of brokering marriages. Nearly 200,000 foreign brides have married Korean men as a result of arrangements made by international matchmaking agencies, friends, or relatives.

In this chapter, these new trends in Korean marriage, family, and kinship will be described. However, some traits of contemporary Korean marriage, family, and kinship can only be properly understood within the long view of historical context. Let me begin, therefore, by providing some of that context with a discussion of the traditional Korean kinship system.

Kinship

Outward appearances notwithstanding, one should not assume that contemporary middle-class Seoulites—with their Western-style clothes, personal automobiles, and Western-style apartment complexes—are just like Westerners. One has to see what they do after they come home from work. Once at home, they take off their

Western clothes, sit on the floor (even though their apartments are furnished with suites of Western furniture), and deal with their family members in accordance with traditional Korean family and kinship rules. Contemporary Koreans are complicated beings.

Many Korean ancestral lineages have launched campaigns to update their genealogies as symbolic reflections of a revitalized interest in kinship. Social gatherings of lineages occur more often now than in the past, despite Koreans' increasing participation in various formal organizations not based on the family. Walking along the streets of Seoul, one can easily find more signs for lineage offices than signs for the Rotary, Kiwanis, and Lions Clubs. I receive more letters of solicitation from lineage and clan, from both their regional and national headquarters, than I do from the alumni organizations of all the schools I attended.

Faithful remnants of the kinship system

Traditionally, anthropologists have been interested in studying kinship mainly because in traditional, non-Western, and noncommercial societies, kinship systems that connect people through genealogical lines have been the dominant form of social organization for many areas of life. Anthropologists note that in some societies "kinship connections have an important bearing on matters of life and death" (Ember and Ember 1996:393). Francis L. K. Hsu (1983:211) believes kinship "holds the key to social and cultural development in the same sense that the germ cell holds the key to the biological organism and provides us with some ideas of what the unfolding animal is going to be like." Marital and consanguineous (that is, biological or blood) relations are the two major structural components of kinship, the very pillars of the kinship system.

Since the early modern period, with the introduction of legislation and court orders, the structure and function of the Korean kinship system has undergone significant transformation. Despite these changes, though, enduring remnants of Korean kinship still profoundly influence the Korean way of life.

Marriage

The Korean kinship system dictates certain rules and taboos regarding marriage.

Marriage between relatives

Koreans during the Goguryeo and Baekje periods practiced, relatively speaking, free-choice marriage, although marriage within the same lineage (or clan) was prohibited. The Silla period permitted free choice of marriage partners and also encouraged within-kin marriages beyond the third degree of relations (that is, beyond uncle and aunt, and with members of the same clan), especially among royal and upper-class families (Lee 1983). In its early dynastic period, Goryeo also allowed; close kin marriage even within a two-degree relationship (including half-brothers and half-sisters, if the mothers were different) in royal families in an effort to maintain the "same blood," so to speak (Lee 1983). In fact, King Taejo of the Goryeo dynasty encouraged such close kin marriages.

Prohibition of marriage between members of the same clan (the same surname group) came into being in the Joseon dynasty after the Da Ming Lü (Law of the Great Ming), the comprehensive body of administrative and criminal law of the Ming dynasty (1368-1644) of China, was adopted. Martina Deuchler (1977b) offers an explanation for the adoption of this law: the Joseon literati-officials (sadaebu) became aware that indigenous Joseon customs often stood in the way of implementing reform policies, which could not be carried out successfully without legal sanctions. The adoption of the Da Ming Lü was therefore an introduction of the "rule of law" to supplement the "rule of goodness." Joseon interpreted the entire Da Ming Lü so literally that lineage and clan exogamy, the rule of marriage that requires a person to marry outside the family group, was institutionalized in Korea (Lee 1983). Nevertheless, *yangban* continued

to marry matrilineal cousins (siblings of mother's sisters and father's sisters) (Deuchler 1977b).

Before July 1997 when the Constitutional Court of Korea handed down a landmark decision that prohibition of marriage between clan members beyond eight-degree relations (third cousins) was unconstitutional, even some prodigious clans with millions of members had been prohibited from intermarrying. Since then, clan members whose kinship was beyond eight degrees have been able to marry legitimately, and family registers could issue marriage licenses for same-clan couples. Furthermore, on 3 February 2005, the Constitutional Court ruled that the *hojeok* system, a male-oriented family registry, was unconstitutional and violated the spirit of gender equality in the Korean constitution. Until this decision, in Korean families only male members could be the "head" (*hoju*), and children had to take their father's surname. Concurring with this court decision, and after strong lobbying from women's organizations, on 2 March 2005, the Korean National Assembly passed a statute abolishing the *hoju* system, effective beginning 1 January 2008. Now, children can legally choose their mother's surname if they wish or combine their father's and mother's surnames. Some women already use their mother's surname in their name, and others use both father's and mother's surnames together in combination.

Arranged marriage

In my comparative family class at The University of Tennessee at Martin, my students expressed curiosity about the system of "arranged marriage." Some of them asked how one could marry someone without first experiencing "love" or "affection," without realizing that even Western societies once practiced arranged marriage. It would also be incorrect to claim the romantic love never existed in the non-Western world.

Indeed, "romantic love" is no foreign concept to East Asians, especially Koreans, Chinese, and Japanese. In fact, one of the

most popular and beloved Korean novels, *Chunhyangjeon*, tells the romantic love story of the son of a local magistrate and the only daughter of a retired *gisaeng*, a female entertainer and escort at men's drinking parties. Although the man was of noble origin (*yangban*) and the woman was of humble birth (*cheonmin*), the man was able to marry her after all by overcoming many obstacles simply because he loved her so dearly. This story has generated many movies, TV soap operas, and musicals over a long period, and is still popular among Koreans. As Stuart A. Queen and Robert W. Habenstein (1974:105) have reported, "In ancient feudal China, falling in love was not an unusual antecedent to marriage, although parental consent was necessary before the various ceremonies preparatory to marriage could go forward."

Even in the West, marriages based on romantic love were not common before the end of the Middle Ages in Europe. In fact, "marital selection in medieval England was a matter of clear bargaining and formal routines, in contrast to the romantic adventure it has become in modern England and America" (Queen and Habenstein 1974:255). In colonial America, marriage required parental permission.

One may surmise that since Korea has experienced rapid industrialization, intense urbanization, and increasing globalization, the traditional system of arranged marriage is waning. Indeed, as Laurel Kendall (1996a:109) has observed, "Today, as the workplace and the coeducational university provide unprecedented opportunities for romance, increasing numbers of women and men have love marriage without a matchmaker's introduction." It appears that a great majority of Koreans of marriageable age now favor love marriage over arranged marriage, but statistics regarding the number of people who enter into arranged marriages as opposed to love marriages vary considerably.

The origins of arranged marriage in Korea

Historically in Korea as elsewhere certain privileged classes have used arranged marriage as a major mechanism for maintaining or

improving their own class status. This was further evidenced during the Joseon dynasty when arranged marriage came to be considered an ideal form and was firmly institutionalized, after the *yangban* class emerged, as a means of maintaining its status quo. Consequently, during the Joseon dynasty, the system of arranged marriages contributed to class endogamy, in which most Koreans married within their own class. Nevertheless, for commoners free-choice marriage remained the norm.

The Korean arranged-marriage system began to decline when Korean society started to transform from premodern to modern. Certain socioeconomic and demographic changes led to a transitional form of arranged marriage. An individual might select several candidates and then ask his or her parents to choose from among them, or parents and kin members would recommend several marriage candidates and the individual would select from among them. Today, while arranged marriages are still the means by which less educated, rural people often acquire their spouses, highly educated, urban Koreans tend to choose their spouses themselves. Nevertheless, even today, well-to-do Koreans often choose to make an arranged marriage in order to maintain their status or improve their socioeconomic standing.

In traditional arranged marriages, matchmaking was done by relatives, most often older females, who would search for matches among their natal kinfolk and their husband's relatives. The paired bride and groom would marry with the approval of the elders of both families. Most of the time, such approval was no more than a formality because male elders trusted that the matchmakers knew the betrothed well enough since they had ties to both clans (Kim 1974). In effect, the matchmakers served as a sort of collateral for both families given their dual family membership. Also, because of such a selection process, the bride and groom tended to be of the same rank socially and economically. Cho Kang-hŭi[Jo Gang-hui] (1984) has documented an elaborate network of marriage among *yangban* groups in

Gyeongsang-do from the later period of the Joseon dynasty to the present. He claims that the boundaries of marriage were limited to some thirty clans, living in geographic proximity within the same province, through a "chain-string" form of marriage arrangement (*yeonjulhon*), which operates by mobilizing networks of relatives, mainly females.

Because increasing urbanization and diminishing the tradition of arranged marriages, during the 1970s and 1980s a legion of unlicensed semiprofessional matchmakers emerged in urban areas. A Madam *Ttu* or Madam Procure, as such a matchmaker was popularly known, mostly arranged marriages between children of the newly rich and privileged. Madam *Ttu* matchmakers did not charge any fee for their activities until the arrangement was successfully finalized. Commissions collected would run about ten million *won* (about $9,523). However, at times, their fees became so steep that it was considered a social problem (Kim 1988a). Laurel Kendall (1996a:133 n.10) has characterized the era of the Madam *Ttu* as follows: "In 1980, after Chun Doo-hwan's coup, the new government identified illegal matchmakers as 'elements corrupting society' and began a major crackdown. . . . Seoul gossip held that the list of marriage prospects carried by a Madam *Ttu* brought to judgment included the names of the unmarried judge who presided at her trial. The Madam *Ttu* has, by all accounts, continued to flourish." Nowadays, this kind of matchmaking has declined but has not disappeared altogether. It has been reported that some former Madam *Ttu* matchmakers have become consultants for commercial marriage consulting centers.

Matchmaking as a corporate enterprise

After the decline of the Madam *Ttu*, licensed commercial enterprises (*gyeolhon Jeongbo hoesa*), which use computerized matchmaking and multimedia technologies, have become increasingly popular in the business of arranging marriages. The marriage consulting center originated in Japan during the early 1980s, where it became popular

and prosperous, with many branches opening throughout the country. The first marriage consulting center in Korea was founded in 1986, and a few others followed soon after. In 1999, when the Family Ritual Code (*Gajeong Uirye Junchik*) that regulated marriage rituals was suspended in Korea, government licenses were no longer required to engage in the commercial matchmaking business. Since then, consulting centers have sprung up throughout the country, and their numbers have increased dramatically. As of November 2011, there were over 1,054 centers, ranging from small local outfits with a few members (or applicants) to those with over 40,000 members that operate globally, with locations in the United States (Los Angeles and New York City) and New Zealand. Some centers also support homepages and videotaped narratives in English. In 1994, during the formative era of these centers in Korea, I visited one such center in Seoul with my students while a visiting professor at Yonsei University. At the time, it looked like a small private consulting center; now it has become a genuine business enterprise.

Anyone seeking a spouse who wants the help of an agency has to be a member. Annual membership fees vary from center to center and by category of membership. An average membership fee runs from 880,000 *won* (about $838) for a general membership to as high as 5.5 million *won* (about $5,238) for a special membership for unusual cases, such as those with outstanding educational credentials or those with disabilities. One center that specializes in remarriage offers three different categories of membership for women (though not for men for some reason) and charges different membership fees. The center's services vary according to membership category. Patent proof of the industry's overall success is easily quantified: the total annual earnings of all Korean marriage consulting centers in 2011 were estimated to be 100 billion *won* (about $92,157,404).

International matchmakers have arranged some 200,000 international marriages

Many Korean men who live in farming and fishing villages have difficulty finding mates due an ongoing exodus of young women from the countryside to cities and industrial zones. To compensate for the shortage of marriageable women and to keep men on the farm, the Korean government, especially local government, has spearheaded a campaign to recruit foreign brides. Early on, the recruitment of foreign brides depended largely on international marriage brokers. Later on, however, the Korean government and civic organizations realized that commercially minded brokers were supplying inaccurate, sometimes deceptive, information about prospective grooms, despite the Management of Marriage Brokerage Act that prohibited the dispensation of such false information. In 2009, a total of 316 (28 percent) out of 1,128 known international matchmaking firms were found to have violated existing law (Kim 2011b). In order to better regulate marriage brokers, the government enacted several tough measures, including an executive order from the president of South Korea; even so, these measures have not put a stop to illegal and unethical marriage arrangements. Tragically, there have been cases of brides being killed by mentally disturbed grooms. Meanwhile, the number of brokers continued to increased—from 1,128 in 2009 to 1,253 in 2010.

In a further effort to eliminate illicit and unethical practices by international marriage brokers, the Ministry of Justice announced, as of August 2010, that any Korean man interested in marrying a foreign bride must attend a four-hour "courtesy orientation session" (*soyang-gyoyuk*) on the proper procedure for international marriages, related laws, and cases of failed international marriages. This orientation session must be attended prior to engagement or marriage, and it is a prerequisite for obtaining a F-2 visa for a bride. Also, the Ministry of Justice announced a restriction on issuing visa requests made by Koreans registered as sex offenders, domestic abusers, ex-criminals,

Multicultural Family

and mental patients (Kim 2011b).

Regardless of the dubious practices of some, international matchmakers have been largely responsible for nearly 200,000 foreign brides from 67 countries marrying Korean men and moving to Korea. Broken down by country of origin, before 2012 the largest number were Korean Chinese (59,346, or 32.2 percent), followed by Han Chinese (51,348, or 28.3 percent) and Vietnamese (34,640, or 19.1 percent). In 2012, for the first time, the number of marriages between Vietnamese women and Korean men (7,636) exceeded the number of marriages between Chinese women and Korean men (7,549). Also, the total number of international marriages in 2012 (30,695) was lower than it was in 2011 (35,098). The slowdown of international marriage comes from two sources. The first, according to Lee Sang-rim at the Korea Institute for Health and Social Affairs, is that the number of bachelors from 25 to 44 years old in rural and fishing villages is decreasing, so international marriages will also decrease. In fact, in 2010, the number of bachelors was 1,193,513, but it has been predicted that number will decline by 10.3 percent by 2015, 17.8 percent by 2020, and 31.5 percent by 2030. If that happens,

the number of foreign brides coming into Korea will be reduced proportionally. The second source of the international marriage slowdown is tougher industry-wide regulations, which led to a downturn.

In a study of brokered marriages, Kim Yong-hak, a Korean sociologist, analyzed almost 800 megabytes of data compiled at a marriage consulting center between 2004 and 2005, and published the results in *JoongAng Daily* (22 July 2005) and *JoongAng Weekly* (22 July 2005). According to his analysis, men and women seeking a compatible marriage partner cared less about a person's appearance or wealth than the person's educational background, which has become an important measure of social status for Koreans.

This finding represents a new variant on an old theme in Korean marriage. Traditionally, arranged marriages in Korea, whether mediated by relatives, a Madam *Ttu*, or a professional, have tended to be endogamous, meaning that one marries within one's own social group. Historically in Korea, social class, particularly *yangban* status, was one such defining category, but in recent times education has come to serve as an important group definer, as demonstrated by Kim Yong-hak's study.

Parenthetically, in America, since mate selection is a "free-choice" based on romantic love, an American youth is free in principle to choose a spouse from any socio-economic or educational background. In fact, marriages often happen across ethnic, racial, and religious lines as well as across class lines, which are hazier. Nevertheless, eligible mates do not exist randomly in society but are located in culturally defined groups or cliques such as college and the workplace. One tends to marry someone known through long association as a member of such in groups. Consequently, this situation results in a sort of "social endogamy."

Patrilineal past

Historically, according to Martina Deuchler (1977b:8), "Marriage

during Goryeo seems to have been a rather loose institution which was not restricted by a multitude of rules and regulations. It was easily entered into and easily gotten out of. This relationship between men and women was open and unceremonious." Marriages were monogamous in general during the Goryeo dynasty, but some wealthy and powerful men did have more than one wife. These wives were not ranked and seem to have enjoyed roughly the same status. Deuchler (1977b:8) tells us that the wives' "social origins were apparently not indicated by different hair and dress styles." However, during the Joseon dynasty, in the spring of 1413, "a law was enacted according to which a man who had a legal wife was prohibited from taking a second wife (Yucheo chwicheo): a man who broke this law was forced to separate himself from his illegally acquired second wife " (Deuchler 1977b: 31).

Age of marriage

In traditional Korean society, people tended to marry at an early age, especially among elite or aristocratic families. Any person beyond marriageable age was labeled an old bachelor (nochonggak) or old maid (nocheonyeo) and stigmatized. Unmarried persons, whatever their age at death, were not granted the full ritual for a dead person and never became subjects for ancestor worship. Laurel Kendall (1996a) has noted that in the day when early marriage was the norm, a bride and groom might still technically be children. In 1925, for instance, most Korean women were married before the age of sixteen. The median age at marriage for women rose by about one and a half years between 1925 and 1940. In 1925, the median age at marriage for men was twenty-one; by 1940, it had risen by a little more than half a year. Ever since Statistics Korea started keeping the official census in 1970, the average age at marriage among Koreans has steadily increased. In 1972, for instance, the average age at marriage for men was 26.7 and 22.6 for women. By 2004, it had increased to 30.6 for men and 27.5 for women. By 2011, the average age of marriage for men was 31.9 and for women, 29.1.

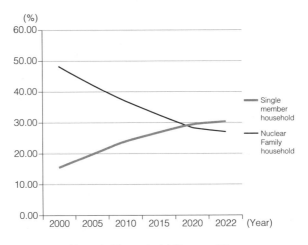

(%)

| | Single member household |
| | Nuclear Family household |

2000 2005 2010 2015 2020 2022 (Year)

Korea's Household Composition

Another prominent social change of late is that a growing number of women are choosing to remain single for life. According to a survey conducted by the school newspaper of an elite university in Seoul in March 2005, nearly one-third of the respondents did not plan to marry. In 2012, the total number of single-person households is 4,538,642 (25.28 percent), which is the second largest category among various types of households, including married couples without an unmarried child or children (2,873,980, or 16.01 percent), married couples with an unmarried child or children (6,294,217, or 35.06 percent), and extended family households consisting of three or four generations (627,495, or 3.49 percent). In 2012, nuclear families consisting of married couples with their unmarried child or children are the largest category in absolute number and proportion, but single households follow as the next highest category. However, as indicated in <Korea's Household Composition>, Statistics Korea estimates that by 2022 the single-person household will be the dominant type of Korean household, comprising 30.37 percent of all households. All categories other than single-member households are projected to decline over the same period.

The reasons why young women want to remain single are varied; most, though, do not want to be tied down by a family. For men, reasons against marriage include the financial burdens of paying for a pricey wedding and providing housing after marriage. In a survey made by the Korean daily *Chosun Ilbo*, reported in September 2012, some 82 percent of men and women respondents expressed a preference for remaining single because it is too expensive to get married and too burdensome to pay for housing. A good many of those single women considered it difficult to manage a family and maintain a career simultaneously on account of inadequate childcare. Many young Korean women now consider a career more important than marriage and want to enjoy the economic freedom that it brings. Such an economically independent single woman is more aptly called a "gold miss" than an "old miss." By the end of 2011, the Korean female workforce had reached a little over ten million (10,091,000), the highest ever in the history of Korea.

Wedding day details

Some people prefer to have a traditional wedding ceremony, wearing traditional wedding outfits, while others choose a modern-style wedding with a Western-fashion wedding gown for the bride and a tuxedo for the groom. Interestingly, while many rural Koreans are opting for modern-style weddings in commercial wedding halls, some urban, well-educated elite Koreans are choosing traditional weddings, a manifestation of nostalgic feeling for past tradition. Many couples, after their modern-style wedding ceremony, change into traditional Korean wedding dress for yet another ceremony called *pyebaek*. With this ceremony comprised of the presentation of gifts (wine and some other food) and a series of traditional Korean bows by the bride to each and every member of the groom's family, the bride is formally incorporated into the groom's family. The groom's parents who are the first to take the bow, will throw dates and chestnuts (prepared by bride's family) into the skirts of their daughter-in-law, wishing

Modern Wedding

the newly-wed many children.

In weddings at commercial wedding halls, a master of ceremonies, the *jurye*, conducts the wedding rites from behind a podium, as does the minister or preacher in a church wedding. The *jurye*, who is selected by the groom or his family, has to have a reputation for virtue and a flourishing family. Up until the present, the *jurye* has usually been a man. Recently, though, it has been reported that some females are also serving as the *jurye*. Instead of throwing a bridal shower or giving gifts as in the West, the invited guests from among the bride's and groom's families, relatives, and friends tend to give cash money in white envelopes. There is no upper limit, but in most cases the amount is less than 100,000 *won*. Those who cannot afford such an amount do not attend the wedding. Now, though, the campaign for small weddings offers the option of requesting that no cash gifts be given as part of the nuptial plan. A good many well-to-do Koreans have begun to follow this trend.

The wedding and associated costs

The average price of weddings grew significantly along with

Korea's economic growth and rapid industrialization. Laurel Kendall (1996a:168) reported that "in 1990, weddings, with all their attendant exchanges, cost the average couple and their families 18.32 million *won* (roughly $26,000)." According to a survey by one of the major marriage consulting centers, of 294 couples from five major Korean cities, in 2000 the average wedding cost per couple was estimated to be 78.45 million *won* (about $74,714). In 2011, according to the Ministry of Gender Equality and Family, the average cost per couple was 110,140,000 *won* (about $104,895)—around three quarters of which was paid by the groom and his family, and one quarter by the bride and her family. For ordinary Koreans with more modest ceremonies, the average cost is still over $30,000. It is thus understandable why the cost of getting married would be prohibitive for many Koreans.

The *Chosun Ilbo*, one of the major Korean daily newspapers, together with the Ministry of Gender Equality and Family, launched a campaign for "small weddings" to reduce the cost of getting married. The campaign urges couples to invite only close relatives and friends and to hold the event in modest places such as a garden, yard, city hall, and even a library. The paper has asked for 1,000 participants to join the campaign, and so far a good many people, especially celebrities, have joined up.

In addition to the cost of wedding ceremony there are important financial considerations concerning marriage. Many Koreans used to believe that the groom or his family should be responsible for the new couple's residential space (whether purchased or rented) while the bride and her family should be responsible for furniture and everything else. The situation actually differs significantly according to the relative status and wealth of the families involved as well as to the "value" of the groom (education, job, etc.) in the unofficial "marriage market." A familiar tale concerning the dowry for the upper and upper-middle classes is the so-called three keys story. Laurel Kendall (1996a:168) relates that she heard it during her fieldwork in Korea:

I soon learned the urban folklore of the "three keys," that if one wishes to marry one of the three *sa* (the three professions of doctor *uisa*, lawyer *byeonhosa* or professor *baksa*), then one must provide the house key, the car key, and the office key (purchase a professional practice) . . . The ubiquitousness of this folklore is indicative, rather, of the cynical and hyperbolic humor regarding matchmaking. I learned recently, when I made reference to the three keys in a public lecture, that at least in the popular imagination, the ante has now been upped to five keys, including the golf club key and the vacation condominium key.

Even working women have to prepare the basic dowry, which includes a large wardrobe cabinet, a dressing table, a dish cabinet, quilts and sleeping pallets, dishes, cooking utensils, a television set, an electronic rice cooker, and a *kimchi* refrigerator—a list that potentially has no end.

Often the dowry inventory serves as a yardstick to measure the "market value" of the bride. If the list does not measure up to the expectations of the bride's mother-in-law, this could lead to a squabble between the two families and ultimately the dissolution of the couple. According to the director of a marriage consulting center, the exorbitant cost of marrying has become yet another reason why Koreans, especially women, are delaying or deferring marriage, or deciding to remain single for good.

Family

Decline of the extended family

The traditional Korean family structure was extended, meaning that more than one generation typically lived under the same roof. When Korea was an agrarian society, extended families engaged in a single economic activity such as farming. As Korean society evolved economically and socially, the pattern of the extended family shifted toward that of the nuclear family. In the move toward nuclear family

organization in Korean society, a transitional stem family system has developed, once considered an ideal form in Japan, although it is disappearing rapidly (Befu 1971). In the stem family arrangement, after the retirement or death of the head of the family, the family continues through succession and inheritance, usually by one of the offspring who stays with the parents after marriage and maintains the family line. In rural Korea, before rapid economic growth and industrialization took place starting in the mid-1960s, many firstborn sons and their brides lived with the groom's parents, while other sons moved elsewhere to establish their own nuclear families. However, recently, almost all sons, regardless of birth order, move out of their parents' home to establish their own nuclear families.

This trend toward nuclear families living in separate domiciles is a preference shared by Koreans of an older generation as well. According to a survey made by the Korean Institute for Health and Social Affairs (*Bogeonsahoe Yeonguwon*) in June 2012, only 3.6 percent of the baby-boom generation of Korean parents (those born between 1955 to 1963) want to live with their children by forming extended families. In a related study conducted by the Ministry of Health and Welfare, only 39.8 percent of elderly parents in 2011 received some sort of "allowance" from their offspring. This is in stark contrast to the traditional Korean extended family, with two or more generations living together, where respect for the elderly and filial piety were norms expected to be honored. To have deviated from this norm would invite social scorn. However, as the results of the baby-boomer survey indicate, older parents, just like their children, prefer not to live forever with their progeny.

In counterbalance to this trend, however, a growing number of young Korean couples are opting to live near their parents or parents-in-law, mainly because couples with small children can take advantage of the free babysitting services offered by mothers and mothers-in-law. Some young couples even prefer to live in the same apartment complexes with their parents or parents-in-law. This situation

of proximal living instead of cohabitation complicates any pat predictions about the changing direction of future Korean families.

Changing authority pattern

The traditional authority pattern of the Korean family is patriarchal, which means authority is vested in the males. Such an authority pattern is reinforced in the relationship of parents and their children; in particular, the relationship of father and son is considered to be of the utmost importance. Such absolute control has been described by Francis L. K. Hsu (1983:338) in this way: "no parents are wrong vis-à-vis their children (*tian-xia wu bu-shi-de fu-mu*)." Roger Janelli and Yim Dawn-hee[Im Don-hui] (1982:50) report that "the proper relationship between father and son soon became the paradigm for all hierarchical relationships in a moral society." The relationship between father and son was governed by the virtue of filial piety (*hyoseong* in Korean and *xiao* in Chinese), which was greatly emphasized after the seventh and eighth centuries under the influence of Confucianism.

However, it appears that in contemporary Korea the virtue of filial piety is changing. For instance, the *Dong-A Ilbo* reported on 19 January 2012 that according to a nationwide survey conducted in 1998, about 89.9 percent of the respondents said that they were obliged to support their elderly parents. However, in the same survey conducted in 2010, only 36.0 percent of the respondents indicated that they had an obligation to support their elderly parents. Over the course of twelve-years, the concept of traditional Korean filial piety must have been changed in accordance with changes in society.

Korean patriarchal rules are closely related to the position of women in Korean society in general, and they set the tone for gender discrimination in particular. Patriarchy was the basis and justification for discrimination against daughters, which in turn created a preference for male children. However, women's rights movements challenged traditional patriarchal rule and have been successful in achieving an equal rights system, or egalitarian system (*pyeongdeung juui*).

Emerging women's rights

As a consequence of patriarchal rule and the preference for males, traditional Korean families discriminated against their daughters. Roger Janelli and Yim Dawn-hee (1982:36) learned of female infanticide, or attempted infanticide, resulting from extreme poverty during their fieldwork in a rural Korean village: "One lineage woman, in the presence of her seven-or-eight-year-old maternal granddaughter, told us how she had placed the girl on a cold floor immediately after birth, hoping she would die." The woman said without any hesitation, "But look how well she grew up." Unwanted female babies were sometimes abandoned at the gate of a stranger's house (Harvey 1979:63, 260-269). Even in ancestral worship, "women were excluded from officiating at the rites, and ritual responsibility could not be assumed by a wife or a daughter's son in the absence of an agnatically related [i.e., patrilineally descended] male heir" (Janelli and Yim 1982:13). Clark Sorensen (1983:64), an anthropologist and expert on Korea, has observed that "At meals . . . women serve the men first, in sequence by status and seniority within the family."

Recently, however, such discrimination against women has diminished dramatically in step with the improvement of female status in Korea. While older Korean women still prefer to have boys, younger Korean women clearly indicate a preference for girls, observing that in general girls tend to understand parents better than boys do (33.5 percent) and girls can be good "friends" with the mother (20.1 percent). Another challenge to patriarchal rule has been a sequence of court rulings and new statutes upholding equal rights. On 21 July 2005, there was another Supreme Court ruling to abolish a century-old system that denied women, especially married women, the right to an equal share of the clan property, which was a major step in ending gender discrimination in the Korean kinship system.

After the fall of the Joseon dynasty and under Japanese rule, male-centered norms regulating divorce persisted. After liberation from Japan and under the influence of the Western concept of

egalitarianism, the South Korean Civil Code was revised to specify conditions for divorce that were equally applicable to men and women. For instance, in an extensive study of divorce cases presented to the Seoul District Court during the ten years after the liberation of Korea from Japan in 1945, Lee Tai-Young[Yi Tae-yeong] (1957), the first Korean woman lawyer, found a total of 144 divorces. Except for a few cases, the defendants were all women. This study focused on the heart of urban South Korea but still revealed a male monopoly in initiating divorce suits. If the study had been done in rural districts, male domination in divorce would have been even greater (Choe 1966).

Even in the 1950s and early 1960s, divorce in Korea was uncommon, and cases were mostly male centered and male initiated. That has now changed, though. The divorce rate in Korea is fairly high now—the highest in Asia and the third highest among members of the Organization for Economic Co-operation and Development (OECD), after the United States and Great Britain. In a reversal of the older pattern, Korean women now initiate more divorces than do men, and the figure is on the rise.

Achievement of Korean women

Much credit should be given to Korean women in achieving an egalitarian authority pattern in society. Overcoming all obstacles, Korean women have recently attained many distinctions in society and excelled in various fields. Korean women have performed particularly well in fields where there are open and competitive examinations, including the higher civil service examination (*haengjeong gosi*), the bar examination (*sabeop gosi*), and the higher civil service examination for diplomats (*oemu gosi*). Almost always, women outscore their male counterparts. Consequently, in 2007, for instance, 55.6 percent of all newly appointed Korean judges were women. In Korea, judges are not elected but appointed by the government on the basis of bar examination scores, together with other credentials.

In other career fields there are also notable developments arising

from greater gender equality in Korea. For instance, women dominate teaching positions in elementary and middle schools. The success rate of women who took the qualifying examination for elementary and middle school teachers in the Seoul School District was overwhelmingly high (89.3 percent). Currently, 60 percent of all Korean elementary and middle school teachers are women. Among all physicians, 18.4 percent are women, while 21.9 percent of dentists and 62.1 percent of pharmacologists are women. In politics, women constituted only 1 percent of all National Assembly members in 1992, but in 2012's National Assembly, 47 (15.7 percent) members out of 300 are women. This amounts to a fifteen-fold increase of women assembly members from 1992 to the present. What is more, on 20 April 2006, a sixty-two-year-old woman, Han Myeong-sook[Han Myeong-suk], became the first woman prime minister of Korea, and Park Geun-hye[Bak Geun-hye] was elected president of Korea in the presidential election on 19 December 2012.

Despite such progress, a majority of Korean women feel that gender discrimination still exists in contemporary Korea. Disparities of gender representation remain in the executive ranks of business and industry. In the twenty top Korean business firms, women constitute nearly 20 percent of the total workforce but occupy less than 1 percent of managerial positions. According to the *Korea Herald's* report on 3 December 2012, "CEO score, an on-liner corporate management evaluator, said its recent survey of the top 1,000 Korean companies by revenue found that only eight companies are led by a woman CEO. Furthermore, most of the female CEOs were found to be a family member of the company's owner."

Kin Group Organization and Kinship System

Pattern of descent

The major pillar for every kinship system is the rule of descent that connects individuals with particular sets of kin on the basis of

known or presumed common ancestry. Within the kin group, each member addresses the others using kinship terms instead of personal names. The rule of descent also determines the scale and complexity of kin groups, including lineage (a set of kin whose members trace their descent from a common ancestor through known links) and clan or sib (which is made up of related lineages). Under the bilateral rule of descent, as seen in most Western societies, kinship links a person with relatives through both sexes, i.e., both sides of the house, as the expression goes.

The Korean rule of descent is a patrilineal system: within a given kin group, a member affiliates with other kinsmen who are related to him through males. The origin of the patrilineal system in Korea may have been prehistoric, although the bilateral descent system was practiced in Goguryeo and Silla. The patrilineal system was strengthened under Chinese influence at the beginning of the Three Kingdoms period around the first half of the first century BC. The system was further developed during the early seventeenth century (Janelli and Yim 1982; Osgood 1951). Since the patrilineal system by definition requires tracing one's kin relationships through males, up until most recently it has fostered a preference for males.

In the past, an heirless family would usually adopt a male heir, a widespread custom since the middle of the Joseon dynasty. But the number of males available for adoption tended to be few when limited to agnates (persons related by patrilineal descent). In earlier times, Korean adoption was not so rigidly agnatic. A sister's sons, daughter's sons, wives' natal kin, and even non-kin were adopted heirs. But a strict agnatic rule became established over the last few hundred years (Lee 1982; Peterson 1974).

This practice of adoption began to change, however, with the revision of the South Korean Civil Code in 1977, which allowed for the adoption of someone with a different surname and permitted the entry of a husband's name into his wife's family registry. In Japan, for instance, if there were no son, a son-in-law could technically be adopted into the family at marriage. "If a family had a daughter

she ordinarily would take over the family name and continue the *ie* [household]" (Vogel 1965:288). More recently, the Korean Constitutional Court abolished male headship in the household and the male-oriented family registry, and the National Assembly passed a statute abolishing the limitation on the range of adoption. However, Koreans still mostly adhere to the agnatic principle in adoption.

An even greater influence of patrilineal rule in the Korean kinship system is that it gave rise to a number of extensive kin groups, such as lineage (*munjung*) and clan or sib (*ssijok* or *chinjok*). In Korea, there are about 1,100 clans, each of which includes scores of lineages (Kim 1988a), although how many Koreans are actually affiliated with active lineages or clans is difficult to ascertain (Kim 1974). The most important mechanism for promoting a sense of belonging to a kin group is using kinship terms to encompass the entire membership of the kin group, as substantiated by the genealogical record (*jokpo*). Lineage and clan members address one another by using kinship terms, regardless of how remote the relationship may be. Most Koreans tend to believe members of the same lineage or even the same clan are all really kin, even though they may be many generations removed from a common ancestor.

Solidarity of kin group members is further fostered by participation in worship of the common ancestor and in communal ownership of property. Members feel they are part owners of that communal property even when they are too poor to own property of their own. In the rural Korean village where I conducted my fieldwork in the early 1960s, a lineage owned three different communal properties: ritual land for the lineage, land for the support of formal education of capable young members, and land for the common welfare of all the members (Kim 1968). If young members are smart and capable of pursuing further education but cannot afford it, the lineage gives such individuals scholarships provided by profits from land designated for this purpose. The idea behind supporting the education of young members of a lineage is based on the belief that if they obtain high

positions in government or gain prominence as scholars, prestige and fame are automatically bestowed on the entire membership of the lineage. Recently, the headquarters office of my clan led a cash fundraiser for scholarships for young and capable members of the clan since returns from communal land would not fund enough scholarships.

My own clan's lands may not generate a lot of revenue, but some clans own property so sizable and valuable—owing to its propitious location in developmental hotspots of Seoul—that they have made billions of dollars from it. Since the Korean kinship system has been patrilineal, with the rule of inheritance favoring male members, female members of their natal lineages and clans have felt discriminated against. Quite a few women from several kin groups have challenged the inequity of property sharing within the patrilineal kin groups. Finally, on 21 July 2005, the Korean Supreme Court abolished such discrimination against women members of kin groups. From that point on, even a married woman has the same rights as an adult male to claim an equal share in property owned by her natal (father's) kin group.

Not only does this court ruling affect the property ownership of Korean kin groups; it may eventually bring about a larger transformation in the Korean rule of descent from a patrilineal to a bilateral system. Immediately after the court ruling, the spokesman from the Korean Confucian Society (yurim) at the Seonggyungwan called the court decision "outrageous," claiming that it would bring "chaos" to South Korea's male-dominated social order. However exaggerated this claim may be, it speaks to an important fact of Korean life. Despite all the changes that have happened to the traditional Korean kinship system, the old system has been with Koreans for so long that it remains a profound influence in their way of life (Kim 1995).

6
Urbanization and a Balanced National Development Plan

Before Korea took a major step forward in successful industrialization, rural Korean villages or hamlets (*maeul* or *burak*) had been the center of socioeconomic, cultural, and political activities. Unlike other countries, Korea had villages that were home not only to a large peasant population, but to a good many members of *yangban* (noble) families as well. These families established private academies (seowon) to educate promising young men (always men) to become future scholar-bureaucrats. Telling in this regard is that, even in the modern era, all Korean presidents except one have come from rural villages. Also, the founders of the top three Korean business conglomerates—Samsung, Hyundai, and LG—had rural roots. In all, vast numbers of Koreans who have achieved distinction in Korean society have come from rural backgrounds.

In the early 1960s, when Korean economic development and industrialization began to accelerate, the great majority of Koreans lived in rural villages. The ratio of rural to urban dwellers was seven to three. By 2005, the ratio had reversed: two (rural) to eight (urban). By 2012, the disparity of rural to urban had widened still further to one rural for every nine urban residents. The speed of Korea's transformation from a rural, agrarian economy to a modern, industrialized economy was equally impressive.

Over the thirty-year period of rapid transformation, one of

the most notable changes was a precipitous decline in the number of farmers in Korea. In 1965, one year before the first five-year economic development plan (1962-1966) had been completed, the farming population was slightly more than 55.1 percent of the total Korean population. From 14 million in 1970, the farming population fell to less than 4 million in 2001, a 75 percent decrease over the previous thirty-five years. By 2011, the total population of farmers in Korea was estimated to be around 2,965,000, which was the first time in the history of Korea that the farming population had dropped below 3 million.

This sharp decline in the rural population created a serious workforce shortage in Korean agricultural villages. According to a survey made by the Korea Rural Economic Institute (*Hanguk Nongchon Gyeongje Yeonguwon*) in March 2010, based on a sample of 1,551 members of the farming population, 88.3 percent of the respondents indicated that they had some difficulties in farming owing to a shortage in the available workforce. According to a report by Statistics Korea on 20 March 2012, out of 3,606,000 rural people, those aged 50 or older accounted for 61 percent of the total, while those 60 years or older represented 20.3 percent.

Despite this bleak statistical picture for Korea's farming villages, there is some hope of revitalizing Korean farming on a smaller scale. Among the baby-boom generation of Koreans, who were born between 1955 and 1963, there has been a movement to reclaim farming as a vocation. In 2011 alone, for instance, nearly 20,000 baby-boomers who are well educated and urbane went to live in rural villages. Their numbers were nearly double what they had been the year before.

Another development is a plan introduced by the government to discourage the development of hyper-urbanization. Under the banner of "balanced national development," the government has made a momentous, if somewhat desperate, effort to disperse the branches of the government beyond the metropolis of Seoul. The major initiative

has been to create a special administrative city, officially called Sejong Metropolitan Autonomous City (Sejong-si), in formerly Yeongi-gun and a part of the city of Gongju in Chungcheongnam-do. Into this newly built administrative city, sixteen government ministries and twenty related agencies will be transplanted by the end of 2014. About 10,000 civil servants and their family members will eventually reside in the new city, which is designed to accommodate about half a million citizens. In addition to creating Sejong-si, the government developed a further plan to disperse 409 government agencies throughout the regional cities in the interest of decentralizing and balancing national development. The ultimate impact of these governmental efforts remains to be seen.

I begin this chapter by reviewing traditional Korean villages in terms of their origin and type, but the central focus of the chapter is on the transformation of rural villages that took place in the latter twentieth and early twenty-first centuries. In particular, I chronicle the transformational, nearly revolutionary New Village Movement in Korea. Despite criticisms that have been leveled at this movement at home, abroad it has drawn the attention of many developing countries in Asia and Africa as a possible role model for modernization.

Villages (Maeul) as the Center of Social Life in Rural Korea

The origins and development of Korean villages

The origin of the Korean village goes far back into prehistoric times. Archaeologists believe that settled villages on the Korean peninsula appeared as early as 12,000 years ago. During the Early Village period (6000-2000 BC), villages were closely related to specific habitats, often situated on riverbanks, along coasts, and on coastal islands (Nelson 1993). Historically, most Korean villages have been small in size, a fact related to topography and climate: over 70 percent of

the Korean peninsula consists of mountains, hills, rivers, and small streams, and Korean villages have been built on a rugged terrain. As geographer and Korean specialist Shannon McCune (1980:15) has pointed out, "the Korean mountain system is over six thousand feet in altitude in some sections. . . . There are no plains deserving of the name and much of the land is in slope." Even in the late Goguryeo period, a good many villages consisted of fifty or sixty households, and villages with fewer than ten households were not uncommon (Lee 1996). Village size gradually increased during the Joseon dynasty.

Until recently, due largely to the natural barriers of rugged mountains and mighty rivers, transportation and communication were difficult. As a result of this relative isolation, each village developed unique characteristics. Some Korean villages are located on flat land, but most are located at the base of a mountain facing south and overlooking a plain. Having the mountain on the north side of the village protects it from cold winter winds, and the plain to the south provides lots of sunshine. Since Korea is located in the northern hemisphere, the sun rises higher in the sky in summer time: roofs and long overhangs block the direct sunlight, creating shade for the house. In winter, the direct sunlight from the south works likes natural solar heating. Therefore, a site with mountains behind and water or a plain in front has traditionally been ideal for a Korean village or house.

There are no really accurate statistics on the number of villages in Korea. Whang In-Joung[Hwang In-jeong] (1981) reckoned there to be 34,871 villages in 1979; Lee Kwang-kyu[Yi Gwang-gyu] (2003) estimated there to be about 50,000 villages in South Korea alone. It is difficult to tally villages with much accuracy because new ones have been established while others have disappeared, often due to the construction of dams, highways, and other development projects. In other cases, villages have combined to form *ri* or *tong*.

Types of villages

In addition to the typical farming village, where peasants engage mainly in wet-rice cultivation, there are other types of villages defined by their locale and the occupations of their residents. There are suburban villages, mountain villages, slash-and-burn-cultivation villages, and fishing villages. In the past, according to Lee Kwang-kyu (2003:144), "suburban communities were settled primarily by outcasts. They were villages composed of special workers, such as leather workers, basket weavers, shamans, etc. At a distance of about four kilometers from the cities were located villages for manufacturing and villages which processed and provided wood for fuel. Especially around Seoul, there were lots of satellite villages which had facilities for lodging and food for the benefit of travelers going between the city and outlying areas." Nowadays, however, because of the development of modern transportation and the expansion of city limits, such suburban villages have mostly been incorporated into larger cities.

Mountain villages are located at higher altitudes and are sparsely populated, with their constituent houses scattered at the foot of a mountain or in a valley. Unlike the occupants of farming villages on the plains who mainly cultivate rice, farmers living in mountain villages have historically grown mostly barley, wheat, Indian millet, millet, potatoes, and corn. They also collect and gather bee honey and mushrooms. Always thinly populated, nowadays these mountain villages are home to even smaller populations, and the crops grown there may be limited to items such as herbal medicines or cabbages, which can grow in the highlands. In the past, the roofs (made of tree bark, called *neowa*) and buildings of mountain villages were distinctive, made from natural elements found in the mountain environment. Nowadays, however, bark roofs have been replaced with the same tin, plaster, and tile roofs found on most farmhouses in the plains. From 1976 to 1977, Clark W. Sorensen (1988) conducted anthropological fieldwork in a mountain village in Gangwon-do.

Because these villages are disappearing so rapidly, his work is valuable documentation of the mountain culture and ecology of Korea.

During the Japanese occupation, farmers who lost their lowland farms often went to mountainous regions to become slash-and-burn cultivators - farmers cultivate a field for a while, then move on to a new field, letting the bush reclaim the old one; later they return to cultivate the first field again, slashing and burning it so that minerals can be re-deposited without the use of fertilizers. In 1933, while Korea was under Japanese occupation, the number of slash-and-burn cultivators amounted to about 82,000 households. Beginning in 1968, however, the Korean government prohibited such farming methods, and in 1974 the government introduced a new bill calling for slash-and-burn cultivators to be relocated. Today, such villages no longer exist in Korea. Besides, a new ecological awareness that emphasizes resource conservation and reduced pollution would not tolerate such a method of cultivation.

The spatial arrangement of fishing villages, both on the seacoast and on islands, is one of clusters, and most houses there are smaller than those found in villages of the mountains, valleys, and plains. Even if a village is classified as a fishing village, very few of its inhabitants engage solely in fishing for their livelihood. Most families have some rice fields or a dry paddy that they cultivate in addition. Generally, fishing exists as an alternative means of income for those with insufficient land, and the income of fishing families tends to be determined by the amount of land they own. Traditionally, fishermen have been regarded as poorer, less educated, and of lower social status than farmers (Lee 2003).

In the mid-1960s, Vincent S. R. Brandt conducted fieldwork in a small farming and fishing village in Chungcheongnam-do. His study delineates the contrast between the strictly traditional agrarian way of life and the increasingly money-oriented fishing economy in a rural village. His writing reflects the prejudice held by the local inhabitants against the fishermen. "There is considerable difference between farmers and fishermen in their personal conduct . . . Idleness

(often enforced), drunkenness, its behavioral corollary quarreling, and adultery all are more prevalent in the neighborhoods where fishermen are preponderant" (Brandt 1971:65).

Currently, however, the Korean fishing industry is flourishing, thanks to technological advances in aquaculture (seaweed, shrimp, and oysters) and changes in societal dietary patterns, notably an increased consumption of fish. In fact, fishermen's annual income per household in Wando-gun, in Jeollanam-do, which consists of more than 200 islands, was almost twice that of the national average for rural farm household. Fishing villages have persisted and prospered.

The village social structure

"Yangban"-dominant lineage villages. Lee Man-gap (1960) identified three distinct social structures that defined Korean villages: (1) villages where a formally aristocratic (*yangban*) lineage is predominant, (2) those where a commoner lineage is predominant, and (3) those where power and wealth are shared by more than one lineage. A simpler way to classify the majority of Korean villages is to assign them to one of two types: 1) lineage-dominant villages dominated by one or more *yangban* lineages or 2) commoner villages that lack any dominant *yangban* lineage. Lee Kwang-kyu (2003:151-152) calls the latter category "mixed villages." These two types of villages are distinctively different in their history, culture, and structure.

Comprehensive ethnographic research has yielded much information on lineage-dominant Korean villages. Fieldwork conducted by Korean anthropologist Kim Taek-kyu[**Gim Taek-gyu**] (1964, 1986) resulted in an ethnography on the Ryu lineage-dominated village of Hahoe, a compact village cloaked in a mysterious aura of ancient folk culture that was founded near the end of the Goryeo dynasty, 1355. The village included residents of two lineages in addition to the Ryu lineage, but the Ryu clan came to dominate sometime between 1635 and 1642, after one Ryu member, Ryu Seong-ryong (1542-1607), had served as prime minister in the Joseon dynasty during the Japanese

invasion in the mid-sixteenth century. Designated a Korean folk village by the government in 1972, Hahoe has aroused keen public interest throughout the country and received intensive international media exposure when Queen Elizabeth II of Great Britain visited on 21 April 1999. Since then, the village has had a record number of visitors (Kim 1992, 2002).

An Overview of the Village of Hahoe

In lineage-dominated villages, behaviors and interactions among the inhabitants are largely governed by kinship rules and follow a clearly structured hierarchical system of rank and authority rooted in Korean aristocratic traditions. Ranking by age is important, but generational order from the common ancestor in the clan and lineage takes precedence over age. Lineage members address each other using kinship terms rather than personal names. For instance, sibling terms extend to every lineage member who belongs to the same generation from the common ancestor. Most prosperous and well-to-do lineages possess communal properties that provide the material basis for

Tiled-Roof House of the Yangban-led Lineage Village

Thatched-Roof Houses in the Mixed Village

ancestor worship rituals, scholarships for bright young members, and other welfare for lineage members.

In lineage-dominated villages, the overall sense of "community" is known to be rather weak. It is generally true that members of lineage-dominated villages, which tend to be more static and rigid than non-lineage villages, are less harmonious in their relations and less willing to cooperate with one another (Lee 1996). Vincent S. R. Brandt (1971:25) reported, "Without a strong sense of community, conflict between kinship groups and after World War II, tensions between the *yangban* and commoner classes and among political factions were all readily expressed in strife within such villages." Recently, those conflicts and tensions have been reduced, if not eliminated altogether.

Commoner villages, or mixed villages. In Zenshō Eisuke's survey of the mid-1930s, when Korea was under Japanese colonial rule, two-thirds of Korean villages were commoner villages, or "mixed villages," composed of members of several lineages, none of them dominant in number, wealth, or influence over the others. Traditionally, mixed villages are composed largely of commoners, without the presence of a *yangban* lineage, and are smaller and poorer than lineage-led villages. The houses in these villages are generally smaller in size, too, and until very recently were topped with thatched roofs made of straw, not tiled roofs as are common in lineage-dominant settlements. The characteristics that distinguished lineage-dominant from mixed villages were more pronounced before passage of the 1949 Land Reform Act, which abolished institutionalized class distinctions. Nowadays the differences between them are much less apparent.

Rural villages as objects of exploitation

Beginning in the Three Kingdoms period, a time when administrative districts were regularly redrawn, villages were subject to reorganization, subdivision, or consolidation. No detailed information

about these villages is available, but the "Castle lords exercised economic jurisdiction in the villages over which their power extended. They both levied taxes on the peasant population and exacted corvee labor service from them" (Lee 1984:97). Rural farmers were the objects of this exploitation, which continued during the Joseon dynasty and intensified as *yangban*-led villages emerged. When the Joseon dynasty redrew districts in provincial counties, semiautonomous villages were variously labeled as *dong, ri, po, pyeong, chon,* or *hyang,* all Chinese loan words, but no efforts were made to improve life in these villages. Although the peasants were freeborn, most of the farmers other than *yangban*-led lineage members were virtually denied freedom of movement. "Peasants were fixed on the land and were unable to move as they wished" (Lee 1984:184).

Peasant rebellion. Because Korean peasants were exploited for so long, Korea has a long history of peasant rebellion. The first peasant rebellion goes back to 889, in the late Silla dynasty, the result of protests against heavy taxes levied by local governments. The peasants abandoned their land and roamed the countryside, seething with rebellion, but the revolt did not accomplish anything that improved their lives. Numerous intermittent uprisings occurred throughout subsequent dynasties, most of which followed the same pattern: several thousand discontented farmers would attack local government offices; the central government would send troops to put down the rebels; the rebel leaders would be arrested and some executed; and the peasants would ultimately accomplish little beyond demonstrating their frustration and anger.

One of the largest rebellions, which took place during the Joseon dynasty in 1894, grew out of a syncretic religious belief called Donghak (Eastern Learning) and erupted into a revolutionary peasant struggle that employed military operations on a large scale. Under the leadership of Jeon Bong-jun, the head of Gobu-gun's Donghak parish, the peasants occupied the county office, seized weapons,

and distributed the illegally collected tax-rice to the poor. When they took up arms, the peasant armies demanded that the *yangban* be prevented from draining the life blood of peasants through illegal extortions. Later, the activities of the peasant armies evolved into a patriotic movement for national independence from foreign domination. These peasant armies fought against the political and economic aggression of the Japanese, but they lacked the strength to successfully confront the modern weapons and training of the Japanese troops.

Farmer protests subsequent to the 1949 Land Reform Act, which marked the beginning of the new republic, have been documented by Nancy Abelmann (1996), a cultural anthropologist and expert on Korea. She discusses a farmer protest in the late 1980s against corporate ownership of tenant plots exempted from the 1949 Land Reform Act. These protests were not limited to rural farmers but also included student activists and organizers who joined the protest and raised broader questions about class, nation, capitalism, and democracy in the context of modern Korean history. Another scholar of this subject, Shin Gi-wook, has written a book (1997) tracing the roots of peasant activism in Korea from 1910 to post-1945.

Recently, Korean rice farmers and farmers' organizations felt so threatened by the 2004 World Trade Organization (WTO) and FTAs for market liberalization that they staged demonstrations that extended even overseas. During the six days of WTO ministerial meetings that began on 14 December 2005 in Hong Kong, some 1,000 Korean protesters clashed with riot police. Over 800 Korean protesters were detained at police stations then subsequently released. When Korea and the United States began formal negotiations on a bilateral FTA in June 2006, a 146-member delegation of Korean activists, workers, farmers, and students went to the United States to protest. Despite the opposition, on 2 April 2007, Korea and the United States announced an FTA between the two nations, by the congressional approval of the two countries, that finally went into

effect in March 2012. This FTA signed with the United States fits a larger pattern in Korea's FTA dealings: Korea has entered into similar agreements with countries of the Association of Southeast Asian Nations (ten nations) and twenty-seven nations of the European Union.

The Japanese land grab and exploitation of peasants

Japanese interest in Korean real estate, especially farmland, had begun before Japan officially annexed Korea in 1910. In order to acquire Korean farmland, in 1908 the Japanese government established the Oriental Development Company. Within the first eighteen months of its operation, the company acquired 73,500 acres of Korean farmland, and an increasing number of Japanese immigrant farmers relocated to Korea as landlords (Lee 1984). To expand their possessions of Korean farmland, the Japanese established the Land Survey Bureau in 1910, the year of Japan's annexation of Korea. Japan then promulgated the Land Survey Law in 1912.

The Land Survey Law allowed the Japanese to grab even more Korean farmland, which they did swiftly by expropriating it from Korean peasant farmers. Consequently, the Japanese Government-General became Korea's largest landowner, owning 40 percent of the total land area in Korea. By 1941, Japanese ownership had swollen to 54 percent. A good many Korean peasants ended up working their own land for their new Japanese landlords (Lee 1984; Huh 2005).

With the development of dams and waterways on farmland, along with the introduction of new varieties of higher-yield rice and new farming methods, Korean rice production increased 24.9 percent from 1910 to 1944, but the beneficiaries of this increase were mostly the Japanese, along with a few Korean landlords. Huh Soo Youl (2005) methodically and persuasively delineated both Korean farm production and the circumstances of Korean peasant life in the period of Japanese exploitation.

Despite the increase in farm production and economic growth, this period is recorded as the most difficult that Korean peasants

had to endure. David Steinberg (1989:46) describes these conditions in quantitative terms: "By 1930, 75 percent of farmers were in debt, and three-quarters of that debt was to Japanese financial institutions. Tenancy and partial tenancy became the norm: some 12 million people (2.3 million families) were tenants, paying exorbitant rents. There was migration out of such rural areas: in 1925, 2.8 percent of such migrants went to Manchuria and Siberia, 16.9 percent to Japan, and 46.4 percent to Korean urban areas, where living standards were so low." Korean peasants were not only exploited by the Japanese but uprooted from their own farms, which marked the beginning of the Korea diaspora as more farmers left rural communities. Korea was basically forced to become a rice-supplying colony for Japan, which had a rice shortage.

Transformation of Rural Villages

Land Reform Act of 1949 and egalitarianism

The Japanese colonialists not only robbed Korean peasant farmers by charging them 50 percent or more of their crop in rent, while leaving them no security of tenure on their land, but they also made no effort to ameliorate social injustice by eliminating *yangban* privileges institutionalized during the Joseon dynasty (Brandt 1971). During the entire period of Japanese domination, the *yangban* class was left intact.

A major transformation in rural Korean communities took place through land reform that occurred after Korea's liberation from Japan. The Land Reform Act was introduced in 1949, one year after the establishment of the Republic of Korea and following the U.S. Military Government policy to distribute Japanese-owned land to Koreans. Initiated by the leading right-wing Korean Democratic Party, the reform initially restricted the maximum amount of land a family could own to 29,752 square meters (9,000 *pyeong*). The tenant

who received ownership of the land from the existing landlord would pay over five years a price equivalent to 1.5 times the average annual product of the land.

Unlike the North Korea Land Reform Act of 1946, which confiscated land from landlords without compensation, the Land Reform Act of 1949 allowed landlords in South Korea to receive bonds from the government, which took on the task of collecting the payments from the former tenants (Kim 1992). Edward S. Mason and his associates (1980:237) have calculated that "In actual practice, landlord bonds with a face value of 30*seok* (equals 5.12 bushels) of rice sold on the market for the equivalent of only 3.5*seok*, in effect virtually wiping out landlord assets. An average former tenant, on the other hand, might be paying 6*seok* a year to the government, 30 percent of his harvest."

Many believed that the Korean Land Reform Act of 1949 was very successful, because "confiscation and redistribution of the land and income of a relatively small number of landlords thus can be seen to have had a large impact on a great many people" (Mason et al. 1980:237-239). Steinberg (1989) also concurs with the view of Mason and his colleagues. Most of all, the Land Reform Act officially eliminated some residual aspects of former *yangban* class status and brought about egalitarianism in the minds of peasant farmers. In this sense, the Land Reform Act brought revolutionary change to the long-rooted *yangban* tradition and its legacy.

New Village Movement

As the military-led Korean government was bringing about unprecedented economic growth and rapid industrialization via the successful implementation of the first and second five-year economic development plans (1962-1971), it was able to give some attention to Korea's rural sector development. In 1970, because of his own personal zeal to bring about modernization in rural Korea, President Park Chung-hee introduced the New Village Movement (*Saemaeul*

Undong). Perhaps it was no accident that President Park initiated the movement because he was born and grew up in a remote village, and later taught there for a few years as an elementary school teacher. The experience of rural poverty was in his bones, so to speak, and he believed it necessary to improve the condition of rural villages and their infrastructure (Kim 2002).

The New Village Movement was a nationwide movement that mobilized over 30,000 Korean villages. Centered primarily on rural development, it was devoted to improving the welfare of rural people. It was a deliberate process in which different kinds of agents and personnel (often young and vigorous with military experience, but not members of the traditional village elite) were mobilized to bring about fundamental changes in various aspects of village life. The central training headquarters were established at Suwon in 1972, and eventually there were eighty-five training institutions throughout the country. The New Village Movement's projects ranged from improvements to the physical environment—such as building farm roads, village entrance roads, sanitary water systems, rural electrification, village halls, small bridges, and small-scale irrigation system—to income-generating projects such as special crops, livestock, and marketing arrangements. Whang In-Joung(1981) provides a full list of various ventures.

Beginning in 1974, as it spread across the nation, the New Village Movement expanded to urban and suburban areas, including industrial plants and schools, and even to military bases. The objectives of the movement were broadened in scope to include spiritual enlightenment and urban factory projects. The movement extended to social leaders such as university professors, journalists, and lawyers. At its height, government officials wore uniforms to symbolize the movement. Even taxi and bus drivers wore distinctive caps. Eventually, the movement, no longer focused only on rural development projects, became a national mobilization project for political purposes.

Although the Korean government allocated a huge budget for

the movement, a large share of the investment in the project was made by rural people themselves in the form of donations of labor, land, and even cash. For instance, the government provided each of over 30,000 villages with more than 300 free bags of cement for the improvement of dikes, roads, and community wells. An unfortunate byproduct of this development was so-called concrete mania, which destroyed the ecological and aesthetic beauty of the rural villages.

Even after the assassination of President Park Chung-hee in 1979, during the Fifth Republic under President Chun Doo-hwan, the emphasis of the New Village Movement was on various welfare projects, including the extension of medical care centers to rural areas and special education programs for rural young women. However, in the Sixth Republic under President Roh Tae-woo, the movement ground to a halt largely due to the scandal resulting from the overcharges, abuse of funds, corruption, and tax evasion committed by the former President Chun's younger brother, who had been head of the organization from 1981 to 1987. He was finally sentenced to seven years in prison for the illegal appropriation of $5.8 million (Lee 2003; Steinberg 1989).

There is no question that the New Village Movement brought about many improvements in rural villages. Most obvious were physical changes: straw-thatched roofs were replaced with roofs of cement tiles, tin, plaster, or galvanized sheets of iron in various colors; easy-access roads were made for vehicles and roto-tillers; culverts and bridges were built with cement; latrines were dug; village wells were remodeled; new varieties of higher-yield rice were cultivated. A more significant if less visible change affected the spirit of the villages. The villagers' tendency to depend on government initiation for every project was replaced by a reliance on their own initiative and cooperation. Furthermore, the New Village Movement, "by providing status to young, non-traditional leadership, has been of the most effective means of destroying the traditional-oriented social system, one of the goals of the movement" (Steinberg 1989:149-150).

On a personal note, when I visited my home village in the late

1980s after having been away since the early 1960s, I was shocked by changes to the village's landscape brought about by the New Village Movement. A classic countryside village, it is located in a remote mountainous region in southeastern South Korea. But because of the movement, access roads to the village had been widened and paved. The houses now had both hot and cold running water in indoor kitchens, refrigerators, and TVs, because electricity was available, and telephone service connected houses to the outside world. Since the mid-2000s, virtually every household has a home computer with broadband Internet service and email. Today almost every adult living in the village has a mobile phone, a good many of those being iPhones.

Struck by feelings of nostalgia, I found myself yearning for the old thatched roofs. I was disappointed by the odd-looking housing styles of dubious aesthetic quality. Villagers assumed they were built in a Western style, but to me the style was neither Western nor Korean. Villagers complained that the new roofs that had replaced the old thatched ones were inefficient for heating and cooling. The old roofs provided insulation against heat loss in winter and served as a barrier to blazing sunlight in summer. Now, the roofs of the houses are so thin that people can hardly endure the summer heat. Clearly, some changes brought by the New Village Movement were incompatible with the traditional way of life in rural Korea, which had evolved for thousands of years in harmony with the weather and other ecological conditions.

Despite the obvious improvements of the New Village Movement, it has also attracted criticism. Kim Kwang-Ok[Gim Gwang-eok] (1998:18) sums it up this way: "the *Saemaeul* Movement was far from being a civil movement as its communal ideology was produced and controlled by the state. Furthermore, the state evaluated and justified the legitimacy of the communities. In short, individuals became the object of state management through the medium of competitive performance. . . These changes led to the migration of people

from villages to cities. Thus, traditional sociocultural elements that constituted traditional life-style were lost." Steinberg (1989:15) points out that in such a movement, "the potential for mobilizing is obvious. Few societies in ostensibly democratic states are so mobilized and controlled."

Mass exodus of rural peasants to urban and industrial zones

Despite the deliberate effort of the Korean government to revitalize rural villages through the New Village Movement beginning in 1970, these villages have nonetheless faced a most difficult time, largely because of the mass exodus of rural peasant farmers to urban and industrial zones. It was a side effect of the inequity of Korean income distribution between urban and rural areas. Before the New Village Movement, the income of rural peasant farmers was about half that of urban salaried wage workers (Steinberg 1989). However, improvements in the rural sector brought about by the New Village Movement along with increases in rice prices reduced the income gap between rural and urban areas. The average annual household income in rural areas in 1970 when the New Village Movement was initiated was 75.6 percent of what it was in urban areas. From 1974 to 1988, except for three years (1979, 1980, and 1987), the average annual household income in rural Korea even exceeded the urban average. Nevertheless, rural household income started to lag behind urban areas once more beginning in 1989. In 2000, rural household income had returned to its level in 1970, and this disparity continues.

On the one hand, rapid economic growth gave the Korean government energy and resources to spare for the improvement of the rural economy and way of life. On the other hand, unprecedented economic growth and industrialization through a series of successful five-year economic development plans also had detrimental consequences for rural development. The lower income and poor living conditions in rural areas — despite improvements of the New

Village Movement—motivated rural farmers to leave their villages for urban areas, where higher wages and modern living conditions, especially a better prospect for the education of their children, were major attractions. Urban and industrial zones have become a "black hole" into which massive numbers of rural migrants are absorbed. Some farmers simply abandoned their farmhouses when they left their villages. There are no reliable statistics on how many rural houses have been abandoned, but one can easily see them in the countryside.

Consequently, the largest proportion of the rural population is older, while young productive workers leave, thereby creating a critical shortage of farm labor. As noted at the start of this chapter, the demographic statistics of rural areas have followed a steady trajectory—a decrease in overall population and an increase in the average age of that dwindling population. The village of Oma-ri in Goheung-gun of Jeollanam-do is a case in point. In Oma, 70 percent of the 160 villagers are sixty-five years and older. It is projected that by 2040, the median age of the entire Jeollanam-do will be 60.2. As of 5 December 2012, since the average life expectancy of Koreans has increased to 81.05 years (77.6 for men and 84.5 for women), the proportion of the elderly in rural Korea continues to increase. Increasing life expectancy has been a trend in Korea for decades.

As the rural population is getting smaller, and older, the amount of farmland under cultivation is also shrinking each year. It went from 2,298,000 hectares in the 1970s to 1,876,000 hectares in the 2000s, with an average annual reduction of around 21 percent. Free trade agreements with other countries have resulted in less demand for domestically produced rice; this is a reason why farmers have generally opposed such agreements.

In 2010, the number of Koreans aged sixty-five and older was 5,450,000; by 2040, it has been estimated that the same age group will number 16,500,000, constituting 32.3 percent of the total population. The number of senior Koreans who are eighty-five and older was 370,000 in 2010, but the number could swell to 2,080,000

in 2040. While Koreans are getting older and living longer, they are also becoming more concentrated in rural areas. By 2040, the largest category of the Korean population, both male and female, is predicted to be elderly Koreans aged eighty and older.

Since in rural areas there are fewer children of elementary school age, those between the ages of six and twelve (only 8.4 percent of the total population), many elementary schools located there have already closed, and the number of such closures is on rise. For instance, in Gangwon-do, 310 elementary schools were closed from 1990 to 2000, and many others are still in danger of closing. This problem is not limited to Gangwon-do but is rather a nationwide phenomenon. In fact, the Ministry of Education, Science and Technology has to decide whether to close or merge nearly 2,000 elementary schools throughout the country. The crisis extends to middle and high schools as well.

Furthermore, there are a limited number of women of child-bearing age living in rural areas (16.6 percent of the total female population in rural villages), and that number is decreasing every year. There is no specific limit for child-bearing age, but Statistics Korea provides data on child-bearing ages ranging from fifteen to forty-nine years old. Newborn babies are deemed precious, literally, because they are scarce, so much so that some municipal governments, such as Donghae, Inje, Yangpyeong, Yeoncheon, Mokpo, and eight other cities, began to give mothers of newborns gold bracelets, silver necklaces, and other precious gifts to congratulate them for bearing children. In the 2012 presidential election campaign, in an effort to promote the fertility of families, a leading candidate had a campaign pledge that when a family has a third child, the third child will have free tuition for a college education. However, some look upon such incentives to promote fertility with skepticism.

In addition, in rural Korea there are fewer marriageable women than men between twenty and thirty years of age; consequently, there is a shortage of women that these men can marry. What is more, rural women tend to avoid marrying rural men because they know

that if they do, they will have the same difficult life as their parents, with hard work on the farm, few rewards, and limited educational opportunities for their children. This exacerbates the scarcity of marriage partners for rural men. Because of this imbalance between supply and demand, an increasing number of men from rural areas are marrying foreign women, a trend already noted in earlier chapters.

The Changing Paradigm of Rural Villages and Their Future Prospects

Rice: A sentimental crop for Korean farmers

Traditionally, Koreans have considered rice to be more than just a staple food. Vincent S. R. Brandt (1971:80) recognized that rice has been "an essential element in the moral order of the farmer's universe. . . . Most wealth is still calculated in terms of rice - a commodity that is, of course, readily transferable into other forms of property." Korean anthropologist Hahm Han-hee[Ham Han-hui] (2005) reports that since rice has been so deeply embedded in Korean culture for so long, Koreans' morality, values, and even worldview are attracted to the culture of rice farming.

Korean preoccupation with rice has been so profound that Korea's yearly rice production steadily increased from 1970 (4,090,000 tons) to 2002 (7,004,000 tons), which saw the largest yield ever in the history of Korean rice production. Such high production was due largely to an adequate supply of fertilizer and insecticide, mechanized farming methods, and the introduction of new varieties of hybrid seeds that produce larger yields than older varieties. From 1970 to today, Korea has supplied over 90 percent of its own rice, except for a couple of bad years, 1980 and 1993. However, since 2002, the total yearly rice production has decreased gradually, a little bit each year, except for two years, 2005 and 2010. In 2011, total production

remained around 6,131,000 tons, which is about one million tons less than it was ten years ago. Since Korea produces less rice each year, the surplus of rice has also decreased each year. In 2002, Korea had a stockpile of some 1,447,000 tons of surplus rice, which has since been reduced to 952,000 tons.

Furthermore, Korean wet-rice farmers have been discouraged by the external pressure imposed by the Uruguay Round Agreement (URA). The URA, named after the 1986 negotiation site in Punta del Este, Uruguay, is the world's largest trading system. Since its formation in 1993, it reached an agreement for negotiations on market access for goods and services. In April 1994, the deal was signed by ministers from 123 participating governments at a meeting in Marrakesh, Morocco. The URA requires the implementation of a minimum market access of 1 to 4 percent of the total consumption of rice. Since the 2004 WTO and FTA push for market liberalization, Korean rice farmers have felt threatened by such agreements. Most Korean farmers worry about the imminent opening of the domestic rice market to foreign imports. In December 2004, Korea reached an agreement with nine rice-exporting countries, including the United States, China, and Australia, to keep its tariff-waiver status on rice imports in exchange for expanding market access.

Beginning in October 2005, a series of farmers' protests were aimed at stopping the ratification of the rice pact agreement by the National Assembly. Korean farmers worry about opening the domestic rice market to relatively inexpensive foreign rice. For instance, the Korean rice price is more than six times the U.S. market price. Korean farmers predict a gloomy future in which Korea might be forced to open its market to other agricultural products as well. On 1 April 2004, Korea and Chile signed an FTA, but rice was excluded from that agreement because Chile is not a rice-producing country of any account. In the FTA between Korea and the United States, rice was excluded from the terms of the agreement.

Even though rice has been excluded from various FTA agreements,

there are other societal pressures devaluing rice in Korea. There is currently an overproduction of rice—driven by its under-consumption—that has followed a radical change in Koreans' dietary patterns, from rice-centered Eastern food to Western food, including bread, pizza, and American-style fast food. McDonald's, for instance, the American fast-food giant, opened its first restaurant in Seoul in 1988. One year later, in 1989, its annual sales volume reached 100 billion *won* (about $106 million at the exchange rate then); a decade later, in 2000, its sales had doubled to 200 billion *won* (about $213 million), with 300 restaurants in Korea. Pizza Hut has turned the most profit of fast food giants: in 2004 it sold nearly 400 billion *won* (about $426 million) worth of pizza to Koreans, especially young Koreans. The market share of non-rice fast food may be the biggest challenge to Korean rice consumption. Most Korean rice farmers see bleak prospects for the future of domestic rice farming; accordingly, the size of Korean rice farmland has shrunk each year. In 2001, the size of rice farmland was 1,059,000 hectares; in 2012, it had shrunk to 849,000 hectares. Jeollanam-do, the province with the highest rice yield, has seen the most severe decline in production.

Commercialization. As the rice-centered agricultural paradigm is changing, Korean farmers have begun to cultivate various other cash crops. They have recognized that, for market-oriented cash crops, non-irrigated paddy farmland (*bat*) is more valuable than irrigated wet farmland (*non*). Using paddy lands, farmers have started to raise cucumbers, tomatoes, watermelons, strawberries, mushrooms, Chinese cabbage, bell peppers, turnips, herbal plants for herbal medicines, and other vegetables. Korean farmers exported bell peppers, eggplants, cucumbers, and pears to Japan, which accounted for almost the entire Japanese import market share of those products. Together with those crops, by exporting lilies (92.6 percent of the Japanese import share), paprika (63.9 percent), and watermelons (58.1 percent), in 2007 Korea farmers earned some $1.2 billion from Japan.

Japanese importation of Korea produce grew after the massive earthquake and tsunami devastated the coast of the Tohoku region in 2011, and subsequent problems at the nuclear reactor in Fukushima raised worries over possible radioactive contamination of foods supplies. For a time, Koreans had some difficulty finding the popular bottled water brand *Samdasu* because much of the available supply was exported to Japan. In 2011, Korean export of fruits, vegetables, and other produce increased 22.2 percent, amounting to around $2.2 billion.

Several conditions have brought about a generalized movement toward market-minded commercialism in Korean farming. First, demand for non-staple, non-grain items such as fresh fruits, vegetables, and fish has increased due to the greater, denser urban population. Second, with the development of transportation and expansion and paving of highways, farmers can now easily access urban consumers in a matter of a few hours, thus ensuring the freshness of the produce. Such a speedy delivery system has revolutionized cash crop farming (Keidel 1980). Third, urban demand for a variety of foods is being met by technological advances, especially the introduction of vinyl greenhouses. Market-oriented cash crops can be grown year-round using greenhouses; even in cold winter weather, farmers can supply fresh fruits and vegetables to customers.

Likewise, most fishermen have taken advantage of advances in the technology of aquaculture instead of depending on traditional fishing methods. Seaweed, shrimp, and other shellfish, especially high-priced abalone (*jeonbok*), are commonly raised in today's aqua-farms of Korea. The income of fishermen has risen steadily since the introduction of aquaculture on a large scale. There are many aqua-farms in inland ponds that raise all sorts of freshwater fish through the application of new fish-farming technologies.

Technological innovation. Not long ago in Korea, human muscle and oxen were the major sources of energy for tilling farmland and

harvesting crops. Now, roto-tillers have replaced oxen for tilling farmland, and combines are commonly used for harvesting. Currently, many farmers also take advantage of information technology. A growing number of Korean farming villages now have the skills and technology to connect to commercial opportunities in cyberspace.

Beginning on 27 December 2001, the provincial government of Gangwon-do and the city of Wonju redesigned the mountain village of Hwangdun-ri, near Wonju, as a "cyber village" to demonstrate how modern information technology could be applied to farming. Computers with broadband connection were installed in the village's 160 households. The village headquarters trained villagers in the use of information technology. The results have been astonishing. The villagers can now find all the necessary information about farming, including the prices of farm products, on a daily basis. Also, each household has an email address to communicate with the outside world, thus freely overcoming physical isolation. Government documents can be readily requested or acquired online without villagers having to make trips to various offices. Village students can submit their homework to school via the school homepage. Parent-teacher conferences can also be conducted online. The village health office monitors the community's patients, diagnosing and consulting with physicians who work in large hospitals in Wonju, the largest city in the region, over the Internet.

Farmers in Daeheung-ri in Gyeongsangbuk-do are reportedly now in the habit of checking the daily weather forecast and the price of farm products on their computers every morning at six o'clock. Recognizing farmers' growing interest in information technology and its practical application to farming, the Ministry of Public Administration and Security (under the Park Geun-hye administration, it has been renamed the Ministry of Security and Public Administration), along with provincial and municipal governments, have selected additional villages to receive information technology. As of 13 March 2003, over seventy such villages were chosen. As of 2012, the total is around

370 villages. Eventually, this will become a nationwide campaign.

Farmers have also begun to see the impact of information technology on produce sales, as demonstrated by an increase in mushroom farmers' income in Dosim-ri, a village located 1,000 meters above sea level in Bonghwa gun, my home county in the northeastern corner of Gyeongsangbuk-do. The county is known to be one of the most remote and resource-poor counties in Korea. Nonetheless, it is well known for its pine-tree mushroom (*song-i* or *Tricholoma matsutake*), which gives off an aroma of pine. This species only grows under pine trees and cannot be domesticated. Because of its remoteness and isolation, the village was selected by the government to be a cyber village in August 2003. One hundred twenty villagers received home computers from the government, and the villagers have been trained to use them.

Since learning to use the computers, villagers have begun to sell their mushrooms over the Internet directly to urban consumers, even to those in Tokyo, Japan. Now that villagers are using this digital platform, the villagers' income from the mushroom sales have gone up 60 times over the past ten years.

There is another, more recent application of information technology that promises to be a boon to farmers in rural villages. In October 2005, SK Telecom together with Green-net introduced an electronically networked system that can control the temperature inside greenhouses and poultry farms from anywhere, at anytime by cellular phone. If this system is widely adopted by rural farmers, there is no telling what future advances will come of it.

Back to the village movement

Though nowhere near the magnitude of movement away from the countryside, the recent return to rural Korea by some citizens of the baby-boom generation is beginning to have an effect. During the financial crisis of 1997 and 1998, Korea received a loan from the International Monetary Fund to make up for a critical shortage of

foreign currency in the country. At the time, some highly educated people decided to seek employment in the rural sector where there was less competition for jobs. Some chose to go to rural areas in order to take advantage of government aid of some 60 million *won* (about $63,965 at the time) that would be provided for their relocation and adjustment to a new life. Although their numbers may be relatively small, some urban elite now choose to live in rural areas and raise their families.

According to a 2005 report, the number of highly educated people, those with two or more years of college, had increased in rural areas by 7.7 percent. The proportion of college graduates was 15 percent (87,000), the highest ever. Some educated Koreans have relocated to rural areas to improve their quality of life by avoiding crowded conditions, traffic jams, pollution, congestion, and other ills of city life. Despite the challenges of rural life, they prefer this environment to an urban one. To smooth the transition for these city-to-country transplants, the National Headquarters for Back to Rural Farming (*Jeonguk Gwinong Undong Bonbu*), a nonprofit organization founded on 19 September 1996, provides various adjustment programs and offers vocational training in various schools. Several major Korean daily newspapers such as the *Maeil Business Newspaper* (12 December 2012), and the *JoongAng Daily* (8 December 2012) have reported that the number of people moving to rural villages is "increasing."

In 2012, there were events held in Korea that catered to those with an interest in moving to the country and taking up farming as a way of life. In early May 2012, the Seoul Trade Exhibition & Convention (*Seoul Muyeok Jeonsijang*) venue in Daechi-dong held the "2012 Festival for Going Back to Rural Villages for Farming" (2012 *Daehanminguk Gwinong Gwichon Festival*). Over 28,000 Seoulites attended. My translation of "Going Back" to rural villages is inaccurate, if not misleading, rendering of the Korean into English. Koreans often speak of returning to the country (*Gwichon* or *Gwinong*) even though many who do so are living there for the first time in their lives.

Among these so-called returnees, according to a May 2012 feature article in the *Korean Economic Daily*, some were earning bigger incomes now as blueberry farmers than they had previously as branch managers of insurance firms and banks.

What is more, according to a report on 16 June 2012 in the *Maeil Business Newspaper*, fifteen deputy directors (samugwan) from the Ministry for Food, Agriculture, Forestry and Fisheries spent several months in rural villages learning how life is lived there—not unlike cultural anthropologists doing fieldwork in a foreign land. I believe such a country immersion for city dwellers is promising for rural development in Korea. When those bureaucrats return to the city better acquainted with rural life, they are apt to enact policies more favorable to its welfare.

It is just possible that rice production might even have a comeback in Korea. Given the shift to more productive varieties of rice, and the decreased use of potent pesticides, health-conscious Koreans might turn once again to rice as a staple food.

Government efforts at balanced national development

Apart from the grass-roots movement led by some city dwellers resettling in rural villages, the government is making its own concerted effort to develop South Korea in a more balanced fashion. The first major effort was to create a new administrative mini-capital, Sejong-si. It is not far from Daejeon, a one-hour train ride from Seoul aboard KTX, Korea's version of the bullet train. When the 465.23 square kilometers of the mini-capital are completed (making it around 77 percent the size of Seoul in land area) by 2014, the city will host thirty-six governmental agencies and sixteen cabinet ministries, including that of the prime minister. The city is designed to accommodate about half a million citizens. By 2015, the city will be the residence of 10,000 full-time civil servants and their families.

The idea of creating a mini-capital grew out of former president Roh Moo-hyun's pledge during his presidential campaign in 2002

to redistribute the population outside overcrowded Seoul. While there is no question that having the whole of national government concentrated in one city is convenient, the progressive overcrowding of Seoul had become unsustainable. President Roh planned to relocate the national capital to Sejong-si, but his plan was never realized in its original form. Sejong-si is a compromise of Roh's original plan, and since its official opening on 1 July 2012, Sejong-si and Seoul have shared the power of governance in a somewhat unsettled and unsettling manner. Some heads of units now located in Sejong-si have business in Seoul as well, particularly when the National Assembly is in session. For now, many are commuting a long distance virtually every day. It will take a while to work out the sharing of political power between the two cities. Only in years to come will the full impact of Sejong-si, built in the interest of balanced national development, become known to Korea.

7
Religions and Beliefs of Koreans

Perhaps it is no exaggeration to say that the Korean peninsula is something of a "repository" for world religions. As a multi-religious society, Korea is presently host to all sorts of religious beliefs: shamanism, a belief in the dual existence of all things as having a physical, visible body, and a psychic, invisible soul; polytheism, which recognizes many important gods, no one of which is supreme; and monotheism, a belief in one god. Some beliefs in Korea are homegrown while others have been introduced from abroad.

Not only are there many religions in Korea, but a large percentage of the population follows one or more systems of beliefs. The number of Christians, both Protestants and Roman Catholics, is the largest in Asia, with the exception of the Philippines, both in proportion as well as absolute numbers. According to the most recent statistics on Korea's religious population, as of 2005, nearly 14 million Koreans (about 29.2 percent of 47 million at the time) claimed that they were Christians (Protestant or Roman Catholic). Although the official Korean census is released every five years, data about religious affiliation are publicized only once every ten years. The next official record of religious behavior in Korea will come out in 2015.

According to Statistics Korea, there are some 72,966 religious organizations across the country, including churches and temples. That includes 57,410 Christian organizations, 13,520 Buddhist organizations, and 2,036 other religious organizations. In Seoul alone there are over 7,000 Christian organizations and churches,

Several Buddhist Monks Decorate a Christmas Tree
in Jogyesa(Seoul) to Celebrate Christmas

1,000 Buddhist organizations and temples, as well as the Confucian headquarters of Seonggyungwan, the headquarters of Cheondogyo, and several Muslim mosques. All these religions coexist in peace, yet none of them is exclusively representative of Korean culture. Regarding Koreans' religious beliefs, the most difficult question to answer is, "What accounts for the phenomenal growth of the Christian faith in Korea?" To answer this, we have to examine the historical context of Korean religious belief.

Inclusiveness and Syncretism

Inclusiveness

Inclusiveness means the "act of incorporating or the attitude of wishing to be incorporated," and reflects attributes of the father-son dominant relationship found in the East Asian kinship system

(Hsu 1965). Korean religious inclusiveness is one reason why Korea is a multi-religious society. There is a general assumption that all gods, whether one knows something about them or not, must be honored equally or at the very least not made objects of contempt. Koreans trust that all religions benefit humanity in some way, so they are all equally good. To a certain extent, Koreans respect the religious beliefs of all other people, so there is no particular reason to foist one's own particular religion onto others. Such a view is in stark contrast to the Western, and especially American, notion that "religion is to be more and more exclusive" (Hsu 1981:254).

Korean religious inclusiveness is such that different members of a family can believe in different religions. By way of illustration, Cho Hung-Youn[Jo Heung-yun] (1994) and his colleagues (Yun et al. 1994) offer this hypothetical scenario: on a given weekend within a family, the mother-in-law goes to a shaman to attend a *gut* (a shaman ritual), one daughter-in-law attends a Christian church, another joins a new religious group, and yet another visits a Buddhist temple. Meanwhile, the father, head of the household, participates in a discussion of Confucianism while mountain climbing. Michael Breen (2004:42), too, has observed that people in the same family may follow different faiths: "It is common to find a husband who could loosely be called Confucian, a Buddhist wife and Christian children. What is striking is how similar Koreans are, whatever their formal religious affiliation." Such religious independence among family members seldom disturbs the harmony of family relations. Usually no one in the family coerces or antagonizes other members because of different religious preferences.

It is interesting that China and Japan practice a similar religious inclusiveness. Francis L. K. Hsu (1981:254) reported that a Chinese man "may go to a Buddhist monastery to pray for a male heir, but he may proceed from there to a Taoist shrine where he beseeches a god to cure him of malaria." Japanese anthropologist Harumi Befu (1971:96) has observed that in Japan "the same person may worship

deities of different religions without any feeling of conflict. For example, a Japanese might pray at the Buddhist altar at home in the morning and go to a neighborhood Shinto shrine in the afternoon. . . . Moreover, there are religious edifices which enshrine deities of different religions. For instance, there may be a Buddhist temple on the premises of a Shinto shrine, or vice versa."

Syncretism

Korean religious syncretism is another factor contributing to Korea's multi-religious society. In a sense, all religions are syncretic, yet syncretism is more prominent in the religious attitude of Koreans than that of any other people. A Korean religious concept of a deity may combine elements derived from different religions.

The distinction between indigenous Korean beliefs and shamanism, for instance, is so blurred that sometimes it exists only in the mind of the scholar analyzing Korean folk beliefs. Anthropologist Kim Seong-Nae[Gim Seong-rye] (2002), for example, has provided detailed information about whether shamanism is part of Korea's indigenous beliefs or imported. Most ordinary Koreans, however, are unconcerned with the historical derivation of a religious concept.

In addition to shamanism, most new religions, such as Donghak (later Cheondogyo), Wonbulgyo (Won Buddhism), Daejonggyo, and many minor religions, founded in the late nineteenth century and the early twentieth century, are syncretic, arising from the combination of two or more other religions. The number of new religions formed in this way is estimated to be over 300. The socioeconomic and political environment of nineteenth-century Korea, which was facing challenges from the West and Japan, made Koreans more receptive to new religious hope and promises in the same way that the masses of Tang Chinese were inclined by the tenor of the times to accept Buddhism.

Korean religious inclusiveness and syncretism make it difficult to determine the precise numbers of believers in Korea. If Koreans were

asked about their religious preferences, a great many would say that they do not have any particular religion. In fact, according to the 2005 Korean census, 46.9 percent of the total population responded in just this way. For this reason, assessing the size of Korea's religious population is more an art than a science.

Korean Native Beliefs

Anthropologists have demonstrated that although culture, including beliefs and religions, varies from society to society, the human personification of supernatural power in the form of gods or deities is a cultural universal, and Korea is no exception. Archaeologists have found signs of religious beliefs in cave paintings in which the predominant images are animals of the hunt. Many scholars think that this reflects a belief that the image was thought to have some power over events. Bangudae, a Korean archaeological site located in Ulju in Gyeongsangnam-do, which is dated earlier than the Megalithic (2000 to 500 BC) by Sarah M. Nelson (1993) or from the late *Bissalmunui* (comb and pit market pottery) pottery period, is home to an incised rock drawing that probably represents sun worship (Choe and Bale 2002). The Dangun mythology symbolizes a sun god for the nation at its origin. Nevertheless, since the details of religions practiced in the distant past cannot be reconstructed by archaeologists simply from the remains of material culture, this chapter will cover only a few select indigenous religious beliefs.

Ancestor worship and house gods

Ancestor worship is one of the oldest Korean indigenous beliefs. Although Confucianism also emphasizes and promotes ancestor worship, Koreans practiced ancestor worship long before Confucianism was introduced to the peninsula. The practice of lavish burials in Goguryeo is indicative of belief in ancestor worship, which in turn

was based on the conviction that the living soul of an ancestor exerts a continuous influence on the well-being of descendants of a later generation (Lee 1984:34). Ancestor worship through elaborate ritual in the Goryeo period was further enhanced during the Joseon dynasty as Confucianism provided a guiding metaphor for the destiny of the dynasty. Most wealthy *yangban* families built their own family shrines to store the tablets that symbolized their ancestors.

As part of ancestor worship, in an ordinary Korean household there is a jar called *josangdanji*, which symbolizes the spirits of the ancestors of the house. This jar of ancestors has various names in different regions of Korea. In some it is called "grandmother" and is related to the fertility of the house (Lee 2003). Rice is stored inside this jar, which is covered with white paper and placed in one corner of the inner room on a high shelf. Food is served in honor of the ancestors once a year in October by the housewife, who prays for good luck for her family.

There are also numerous deities for the house. The House Master God (*Seongju*), which is supposed to protect the head of the family, is symbolized by another jar filled with rice and barley and placed on the wooden floor (*maru*). In Gyeonggi-do, a white paper vessel is used instead of a jar. The housewife pays homage to this god with food. The Fire God (*Jowang*), which is supposed to protect the housewife, is placed in the kitchen, and the housewife serves it clean water in a white cup every morning. The House Site God (*Teoju*) and the God of Wealth (*Eop*) are placed side by side in the backyard, near the platform that holds jars and crocks of soy sauce, soy bean paste, and other salted food. Both of these gods are also honored and recognized by the housewife once a year in a special ceremony. There is also the Young Lady of the Toilet, a goddess who metes out punishment to those who disturb her by letting them fall into or lose their shoes in the toilet. She might take lives when she is really upset. Ritual services for all house gods are performed by housewives, except in the Confucian style of ancestor worship.

Village gods

In the past, almost all Korean villages had gods whose role was to protect the village. These gods were called mountain gods, or *Seonangdang*, also the name of a ritual performed in their honor on the fifteenth of January in the lunar calendar and overseen by a master selected by the villagers. Nowadays, however, the observance of rituals concerning house gods and village gods is fading away, especially after the advent of the New Village Movement. For many Koreans, particularly young and educated villagers, worshipping both house gods and village gods is considered superstitious rather than genuinely religious. Recently, however, there has been a revival of these activities in what is called the "village-coming" gathering (*hyangto moim*), influenced by the Korean popular culture movement.

Dangun myth and a belief for the nation

In Dangun mythology, the sun god symbolizes the origin of the nation. Dangun was the son between Hwanung who came down from Heaven and a bear-turned-woman who lived on earth. The myth represents not only the beginning of the first Korean kingdom, supposedly established in 2333 BC, but is also the source for the national shrine to Korea's ancient religion at Pyeongyang and other places. This mythology appears to be an attempt to enhance symbolically the divinity and authority of Dangun as a political leader in the first kingdom. According to Charles Allen Clark (1961:139), an American missionary, "In 2265 BC, according to tradition, Dangun first offered sacrifice ot 'Hananim,' the God of the Heaven, at Hyeolgu on the island of Ganghwado in the mouth of the Hangang, twenty-five miles below the modern Seoul. Later he erected on that island on the Manisan (Mani Mountain, formerly Marisan[**Mari Mountain**]) a great altar of stone and earth seventeed feet high and six feet six inches square at the top, and that altar is still standing today."

Throughout Korean history, there have been numerous "founder's

altars" erected by founders and/or kings who then visited these altars to worship, an act that in turn promoted the unity of their subjects. Most of these altars developed into shrines, some of which were dedicated to the king's forebears and others to *sajik*, the gods of land and harvest. As late as the Joseon dynasty, emulating an old Chinese practice, the founder-king Taejo (Yi Seong-gye) built an altar, *sajikdan*, in 1395 to worship the gods of land and harvest, offering prayers four times a year. This shrine-like altar of *sajikdan* was erected to the west of the main palace in Seoul, and the city block where the altar is located has been called Sajik-dong, after the altar, which is preserved to this day.

Shamanism

Shamanism is one of the oldest religious beliefs in Korea and can be traced back to 4000 BC in the Neolithic period (Lee 1984). Although shamanism is widely dispersed on the Eurasian continent, Korea has preserved it well, and it is still active. Kim Seong-Nae (1999) has summarized the scholarly work on Korean shamanism undertaken by scholars at home and abroad over the past 100 years.

Shamanism has a dualistic religious worldview in which the body and soul are seen as separate. Therefore, a particular soul or spirit can enter another body in an act of "possession." One particular characteristic of shamanism is that the medium, known as *mudang* (female shaman), perceives this possession physically. The functions of a shamanistic ritual service are performed for the purpose of securing good luck, effecting a cure of physical or mental illness, or pacifying the spirits of deceased family members.

Shamans make contact with gods (benign spirits) or civil spirits through special ritual techniques: *gut*, a major shaman ritual, and *chiseong*, a minor offering. *Gut* includes paraphernalia that echo the distant past and use ancient percussion instruments. The whirling *mudang*'s ritual performance is very noisy because of the sounds of the large drum (*janggu*), fiddles, gong, pipes, and dancing ornaments

Scene of a Shaman Ritual

attached to clothing that glitter and make rhythmic sounds during the whirling dance. The ritual service usually lasts for two days, and since one shaman alone cannot dance for two days straight, usually four or five shamans, along with musicians, perform together as a group.

Since ancestor worship, Dangun mythology, and other native Korean belief systems all include some shamanistic elements, it is difficult to deny a close relationship among them (Kim 1982). Nevertheless, many foreign scholars indicate that ancestor worship and shamanism are different ritual systems (Akiba 1957; Brandt 1971; Dix 1980). Roger Janelli and Yim Dawn-hee (1982) point out this difference: while ancestor worship idealizes ancestors who are benevolent and never harm their descendants, in shamanism ancestors are sometimes threatening and a supplicant may seek out a shaman to appease them.

To become a shaman, one has to experience the "shaman illness." During her lifetime, most often in adolescence or late in life, a

Religions and Beliefs of Koreans

woman might suffer from an unknown illness, either bodily pain or mental exhaustion, dreaming of demons or gods and experiencing hallucinations and visions. Knowing that there is no cure for these symptoms, the woman visits a shaman to ascertain whether or not she has a shaman illness. If so, she becomes a novice shaman, and the older shaman she consulted becomes her godmother. The novice takes the god who appeared in her dream as her guardian deity (Lee 2003).

In the Joseon dynasty, shamans and shaman devotees were classed with other outcast groups and subject to discrimination. During the Japanese occupation, the Japanese attempted to eliminate shamanism in their effort to eradicate Korea's native beliefs. The Japanese imposed their Shintōism—Japanese traditional belief that is a composite of indigenous beliefs grouped under the name of Shintō, or "way of the gods"—on Koreans under the pretext of creating a single Japanese entity (*naeseon ilche*[*naisen ittai* in Japanese]). Arresting Korean shamans was a common occurrence (Yun et al. 1994). The liberation of Korea from Japan after World War II did not liberate shamanism. In 1970s, shamans had to face yet another challenge, this time from the New Village Movement. Believing that shamanism and its rituals were in the same category as excessive drinking and gambling, the movement declared war on the practice. Leaders of the movement together with some civil servants destroyed numerous shaman shrines and prohibited the performance of *gut* rituals.

After enduring all these hardships imposed on them for so long, Korean shamans finally have allies and sympathizers. International scholars and tourists from Japan and the United States were the first groups in recent times to be sympathetic to shamanism (Kendall 1985a, 1985b, 1996b). Another group sympathetic to shamanism, mostly young, anti-government protesters and intellectuals who initiated the Korean popular culture movement, emerged in the 1970s. These proponents often romanticized shamanism as the most victimized segment of Korean culture. During their anti-government demonstrations and

rallies, they utilized *gut* rituals, including shaman dance and music. College students often invited shamans to their festivities, believing that shamanism represents traditional Korean culture.

Shamanism has also been rejuvenated by the Cultural Heritage Administration (*Munhwaje Gwallicheong*) of the Ministry of Culture, Sports and Tourism, which in 1980 designated *gut* as one of the "intangible cultural properties" (assets), or *Muhyeong munhwajae*. This designation means that shamanism and its rituals are protected by the government and that shamans receive some financial assistance from the government for performing rituals, which has given Korean shamanism a great boost. Shamanism is being transformed as shamans adjust to Korea's increasing urbanization, industrialization, and commercialization.

Nowadays, rural-based shamans move to cities and perform *gut* for urban clients engaged in high-risk, petty capitalist enterprise. Laurel Kendall (1996b) has traced the movement of shamans from rural villages to cities. Some shamans now work in women's beauty parlors, telling the fortunes of foreign clients from Japan and Taiwan while these tourists receive massages. Some shamans have their own websites to advertise their services, and others teach short courses in becoming a shaman at private tutorial schools. The Korean Overseas Information Service estimates that in the early 2000s there were well over 50,000 dues-paying members of shaman organizations in Korea.

Foreign-born Religions and New Religions in Korea

Confucianism

Originating in China, Confucianism was founded by Confucius. The name by which he is commonly known is actually a Latinized form of his real name, Kong fu-zi (551-479 BC), which means Great Master Kong. Nevertheless, Tu Wei-ming (1984:3-4), one of the foremost authorities on Confucianism, points out that "Confucius

was not the founder of Confucianism in the sense that Buddha was the founder of Buddhism and Christ was the founder of Christianity." Rather, the story of Confucianism does not begin with Confucius alone but with the "family of scholars" or disciples who followed or advocated Confucian doctrines.

Confucianism does not have clergymen and does not teach the worship of a god or gods, so, for this reason, there is debate over whether Confucianism is actually a religion in the Western sense. Tu Wei-ming (1998:3) states that although Confucianism is often grouped together with Buddhism, Christianity, Hinduism, and Taoism as a major historical religion and has also exerted a profound influence on East Asian spiritual life, "it is not an organized religion." If Confucianism is a religion, it is one without a god, without an organized missionary tradition, and without a promise of life after death. Nevertheless, millions of Confucian devotees in China, Korea, Japan, and other Asian countries honor Confucius in much the same way that other peoples honor founders of religions.

The basic tenet of Confucianism teaches that humans are compelled by their nature to live with other humans in society. The universal human quality that leads them to do so is *jen*[ren], which can be rendered in English as "benevolence," "human-heartedness," "person-to-personness," and "perfect virtue." "Right action" is defined by Confucians in terms of the duties and obligations implicit in five basic relationships: ruler and subject, father and son, elder person (elder brother) and younger person (younger brother), husband and wife, and friend and friend. Except for the category of friend and friend, all these relationships involve the authority of one person over another.

Confucianism was introduced to Korea during the Three Kingdoms period (37 BC-AD 935). Goguryeo established a Confucian academy in 372. In 682, a Confucian academy was also built in the Silla capital of Gyeongju. During the late Goryeo and early Joseon periods, numerous exchanges between Korean and Chinese scholars stimulated the growth of Neo-Confucianist studies in Korea. By the

fourteenth century, Confucianism had become an integrated part of Korean culture, and since the sixteenth century, it has almost completely dominated Korean thought and philosophy (Yang and Henderson 1958). In a sense, Koreans were more Confucian than the Chinese, particularly in their devotion to Neo-Confucianism (Janelli and Yim 1982; Osgood 1951; Peterson 1974; Reischauer and Fairbank 1960). Neo-Confucianism was developed by scholars such as Han Yu (768-824) and Zhu Xi[Chu Hsi] (1130-1200) to rediscover the meanings of Confucianism that had been lost over the centuries. Tu Wei-ming (1984:10) writes, "Confucianism, for example, featured prominently in Korea, especially in the Yi dynasty[Joseon] . . . Indeed, from roughly the end of the 14th century to as recently as the 20th century, Korean culture has been greatly shaped by Confucian thought."

Neo-Confucian scholar officials were allies of the founder of the Joseon dynasty. The best-known Confucians of the time were appointed teachers at the highest National Confucian Academy (Seonggyungwan). Teachers and students of the academy gathered together to debate outstanding problems of Neo-Confucian thought. The kings of Joseon were pressured by the Confucians to replace traditional aspects of the people's religious life with Confucian principles (Deuchler 1992). Throughout the Joseon dynasty, the two most prominent Neo-Confucian scholars were Yi Hwang and Yi I. Yi Hwang was the foremost Korean Confucian philosopher of his age and interpreted Neo-Confucianism in Korea. He has often been called the Zhu Xi of Korea, and he maintained a position that emphasized personal experience and moral self-cultivation as the essence of learning. His views had a great influence on Confucian scholarship in Japan, eventually evolving into one of the main schools of Japanese Confucian thought.

Korean Confucianism emphasizes traditional social relations, teaches the importance of a hierarchical order, and contains five basic principles of human social relations, of which the parental authority of father over son is the most valued. The highest virtue is filial piety.

Dosan Seowon Where Yi Hwang Taught His Students

Specifically, Confucianism highly values (1) education and training; (2) emphasis on the group—such as the family, organization, and state—over the individual, in contrast to individual-centered Western values; (3) the family as the most important unit for economic activities; (4) five basic principles of social relations to promote comity; and (5) a positive rather than a pessimistic worldview (Kim 1992).

The dynamic between Confucianism and Korea's economic growth has not yet been fully evaluated. Some scholars, following Max Weber (1951), view Confucianism as a hindrance to economic development. Chung Young-iob (1989:152), for one, is critical of the role of Confucianism in Korean economic development: "Confucian teachings rejected training in economics for the pursuit of wealth and held business people in low esteem. The ruling elite, *yangban*, did not allow themselves to participate in profit-making enterprises." Han Kyung-koo (2003:9) reports that while the *yangban* "took great pride in the high degree of the Confucianization of Koreans" during the

Joseon dynasty, many Koreans subsequently changed their evaluation of Confucianism. Even its critics agree that Confucianism had some indirect positive influence on Korean economic development, especially through its effect on education (Kim and Kim 1989; Steers et al. 1989): "the Confucian emphasis on learning and competitive examination as a means of social achievement has long motivated the Koreans to pursue scholarly and educational endeavors, which are crucial to the acquisition and diffusion of knowledge — skills indispensable to development" (Chung 1989:130). Dwight H. Perkins (1986:7) observes that leaders of economic development in Japan, Korea, Hong Kong, Taiwan, and Singapore "were influenced by Confucian values, used Chinese characters, and ate with chopsticks." In explaining the role of Confucianism in East Asian economic growth, Tu Wei-ming (1984) distinguishes politicized Confucianism from the Confucian ethic:

> Political Confucianism is the power of the state over society; politics over economics; and bureaucratization over individual initiative. This type of Confucianism, as political ideology, needs to be thoroughly critiqued before a country can be made dynamic. The other is the Confucian personal ethnic which values self-discipline, going beyond egoism to become actively involved in the collective good, education, personal involvement, the work ethic and communal effort.

Tu believes the ethical aspects of Confucianism promote economic success. In fact, unexpectedly, the Confucian ethic has contributed to the rise of modern capitalism in East Asia. "This is analogous to the influence of what Max Weber has described as the Puritan ethic in the rise of traditional Western capitalism" (Tu 1984:142). Carter J. Eckert (1990:410) has expressed a similar view: that the effect of Confucianism on East Asian economic growth, including Korea, was a case of "unintended consequences, similar to that of Calvinism on early Western capitalists."

Any estimate of the number of Confucians and Confucian devotees is hard to come by, for unlike Christians, Confucians do not have any formal notion of membership. Nor do they have churches, temples, or shrines where they gather together on a regular basis. There are numerous Confucian organizations, including Yurim, which has 234 regional branches (Hyanggyo), and about 12,000 officials work within them. Judging from the number of people who practice Confucian-style ancestor worship, Yurim estimates that the number of Confucians and Confucian devotees is over 10 million. Again, this is based on the census statistics compiled in 2005. Others estimate that at least 91.7 percent of Koreans practice and believe in Confucianism (Yun et al. 1994). Kum Chang-tae[Geum Jang-tae] (Yun et al. 1994) reports that there were nearly seven million Confucians in 1982, but according to the 2005 census, only around 105,000 (0.2 percent) of Koreans were classified as Confucians.

Buddhism

Buddhism, an offshoot of Hinduism, was founded in the sixth century BC by Siddhartha Gautama (Gautama Buddha, 624-544 BC), son of a chieftain of the Sakya tribe, who was dissatisfied with Hinduism and founded the new religion by practicing asceticism. Buddhism in its original form was a highly esoteric, philosophical formula for personal salvation through the renunciation of worldly desires, thus avoiding rebirth in the endless cycle of reincarnation of the soul and resulting in the enlightened state of nirvana, or "desirelessness." Buddhism was originally a religion without a god, as was Confucianism, and consisted of a set of premises on how to avoid earthly suffering by following the proper procedures of spiritual discipline specified in the Four Noble Truths and the Eight-fold Path. The Four Noble Truths include the following tenets: (1) existing is suffering; (2) suffering is due to selfish desires; (3) the cure for suffering is to destroy selfish desire; (4) the cure can be accomplished by practicing the Eight-Fold Path. The Eight-fold Path consists of (1) right view; (2) right thought;

Parents Pray for Their Children to Score Well on the College
Entrance Examination at a Temple

(3) right speech; (4) right action; (5) right means of livelihood; (6) right exertion; (7) right mindfulness; (8) right meditation.

Buddhism in Korea has been largely practical in nature. Its aim at the individual level has been to attain Buddhahood and at the social level to save living things. Individuals, the objects of salvation, are in the category of living things; thus, regardless of their religious preference, people are regarded as objects of Buddhist salvation. In the spirit of inclusiveness, Koreans have incorporated Buddhism into ancestor worship services for dead spirits. Descendants may have ritual services performed for their dead ancestors at any time. Although Buddha himself never mentioned it in his original writings, a characteristic of Korean Buddhism has been the addition of geomancy and superstition; thus, the most popular prayers are for childbearing (for a male offspring in the past), for the welfare of the family,

and for expelling bad spirits and illness, the same prayers that are popular in shamanism (Lee 2003). Nowadays, many Koreans go to Buddhist temples to pray that their children score well on the college entrance examination required for admission to Korea's prestigious colleges and universities.

Buddhism arrived on the Korean peninsula in the fourth century during the middle of the Three Kingdoms period. The northern kingdom of Goguryeo, which bordered on China, made the first contact with Buddhism when the Chinese monk Sundo[Shun-dao] visited the kingdom in 372, bringing with him a Buddha statue and Buddhist scriptures. Eventually, Buddhism was accepted by the royal house of Goguryeo. In 384, a dozen years after Goguryeo had first encountered Buddhism, an Indian missionary, Marananta, came to Baekje via China. Buddhism was eventually accepted in Baekje without any significant discord. A century later, Buddhism was brought to the Silla royal house, with the arrival of the monk-envoy Wonpyo from Liang (502-557). Beopheungwang (King Beopheung) (514-540) made every effort to secure the acceptance of Buddhism, but he was thwarted by the opposition of the Silla aristocracy, which led to the storied martyrdom of the high court noble Ichadon in 527 (Lee 1984). After that event, Silla officially recognized Buddhism in 535.

Buddhism flourished in the Three Kingdoms period under royal patronage. Many temples and monasteries were constructed and hordes of believers converted. Buddhism became rapidly and deeply rooted in Korean society, eventually spreading to Japan. By the sixth century, Korea was exporting priests, scriptures, and religious artisans to Japan, forming the basis of early Buddhist culture in that country. Eventually, Buddhism became the state religion in all the Three Kingdoms, although government systems were still run along Confucian lines. United Silla produced magnificent Buddhist arts and temple architecture. Bulguksa, the most famous of the Korean Buddhist temples, was built between 751 and 774 during the Silla period. The temple also boasts many treasures and was put on the

Bulguksa

UNESCO World Cultural Heritage List in December 1995, which is also the case for Seokguram, the stone Buddha statue that sits in a grotto with a domed ceiling. This sculpture sums up the religious enthusiasm, architectural technology, and aesthetics of the Silla people.

Another cultural influence of Buddhism in Silla was the development of the *hwarang* warrior, a youth movement established by the Buddhist monk Wongwang in the early 600s. *Hwarang* consisted of young elites, often in their mid-teens, who primarily served a military function. The *hwarang* also had religious elements, however, and made pilgrimages to sacred mountains and river sites to pray for national peace and prosperity by performing ceremonial songs and dances (Lee 1984). The ideal of *hwarang* combined the traditional age-rank system with the Buddhist concept of charity and the Confucian concept of order.

The Goryeo dynasty that replaced Silla supported Buddhism so enthusiastically that it created a Buddhist state. Sometimes the princes became monks, or the monks became important players in politics.

In the thirteenth century, when the Mongols invaded Goryeo, the reaction of the Buddhist-oriented court was to seek divine assistance by carving the Buddhist scripture onto wooden blocks for printing. The resulting *Tripitaka Koreana,* which consists of 81,258 panels and took sixteen years to complete, is considered to be one of the most outstanding contributions to the Buddhist cannon. It is still on display at Haeinsa and was also registered on the UNESCO World Cultural Heritage List in 1995.

Revival of Buddhism. During the 500-year history of the Joseon dynasty, Buddhism was suppressed, and the vast wealth and land holdings of the temples were seized. Buddhist monks were treated the way shamans had been earlier and denied entrance to the capital city by the Joseon court. After the Korean War, Buddhism experienced a considerable revival among the young. There has been a deliberate effort to turn "mountain Buddhism" into "community Buddhism" and "temple-centered Buddhism" into "socially relevant Buddhism." As evidence of this effort, there are forty-six Buddhist organizations for young members, thirty organizations for college students, and sixty-six organizations for middle and high school students. Buddhist organizations sponsor various schools, including universities, high schools, middle schools, primary schools, and kindergartens. They also manage three major hospitals, two daily newspapers, and one radio and television station (Yun et al. 1994).

As with Confucianism, it is difficult to ascertain the number of Buddhist adherents. Even if a good many people commit to Buddhism as their religion, a large number of them seldom attend the temples to pray. Currently, there are eighteen different Buddhist sects in Korea. According to Lee Kwang-kyu (2003), in 1980 there were 1,912 Buddhist temples, of which 1,093 belong to the Jogyejong sect within the *Seon* (or Chan in Chinese and Zen in Japanese) Buddhism school, and 18,629 monks. In 2005, it was reported that there were over ten million Buddhists (or 22.8 percent of the population).

The cultural contribution of Buddhism as a major religion for millions of Koreans for over 1,600 years has been profound. As one scholar has noted, over 90 percent of Korean material cultural relics and national treasures are related to Buddha and Buddhism (Yun et al. 1994). Nearly 2,000 Buddhist temples occupy beautiful sites deep in mountainous regions. In an atmosphere of beauty and tranquility, over the centuries Koreans have created world treasures of art: temples, pagodas, paintings, sculptures, carvings, and more.

Christianity

Catholicism. In Korea, Catholicism was first understood as "Western learning." Korean Confucian scholars such as Yi Ik and An Jeong-bok, who were oriented toward the practical-learning school of thought, were exposed to Catholicism in the eighteenth century by European Jesuit missionaries in Beijing of Qing China, before foreign missionaries carried out their work in Korea. However, their initial interest in Catholicism was more intellectual than spiritual.

Catholicism as a religion was not introduced to Korea until 1784, when Yi Seung-hun (1756-1801) was baptized by a Western Catholic priest while on a court visit to Beijing. Following Yi, several other Koreans converted to Catholicism. Most early converts were not *yangban* but belonged to the *jungin* class (middle-class commoners), mostly technical specialists who had little access to political power (Lee 1984). Nevertheless, no priests or foreign missionaries came to Korea until 1785, when the Jesuit Father Peter Grammont crossed the border and began baptizing believers and ordaining clergy. During the late eighteenth and early nineteenth centuries, the promulgation of foreign religion in Korea was still technically against the law. Many ruling Confucians in the Joseon court viewed Catholicism with suspicion, believing that the religion would undermine existing social norms, particularly ancestor worship, and eventually lead to the destruction of the dynasty. Nevertheless, a lax administration allowed for a relatively tolerant view of the Catholic movement, although

there was sporadic government persecution.

Despite the efforts of the government to suppress Catholicism, it continued to spread, appealing to many from the lower classes. By 1795, following the martyrdom of a Chinese priest, Peter Ju Mun-mo[Zhou Wen-mo], there were 4,000 believers in Korea, and by 1863 membership had increased to 23,000. As the number of Catholic believers grew, government persecution intensified, especially after Hwang Sa-yeong's persecution in 1801. Hwang (1775-1801), who was born into a *yangban* family and had the potential to become a successful scholar-official, converted to Catholicism and attempted to send his "silk letter" (so called because it was written on silk) to a Catholic bishop in Beijing, asking Western nations to dispatch naval and land forces to compel the Joseon court to grant religious freedom. However, his letter was intercepted, and he was eventually executed for his actions. Another notable persecution, after Hwang's, was the 1839 persecution of three French priests and 300 Korean believers (Lee 2003).

Beginning in 1880, after years of persecution and martyrdom, Korean Catholics gained some degree of freedom to participate in religious activities, a freedom further enhanced after the signing of a treaty between Korean and France in 1886. In 1898, a cathedral was built in Seoul, and Catholicism in Korea grew in popularity until the Japanese interference started in 1910. Beginning in 1940, as part of Japan's assimilation policy under the slogan of *naeseon ilche*, Shintōism was imposed upon the Korean people, and Catholic believers were forced to attend and observe Shintō religion services and practices. Many Catholics joined the forces fighting for Korean independence.

The visit of Pope John Paul II in May 1984 during the bicentennial commemoration of Korean Catholicism is the biggest event in the history of Catholicism in Korea to date. During his visit, the Pope canonized 103 Korean martyrs, making Korea the fourth country in the world in total number of saints. On 24 March 2006, the Korean Catholic Church received additional recognition when Pope Benedict

XVI appointed Archbishop Nicholas Cheong Jin-suk[Jeong Jin-seok] cardinal. With Cardinal Cheong and Cardinal Stephen Kim Sou-hwan[Gim Su-hwan], who was appointed in 1969, the Korean Catholic Church had two cardinals at one time. Since the Korean Catholic church had long wished for a second cardinal, the appointment of Cardinal Cheong has done much for its morale. Unfortunately, however, Cardinal Kim died on 16 February 2009. In January 2014 Pope Francis appointed Archibishop Andrew Yeom Soo-Jung[Yeom Su-jeong] as a new cardinal. By this Korea now has two cardinals, three parishes, about 4,000 priests, and over five million Catholics.

In addition to its religious function, the Catholic Church in Korea has provided various socio-cultural, educational, and social welfare projects. The church sponsors twenty-seven hospitals, fifteen nursing homes, 220 kindergartens, 652 Sunday schools, seven primary schools, sixty-five middle schools and high schools, ten special and vocational schools, and nine universities (Yun et al. 1994). Most of all, the Catholic Church served as a source of strength during the turbulent political upheavals of the 1980s by providing sanctuary to many dissidents. In particular, Myeong-dong Cathedral (Myeong-dong Seongdang) provided such sanctuary from the mid-1970s through much of the 1980s, and up until the mid-1990s, when the military-led government was replaced by a civilian government. Notably, in 1975 when President Park Chung-hee's *Yusin* policy was at its height, the Catholic Priests' Association for Justice in Korea (*Cheonjugyo jeongui guhyeon jeonguk sajedan*) used the Church to demand the restoration of civil rights and to boycott a proposal for a referendum to amend the Korean constitution. In 1972, the *Yusin* Constitution was passed with the overwhelming support (91.9 percent) of Korean voters. In response, the Catholic Priests' Association for Justice in Korea was organized in 1974 upon Archbishop Daniel Tji Hak-soun[Ji Hak-sun]'s arrest for his declaration that President Park Chung-hee's *Yusin* Constitution was null and void.

The initial martyrdoms of Catholic believers in Korea were due

largely to their refusal to observe ancestor worship rites. But in 1995, the Catholic Church in Korea officially allowed its members to observe ancestor worship as they pleased. This effort to embrace local customs and tradition has contributed to an increase in Catholic believers.

Protestantism. Unlike Catholicism, Protestantism was introduced to Korea by American missionaries: Horace N. Allen in 1884 and Horace G. Underwood and Henry G. Appenzeller the following year. Protestantism was introduced a century later than Catholicism in the relatively tolerant political environment of the late nineteenth century. Protestant missionaries did not have to endure the persecution that Catholics experienced a century earlier. Allen and Appenzeller were physicians, and they combined their missionary work with medical practice. With permission from the king they founded a medical clinic (Clark 1986). Early Catholicism was popular socially, politically, and economically with the underprivileged class. However, "Protestantism was most warmly received by the new intellectual class and by the business community" in the midst of modernization efforts (Lee 1984:335). By then, Koreans viewed the late-arriving Protestants as bearers of modern knowledge, which was desperately needed in Korea's efforts to modernize and protect its independence.

The role of early missionaries was not limited to evangelism. Early missionary organizations established the first Western medical clinic, Gwanghyewon, and founded several schools: Paichai**[Baejae]** School for men in 1885, and a year later, Kyungshin**[Gyeongsin]** School and Ewha**[Ihwa]** School for Women, which was Korea's first educational institution for women. Between 1885 and 1909, Protestant missionary organizations established thirty-nine schools. Many national leaders attended and graduated from these missionary-founded schools, including the former independence fighter and first president of the Republic, Rhee Syng-man, who was a graduate of Paichai. Indeed, Koreans are well aware of the positive

contributions made by Christianity to Korean modernization.

After the annexation of Korea by Japan in 1910, many missionaries offered assistance to the Korean independence movement. Many Christians played a vital role in the March First Independence Movement. Of the thirty-three signers of the March First Declaration of Independence, fifteen were Christians. The missionaries' support for Korean independence continued until 1938, when Japanese authorities began to enforce Shintō worship. The Japanese expulsion of the missionaries took place in 1940, on the eve of World War II. There had been many persecutions of Korean Christians because Japan assumed that the Korean Church was opposed to Japanese dominance over the Korean peninsula. Incidentally, in Japanese retaliation for the March First Independence Movement, forty-seven churches and two missionary schools were burned, one such incident being the Jeam-ri massacre.

After World War II, Protestantism in Korea was revitalized after Korea's liberation reopened opportunities for missionary work, and many missionaries returned after 1946 with permission from U.S. military authorities. Protestantism received another boost from the Korean War, which brought the country to the attention of many foreign missionaries, and new denominations began to flow in after 1953. Donald N. Clark (1986:18) wrote that "Protestant Rhee Syngman, a member of the First Methodist Church in Seoul, supported the church and wished it well. Many of his closest associates were Christians and much was said about the Christianization of South Korea while he was President."

During the endless series of upheavals, student demonstrations, and labor disputes that erupted in the process of modernization and rapid industrialization beginning in the mid-1960s, Protestant churches supported the underdogs: workers, students, protestors. Notably, the Urban Industrial Mission (Dosi saneop seonggonghoe), which originated in the United States in 1956 and was introduced into Korea in 1957, was created to carry out missionary work among workers in

an industrial setting. In the earlier years, the mission focused mainly on providing religious services at factories instead of churches, and offering social services and consultations. However, since their mission activities were directed at industrial workers, they became involved in organizing labor movements and strikes, and negotiating disputes between employers and employees. In 1979, when women members of the mission occupied the main office of Korea's opposition party, the mission attracted much national attention. Some industries, including YH trading company and several others factories, went out of business because of prolonged labor disputes.

Since then, government and industry have been well aware that the mission played a major role in instigating labor disputes. Consequently, the mission had to face government repression in the 1970s and 1980s, years during which many college students, dissidents, labor leaders, and activists were involved in the Urban Industrial Mission. At one point, the mission had fourteen branches throughout the nation with around 3,000 members. Nowadays, its mission has become moribund because the civilian government has been replaced. Regardless of their own religious preferences, a good many Koreans credit Protestant organizations with trying to ensure Korea's survival.

With nearly nine million members (about 11 percent of Korea's religious population), the Protestant church is currently the most active religious organization in Korea. A church in Yeouido, in downtown Seoul, has nearly 800,000 members. Korea may be the only country in the world where daily prayer services begin at 4:00 a.m. in many churches, a testament to the ardent enthusiasm of Korean Protestant churchgoers. A foreign observer, Michael Breen (2004:44), made a similar observation: "Many women go to 5 a.m. worship services before starting their children off to school."

Many Westerners wonder how the Christian Church, Protestantism in particular, has enjoyed such phenomenal growth in traditionally Confucian Korea. There are plausible theories, if no one definitive answer. David Chung and Oh Kang-nam[O Gang-nam] (2001) believe

that the syncretic worldview of Koreans may be the main reason for the remarkable growth of Christianity in Korea. Donald N. Clark (1986:36-37) offered the following explanations:

> . . . a spiritual hunger among Koreans arising from suffering through colonialism and civil war, the attractions of Christian ideas of salvation, the echoes in Christianity of other faiths such as Buddhism (heaven and hell) and shamanism (miracles, sacrifices and priesthood), and the fact that the use of *Hangeul* made scriptural study possible for large numbers of people. The church's stress on personal evangelicalism on a one-to-one basis has been especially effective in urban areas, where migration from the countryside has created large communities of strangers who miss their village neighbors and are desperately lonely in the cities.

In his recent book, Clark (2000:50-52) cites the Church's record on civil rights as a reason for its evangelical success:

> Another circumstance was the Catholic and Protestant commitment to human rights at a time when South Korea was suffering under a strict military dictatorship. . . . Christians actively supported people who were persecuted under this law, demanding not only democratic reforms that would permit free speech, freedom of religion, and human rights but also demanding that Korean workers be treated more fairly with better wages. Christians took these stands because of their religion's respect for individuals in the sight of God.

Islam

Muslim merchants were Korea's first contact with Islam, which occurred around 1024 during the Goryeo dynasty. About 100 Koreans who were agricultural immigrants in Manchuria were exposed to Islam through contact with Arabic people there and showed some interest in Islamic religion (Yun et al. 1994). However, there was no mission work to introduce Islam to Korea until the

early 1950s during the Korean War, when Islam was introduced to the peninsula by an imam attached to the Turkish army, one of the sixteen nations that comprised the U.N. forces. Through the imam's efforts, some Koreans worshipped with the Turkish soldiers and converted to Islam. In 1966, a Korean Islamic organization was formed, and a mosque was established in Seoul. Since then, seven more mosques have been erected throughout Korea. It is estimated that there were some 20,000 Muslims in Korea by 2005. There is no sign, though, of an increase since then.

New Religions

There are about 300 new religions in Korea whose membership ranges from less than ten in some sects to more than 600,000 in others. The total number of believers in new religions has been estimated to be between one and one and a half million. Despite their variations, these new religions have two common characteristics: they appear to be nationalistic, if not ethnocentric, because most were founded in response to or in reaction against foreign-born ideology, religion, and political dominance; and they are syncretic in their theology, combining several elements of existing religions. I will limit my attention to those sects with the most adherents according to Statistics Korea.

Donghak. Donghak (Cheondogyo) was founded in the 1860s by Choe Je-u (1824-1864) as a movement of Eastern learning in reaction to Western learning, as exemplified by Catholicism, and the dominance of Western power. Choe's main belief was "in the unity of man with God, that mankind and the Supreme Being are one and the same" (Lee 1984:258). It was a nationalistic proclamation that only Eastern learning could stop the negative influence of Western learning on the minds of Koreans. Donghak is a syncretic religion that includes elements of Confucianism, Buddhism, and Taoism. The government was so alarmed by the popularity of Donghak that in 1863 Choe was

arrested on the charge of misleading the people and sowing discord in society. He was executed the following year (Lee 1984).

After the execution of Choe Je-u, under the leadership of Choe Si-hyeong (1827-1898), the second leader of the movement, Donghak became a well-organized force and sought to restore its good name and correct the distorted image of its founder that had been propagated by the government. At the same time, Donghak followers organized and pressed the government to prevent the *yangban* from draining the peasants' lifeblood with illegal extortions and to expel the Japanese and Westerners. In the meantime, membership in Donghak increased to several thousand, and in 1894 the movement erupted in a peasant revolution, employing military operations on a large scale. Jeon Bong-jun, head of Gobu-gun parish, and his peasant army occupied the county offices, seizing weapons and disturbing to the poor rice that had been taken from them by illegal taxation of the Gobu-gun magistrate.

As the peasant army gained strength, its influence spread to other provinces. When the panicky government sought military support from China and Japan, Japan intervened, and the Donghak peasants ended up fighting well-trained Japanese soldiers equipped with modern weapons, and they were no match for them. The Donghak uprising was a revolutionary movement of peasantry against Joseon's oppressive *yangban* society that demonstrated the power of the peasants.

Donghak changed its name to Cheondogyo in 1905 under the leadership of Son Byong-hi[Son Byeong-hui], who took a religious-nationalist approach and played a leading role in the March First Independence Movement, serving as head of the thirty-three signers of the Declaration of Independence. At one time, membership swelled to two million but later declined to 600,000 when Japanese suppression was lifted. Membership became stagnant after liberation (Yun et al. 1994:214). Cheondogyo followers were estimated to number 28,184 in 1995 according to Statistics Korea. Figures for membership do not appear in the 2005 census.

Wonbulgyo. Wonbulgyo (Won Buddhism) is an offshoot of Buddhism that was founded by Pak Chung-bin[Bak Jung-bin] in 1916 at Iri (currently Iksan-si), Jeollabuk-do. As a syncretic religion combining elements of Confucianism, Buddhism, and Taoism, Wonbulgyo emphasizes modernization and revitalization of Buddhist doctrine. In addition to religious activities, Wonbulgyo runs a university, hospital, high school, and middle school and also sponsors various welfare programs, including a nursing home and orphanage. Lee Kwang-kyu (2003:249) reports that "there are 681,000 believers in Wonbulgyo." The 2005 Korean census recognized 130,000 members.

Daejonggyo. (Dangunism or *Religion of the Divine Progenitor)* This religion was founded in 1904 by Baek Bong, and in 1909, Na Cheol and Jeong Hun-mo promulgated a version of it in Seoul centered on the mythology of Dangun, founder of Gojoseon. "The main doctrine was to return to three truths, the three truths being the basic elements of a human being one's disposition, life, and energy" (Lee 2003:250). To avoid Japanese suppression, believers changed the name of their religion to Daejonggyo and moved the center of its mission to Manchuria, where they engaged in anti-Japanese independence fighting. Daejonggyo once had 145,000 believers (Lee 2003:250). The 2005 census, however, does not list Daejonggyo as a separate category.

Daesun Jinrihoe. The Jeungsando (Jeungsan religion) was founded in 1902 by Kang Il-sun, who was once a believer in Donghak but recognized its limitations and proposed a new religion that preached belief in a paradise in the afterlife. Jeungsando is a combination of Confucianism, Buddhism, and Taoism, along with the realm of diviners, geomancers, and medicine men. It teaches that the universe is a heaven that can be realized in the mind of a person through homage and prayer (Lee 2003). A branch of Jeungsando headquartered in Seoul, Daesun Jinrihoe, has grown steadily since it was established

in 1969 and includes 650,000 members (Yun et al. 1994). The Daesun Jinrihoe sponsors regular seminars and lectures.

Unification Church. As a new religious movement, the Unification Church (Tongilgyo) was started by Moon Sun-myung[**Mun Seon-myeong**] in 1954. It was formally and legally established in Seoul as the Holy Spirit Association for the Unification of World Christianity, reflecting Moon's original vision of an ecumenical movement. The doctrine of the church is explained in the book *Divine Principle,* which draws from the Bible as well as from Asian traditions. The doctrine espouses a belief in a universal God. According to Michael Breen (2004:44), "Moon's view of God is quintessentially Korean, combining shamanist passion and Confucian family patterns in Christian form." In the 1990s, Moon began to establish various peace organizations, including the Family Federation for World Peace and Unification. According to the *Maeil Business Newspaper,* dated 3 September 2012, members of the Unification Church are estimated to be over three million and are found in 194 countries. Japan has the largest number of adherents with over 500,000, and Korea has about 200,000.

Among the practices of the Unification Church, the blessing ceremony is considered to be the most important ceremony in a person's spiritual life. The blessing ceremony removes the couple from the ranks of sinful humanity and makes them part of God's sinless lineage. Any children born to the blessed couple are free from original sin. Those who espouse the faith believe that matchmaking and marriage are the direct and perfect manifestation of a profound theology and worldview. The blessing ceremony was first held in Seoul in 1960 with three couples and in 1961 with thirty-three couples. Since then the scale and size of the blessing ceremony has become larger as evidenced by a 2009 ceremony for forty thousand couples at Sun Moon[**Seonmun**] University in Asan, Korea.

Most Korean think that the phenomenon of multiculturalism in contemporary Korea began in the late 1990s and became more

popular after 2000, as a large number of foreign brides, mostly from East and Southeast Asian countries, married Korean men and came to Korea. However, international marriages conducted by the Unification Church began in 1961. Through my participation in the Cyber University of Korea's campaign, I found that a good many Japanese women who marry Korean men are married by way of the Unification Church. It is estimated that over 60 percent of international marriages between Japanese brides and Korean men are conducted by the Unification Church (Kim 2011b).

By the way, on 3 September 2012, founder Moon died at ninety-two years old. His funeral took place thirteen days after his death to allow time for his adherents from all over the world to attend. Some 350,000 followers and well-wishers came from various parts of the world, 10,000 from Japan alone. Since Moon's death, it is reported that his thirty-three-year-old seventh son will be in charge of religious matters and business operations will be handled by his forty-two-year-old fourth son.

In sum, with its more than 300 religions, Korea is indeed a multi-religious society. Unlike some other multi-religious nations where the threat of disintegration exists, in Korea multiple groups coexist peacefully and even show respect for other religions. Koreans practice inclusiveness in religion and trust that all religions benefit humans in one way or another. Therefore, from the Korean perspective, all religions are equally good.

Not only has religion granted Koreans spiritual enrichment, but it has brought tremendous cultural enrichment to the country as well. Koreans have incorporated foreign cultural elements that came along with these religions into their native culture, adopting them and making them their own. When the country faced an imminent threat from foreign powers, various religions groups joined together and fought for Korean independence. Religions have indeed made a profound contribution to Korean history.

8
The *Yangban* Legacy and Education for Upward Mobility

My generation of Koreans might be the last to have witnessed the remnants of the *yangban* class in practice. Nowadays, most Koreans trust that social stratification in Korea is not based on a hereditary caste-like system, as it was with the *yangban* system; rather, one's social ranking will be influenced, if not governed, by factors related to one's achievements—high aspirations, hard work, some talent, and a little bit of luck. Most Koreans today believe that in determining one's social standing in an open class system, education plays a pivotal role. Therefore, Koreans as a people spend some $19 billion annually for private educational expenses. To non-Koreans, this amount might seem extravagant or even wasteful since Korea as a whole allocated 8.0 percent of its total GDP to public education in 2012, the second highest amount spent by nations (next to Iceland at 8.1 percent) belonging to the OECD. However, most Korean parents tend to think of such large educational expenses as money invested, not wasted.

A Historical Survey of Korean Social Class

Social stratification in Korea has a long history. Early class distinctions were hereditary in nature and largely fixed, with limited

upward social mobility. By examining various kinds of burial markers, dolmens, and cairns, Sarah M. Nelson (1993) observed that social class began to appear on the Korean peninsula in the second millennium BC. Later, the Three Kingdoms created centralized aristocratic states in which power and prestige were exercised by a limited number of aristocratic families and lineages of kings and queens. However, very little is known about the Goguryeo social class order other than the upper aristocracy. Baekje aristocracies were limited to eight renowned families, and power was vested only in members of those families (Lee 1984).

Silla developed a unique, rigid, and hereditary class system, manifested in what was called the "bone-rank" (golpum) system. There were eight levels of bone-rank: at the top were "sacred-bone" (seonggol, or hallowed-bone) and "true-bone" (jingol). Only those of sacred-bone could ascend the throne in early Silla; when they died out, those of true-bone could come to the throne. According to Lee Ki-baik (1984:50-51), "Not only this, but bone-rank also determined the scale of the residence in which a Silla citizen might live. For example, a true-bone house could not exceed 24 'feet' in length or width, a head-rank six house 21 feet, a head-rank five house 18 feet, a head-rank four or commoner's house 15 feet. Moreover, sumptuary regulations based on bone-rank governed the color of official attire, vehicles and horse trappings, and various utensils." Below bone-rank, there were several grades and classes, which were rigid and clearly demarcated.

During the Goryeo dynasty, aristocrats expanded their power base to many prominent lineages. The Goryeo system allowed a large number of men to become government officials, which required a new method of selecting personnel: the civil service examination. This examination provided a means of advancement for members of all the hereditary aristocratic families. Below the aristocratic families were petty officials and low ranking military officers. Sons of the peasants were able, in theory, to take state examinations and become government officials. Artisans, however, had their occupations

determined by heredity and could not change them. Below these were outcasts and slaves.

Joseon social classes with "*yangban*"

Joseon's social class system was dominated by *yangban,* which consisted of two orders, the literati and military officers. The Joseon dynasty broadened the base of recruiting officials to serve the government by instituting a state examination system. There were only two official categories of people in early Joseon; the freeborn (*yangin*) and the lowborn (*cheonmin*). In time the former developed into three, and thus came into being the four major classes: *yangban* (upper class), *jungin* (middle class), *sangmin* (commoners), and *cheonmin* (the lower class or outcasts).

Yangban: the first class. In the Joseon dynasty, *yangban* directed the government, economy, and culture. In principle, a person could serve the government as an official if he (always he, not she) could pass the state examination. But this opportunity was in reality limited to those of *yangban* rank. Since *yangban* were exempted from the usual service obligations to the state, including *corvée* labor and military duty, they could devote themselves exclusively to study and preparation for the examinations. *Yangban* discriminated against the other classes in all aspects of social life, maintaining their own areas of residence in the southern and northern sections of the capital and creating their own villages in the countryside.

Jungin: the second class. Second in status to the *yangban,* the *jungin* were engaged in science and technology. People in the *jungin* class were eligible to take the civil service examination but in the miscellaneous category. If they passed, they could become low-ranking government officials or take jobs as interpreters, medical officers, astronomers, geographers, mathematicians, lawyers, musicians, and painters.

Sangmin: the third class. This class included people who were engaged in production, such as farmers and workers in manufacturing. Among the commoners, there was also a rank order: farmers were considered the highest, followed by workers in manufacturing, then merchants at the bottom. All commoners were obliged to pay taxes, were subject to compulsory labor, and had to serve in the military.

Cheonmin: the fourth class. This class included slaves, butchers, shamans, singing girls, and performers. Slaves, who occupied the lowest layer, were sold, given as gifts, and inherited. People who belonged to this class were discriminated against by the people above them.

The tradition of the four-class system of the Joseon dynasty led to the development of a distinct classification of occupational prestige in Korea: *sa* (scholars and literati-bureaucrats) was considered the highest occupation; *nong* (farmers) was regarded as the second highest; *gong* (artisans) ranked third; and *sang* (merchants) occupied the bottom of the social ladder.

Emergence of the open class system and change in occupational ranking

The *yangban*-led Joseon class system was reevaluated by scholars of the Practical Learning School (Silhak) during the eighteenth century in an effort to reform Joseon dynastic social institutions. These scholars recognized that the nation could no longer ignore people who were engaged in farming, science and technology, commerce, and industry by treating them as second-class citizens.

Silhak thinkers focused their attention not on the landlord class but on the farmers who actually cultivated the soil. They proposed to abolish all distinctions of social status, in other words, all social classes. Lee Ki-baik (1984:236) sums up Silhak thought as follows: ". . . they took the position that the well-being of the people was to be achieved through abolishing the social status system and

determining the division of labor in Yi[Joseon] society on the basis of ability alone." Eventually, under the influence of Silhak thought, as well as government policy permitting slaves to perform military duty in exchange for their freedom, government slaves (*gong-nobi*) were set free. Private slaves (*sa-nobi*) as well as government slaves, if any still remained, were eventually freed as part of the *Gabo* reform in 1894. The reform program also included the elimination of class distinctions between *yangban* and commoners, and made it possible to open the ranks of officialdom to men of talent regardless of social background (Lee 1984; Lew 1990).

The fall of the Joseon dynasty in 1910 brought with it the abolishment of the Joseon class system, but the Japanese, then occupying Korea, did little to acknowledge its disappearance. Nevertheless, some lower-class Koreans such as butchers did try to escape from the stigma of their class status. Despite many instances of being barred from schools, by the mid-1920s some 40 percent of butchers' children were in school (Breen 2004). After the liberation of Korea, the Western concept of equality was introduced, especially through Christianity. As a new republic was born in 1948, equality was guaranteed in the Korean Constitution, and Article 11 is specific about not recognizing any privileged class. Before the 1949 Land Reform Act took effect, landlords were mostly of *yangban* origin and still exercised certain power and privileges. It was the Land Reform that finally "undermined the economic base of the former aristocracy [*yangban*]" (Brandt 1971).

Ranking of occupational prestige

The previous social ranking order of the Joseon period—*sa*, *nong*, *gong*, and *sang*—became obsolete as Korea underwent rapid economic growth and industrialization beginning in the mid-1960s. As a reflection of changing trends, according to survey data from 1964 to 1971, the occupation that most students at Ewha Womans University ranked highest for a prospective spouse was "businessman,"

a category at the bottom of the ranking system during the Joseon dynasty (Jones and Sakong 1980).

Recently, contemporary Koreans tend to rate professional specialists such as physicians, lawyers, university professors, executives in big business, and high officials in government as most prestigious (Choe 2002). Interestingly, three out of five of the topmost prestigious occupations once belonged to the second class, *jungin*, and the third class of *sangmin* during the Joseon period. An entertainer was considered a member of *cheonmin* in Joseon but currently that occupation's prestige is fairly high (below that of a radio or television producer but above that of a newspaper reporter): twelfth out of thirty-three listed occupations.

Recent social classes

Unlike the bone-rank system of the Silla dynasty and the *yangban*-led four-class system of the Joseon dynasty, under the current open class system, an individual's class affiliation is determined by several informal criteria such as income, occupational prestige, educational attainment, residential area, and family background, among others. There has been no anthropological study of social status in contemporary Korea comparable to the classic case study in the United States by American anthropologists W. Lloyd Warner and Paul Lunt (1941), the *Yankee City* study, which showed six different classes that Americans commonly consolidate into three: lower, middle, and upper. Nonetheless, most Koreans tend to classify their class membership along similar lines: lower, middle, and upper class, based mainly on income.

Most discussions of social class in Korea by social scientists, policy makers, and politicians (particularly in election years) focus on the middle class, often expressing a concern for its erosion. While the lower and upper classes have been continuously increasing, according to the Hyundai Research Institute report dated 8 August 2011, for the past twenty years (1990-2010), Korea's per capita GDP has increased

threefold. Nevertheless, the Korean middle class has decreased by 8 percent. Several explanations for this trend are plausible, including the high unemployment rate for educated white-collar workers and the impact of the restructuring of business and industry after the IMF bailout in 1997.

Most troubling is a widening disparity in income between a limited number of highly paid earners and a growing number of poor people. According to a report by the *Korea Herald*, dated 7 July 2014, the South Korea's top earners made 4.85 times more than those in the bottom 10 percent did on average in 2010. Furthermore, it has been predicted that the income of South Korea's richest 10 percent will be nearly 6.5 times larger than the bottom 10 percent of the income ladder over the coming fifty years. A newly-released report, dated 7 July 2014 from the OECD, predicts that South Korea's income gap will be the third largest among the twenty-nine OECD member countries by 2060.

Despite these troubling statistics on poverty, most attention, as already stated, has focused on the shrinking size of the middle class. From 1990 to 2010, several changes, which might be attributed to an eroding Korean middle class, have taken place. Most notably, in 1990, the middle class consisted mostly of persons with these demographic characteristics: aged thirty-something, high school graduate, working in manufacturing fields, and male. However, in 2010, the middle class was comprised of those with these characteristics: aged forty-something, college graduate, working in the service field, and working couples. Also, by 2010, the middle class owed 23.3 percent more than it owed on average in 1990: 15.8 percent. Moreover, the middle class in 2010 had a burden of expenses almost three times more than in 1990 — a burden that includes personal debts, health insurance fees, and ever-increasing expenses for children's private education. According to data from Statistics Korea, as of 2011, the average Korean spent nearly three million *won* (about $2,857), which is equivalent to 12.5 percent of Korea's per capita GDP.

As the composition of the middle class changes from primarily high school graduates to primarily college graduates, education plays a major role in determining social class. For that reason, some discussions of Korean education are in order.

Education for Upward Mobility

While education may have become a near obsession in the minds of contemporary Koreans, an emphasis on education has in fact been a long tradition in Korea.

Confucianism and its emphasis on education

The recognition of the importance of education in Korea can be traced to the impact of Confucianism. During the Three Kingdom period, education was not available to the general public, but each kingdom did establish a Confucian academy for the education of the elite.

During the Goryeo dynasty, the school system was institutionalized in Taejo's reign (918-943), and the nation's highest academy, Gukjagam (National University), designed principally for the study of Chinese tradition and Confucian classics, was established in 992, under King Seongjong (981-997). The state's civil service examination motivated youth to obtain a university education.

During the Joseon period, in 1398 the National Confucian Academy of Seonggyungwan was established. In order to prepare for the civil service examination, "from an early age *yangban* youth attended private elementary schools (seodang) where they learned the basic Chinese characters and practiced writing them. Then, from age seven, they advanced to one of the Four Schools (Sahak) in Seoul or to the County School (Hyanggyo) established in each county. The Confucian students of these schools, after several years of study, were thereby qualified to sit for the licentiate examinations. If they passed

the first stage of the examination held at the provincial level, they proceeded to Seoul for the second stage, which determined those who would receive a degrees" (Lee 1984:180). These licentiates might then enter the nation's highest academy, Seonggyungwan, in Seoul, where they could excel even further.

Also, many Neo-Confucian literati played an important part in teaching the scholarly tradition to members of their own clans or lineages in order to retain social power. In the vicinity of their homes in the countryside, these literati established Seowon (private academies), where they educated youth in Neo-Confucianism, thus perpetuating the scholarly tradition in which they played an essential role. During King Sukjong's reign (1674-1720), there were about three hundred Seowon throughout the nation that taught Confucian scholarship. Teaching was centered on the Confucian classics, not the practical fields of science and technology, medicine, law, and commerce. Education was limited to aristocrats and *yangban* and served as the major route to government office.

Hunger for education

Modern education was introduced to Korea by American Protestant missionaries: the first Western medical clinic opened in 1885; the Paichai School for men in 1885; and the Kyungshin School for men and Ewha School for women in 1886. At the same time, Koreans themselves recognized the importance of education as the vehicle for modernization and national independence and strength. In 1895, King Gojong (1863-1907) proclaimed in an edict that education was essential to the nation's future. During the period of Japanese domination in the early 1900s, Koreans further emphasized education, trusting that it would eventually provide the foundation for future Korean independence. Many Korean nationalist intellectuals who were once active in political movements decided to devote themselves to education. In the short time before Korea fell completely under Japanese colonial domination, the number of private schools reached

3,000, and they were fairly numerous in the northern half of the country (Kim 1998).

In addition to disseminating new learning, many private schools in the years of Japanese domination served as hotbeds for the nationalist movement. Naturally, Japan frowned on these schools and felt it necessary to control Korean education, particularly private educational institutions during the Residency-General. As a consequence of this control, the number of schools diminished. In 1907, missionaries alone operated 508 primary schools, twenty-two high schools, and two theological schools. By 1917, this number had been halved, and by 1937 only thirty-four missionary schools remained (Eckert et al. 1990). Also, after the annexation of Korea, Japan changed its educational policy by directing its efforts toward elementary and vocational education for Koreans to teach them how to perform menial tasks in the Japanese language for the benefit of Japan.

In order to "Japanize" the Koreans effectively, Japan made primary education in Korea a minimum requirement for everyone, and the Government-General built hundreds of public schools in the first decade of its rule. By 1910, some 110,800 students attended these schools, and this number increased to nearly two million by 1941 (Eckert et al. 1990). By contrast, the Japanese strictly limited higher education opportunities for Koreans. It was estimated that "Only five percent of Korean students passed beyond the primary level, and although there was a tremendous expansion of student numbers over time, in 1945 only about twenty percent of the population had received some schooling, while the general rate of literacy was still below fifty percent" (Eckert et al. 1990:263).

Higher education as "*han*"

In response to the discriminatory policy of the Japanese that banned higher education for Koreans, Koreans started a movement in November 1922 to establish a Korean People's University (Minrip daehak). The rationale for this attempt was that "although mass education was

necessary for overall development, a society is judged, in the end, by the quality of its upper level educational system, which, in turn, produced national leaders" (Robinson 1988:86). However, the movement was unable to raise the necessary funds, and its momentum was slowed by the mismanagement of donations, infighting between chapters, and vitriolic criticism from more radical nationalists (Eckert et al. 1990).

Although the Korean drive to establish a people's university was widespread, in 1926 Japanese authorities announced a plan to establish Keijō Imperial University (currently Seoul National University) in Seoul, which further diminished public interest in the Korean People's University, and soon the movement withered away (Kim 1998). Because the door of the imperial university was not open to most Koreans, some Koreans who wished to receive an elite education and could afford to do so went to Japan or Western countries, mostly America, with the help of American missionaries. Because of these limiting circumstances, in 1945, for example, fewer than 1 percent of Koreans had received higher education.

However, there were several Korean institutions of higher education, such as Joseon Christian College (later changed to Yonhi[Yeon hui] College and then to Yonsei University), Ewha Womans Junior College, and Soongsil[Sungsil] Junior College, but Japan did not allow them to become integrated universities. For many Koreans yearning for further education to achieve upward mobility, higher education remained a *han*.

Between 1945, when Korea was liberated, and 1965, before Korea made great economic strides, educational institutions grew dramatically. In 1947, there were 15,400 public schools, compared with 3,000 at the time when Korea fell under Japanese domination. Student enrollment in institutions of higher education increased from 7,819 to 141,626 by 1965 (Mason et al. 1980). With the proliferation of schools following liberation, many Koreans were able to fulfill their long-enduring *han* for higher education opportunities.

Higher education as a means for upward mobility

Although some Koreans have become celebrities, including president, without the benefit of higher education, higher education has played a pivotal role in providing upward mobility and success for many individuals. For instance, according to a survey by Leroy P. Jones and Sakong Il (1980), 69.1 percent of entrepreneurs, 51.1 percent of *jaebeol* leaders, 62.7 percent of high civil servants, and 84.2 percent of public managers had completed college or beyond.

People recognize the importance of education not only because of their cultural heritage and their need to fulfill a longstanding *han*, but also for the economic rewards it brings. People with more education are paid more on average than those with less education; they have greater marketability; and they gain social mobility through economic advancement.

Higher education enhances one's chances of meeting a desirable marriage partner

For many young Koreans seeking a marriage partner through a marriage consulting center (*gyeolhon sangdamso*) or a matchmaking agency (*gyeolhon jeongbohoesa*), educational background is considered to be of the utmost importance. Young Koreans consider the appearance or wealth of a prospective marriage candidate secondary to the person's educational attainments, trusting that a highly educated candidate has a better chance of acquiring a reputable white-collar job, a secure income, and future success. It is assumed that any individual who holds a degree from a reputable and sought-after university must be intelligent and capable, and therefore have a higher potential for future success.

Obsession with Education in Contemporary Korea

According to the results of a nationwide survey conducted by Statistics Korea from May to June 2012, on the basis of a sample of 37,000 persons ages thirteen and older, 86.3 percent of students 15 years and above think that they have to have an education at the college level or beyond, and 92.6 percent of parents surveyed want the same for their children. What is more, of these parents surveyed, 14.6 percent responded that they wish their children to have doctoral degrees. The major reason given for the need of high educational attainment has been to get good jobs (*Dong-A Ilbo*, 21 December 2012).

According to another report released 29 October 2012 by Statistics Korea, for the past forty years, from 1972 to 2012, the total number of Koreans who completed four-year college degrees was sixteen million. Forty years ago, fewer than one person (0.7) out of ten had completed college, but by 2012, four out of every ten Koreans had a four-year college education. In pursuit of education, Koreans spend (or invest) some twenty trillion *won* (about $19 billion) annually for private educational expenses. If this is not evidence of obsession, what would be?

The educational system and first-tier schools

During the Japanese occupation, the Korean school system was structured like the Japanese one. There were six years of primary school, five years of secondary, and several junior colleges such as Ewha, Boseong, and Yonhi, until a Japanese-run Imperial University (Keijō Imperial University) was established in 1924. After liberation, under the initiative led by the U.S. Military Government, in close consultation with Korean members of the Advisory Council for Education, Korean education was restructured into a 6-3-3-4 system: six years of primary school, three years of middle school, three years of high school, and four years of higher education. Currently, medical schools require six years, including two years of preparatory

college before medical school; schools of pharmacology require a four-year education for a student who already has two years of college education and has passed the required test; and law school requires three years of training for students who graduate from a four-year college—the same as American law schools. Besides brick-and-mortar schools (traditional off-line schools), the distance-education Korea National Open University (Bangsong Tongsin Daehak), founded in 1972, and twenty-one all-online colleges and universities, founded since 2001, offer alternative educational options. The growth of online colleges in Koreas reflects the country's well-developed infrastructure of information technology that has extended the reach of the Internet across the nation, including remote inland regions and coastal islands. By 2011, nearly eighteen million Koreans were connected by a broadband Internet network. Indeed, Korea is one of the most wired nations in the world.

As a side note, the Korean Ministry of Education (formerly the Ministry of Education, Science and Technology), responsible for issues and concerns pertaining to both formal and informal education in Korea, is more centralized and powerful than its U.S. federal counterpart, which delegates many of its functions to states, private institutions, and accreditation organizations. The power, authority, and jurisdiction of the Korean education ministry are extensive; it regulates all Korean educational institutions, including higher education institutions and privately endowed schools. The ministry also regulates the admissions policy of private colleges and even appointments to their boards of trustees. The ministry can regulate virtually everything related to education, including the so-called "Three Nots Policy," which spells out what should be prohibited: Administration by universities of their own entrance examination, acceptance of financial donations for admitting students, and making students' high schools a factor in college admissions.

The Three Nots Policy came into being in response to the negative impact of the highly competitive examination system. The

Korean obsession with education has created an "examination hell" whose fires are stoked by Korean parents determined to sacrifice everything so that their children can obtain good scores on the College Scholastic Ability Test. Many Koreans today equate receiving degrees from top-tier universities with passing the high civil service examination (*gwageo*) of dynastic times. As pointed out above, graduates of the nation's leading universities have a better chance of obtaining employment in government and leading businesses, and even of acquiring a desirable marriage partner.

In response to the negative impact of the highly competitive examination system and its attendant "examination hell," Korean education policy makers, particularly members of the "386 generation" who stood up to the privileged and the establishment during the military regime, have made a deliberate effort to oppose the privileging of any group or institution, including first-tier universities. Efforts to level the playing field of public education in Korea have made some important contributions to educational reform.

Most of all, because the entrance examination for middle school was deemed unfair and had many adverse effects on young children, it was abolished in 1969. Such an examination was thought unnecessary because national compulsory education extended to middle school. Only the high school entrance examination remained until it, too, began to be abolished in 1974 in an effort to eliminate differences in rank order among high schools. Instead of the entrance examination, the Ministry of Education initiated a lottery system for admission to high school. However, the college entrance system remains the same, and competition for top-tier universities has not changed and may even have intensified.

In more recent initiatives of reform aimed at higher education, the Roh Moo-hyun government, during its tenure from 2003 to 2008, adopted the Three Nots Policy, President Roh stressed that the Three Nots Policy not only protects equal education opportunities

for the nation; it is also a fundamental element of education policy in maintaining a cooperative society. Several leading members of the ruling Uri Party concurred with the president, saying that considering how bad the polarization of the society has become, the Three Nots Policy should remain enforced.

The Three Nots Policy has not gone uncontested, however, particularly by administrative officials at some universities. They demand that the government guarantee universities freedom in instituting admissions practices and call for an educational policy that allows for fair competition. Most university administrators consider the Roh government's policy an obstacle to fair competition among universities in a globalizing world. It appears that this debate will be ongoing.

Korean education was rated one of the top in the world by Pearson

According to a November 2012 evaluation of the best education in the world by Pearson Education, a world-renowned education publisher and provider of assessment services to schools and corporations, Finland and Korea top the list, being first and second, respectively, of forty developed countries when it comes to education. Pearson's chief education adviser Sir Michael Barber told the BBC that high-ranking countries tend to offer teachers higher status in society and have a "culture" of education. The Pearson study suggests that, while funding is an important factor in a strong education system, having a larger culture supportive of learning is even more critical — as evidenced by the high rankings of Asian countries where education is prized and parents have great educational expectations for their children. Hong Kong was ranked third, Japan fourth, and Singapore fifth. While Finland and South Korea differ greatly in their methods of teaching and learning, they hold the top spots because of a shared social belief in the importance of education and its underlying moral purpose.

As of 2012, there were 20,241 schools in Korea, ranging from kindergarten to university, and over 10.3 million students enrolled in those schools. Those numbers are astronomical compared to the time of Korea's liberation from Japan in 1945, when, out of all the students enrolled in the school system, 93 percent were in the primary grades (Mason et al. 1980). By 2012, students enrolled in primary grades accounted for only 22 percent.

In Korean education, private schools play a major role. Over 30 percent of all students are enrolled in private schools. Of 343 institutions of higher education, 301 schools (87.7 percent) are private colleges and universities. Of 2,952,000 total students, over 85 percent attend private institutions. Koreans' zeal for higher education is reflected in their outlay for educational expenses. As of 2009, Korea, in terms of both state and private expenditure, spent 8 percent of its GDP on education, which is higher than the average of OECD countries (6.3 percent); it is worth noting, too, that the Korean government pays only 4.9 percent of this 8 percent, and the remaining 3.1 percent is paid by private citizens. According to a report by the *Seoul Economic Daily* on 10 October 2012, this outlay of private money for education has been the highest among OECD countries for the past twelve years. On average, each individual Korean pays about 2,880,000 *won* (about $2,743) annually for private education.

Koreans' devotion to education is also reflected in the high rate of student advancement through the school system. In 2012, for instance, 99.9 percent of Korean students who graduated from primary school enrolled in middle school, and 99.7 percent of students who graduated from middle school went on to attend high school. The proportion of Korean students who graduated from high school and proceeded to colleges and universities increased from 79.7 percent in 2003 to 82.1 percent in 2005, 82.8 percent in 2007, and 83.8 percent in 2008, which is the highest ever. Peaking in 2008, the rate of high school graduates going on to college dropped to 81.9

in 2009, 79.0 in 2010, 72.5 percent in 2011, and 71.3 percent in 2012, the lowest rate in the new millennium. Because of an interest in higher education, in 2012 alone, some 12,243 Korean received doctoral degrees at home and abroad.

Also, Koreans' zeal for the teaching and learning of English has been comparable to the pressure to attend top-tier colleges and universities. This emphasis on learning English intensified in the early 1990s after the signing of the URA. Korea was facing the unavoidable challenge of internationalization and globalization. In order to meet this challenge, in November 1994, President Kim Young-sam introduced the neologism *Segyehwa*, which combines several meanings: globalization, internationalization, and an open-door policy toward the outside world. There was a consensus at the time among informed Koreans that *Segyehwa* was to become a major world trend and an unavoidable destiny.

Recognizing that English competency would be essential for survival in the global arena, Korea has emphasized English instruction at all levels of schools, business communities, and government. In 2008, Korea's Ministry of Education made plans to require a two-hour weekly lesson in English starting in the first year of primary school. Currently, private primary schools teach English in the first and second grades for 7.2 hours per week, while public primary school does not teach English in the first and second grades. Parents of public schools worry that their children lag behind their private school counterparts. Before English teaching became an integral part of the primary school curriculum, it had already been instated in private kindergartens and many private tutoring centers (*hagwon*) in most major cities throughout Korea. Because of its popularity, English teaching has become a thriving business.

Parenthetically, however, on 11 March 2014 to be effective by 4 September 2014, the Park Geun-hye's administration introduced a new bill that prohibits any prerequisite learning and teaching (*seonhaeng hakseup*) any foreign languages, including English, prior to

the third grades in primary schools and kindergartens in both private and public schools.

Why are Koreans so enthusiastic about learning English? As one of my Korean friends told me, "We cannot deny the importance of American influence, resulting from intensive contact between the two countries ever since the end of World War II. Also, an unusual zeal for learning English was greatly reinforced when the wave of internationalization and globalization started sweeping the world." Evidence of America's influence also comes anecdotally from an exchange I had with a high school principal who was looking for a native English teacher (Koreans call such an English teacher a *woneomin gyosa*, a native-tongue English teacher). I recommended to the principal an Englishman I knew but was told that the school preferred an American who speaks American English, not English as spoken by the English. That the English are not the authorities on English in Korea was an irony that impressed itself upon me.

Korean enthusiasm for overseas education

It is widely known that a large number of Koreans have attended and still enroll in institutions of higher education in the United States. Korean students studying in the United States represent about 30.7 percent of all overseas Korean students. According to data compiled by the Ministry of Education, as of 1 April 2012, some 73,351 Koreans were studying at higher education institutions in the United States, the third largest number among all foreign students after those from China (157,558) and India (103,895). Considering the much greater population sizes of China and India, the number of Korean students in the United States is truly astonishing. Although the total number of Korean students studying abroad decreased by 8.9 percent in 2012, the number of Koreans studying in the United States increased by about 1.7 percent as compared to the previous year. Nevertheless, in the 2013 academic year, the number of Korean students in the United States from the 2011-2012 academic years

has been decreased 2.3 percent. Now, Korean students in the United States dwindle to 70,000. Peggy Blumenthal, senior counselor at the Institute of International Education (IIE), offered an explanation by commenting that "the decline seems to be attributable to improvements in Korea's higher education system and the rise of Chinese universities as an alternative" (Indirect quote from the Korea Herald, 13 November 2013).

The enthusiasm of Korean students for overseas education is not limited to higher education but is found at every level. According to statistics compiled by the Korea Educational Development Institute (*Hanguk Gyoyuk Gaebalwon*), in 2011, among students at all levels (excluding college students), primary school students (7,477) outnumbered middle (5,468) and high school students (3,570). In 1998, only about 200 primary school students went overseas, but this number swelled to over 12,531 in 2008, a sixty-three-fold rise from 1998. However, since 2009, this number has steadily decreased, to 7,477 in 2011.

Why this recent decrease of the overseas-bound-precollege students? In my earlier chapter on the Korean family, I spoke of the neologisms that describe families where young children and mothers move overseas for the children's education, leaving the fathers behind: "wild geese fathers," "penguin fathers," and "eagle fathers." This geographic separation puts both an economic and an emotional strain on families. The decrease in the last few years of overseas education for young children may be due to the greater availability of quality English-language instruction domestically. For parents who are determined to have their children learn English with native-speaker fluency, there are now more options, from hiring native English-speaking tutors to sending their children to areas such as Jejudo and Songdo of Incheon, where there are schools where English is the sole language of instruction.

New Challenges for Korean Education

A surplus of highly educated workers

Korean higher education has expanded much more rapidly than the economy can incorporate college graduates. According to the 2010 census, of 36,765,374 Koreans twenty years old and older, 15,878,204 (43.2 percent) were college graduates. Forty years ago, fewer than 1 in 10 Koreans were college graduates; now more than four out of every 10 Koreans are college graduates. The proportion of college graduates in Korea was much higher than the 30 percent average of the OECD in 2009. While having many college graduates is good for the country, the unemployment rate among those graduates is alarming.

For the past several years, annual economic growth has slowed, and the number of college graduates has exceeded the manpower requirements of the economy. The number of jobless Koreans hit a four-year high in 2005, with an annual unemployment rate of 3.7 percent, as more people failed to land jobs amid a faltering economy. The rate of unemployment in 2012 was 3.1 percent, a little better. Nevertheless, 2012 was the first time since Korea has kept official statistics on the unemployment rate (since 1999) when the unemployment rate of college graduates surpassed the unemployment rate of high school graduates. Consequently, in desperation, some university graduates seek work that only requires a high school degree. For example, in 2005, when five positions for expressway tollgate clerk became available, three of the 163 applicants had master's degrees and forty-four had bachelor degrees. This scarcity of appropriate jobs for college graduates continues today. According to a report prepared by the Korea Research Institute for Vocational Education & Training (KRIVET, or *Hanguk Jigeop Neungryeok Gaebalwon*), on 17 July 2012, there was a continuing tendency for college graduates to end up taking lower-grade jobs that do not require a college degree. Worried about the lack of employment opportunities, some

students defer graduation, hoping for an improvement in the job market. Beginning 7 December 2012, the Korean daily *Chosun Ilbo* published a series of reports on this issue, claiming that about one million college students had deferred graduation.

Because of this "inflation" in the educational attainment of job applicants, there is growing social pressure to reduce the number of four-year university graduates. In 2005, the Ministry of Education encouraged fifteen national universities to reduce their numbers by consolidating. Each year, the ministry reviews and evaluates every university on the basis of certain criteria and weeds out those that do not meet the standard. Some universities have been notified, and public announcements made, that their students are ineligible for government-guaranteed student loans, which is one way to downsize universities that do not meet the minimum standards.

Offer more jobs to high school graduates and plan for college work later

Considering the soaring level of highly educated youth coupled with a labor shortage in certain industrial sectors, Lee Myung-bak's government supported vocational high school, which trains students in specialized industrial skills, in an effort to cut youth unemployment (7.7 percent in 2012, according to Statistics Korea). High on President Lee's policy agenda was tackling the imbalance in supply and demand of labor stemming from academic inflation, where people receive more education than their vocation requires. President Lee insisted that "academic inflation has elevated private tuition costs, created excessive tuition costs, created excessive competition in education, a soaring level of highly educated youth and a labor shortage problem." The Lee administration launched an elite technical school program called Meister schools in 2008, offering select vocational high schools various incentives, including full scholarships and job placement advantages. There are thirty-five Meister high schools currently in operation. All 142 seniors in this

Meister program have confirmed their employment with various local companies operating in the industrial city near Seoul.

According to personnel officers at industrial firms who hired graduates of vocational and technical high schools, including Meister schools, a good many able young workers are interested in pursuing higher education after they work for a few years. Indeed, according to the results of a nationwide survey conducted by Statistics Korea from May to June 2012, nine out of every ten Koreans think that four-year college or university education is absolutely necessary. In order to accommodate people who want to have jobs right after graduation and not forgo college entirely, the Ministry of Education, in the name of "getting a job first and pursuing college work thereafter" asked online universities to accommodate the needs of these workers who aspire to college. Online universities, or cyber universities, seem particularly well suited to meet this need, for they allow enrollees to work and study at the same time without having to relocate or alter their work schedules. For the academic year of 2013, four Korean cyber universities out of twenty-one were selected to offer various programs such as information technology, new media content, and electronic communication. Not only can the graduates of Meister schools apply for admission, but students at other vocational or general high schools can as well. Though presenting many challenges, this new initiative involving Korean cyber universities may prove mutually beneficial to employees, employers, and the universities alike.

Other challenges

The Korean *han* to acquire better and higher education seems to have been satisfied for many, as attested by statistics. Though a rather small country, roughly the size of the state of Indiana, Korea has 16 million college and university graduates. In 2011 alone, 426,634 Korean students received college or university degrees. Now, however, is a time when Korean institutions might rise to match the

achievements of Korean students. If this were to happen, the many students who currently pursue advanced study abroad (73,351 Korean students in the United States, 62,855 in China, 12,580 in England, 21,290 in Japan, and others) might be educated at home. Before this improvement in Korean institutions comes about, though, several challenges must be met.

First, an effort has to be made to reduce the variation in the quality of education across different schools in Korea. Of the over 300 colleges and universities, some are world class, while others are subpar. As long as there are great differences in quality among colleges and universities, the extreme competition to enroll in the few top-tier universities will continue.

Because of Korea's low population growth, many provincial colleges are facing difficulties in recruiting students that will only worsen in the future. Demographers predict that by 2050 the total number of high school graduates in Korea will be 250,000, while available positions in college and universities will be 640,000. Even if all high school graduates go on to higher education each year, 380,000 positions will remain vacant. The concentration of higher education institutions in Seoul and its vicinity has created an associated problem of overpopulation, a problem addressed in the discussion of urbanization.

A second major challenge to improving Korean higher education is restructuring the content of the curriculum as well as improving teaching methods. Korean textbooks are loaded with factual information, and instructors tend to emphasize memorization rather than creative thinking because it is easier and quicker to check, correct, and assign grades under such conditions: "excellent students" are those who can retain large amounts of information. Perhaps this system had its origins in Confucian teaching, where the main aim was to memorize and recite the Confucian classics. In the words of foreign observers (Mason et al. 1980:372), "Especially at the higher levels of [Korean] education, curriculum and examination content would

248

seem to discourage creativity and innovation." A former consultant of Booz Allen Hamilton Korea, Tariq Hussain (2006:218), is critical of the shortcomings of Korean education, which does not create globally competitive resources. In Hussain's view, the Korean educational system does not encourage critical thinking and problem solving, nor does it foster communication skills, diversity, and leadership.

Third, a third challenge that Korean education has to confront is multicultural and bilingual education for children of foreign-born mothers (mostly) and fathers who represent an increasing demographic in Korean schools. Historically, Korea has been thought to be racially, culturally, and ethnically homogeneous (a belief that I will interrogate in the epilogue), and Korean education has labored to propagate this belief. Nevertheless, as the number born to international marriages has grown to more than 150,000 students, bilingual education for these children has become a pressing need.

Informed Korean citizens consider bilingual language teaching absolutely necessary, because, in the homes of international marriages, mothers and fathers generally do not speak the same language, and children may never learn to speak the language spoken by their mother. Teaching children to speak their mothers' languages will allow mothers and children to communicate with one another, and these children will also be able to interpret for their Korean fathers, grandparents, other relatives, and family friends. Also, if the home languages of these children are taught in school, the children who come from these homes may find a newfound respect from their peers. Furthermore, if bilingualism is fostered in these children of international marriages, their linguistic skills could well benefit the country at large in an age of globalization.

A difficulty arises, however, in that Korea does not have many talented teachers who can teach these various languages, so implementing bilingual language teaching presents problems. One obvious source of such teachers is the foreign-born mothers themselves, but few have any formal training to better enable them

to teach their native language to their children. As these children mature fast the age at which foreign language instruction is easiest and most effective—especially phonologically—Korea stands to lose an important opportunity, if something could not be done very soon.

Fourth, perhaps the greatest challenge Korean education has yet to face is competition from foreign educational institutions in Korea. In order to meet the demands of the new century, Korea has not only lifted restrictions on overseas study but has allowed for the establishment of foreign schools in some parts of the country. In May 2005, the National Assembly passed a bill allowing foreign schools to open in Korea's free economic zones, which include the entire provinces of Jejudo, Songdo, Gwangyang, Busan, and Jinhae. On 18 January 2006, Korean President Roh Moo-hyun announced in his New Year's address that he would eventually allow foreign universities to establish themselves in Korea.

An international school on Jejudo already attracts students from the mainland and appears to be popular, as does Songdo of Incheon. (These schools were mentioned earlier as places where Korean students can seek instruction entirely in English.) Korea's own Yonsei University has established a branch in Songdo, and several foreign universities are preparing to establish branches, too. Such a new development can foster competition in higher education in Songdo and elsewhere. The most challenging competition will take place in cyberspace. Several prestigious universities in the United States offer free college courses over the Internet (massive open online courses or MOOC), and Korean students take them free of charge. If Korean institutions of higher education can meet these enumerated challenges properly and wisely, they may one day attain world-class status.

9
Korea's Economic Miracle: from Foreign Aid Recipient to Donor

O ver the past sixty years *(hwangap,* a sexagenarian life cycle) since the Korean War cease-fire took effect in 1953, Korea has seen many incredible advances. Economically, Korea has transformed from one of the poorest nations in the world, with a $67 per capita GNI in 1953, to the fifteenth largest economy in 2013, with a $26,205 per capita GNI. Six decades ago, Korea's per capita GNI ranked below that of Ethiopia. In fact, during the Korean War, Ethiopia helped South Korea by sending 6,037 soldiers to fight against the communist invasion. Today, in a turnabout, Korea provides some aid to Ethiopia.

Today, Korea ranks seventh in the world in international trade; ranks fifth in producing automobiles; is a global leader in ship building and the manufacture of LCD screens, mobile handsets, and memory chips; has the fastest broadband in the world; ranks eighth in the number of large business conglomerates *(jaebeol)*; and has athletes who win Olympic medals and golf championships. As we saw in the previous chapter Korea was second only to Finland in educational quality according to Pearson Educational Services in 2012; it also has had the best international airport out of 1,700 in the world for the past seven consecutive years. The heads of both the World Bank and the United Nations were born in Korea, and K-pop music and the Korean wave, *Hallyu,* have swept Asia and

beyond. Korea is the only nation to go from being a recipient of foreign aid from the Development Assistance Committee (DAC) to becoming a member of the donor committee. The Korean miracle is not limited only to the "miracle on the Hangang," a reference to Korea's extraordinary economic growth, but also includes Korea's miraculous political transformation from a military dictatorship "to the twentieth most democratic country in the world, and the most democratic in Asia" (Tudor 2012:78).

Korea's success is remarkable because it was achieved by overcoming many obstacles. From the eighteenth to the twentieth centuries, when Korea was serious about modernizing, it was caught up in several major wars: the Russo-Japanese War (1904-1905), the Sino-Japanese War and World War II (1937-1945), and the fratricidal Korean War. For thirty-six years of Japanese colonization, Koreans did not have a fair opportunity to receive a proper education. Even when South Korea was implementing its economic development and industrialization plan, there were numerous threats and disturbances from North Korea. Even now, the provocations of a North Korea armed with nuclear weapons and long- and short-range missiles are very real.

Regarding Korean economic growth and development—a period of fast growth in the mid-1960s and a period of slow growth starting in the late 1990s—the title of a recent book, *From Miracle to Maturity* (2012), by Barry Eichengreen and coauthors, captures well the recent history of Korean economic development. With this two-stage economic development in mind, I focus in this chapter on the period of fast growth and identify factors that account for it. In the process I hope to go some way toward explaining how Korea was able to transform itself from a receiver of international aid to a provider.

Miraculous Economic Growth and Rapid Industrialization

Personal notes on the "mendicant mentality"

Korea's miraculous economic growth and rapid industrialization may mean many different things to different Koreans. For Koreans of my generation and earlier, who lived a marginal existence under Japanese rule and during the devastating Korean War, it has special meaning—full of pride, self-fulfillment, and great relief. I remember that, near the end of World War II, most Korean schoolchildren did not have decent shoes to wear because materials to make them had been confiscated by the Japanese for war supplies. (Ironically, Korea was the world's largest exporter of shoes, $1.1 billion, and leather-wear, $69 million, in 1986 [Kim 1992]).

I want to relate one of my indelible memories of Korea's former poverty. In 1964, when I was teaching assistant to Hahm Pyong-Choon[Ham Byeong-chun] (then professor of law at Yonsei University who later became the Ambassador Extraordinary and Plenipotentiary to the United States of America), Hahm asked me to read his manuscript entitled "Korea's Mendicant Mentality?" before submitting it to *Foreign Affairs* (1964:165-174) for publication. Hahm's article contained the following passage:

> Not long ago, at a social gathering, I overheard a high-ranking U.S. military officer berating the Korean people for their "mendicant mentality." He was deeply annoyed by the inability of Koreans to find a way to live independently, without always looking to the United States for financial help. He did not see how the American taxpayers could be made to carry indefinitely the burden of helping a poor nation that seems unable or unwilling to help itself. He cited the billions of dollars of American aid that have been poured into Korea since 1945. . . . The Koreans must be made to realize, he said, that they had to get onto their own feet very soon; otherwise continued American aid would only create what one American news magazine several years ago terms a "handout mentality."

Hahm's words annoyed and disturbed me, and made me ashamed of the "culture of Korean poverty." By then, Korean per capita GNI was merely $130. Nonetheless, I sent the manuscript off for him.

David I. Steinberg, who was in Korea as director of the Asia Foundation when Hahm was writing his article for *Foreign Affairs*, also ruminates on the Korea of those years: "Per capita income for 1953 was only $67 . . . and one of the lowest in the world. . . . There was in Korea, moreover, a sense of despair and hopelessness, as well as a 'mendicant mentality,' a reliance on foreign patrons, especially the United States, for military, economic, and political support, Korea was at that time a U.S. client state" (Steinberg 1989:122). Assessing contemporary Korea in relation to the past, Steinberg (1989:122) says, "from the dark nadir of 1953, progress of this magnitude was virtually unthinkable; few Koreans radiated self-confidence; few foreigners realized Korea's potential."

Because I have personal memories of that "dark nadir," Korea's economic accomplishment has touched me dearly. In 1987, for instance, when I saw a Korean-made Hyundai Excel parked in our university parking lot when I was a faculty member at the University of Tennessee, I dashed over and touched its exterior. It was an emotional moment for me to see that a Korean-made automobile had come to a southern university town. Perhaps the younger generation of Koreans who never had firsthand experience of the poverty, starvation, and massive destruction caused by war would find it difficult to understand the sentiment of an older Korean.

Korean economic development and rapid industrialization

It is amazing that a resource-poor country like Korea, still bearing the scars of a devastating war, managed to become an economic powerhouse in so short a period of time. Many scholars at home and abroad are interested in knowing what inspired and sustained Korea's impressive record of growth and development. To answer this question, in the late 1970s, a group of American and Korean

scholars began to publish their findings on Korea's success. The most notable of these studies was conducted by the joint program of the Korean Development Institute (KDI) and the Harvard Institute for International Development and by the World Bank (Hasan 1976; Hasan and Rao 1979; Jones and Sakong 1980; Kim and Roemer 1979; Krueger 1979; Mason et al. 1980; Wade and Kim 1978; Westphal 1978). Interest in Korean economic ascendancy encouraged the study of Korean management by scholars of business and management (Chung and Lee 1989; Steers et al. 1989; Yoo and Lee 1987). Some sociologists have discussed the dynamic relationship between the state and *jaebeol* in Korea (E. Kim 1997). Still others have studied the lives of factory workers and labor union movements in the process of industrialization (S. Kim 1997).

Most literature on Korean economic progress and industrialization tends to focus on the period of manifest growth from the sixties onward. Without any doubt, remarkable progress did take place after the 1960s. However, historians tell us that the national movement for Korean economic development, as well as nascent capitalism, began in the late nineteenth century (Eckert 1990, 1991; Eckert et al. 1990). The movement to raise the general level of national consciousness, education, and economic development was inaugurated by moderate cultural nationalists in the early 1920s under colonial rule (Eckert et al. 1990; Robinson 1988, 2007). In those years, entrepreneurs and manufacturers were viewed as patriots, and such a perception still lingers in the minds of many Koreans.

Some sources have traced the infrastructure of Korean industrialization to the Japanese influence during the colonial era (Cumings 1984; Mason et al. 1980), while others strongly deny a positive Japanese role (Huh 2005). Other scholars like to give credit to the various risk-taking activities of entrepreneurs (Kim 1986), while still others believe that Korea's economic success has been accomplished by the exploitation of workers (Choi 1990). All causes that have been suggested may have played a role in Korea's rapid economic development and industrialization (Kim 1992).

The concept of the "privilege of backwardness"—to learn and borrow available technology from advanced countries rather quickly and inexpensively—has been viewed as another possible explanation (Gershenkron 1962, 1968; Sahlins and Service 1960; Trotsky n.d.). Alice Amsden (1989) has characterized Korean industrialization as "late industrialization" because of its practice of appropriating foreign technology from industrialized countries rather than developing its own. She trusts that Korean industrialization is a classic model containing all the characteristic elements. She convincingly uses the example of POSCO, a hugely successful steel company, which was founded by the Korean government in 1968 on a turnkey basis with Japanese technology.

Nevertheless, Korea's exceptional learning ability as an "apprentice" has to be taken into account. Take the case of POSCO. While it is true that over 500 engineers among more than 23,200 employees and frontline supervisors of POSCO had received overseas training prior to its opening, "when operations commenced in 1973, local engineers reached normal iron production level within eight days, an unprecedented record in the history of the industry" (L. Kim 1989:125). Measured against this success story, all apprentices may not be able to implement with the same intensity the technology they wish to adopt (Kim 1992).

If one defines innovation as the refinement of existing cultural traits, e.g., industrial products, then in the process of industrialization Korea may be said to have made many indigenous innovations. Also, efforts have been made to upgrade both products and the production process through "reverse engineering," that is, taking apart and reassembling off-the-shelf foreign products. Kim Linsu[Gim In-su] (1989) has witnessed this process of indigenous innovation by which a small and simple steel pipeline builder evolved into a world-ranking manufacturer of steel machinery.

Contributing factors in Korea's economics development

Importing foreign cultural traits. Among the various cultural traits that Korea borrowed from China, perhaps Confucianism and Chinese characters are the most important. The function of Confucianism and its impact on the Korean way of life, including rules for industrial relations, especially in terms of "harmony" (*inhwa*), have not yet been fully evaluated. However, Geert Hofstede and Michael H. Bond (1988) believe that the notion of harmony originated in Confucian thought. Some scholars, following Max Weber (1951) over a half century ago, viewed Confucianism as a hindrance to economic development.

Some view Confucianism's role as counterproductive and obstructive (Kim 2001). Chung Young-iob (1989:152) writes that "Confucian teachings rejected training in economics for the pursuit of wealth and held business people in low esteem. The ruling elite, *yangban*, did not allow themselves to participate in profit-making enterprises." Bae Kyuhan[Bae Gyu-han] (1987:79) observed a similar view among Hyundai workers that Korean government and industry were taking advantage of Confucianism to exploit industrial workers. Early Korean industrialists were seen more as "developers" than "profit makers." Roger Janelli with Yim Dawn-hee (1993), on the basis of their anthropological fieldwork on a leading Korean business conglomerate, concluded that South Korean corporate culture is based on traditional family life in the village. Nevertheless, even Confucianism's critics do not deny that it has had some positive influence on Korean economic development, especially through its encouragement of education (Kim and Kim 1989; Steers et al. 1989). Even critic of Confucianism Chung Young-iob (1989) acknowledges some indirect benefit to economic development from Confucianism.

Besides Confucianism, the Chinese writing system was also influential for Korean culture. Korea used Chinese characters until it invented its own written language in 1446. Even today, many Koreans opt to use Chinese characters alongside their own language,

as do the Japanese. Chinese characters are difficult to master, yet once learned, one can comprehend their meaning quite easily. Dwight Perkins' (1986:7) comment that Japan, Korea, Hong Kong, Taiwan, and Singapore "were influenced by Confucian values, used *Chinese characters*, and ate with chopsticks" (emphasis mine) may not be a mere frivolous observation. Koreans' ability to pick up the tiniest food particle, such as a pea, using metal chopsticks may be called a sort of special skill, which in turn might lead to an enhanced ability to use micro tools in the manufacturing of industrial goods (Kim 2011a).

Korea's use of historical adversities.   The history of Korea could be told as a series of adversities. Because of its geopolitical situation in the middle of the Far East, it has had to confront larger and often hostile neighbors: Yen, Khitan, Jurchen, Mongol, Manchu, China, Japan, Russia, and, most recently, North Korea. Paradoxically, however, such foreign menaces have also steeled Koreans—in retaining their identity, ensuring their cultural continuity, and overcoming the challenges that confront them. While they were struggling to sustain life itself, Koreans gained the wisdom and courage to cope with their situation, and at times they were able to turn the worst situations to their advantage.

Two examples of this resourcefulness and resilience from Korea's twentieth-century history are the Korean War of the early 1950s and the Vietnam War of the following decade. The Korean War devastated the entire Korean peninsula, literally laying it to waste. In addition to the enormous devastation of property, the war also created one of the worst human tragedies in history. Paradoxical as it may sound, the near-total destruction of existing industry, often small and obsolete facilities inherited from the Japanese, allowed Koreans to build newer, larger, and more modern ones free of the limitations of the former. Almost all Korean industrial plants, from top-ranking steel plants to gigantic shipyards, were built on new industrial sites.

Specifically, during and after the war, some entrepreneurs, most notably Chung Ju-yung of Hyundai, actively participated in "repairing bridges, paving roads, and building army barracks, simple dams, and reservoirs, using 'appropriate technology' specified by the Corps of Army Engineers" (Amsden 1989:266). In part, the skills and technologies acquired by Hyundai during the Korean War allowed the company to win later construction bids worldwide, even a bridge project in Alaska. Diversifying his business interests in heavy industry and the auto industry, Chung, with just a grade school education, became the twelfth richest person in the world as rated by *Fortune* in September 1991.

Regarding the experience of the Korean War and its relationship to economic development, the role of the military should not be overlooked, nor should the military coup led by General Park Chung-hee. The mass of Koran peasants would have had little or no formal training—as was the case during the colonial period—in modern technology had it not been for mandatory wartime mobilization. As a result of this military draft, not only did they become literate, but they also were given opportunities to learn the skills needed to handle sophisticated equipment. This education through three wars—World War II, the Korean War, and the Vietnam War—helps explain in part why Korean construction workers have been so successful in undertaking difficult projects in the Arabian desert under inhospitable conditions. Also, in the New Village Movement, the nationwide development project to improve the welfare of rural people initiated by Park Chung-hee in the 1970s, young and vigorous leaders with military experience, not members of the traditional village elite, were often the ones mobilized to bring about fundamental changes in village life.

The Vietnam War also gave the Korean economy a boost. Between 1965 and 1973 South Korea dispatched about 300,000 troops to Vietnam. In spite of all the human casualties, in 1966 the war accounted for 40 percent of Korea's crucial foreign-exchange

receipts. Many Korean business firms, including two of the largest corporations, Hanjin (Korean Air) and Hyundai, received a big economic boost from the war, just as Japan had from the Korean War. Their construction experiences later paved the way for the various construction projects in the Middle East (Kim 1992).

Geopolitical, managerial and human factors

Strong leadership and a feasible development plan. Due credit must be given to the leadership of the Korean government and its economic development program that was devised and carried out by many able, well-educated, and disciplined technocrats. Aside from his military-oriented autocratic rule, President Park Chung-hee ignited the sparks of Korea's economic modernization with the catch phrase "You can do it!", bolstering an economic growth strategy using social psychology (Hussain 2006:31). President Park's basic goal was to create an economic base for industrialization and self-sustained growth.

In the early stage of Park's economic development plan, he was seeking loans from foreign countries, especially from the U.S. and West Germany. (Korea did not have normal diplomatic relations with Japan until 1965.) Park tried the U.S. first, going there in 1961 to meet President John F. Kennedy. But Park's plea for a loan was denied. Not long after Park's military coup d'état, Kennedy did not want to create an image of endorsing the coup by lending money to the military strongman.

Park also entreated West Germany for a loan. By then Germany had built a wondrous economy on the Rhine River. West Germany, it was thought, might have some sympathy toward Korea, both being divided nations after World War II. As the results of earnest request made by Korean delegates for their government's economic mission to make loan from Germany, finally on 27 October 1962, the German government decided to grant the loan at 150 million Deutschemarks (about $40 million at the current value) as South Korea asked for. However, when, as part of the prerequisite for the loan, German government

asked for a guarantee by an overseas bank. Korea was unable to get any foreign bank willing to do so. Finally, the German government made a suggestion that if the Korean government could promise to send some 5,000 Korean coal miners and 2,000 nurses as foreign industrial trainees for three years, Germany could substitute such a deal for the bank collateral. The deal worked out well, because then Germany needed such a work force to fill the gap created by labor shortage, and Korean unemployed workers needed job desperately. As Korea was willing to send workforces to Germany, at last the loan deal was finalized on 27 October 1962. Eventually, these Korean mine workers and nurses who worked in Germany helped their country in two ways: not only were their wages used as loan collateral; they were also remitting money home beyond the minimal amount they spent to live on. The total amount of money they sent to Korea constituted about 2 percent of Korea' annual GNP at the time.

Parenthetically, since then through the 1970s, the total numbers of 18,000 Korean workers (8,000 miners and 10,000 nurses) worked in Germany. By the way, still some 3,300 remnants of the former working immigrants and their families live in Germany.

Apart from securing a loan, during his visit to Germany on 10 December 1964, President Park secured a very valuable lesson for economic development from German Chancellor Ludwig Erhard. The chancellor strongly urged President Park to construct highways as soon as possible because they would in turn lure the automobile industry and steel industry. According to Paek Young-hoon[**Baek Yeong-hun**], who served as the translator for President Park, Chancellor Erhard had traveled in Korea when he was the minister of economics and knew Korea's rugged mountains. He believed Korea should construct a highway system equivalent to the autobahn in Germany to serve as a strong infrastructure for economic development. With an extensive, modern highway system Korea could facilitate transportation and distribution, and induce the development of other industries. Taking Chancellor Erhard's advice seriously, Park traveled

from Bonn to Cologne on the autobahn. According to Paek Young-hoon, Park's idea to construct a 416-kilometer-long Seoul-Busan Expressway was inspired by the German chancellor's advice. With hard work and the strong support of Chung Ju-yung of Hyundai, the Seoul-Busan highway was opened on 7 July 1970.

Ironically, a half century later since President Park Chung-hee visited to Germany in December 1964, on 28 March 2014, President Park Geun-hye, the daughter of the former President Park Chung-hee, has made a four-day state visit to Germany, aiming at sharing the experiences of Germany in achieving unification and integration to prepare for the unification of North and South Korea.

In the early 1960s, at the time of the first five-year economic development plan, the country's target was an annual growth rate of 7.1 percent between 1962 and 1966. Korea exceeded this target, achieving a higher growth rate beginning in 1963. Successive five-year economic development plans—the second (1967-1971), third (1972-1976), fourth (1977-1981), and fifth (1982-1986)—contained specific goals and directions, but one consistent, basic policy was an emphasis on export-oriented industrialization and growth. This fundamental policy goal remains unchanged even today.

Motivated "*jaebeol*" and dedicated workers

In September 1987, the *JoongAng Ilbo*, a daily Korean newspaper, reported the results of a nationwide survey in which Koreans, asked to rate factors contributing to Korea's economic success, gave considerable weight to the efforts of the Korean people themselves. Koreans' penchant for pluck and hard work is also attested by a more recent survey, which reported that Koreans, ranging in age from twenty to seventy-four, work two hours longer per day than do Americans and Germans, while sleeping fifty minutes less per night. In fact, according to data released 12 December 2012 by the Institute for International Trade in the Korea International Trade Association, on average, Korean workers, compared to those in other countries,

work the second longest hours in the world. Because of such single-minded willpower, Koreans have been able to accomplish their economic goals.

The role of jaebeol. Although Korean *jaebeol* have been criticized, their contributions to Korea's economic development have been indispensable. The *Korean Economic Daily,* dated 13 April 2006, quoted a report by Ikeda Motohiro, the bureau chief of the Japanese newspaper *Nihonkeizai* in Seoul: "if Samsung were not in Korea, the Korean economy would have been at the same stage as that of the Philippines . . . And, if Samsung management would be shaky, then the entire Korean economy would be shaky as well." Ikeda's statement about Samsung may be no exaggeration. A good many *jaebeol* owners work very hard. Some have traveled through many alien societies to develop business relationships, encountering many alien customs, even braving risks, as if they were cultural anthropologists. Reading the autobiography of Kim Woo Choong[Gim U-jung](1992), former chairman of Daewoo group, I learned that he had confronted more difficulties than I have in my years of anthropological fieldwork (Kim 2001).

Jaebeol are analogous to Japanese *zaibatsu*. Although Chinese characters for *jaebeol* and *zaibatsu* are identical and the entities they refer to share many common characteristics, scholars familiar with both forms find that they have some important differences (Hattori 1989). Yoo Sangjin[Yu Sang-jin] and Sang M. Lee (1987) define a *jaebeol* as a business group consisting of large companies, owned and managed by family members or relatives, in diversified business areas, commonly called a management of "octopus tentacles." A review of several available definitions and characteristic features of a *jaebeol* indicates that it has two major features: ownership by a family and a diversified business operation (Kim and Hahn 1989; Lee 1989).

Notwithstanding their contribution, lately *jaebeol* have come to be viewed with great ambivalence and criticism by an increasing

number of Koreans because of a poor system of corporate governance and bribery scandals. Perhaps in this globalizing world, the *jaebeol* might seem to be outdated, for more than half the stock of these Korean companies is owned by foreign investors. Even though the chairmen own a very limited portion of their companies' stock, they control the *jaebeol* through a web of complicated shareholdings and a direct stake. Because of this structure, *jaebeol* groups are vulnerable to the charges of bribery, illegal wealth transfers, and slush funds.

Industrial workers.   Despite many existing theories and explanations, as W. Arthur Lewis (1966:270) has aptly indicated, "the government can persuade, threaten, or inquire; but in the last analysis it is the people who achieved." Thus credit should be given to Korean rank-and-file workers who actually carried out the hard work of industrialization. Koreans have been able to accomplish an ambitious economic agenda because Korea has had a well-educated and disciplined workforce (Kim 1992). A foreign observer, Daniel Tudor (2012:170), praises industrious Korean workers:

> As the hardest working people in the OECD, they are the very model of industriousness. In 2008, the average Korean clocked a total of 2,357 hours at the office. From the 1960s onwards, they have worked under tough, somewhat militaristic conditions. Rank and organizational hierarchy are of great importance, and workers are expected to be loyal to their employers, despite a lack of genuine "jobs for life."

Korean workers not only work hard in Korea; they also work hard when living abroad. Take, for instance, the aforementioned Korean workers in Germany: the coal miners and nurses. Miners though they were, a good many of them were college graduates, and all of them were high school graduates. They put up their wages for their country when it was unable to come up with the bank-guaranteed collateral. How many immigrant workers from other countries would make the same sacrifice? Other Korean workers have

endured inhospitable working conditions—the scorching deserts of the Middle East, for example—creating a manmade river in the middle of the desert and building the world's tallest building on the desert sand. Despite the inhospitable conditions, most times Korean workers finished the job earlier than expected.

Some outside observers may wonder whether Korean laborers have been unduly submissive to management, but the truth is, at times, disputes between management and labor have been furious. I witnessed some of those disputes in my fieldwork. During my fieldwork on the Korean non-steel metal industry in the 1980s and early 1990s, I had the opportunity to witness the most furious labor unrest in Korean history. When I began my study, there was no labor union at the plant I was studying. There was no indication that Korea would see such an eruption of labor disputes. In fact, in the early 1980s, some scholars generalized about workers in newly industrializing countries in Asia, including Korea, portraying them as cheap, docile, loyal, and productive laborers because of their Confucian cultural heritage (Benjamin 1982; Chen 1981; Hofheinz and Calder 1982). As evidenced by the recent rate of wage hikes and the prevalence of labor disputes, however, cheapness and docility are no longer traits of Korean workers, who may have appeared docile until 1987 because of strong control by the military-led government.

What had been a peaceful-looking Korean labor union movement in the early stages of my fieldwork suddenly changed. In the midst of my study, the Chun Doo-hwan regime was brought to the brink of collapse by massive antigovernment demonstrations by students, workers, and intellectuals. When Roh Tae-woo, then the ruling party's candidate for president, issued the "June 29 Proclamation," great labor unrest touched off widespread demonstrations and strikes. In 1987, the total number of labor disputes reached 3,749, the largest number in a single year in the entire history of the Korean labor movement. Since 1987, labor disputes, strikes, and demonstrations have become a common occurrence in Korea.

Some labor disputes have been extreme at times. In the late 1980s, the streets of Seoul looked like a battlefield. This scene provided evidence for some scholars' assessments that Korean labor-management relations followed a confrontational mode rather than the cooperative mode as manifested in Japan (Chung and Lie 1989; Deyo 1989). Since Koreans have paid such a high price for labor disputes, the frequent strikes and demonstrations have been criticized for being too hostile and expensive. But as long as some *jaebeol* are still accused of wrongdoing, labor unions will continue pushing for improved working conditions and higher wages. There are, however, some indications that the confrontational mode is changing toward a cooperative one. It appears that both management and labor have begun working together for common goals as a consequence of foreign challenges.

Other non-economic factors

Location of Korea.   Korea's geopolitical location has been blamed for its vulnerability to foreign interference and invasion, but Korea has been successful in capitalizing on its placement. Among all the Asian countries, Korea is situated closest to three of the world's economic giants: China, Japan, and the United States. This is convenient for trade and commerce. Seoul can easily serve as the dispersal point for other major Asian cities: Tokyo, Osaka, Beijing, Shanghai, Hong Kong, and Singapore. By air, only a few hours separate Seoul from these cities. Seoul also has great potential to serve as a center for commerce and transportation, and as an international money market for Pacific Rim countries. Korea may have the largest number of English-speaking natives, except for Hong Kong, Singapore, and the Philippines. Korea's selection as host of the G-20 Economic Summit in Seoul in November 2010 was no accident.

Patriotism as Koreans' "oneness."   Seeing millions of Koreans cheering during the FIFA World Cup in 2002, I started to understand how they were able to accomplish such a formidable economic task. I also understood more when I (then a faculty member at a U.S. university) heard how Koreans recovered from one of the worst financial crises in 1997 and 1998, a time Koreans aptly call the "IMF" era, alluding to the loan that bailed them out. This is what happened:

> Tens of thousands got caught up in a gold-selling fever launched by KBS TV and the Korean Housing and Commercial Bank to raise dollars to help repay the IMF loans. People queued up to either donate or sell their gold after experts had announced there was an estimated $20 billion worth kept in Korean homes . . . young couples handing in their wedding rings and old ladies handing in items of tremendous personal significance with the feeling that they were helping save their country. . . . People stopped drinking coffee because it is imported. (Breen 2004:159-160).

Some 3.49 million people participated in the three-month-long "gold collection campaign" in which $2.17 billion (225 tons of gold) was collected, according to the *Chosun Ilbo's* report on 12 January 2006.

The Korean sentiment of "oneness" (*Urineun Hana*) appears to be a remarkable motivation for Koreans to work together toward a common goal if there is a clear-cut objective, national agenda, or moral cause to justify it. Such a motivational factor has undoubtedly contributed to Korea's accomplishments. There are, however, many differences that continue to divide Korean society: conservative versus liberal, rich versus poor, urban versus rural, pro-FTA versus anti-FTA, globalization versus localization, and native Koreans versus foreigners.

Economic Maturity

Economic prosperity in the Korean way of life for the past generation is evident even in that generation's physical stature and life expectancy. Koreans are getting taller, healthier, and are living longer than they did in the past. If Korea took advantage of being a late arrival on the modernizing scene in its period of rapid growth, the period of slow growth of the Korean economy may be due partly to the "penalty of taking the lead" as Thorstein Veblen (1915:ch. 2-4) has discussed. In fact, when Korea was backward technologically and economically, self-indulgence might have been viewed as shameful, and a frugal work ethic might have been viewed as virtuous. After Korea reached the mature stage economically, with the middle range of per capita GNI, Koreans might have become complacent.

Because strong economic growth is a central preoccupation of Koreans, recently they have begun to worry about their slow economic growth since the 1997-1998 financial crises, which marked the end of the fast growth era. From 2001 to 2007 GDP growth averaged only 4.7 percent, which is a notable decline from earlier years of over 9 percent growth. For the past five years, from 2008 to 2012, the average GDP annual growth has been 2.92 percent, and slightly increased to 3.0 in 2013; in 2009 it was 0.3 percent, the worst year ever. The most recent crisis that took place in 2008, and which brought only 0.3 percent growth in 2009, was the result of events in the global economy beyond Korea, including the deleveraging by U.S. hedge funds and the failure of Lehman Brothers in September 2008. Banks and corporations experienced a severe shortage of dollars.

Slow growth is a sign of economic maturity

Barry Eichengreen and coauthors (2012:306) have pointed out that "there is a sense of impatience and disappointment about the current performance of the economy. Commentators complain that growth has slowed. They worry that the economy should be growing faster.

They are pessimistic about the future." Nonetheless, it is unrealistic for any nation whose income range is as high as South Korea's to expect fast growth forever. Paradoxical though it may sound, the slow growth of the Korean economy is a manifestation of Korea's economic maturity. Barry Eichengreen and his colleagues (2012:306) characterize the current stage of Korean economy as follows: "One message of this study is that *this sense of pessimism and disappointment is exaggerated.* The presumption inherited from the peak growth period, that Korea should grow at rates approaching double digits, is no longer realistic. Growth at near-double-digit rates can be sustained only in relatively backward economies that have recently broken free of their low-level equilibrium trap" (emphasis mine).

A sign of the maturity of the Korean economy even under the threat from North Korea. Korea's mature economic status has been demonstrated during persistent threats from North Korea, with its testing of nuclear weapons beginning in February 2013 through much of April and May 2013. On 26 March 2014, North Korea fired two midrange ballistic missiles from mobile launchers into East Sea in an apparent show of displeasure with the increasing pressure on it to denuclearize. Kim Jong-un, grandson of Kim Il-Sung (1912-1994) and son of Kim Jong-il (1941-2011), became the supreme leader of North Korea upon the death of his father. Despite unyielding North Korean threats, the Korean stock market did not suffer, and South Koreans remain calm in their normal, routine work. No one stocks up on food for an emergency, *sajaegi* (buying up the essentials of daily life in case of an emergency), in the belief that North Korea will make good on its threats to attack.

Also, on 6 May 2013, during her four-day state visit to the U.S., in a meeting with Korean Americans in New York, President Park Geun-hye assured the audience that the Korean economy is unfazed by the North Korean risk, as evidenced by the state financial markets and businesses' commitment to investment. At a roundtable and

luncheon hosted by the U.S. Chamber of Commerce on 8 May, 2013, Park addressed 170 American business leaders: "Notably, foreigners are increasingly becoming net purchasers of Korean bonds. I am inclined to believe this is a 'vote of confidence' in the resilience of the Korean economy and Korea's track record of turning adversity into opportunity." According to the presidential office, Seoul attracted foreign direct investment worth $380 million from seven U.S. enterprises such as Boeing, Almost Heroes LLC, and Curtiss-Wright on the occasion of the president's U.S. visit. At the meeting with Park, GM's Dan Akerson was quoted as saying the company was "not abandoning" Korea and was planning to invest around eight trillion *won* (about $7.1 billion U.S. dollars) in the country in the next five years. All of this is evidence of the maturity of the Korean economy.

Future prospects for the Korean economy. The Korean economy has been said to be shifting away from a rapidly growing manufacturing economy toward a slower growing, mature economy. This slowing may be perfectly normal for an increasingly mature middle-income country with a per capita income between $10,000 and $16,000 (in terms of year 2000 purchasing power parity). If a slowing economy is any reason for pessimism, consider Korea's formidable inventory of economic strengths. Barry Eichengreen and his colleagues (2012:308) have described Korea's economic strengths as follows:

> It has a skilled and educated labor force. Korean firms are accustomed to competing on international markets. They include a number of world-class manufacturing firms, Samsung, LG, and Hyundai . . . that enjoy brand recognition internationally for their household appliances, consumer electronics, and motor vehicles. . . . The country ranks among the leaders in R & D spending as a share of GDP. It has up-to-date infrastructure, from modern port facilities to an extensive broadband network. . . . Close by is the rapidly growing Chinese market for Korean capital and consumer goods. Above all, history and

tradition cause Korean society to value economic growth. Koreans are willing to sacrifice in order to attain it. The country possesses a government—not just leaders but a permanent civil service—that prioritize[s] growth and formulates policy accordingly.

Counterbalancing this inventory of economic strengths are some negative factors that could hinder Korea's economic growth. Eichengreen and his associates (2012:308) mention several such factors: Korea's aging population, reluctance to embrace immigration, an education system that does not encourage students to think creatively, an ineffective university education system, adversarial labor relations, the influence of family and personal connections in business and politics, the difficulty of attracting foreign direct investment, and the competition of China. The Korean situation could be analogized as a "sandwich," squeezed as it is between low-cost China and high-tech Japan (*Financial Times* 19 March 2007).

Regarding the slow growth, Tariq Hussain (2006:273-313) offers an eight-item agenda, including reforming government, corporations, the labor market, universities; opening up the economy; harnessing the power of women; and budgeting social capital. I also made some similar suggestions to improve Korean economy, including redefining the role of *jaebeol* and reducing government regulations, creating an open policy to meet the challenges of globalization, promoting incoming foreign direct investment, preparing a future labor market in an increasingly aging society, and promoting the rejuvenation of the Korean spirit for a new leap forward toward further development. These two sets of suggestions are both a few years old now, but they are still valid (Kim 2007:320-324).

The forecast for the immediate future does not look promising. In May 2013, OECD predicted that Korea's 2013 economic growth would be 2.6 percent, lower than the world average, mainly because of both external and internal risks. The risks include uncertainty around the 2012 election; the never-ending threat of North Korea

(having three times conducted underground nuclear tests with long- and short-range missiles); household debts of 1,100 trillion *won* (about $1 trillion U.S. dollars), owing largely to expenses of private education; and a widening income gap between the rich and poor (the top 10 percent of Koreans earn ten and a half times the income of the poorest 10 percent), ranking ninth among OECD members. Also, Korea's ranking in terms of economic competitiveness remained at 22, while China ranked 21 and Japan 27, among 60 countries in 2013 for the third straight time, according to the Switzerland-based International Institute for Management Development. Nonetheless, because of its economic maturity, Korea plays several important roles in the global community. Specifically, for the first time in its history, Korea has become a donor of foreign aid to developing countries.

Becoming a Donor of Foreign Aid

At a joint press conference between U.S. President Barack Obama and Korean President Park Geun-hye on 7 May 2013, during Park's state visit to the U. S., President Obama commented that "this visit also reflects South Korea's extraordinary progress over these six decades. From the ashes of war, to one of the world's largest economies, from a recipient of foreign aid to a donor that now helps other nations develop. And of course, around the world, people are being swept up by Korean culture—the Korean wave. And as I mentioned to President Park, my daughters have taught me a pretty good Gangnam Style (laughter)." Indeed, Korea's mature economy has allowed Korea to play a major role in economic, social, political, and other international affairs in the global community. Korea offers monetary and non-monetary foreign aid, technical advice such as teaching the New Village Movement, Korea International Cooperation Agency (KOICA) services, and awards fellowships for those interested in learning Korean language and culture.

Foreign aid that Korea received in the past

Since 1945, when Korea gained its independence from Japan, total foreign aid given to Korea amounted to about $61 billion. Even in 1969, at a time when Korean economic development and industrialization projects were initiated, Korea received some $70 million from the international community. In that same year, one-third of Korea's total annual budget (about $260 million) came from foreign aid, mainly Official Development Assistance (ODA). Without such aid, Korean development would not have been possible, for the aid was used as seed money for economic development and industrialization projects.

As the Korean economy grew during the country's rapid industrialization, in 1995 Korea was finally removed from the list of foreign aid recipients by the World Bank. By 1996, Korea had become a member of the OECD, even though Korea did not become a member of the DAC until November 2009. By becoming a member of DAC, Korea became the only country in the world that was once a recipient of DAC aid and later turned into a donor.

Korea's foreign aid to developing countries via KOICA. Although Korea has offered some aid to developing countries since 1982 through the International Development Exchange Program (IDEP), a strong commitment to international aid to developing countries began when the KOICA was established in 1991, and full-fledged foreign aid started in the mid-2000s. KOICA, the Korean version of the American Peace Corps, was founded as a government agency in April 1991 to maximize the effectiveness of Korea's grant aid program for developing countries by implementing the government's grant aid and technical cooperation programs. As of March 2013, over 10,034 volunteers have been and are serving in sixty-five countries. At first KOICA sent only forty-four volunteers to Nepal, Sri Lanka, Indonesia, and the Philippines, but as it gained in popularity, the number of participants increased over 10,000 in less than a quarter

of a century. It is indeed a phenomenal story of growth and success.

The New Village Movement as a role model. While KOICA volunteers are going overseas to serve in developing countries, the New Village Movement attracts village leaders from developing countries to come to Korea to learn about its rural village development. Ironically, while some Koreans have been critical of the New Village Movement, in 2006 delegations from 133 countries came to Korea to learn about it. In that same year, China likewise looked to the movement as a model to revitalize rural Chinese villages. On 23 November 2012, high governmental officials, university professors, and leaders from ten developing Asian countries, including Mongolia and Nepal, and from five African countries, including Uganda and Tanzania, came to the training headquarters office in Bundang, a suburb of Seoul, and organized a forum called the International New Village Movement. The forum anticipates that each member country will share experiences and acquired wisdom, thereby disseminating ideas for rural development across the developing world. Korea sharing its experience with the world would be more valuable than any gift of monetary aid.

Reflecting the accomplishments of the New Village Movement, on 19 June 2013, "The Archives of the New Village Movement" in the 1960s were added to UNESCO's Memory of the World Register, the Cultural Heritage Administration. The archive includes presidential speeches, government papers, village documents, letters, manuals, photographs and video clips related to the campaign launched in the 1970s by former president Park Chung-hee, who is the father of incumbent President Park Geun-hye.

Foreign aid Korea offers as a member of DAC and ODA. According to data from ODA, Korea's aid to developing countries in 2007 was $696.1 million, with a rate of 0.07 percent. The rate of aid is calculated by using the amount of ODA aid given, divided by the

quantity of GNI (ODA/GNI). For Korea, the amount and rates of ODA/ GNI have risen gradually each year. By 2010, Korea's ODA reached over $1.17 billion (0.12 percent), $1.32 billion (0.12 percent) in 2011, and $1.55 billion (0.14 percent) in 2012. Despite these increases, the total aid given by Korea is still below the annual average of other DAC member countries, which is 0.31. Korea has pledged that by 2015 its ODA/GNI rate will be 0.25 percent. Since Korea has made such a firm commitment, there is reason to believe that it will achieve its goal. More than any dollar amounts, Korea's participation in ODA and as a member of DAC has a significant symbolic meaning: a former recipient turned giver is a good role model for developing countries.

Promotion of Korean culture and Korean studies by Korea Foundation

The Korea Foundation was established in 1991, about the same time that KOICA was established by the Korean National Assembly. The foundation aimed to improve the image of Korea in the world community and to promote and support overseas Korean studies, including Korean language studies. The goals, purposes, and missions of the Korea Foundation are similar to those of the British Council, Goethe Institute, Alliance Française, and Japan Foundation. The foundation was established at the height of Korea's rapid economic growth period, when per capita GNI, which had been $67 in 1953 when the cease-fire went into effect, had increased to $7,000.

Obscure Korea and role of the Korea Foundation. By the time the Korea Foundation was established, Korea had already undergone a significant socioeconomic and political transformation and had hosted the 1988 Summer Olympic Games in Seoul. Nevertheless, the knowledge that people around the world had of Korea was still limited, and an old, clichéd label that still stuck to Korea was "hermit kingdom." In the early 1970s, when I was conducting

anthropological fieldwork on pulpwood-harvesting industrial workers in the rural American South, a worker at a wood yard in a Georgia town wanted to know my ethnic identity. He asked me, "Are you Chinese?" When I said "no," he persisted. "Are you Japanese?" When I said "no" again, he seemed frustrated and asked disdainfully, "What the hell are you, then?" (Kim 1977). That I was Korean was not a possibility that occurred to this man at that time.

Some obscurity still hangs over Korea even in the twenty-first century. Michael Breen (2004:ix) relates a humorous anecdote about this: "A relative of mine once asked me, 'Korea? That's part of Vietnam, isn't it?'" As late as the mid-1980s, a college-level textbook on Asia published by a major publisher in the U.S. States treated Korea along with Tibet in a single chapter titled "Land of Mystery and Isolation" (Tweddell and Kimball 1985:245-262).

A textbook in the Netherlands introduces Korea parsimoniously in just two lines while allocating twelve pages to China and four to Japan (*Dong-A Il bo*, 4 June 2013). On Korea, it states (my paraphrase) that because Korea is a peninsula surrounded by ocean on three sides, the fishing industry is very important. Because of cheap Korean labor and since Korean fishermen sell trimmed fish, we can buy them in our supermarkets.

It is shocking to think that the Dutch have such superficial knowledge about Korea available to them when we consider the long and intimate relationship between the two countries. Historian Lee Ki-baik (1984:241-242) has written about this:

> In 1628 a Dutchman, Jan Janse Weltevree, was shipwrecked on Korean shores; he took the name Bak Yeon and lived out his life in Korea. Since he was experienced in casting cannon he was assigned to the Military Training Command and contributed to development in that area. He was followed in 1653 by Hendrick Hamel and his company of Dutch sailors who were cast ashore on Jejudo. Brought to Seoul, a number of them later made good their escape to Nagasaki, and Hamel's account of

his years of captivity gave the West its first knowledge of Korea.

In fact, Weltevree (1595-?) was the first European immigrant to come to Korea (Kim 2011b:20), and Hamel's account of seventeenth-century Korea is an interesting travelogue that was recently republished (Hamel 2011 [orig. 1653]). Most Koreans have not forgotten that the Netherlands helped Korea during the Korean War.

Two Dutchmen, Guus Hiddink and Dick Advocaat, are the most popular and beloved Korean national soccer coaches that the country ever had. Also, Royal Philips of the Netherlands and Korea's LG have been good business partners. It has been reported that the Korean embassy in the Netherlands works hard to introduce the real Korea to the Dutch public. In the end, in March 2014, it has been reported that a part of geography textbook for elementary students that said fishing is extremely important in South Korea was revised to say South Korea has become a wealthy and an advanced industrialized country. Also, a history textbook for high school students introduced South Korea's economic development and democracy. The Netherlands case illustrates the crucial role of a government institution in effective cultural diplomacy.

Korean studies abroad

The Korea Foundation was established to counter distorted and obscure images of Korea, and since its inception in 1991, the foundation has accomplished this mission successfully. By 2013, college courses on Korean studies had expanded to 845 universities in eighty-one countries; before the foundation came into being, the count was 152 universities in thirty-two countries. Geographically, the distribution of schools offering this curriculum is vast: 550 universities in nineteen countries in Asia; 110 universities in two countries in North America; twenty-three universities in nine countries in Central America; fifty-seven universities in sixteen countries in Western Europe; seventy-seven universities in twenty-

one Eastern European countries; nine universities in two Oceanic countries; and nineteen universities in twelve countries in Africa and the Middle East.

Centers for Korean studies were limited to six universities in two countries in 1991 before the foundation became effective, but increased to forty-four in thirteen countries by 2012. In 1991, there were five Korean studies associations overseas; there were twenty-two by 2012. Also with support from the foundation, from 1992 to 2012, a total of 108 chaired professorships had been created.

The total number of foreign educators who participated in workshops on Korea from 1992 to 2012 is 3,331. When the program was initiated there were only thirty-nine participants, all of whom were from English-speaking countries, including the U.S., Canada, Australia, and New Zealand. There were no participants from East and Southeast Asia, Russia, or Europe. Beginning in the early 2000s, participating countries were from all over the world, and the number of participants increased from double digits to triple, the largest number being 496 in 2010. Perhaps *Hallyu* has generated more interest in workshops on Korea.

Since 1993, 1,473 people have received a Foundation fellowship to study the Korean language. The number of the participating fellows each year varies — from a high of 116 in 2008 to a low of 43 in 2012 — but does not seem to follow an identifiable pattern. It is interesting to note that the 627 fellows from Europe alone is impressive as they compared with the 640 from Asia and Oceania combined.

In promoting Korean studies abroad, the Korea Foundation has played an indispensable role and has made a major contribution to foreigners interested in Korean studies. That said, some credit in promoting Korean studies abroad should be given to the Korean cultural wave, called *Hallyu* or Korean wave. Recently, Korean pop music (K-pop), television drama (K-drama), and movies (K-movies) have generated worldwide interest beyond Korea and its neighboring

countries. Some people around the world who are attracted by the wave have started to learn the Korean language. A further exploration of *Hallyu* is taken up in the next chapter. Without Korea's phenomenal economic growth, there perhaps would be no Korea Foundation, no KOICA, and no *Hallyu*.

10
Cultural Paradox

V incent S. R. Brandt (1971:28), an American anthropologist who did his fieldwork in a small farming and fishing village in Korea in the mid-1960s, characterized the Korean mind-set as riddled with contradictions: "Contradictory forms of behavior are found in all cultures, but they seem to have been more dramatically expressed in Korea than in some other parts of the World." If Brandt were to carry out his fieldwork today, not only would he witness contradictory behaviors, but he would also encounter many paradoxes, because Korean society is transforming so rapidly. Some foreign observers have commented that Korea has an immense capacity for change: "A statement about life in Korea that is true at a particular moment may become completely false far sooner than can be predicted" (Tudor (2012:139).

A true paradox is, of course, evident in a comparison between South and North Korea. In many ways, South Korea is a top-down society, with its constitution, its village restoration projects, its creation of a governmental second city, and its call to citizens to turn in gold to repay a national debt, yet it has succeeded in democratizing itself, equalizing opportunity, and spreading economic prosperity. Confucianism would seem to be antithetical to democracy, capitalism, and technological advancement (Bae 1987; Chung 1989; K. Kim 1998; Weber 1951), yet South Korea is a paragon of a modern, largely free-market, technology-producing economy. However, why has North Korea followed such a different trajectory since the

partition of the peninsula in the mid-twentieth century, although it, too, is also a top-down society? North Korea has become secretive, hostile, repressive, and terribly poor. How did the two countries come to such different ends while sharing ethnicity, history, a common language, and a common culture? How did the two Koreas become so strikingly different when they were so similar to begin with? It is indeed a Korean paradox.

This chapter focuses on South Korea and describes some of these Korean contradictions, confusions, and/or paradoxes. Among them, four characteristics have been selected as illustrations: 1) A good many Koreans have been or still are captives of a belief in a single ethnic nationalism even after multiculturalism has become part of public discourse and discussion among Korean intellectuals; 2) Koreans tend to be inwardly oriented, yet act outwardly; 3) Economic growth and development are a central preoccupation of Koreans (Eichengreen et al. 2012:1), yet their efforts to conserve the environment equal those in other developed countries; 4) The remnants of Confucianism in Korea are strong, yet Korea became the first East Asian country to elect a "madam" president.

The Myth of Ethnic Nationalism and the Emergence of Multiculturalism

Since the early twentieth century, in reaction to Japanese domination, Koreans have been captive to a myth of ethnic and racial nationalism, one that imagines that the Korean people belong to a single ethnic group, a pure race. Recently, however, public discussion of multiculturalism has acknowledged Korea's ethnic heterogeneity in response to a growing number of foreigners living in Korea, especially foreign brides. This recent transformation of Korean mono-ethnic nationalism into Korean multiculturalism presents an interesting paradox to unpack and examine more closely.

Myth of ethnic nationalism

The view that Koreans are a single, ethnically pure people was popular among native Koreans, especially ethnic nationalists. The belief is that Koreans belong to a single ethnic group of "pure blood" (sunhyeol) descended from a common ancestor. Older Koreans living today were deeply indoctrinated by a school of nationalistic historiography (minjok sahak) that stressed the origins of Korean national identity as rooted in a single race (danil minjok).

This version of nationalism came into being when Korea lost its sovereignty as a state to Japan. Consequently, Koreans dwelt on the importance of nationalism. Led by Shin Chae-ho[Sin Chae-ho], many Korean historians and intellectuals supported a nationalistic historiography with the patriotic goal of writing a new history of Korean independence. This new history was influenced by Korea's resistance to the "Japanese imperialistic historical framework" (Pai 2000:1). According to Han Kyung-Koo (2007:13), "Even scholars fail to critically review this misconception and blame the Dangun myth as the source of ethnic nationalism in Korea. This misunderstanding is corroborated by Korean familism, which emphasizes blood relatedness. Familism makes Korean ideology seem preoccupied with blood kinship, an archaic means of solidarity." The Dangun mythology grew stronger along with ethnic nationalism during and after Japanese colonization.

Terms such as mixed blood (honhyeol) and pure blood (sunhyeol), which originated in the ethnic nationalism of the early 1900s, have long been used to describe the ethnic origin of Koreans. This tradition has raised concerns among human rights activists who argue that such terms lend themselves to social and economic discrimination. For this reason, in 2007, the U.N. Committee on the Elimination of Racial Discrimination (CERD) asked Korea to avoid using such expressions as "mixed blood" and "pure blood."

Discrimination against children of "mixed blood."   Despite the popular rhetoric of multiculturalism in contemporary Korea, many children born to cross-racial and cross-ethnic parents, especially those with darker skin pigmentation, have been, and still are to some extent, discriminated against for their ethnic and racial origins. Before the children born today to international couples, there were previously many children born to American military servicemen and Korean women before multiculturalism became fashionable. For this reason, some academics classify them into two groups. The first group includes children born to American military servicemen and Korean women; these children are called "Ko-Americans" or "Amerasians." The second group has been labeled "Ko-Asians" (children born to international marriages between Koreans and other Asians); these are children born to multicultural families beginning in the late 1990s and early 2000s.

The numbers of the first group were estimated to range from 1,400 to 2,300 in the 1960s; this figure fell to 500 in 1990 as U.S. forces in Korea were drawn down (Chun 2008:17, 24). Nonetheless, as officials at Statistics Korea have indicated, it is practically impossible to determine the number of international marriages because birth certificates do not have any place to identify the nationality of the parents, the assumption being that all were Koreans. All the figures vary from source to source since no official records are yet available. Nevertheless, one thing is obvious: prejudice and discrimination against the first group children—Ko-Americans or Amerasians— were worse than for the second group, Ko-Asians, thanks to the rhetoric of multiculturalism and the awareness it has raised (Kim 2011b:65-66). Hines Ward, winner of the 2006 MVP award in American football's Super Bowl XL, for example, was born in Korea to a Korean mother and an African American ex-GI. As a Ko-Asian, Ward is one of the many who went to the U.S. to avoid the discrimination prevalent at that time in Korea.

Were Koreans xenophobic?

Some foreign writers who have lived in Korea for some time comment that Koreans are xenophobic. Michael Breen (2004:20), for one, has said that "Korean intellectuals become more xenophobic and nationalistic, and perpetrate the idea that all of Korea's problems are the result of willfulness by foreigners." According to a survey conducted by the Corea[Korea] Image Communication Institute (CICI), of 213 foreign "opinion leaders"—including foreign companies' CEOs, diplomats, foreign professors, correspondents, branch managers of foreign banks, and business expatriates living in Korea—17.8 percent responded that Koreans are not open-minded and are xenophobic toward foreigners, and 10.2 percent responded that Koreans are not courteous toward foreigners (Kim 2011b).

It is worth remembering, however, that xenophobia is present in virtually every part of the world. Jürgen Habermas (1994:136) wrote an extensive commentary on Charles Taylor's multiculturalism and said, "Xenophobia is widespread these days in the European Community as well. It is more marked in some countries than in others, but the attitudes of the Germans do not differ substantially from those of the French and the *English*" (emphasis mine). Guy Sorman, a leading contemporary French intellectual, said, "When you discuss xenophobia, you are right to mention that it happens in all societies," in a letter to me dated 23 January 2012 in which he commented on my book on Korea's multiculturalism (Kim 2011b). Perhaps the word *xenophobia* has been used indiscriminately at times, so I offer the neologism *xeno-uneasiness* as an alternative (Kim 2011b: 50). It seems to me that in order for an attitude to be labeled as xenophobia, there must be more than a strong suspicion about foreigners; there has to be a systematic or institutionalized form of differential treatment—legally, socially, and otherwise—that applies only to foreigners and strangers.

Koreans' view of foreigners

Despite the prevailing view of traditionalists in Korea, evidence from Korean prehistory, history, and current demographics suggests that the conventional view of Korea as a racially homogeneous society may have no foundation in fact. According to newly revealed archaeological evidence, during the Paleolithic period through the Neolithic era and into Bronze Age, the Korean peninsula was inhabited by two major racial groups, Caucasoid and Mongoloid, who appear to have lived side by side. Also, during later historical periods, various groups of foreigners—the Han Chinese, Mongolians, Manchurians, Vietnamese, Jurchens, Khitans, Yen, Japanese, Arabs, and various groups from the south and southeast—immigrated to the Korean peninsula and were naturalized. The descendants of those foreign immigrants have been identified and amount to almost 12 million of South Korea's 46 million residents counted in the 2000 census. The descendants of those individuals who immigrated to Korea during the last several hundred years made up 26 percent of the country's total population. This figure alone should give one reason to question the accuracy of South Korea's self-description as mono-ethnic and mono-racial (Kim 2011b).

Some foreign scholars such as Bruce Cumings, John Frankl, and Andre Schmid have researched Korean history as well as played a significant role in tracing Korea's multiethnic past. Shin Gi-wook's *Ethnic Nationalism in Korea* (2006) is also an important contribution to this scholarship, as it rethinks and reevaluates the consequences of ethnic nationalism in contemporary Korea. According to this group of scholars, Korea was once open and indeed welcoming to foreigners prior to the late nineteenth and early twentieth century. Apparently, there was no strong nationalistic sensibility in traditional Korean society (Kim 2011b).

John M. Frankl (2008) reports that traditionally Koreans did not make any effort to distinguish between foreigners and themselves on the basis of national boundaries. They did not consider themselves

to be ethnically unified as a people and did not discriminate against foreigners simply on the basis of their ethnic origins. Instead, Koreans were tolerant, open, and even hospitable to foreigners. Because a large number of naturalized Koreans came from elsewhere, Frankl rightly refers to Korea as a society of cultural hybridity, not ethnic homogeneity. According to Andre Schmid (2002:173), the term *minjok*, meaning "ethnic nation," rarely appears in the canonical texts of Korean nationalists in the ten years before the Protectorate Treaty of 1905 with Japan. Recently, with the trend toward multicultural studies, anthropologists, archaeologists, and historians have begun to scrutinize nationalistic historiographies (Kim 2011b).

The myth of ethnic nationalism is being replaced by multiculturalism

There are over 1.5 million foreigners currently living in Korea, including foreign workers, foreign brides and grooms married to native Koreans, and foreign students, from 180 different countries. They make up 2.5 percent of the current South Korean population. Obviously, these numbers pale in comparison to the number of foreigners who have immigrated to countries such as the United States, Australia, or Canada. This number is significant, however, especially in relation to Korea's history. The country's foreign population has doubled twice in the last five years and continues to grow steadily. In response to such shifting demographics, particularly to some 200,000 foreign brides from over 67 countries and their 150,000 offspring, multiculturalism has become one of the most talked-about issues in Korea. Increasingly, the public, government, and many civic organizations are demanding that the country recognize and affirm its ethnic diversity. The notion of a single ethnic nationalism in contemporary Korea is being replaced by an emergent multiculturalism (Kim 2011b).

Korea has indeed had a long history of international marriages. The king of Gaya, Kim Su-ro, married a princess of Ayodhya, India,

in AD 48, according to the *Memorabilia of the Three Kingdoms*, and during the Goryeo dynasty, a succession of five kings married Yuan princesses. Recently, many foreign brides have married Korean men largely because of the shortage of marriageable women in the countryside. In effect, urban and industrial zones became "black holes" into which massive numbers of rural migrants, especially young women, were drawn. To compensate for the shortage and to attempt to keep men on the farm, the Korean government, especially local government, has spearheaded a campaign to recruit foreign brides, relying heavily on international marriage brokers. These foreign brides include Korean Chinese (*Joseonjok*), 32.7 percent; Han Chinese, 28.3 percent; Vietnamese, 19.1; and Filipina, 5.8 percent. There is an ethnographic account regarding marriage and labor migration in *Joseonjok* (Freeman 2011).

Korean version of multiculturalism

Some native Korean scholars are critical of many Koreans' misuse or misunderstanding of multiculturalism as a way of describing an increasingly ethnically and racially diverse Korea. Multiculturalism in this sense is being used in Korea as a counter- or contrasting concept to the idea of a single ethnic nationalism. Until recently, Koreans were not keenly aware of the complexities that come with multiculturalism. The prefix *multi-* was first introduced to refer to the growing number of international marriages involving unions between Koreans and persons of non-Korean ethnicities. The phrase *multicultural family* was adopted before the term *multiculturalism*. Because the term *multiculturalism* originated in and evolved from the concept of the multicultural family, most Koreans tend to think that multiculturalism only pertains to foreigners who married Koreans and to their children. Except for some activists in various NGOs, few members of the Korean public or officials in government recognize some 557,000 foreign workers, legal and illegal, as multicultural or protected by multiculturalism policy. Little effort has been made to

protect their human rights in Korea.

Even if there is some confusion about the concept of multiculturalism in Korea, Korean multiculturalism is moving the country away from its tradition of ethnic nationalism and policies of assimilation toward a genuine liberal multiculturalism modeled on the West. Koreans have come to understand that multiculturalism respects cultural diversity. Not many, though, have yet come to recognize that endorsing multiculturalism also entails respecting the right of minorities not be assimilated into Korean culture at the cost of their native culture. For this reason, Korea is in the early stages of multiculturalism.

Today, many Koreans, especially scholars, intellectuals, NGO activists, and the news media, are determined to implement a liberal multiculturalism. At present, multiculturalism in Korea is still mainly at the level of discourse, with little in the way of policy implementation except for some limited policies on behalf of foreign brides. However, Korea's efforts to achieve multiculturalism are sincere and genuine. Even if Korea is not traditionally an immigrant nation, Korea has a history of accommodating various ethnic and racial groups from the dawn of its civilization until the late nineteenth century, when ethnic nationalism came into being. Now there is a call to return to the ethos of civil harmony among heterogeneous people. What makes this call seem real for many people — realer than mere rhetoric — is the changing demographics of Korea. According to a report released 2 January 2013 by IOM (International Organization for Migration) Migration Research and Training Center, by the year 2030, Korea may need 3 million foreign laborers per year to fill the population gap created by its low birthrate. By 2050, the number needed could climb as high as 5 million.

Of late Korea has witnessed the fruits of multiculturalism in terms of its children. Some 200,000 foreign brides who married Korean grooms have had more than 150,000 offspring; together they have boosted the total Korean population to 50 million. In 2005, Korea had the lowest birthrate in its history, 1.076, which was one of

the lowest rates in the world. Demographers predicted that Korea's population would shrink by 0.02 percent yearly thereafter. Contrary to this pessimistic assessment, Korea's birthrate has crept upward, after hitting that low in 2005, to 1.24 in 2012, but in 2013 again it has decreased to 1.19. Despite of such a decrease, on 23 June, 2012, the total population of the country reached 50 million, and South Korea became a member of the "20-50-club," whose membership includes countries with a population over 50 million and a per capita GDP over $20,000. Current members include Japan (joined in 1987), the United States (1988), France and Italy (both in 1990), Germany (1991), and Great Britain (1996). Korea has now joined these seven countries, despite the devastating Korean War from 1950 to 1953. Korea partly owes its current membership in the 20-50-club to the influx of foreigners and to the children born to them.

Korea's movement toward multiculturalism appears to be meeting the key conditions of establishing successful multiculturalism posited by Will Kymlicka (2005:36). Korea's low birthrate and strong economy mean that foreign immigrants are needed to support the economy. Most Koreans are fully aware of multiculturalism and endorse its basic tenets. Various Korean civic organizations have become strong advocates of human rights for immigrants. Since 1993, Korea has enjoyed a mature democracy. No national minority threatens the mainstream Korean population. Finally, Korea has a cultural legacy and tradition of openness, which can help pave the way for a multicultural society (Kim 2011b).

Also, some big business conglomerates such as Samsung, LG, and Hana Banking Group, have begun to launch a major campaign for multicultural families. Most of all, some foreign brides actively participate in Korean political processes, in local, regional, and even central government. In fact, a woman from the Philippines, who was naturalized as a Korean citizen in 1998, became a member of the National Assembly in the 2012 general election as a ruling party member by way of the party's proportional representation. Of the

299 members of the National Assembly of Korea, 243 represent single-seat districts, and fifty-six seats are shared proportionally by their parties in representation. Becoming a member of the National Assembly would serve as a big booster of morale for multicultural families. Having multicultural citizens participating in government will help to hasten the full implementation of multiculturalism, thereby putting an end to the paradox of ethnic nationalism versus multiculturalism.

Korean Characteristic of Inwardness Versus Outward-Oriented Activities

East Asians—Chinese, Japanese, and Koreans—have generally been centripetal or inward looking. The distribution of world population today bears witness to this. Francis L. K. Hsu reports on the case of China, but the observation might apply equally well to Japan and Korea. Although Hsu's (1977:204) figures are outdated, they remain proportionally valid: "The population of Europe minus Russia stands today at about 450 million. But the white population of the two Americas alone comes to over 500 million. In other words, there are at least as many whites outside of their home continent as within." With the current population of China at 1.3 billion, one can grant Hsu's (1981:303) point that, "had the Chinese been as ready to emigrate as Europeans, it would not be difficult to imagine most of the world being Chinese." By 2012, the overseas Chinese population was only 3.8 percent of its homeland population of 1.3 billion, while the overseas Japanese population was only 2.0 percent of its homeland population of 128 million.

Although Koreans are centripetal and inward looking, the overseas Korean population is a surprising 13.6 percent of 50 million South Koreans. About 7 million ethnic Koreans live in seventy-three countries worldwide, ranging from over two million

in China and the United States, to nearly 1 million in Japan, to one in Kiribati, San Marino, and Guyana. The overseas Korean population is proportionally larger than that of its neighbors, owing partly to the country's unfortunate history of foreign domination by hostile neighbors. Whatever the origins of the Korean diaspora, many Korean business firms have benefited from overseas Koreans in marketing their industrial products.

"Hermit Kingdom" no more

Outwardly directed. In contrast to century ago, nowadays many Koreans participate in globalization through outwardly directed activities. Korea has diplomatic relations with 189 countries, the exceptions being Cuba, Syria, Macedonia, Monaco, and a few others. Over 1,200 diplomatic personnel are stationed in overseas embassies. To promote Korean trade, business, and investment, the state-owned Korea Trade Investment Promotion Agency(KOTRA) had 119 branch offices in 119 cities from eighty-one countries as of 2012. Besides, over 10,000 KOICA volunteers have participated in sixty-five countries, and nearly 23,332 Korean Christian missionaries are carrying out their mission work in 169 countries. In the private sector, among the 11,733 Korean firms with fifty or more employees, 21.3 percent have branches in over 150 countries, with investments of over $44 billion. By April 2012, there were 239,213 Korean students studying overseas: most of these students were in the United States (73,351, or 30.7 percent), China (62,855, or 26.3 percent), and Great Britain (12,580, or 5.3 percent), while some 89,537 foreign students are studying in Korea. The outgoing traffic is heavier than the incoming.

In other efforts to shake off its former isolation, Korea has invited people from all over the world to events held on its peninsula. Past events included the forty-second World Shooting Championship in Seoul in 1978, the 1988 Summer Olympics in Seoul, the 2002 Fédération Internationale de Football Association's World Cup (co-hosted with Japan), the 2002 Busan Asian Games, the 2003 Daegu

Summer Universiade, the summit in November 2010 of the Group of Twenty (G-20), the 2011 Daegu World Athletics Championship, the Nuclear Summit in Seoul in 2012, and the EXPO 2012 in Yeosu. Future events scheduled include the 2014 Incheon Asian Games, the 2015 Gwangju Summer Universiade, and, most notable of all, the 2018 Winter Olympic Games in Pyeongchang. Hosting the Winter Olympics means so much to Koreans after previous bids were twice unsuccessful. The people of Pyeongchang persevered for twelve consecutive years in their effort to win the bid.

Korea's outgoing effort in Free Trade Agreements. As of 2013, Korea has signed an FTA with 47 countries, including Chile; India; four EFTA countries, including Switzerland, Norway, Iceland, and Principality of Liechtenstein; ten Associates of Southeast Asian Nations, including Indonesia, Malaysia, the Philippines, Singapore, Thailand, Brunei, Vietnam, Laos, Myanmar, and Cambodia twenty-eight European Union countries, including Australia, Belgium, Bulgaria, Croatia, Cyprus, the Czech Republic, Denmark, Estonia, Finland, France, Germany, Greece, Hungary, Ireland, Italy, Latvia, Luxembourg, Malta, the Netherlands, Poland, Portugal, Romania, Slovakia, Slovenia, Spain, Sweden, and the United Kingdom; Peru, the United States, and Turkey. Also, Korea has signed additional three countries and currently nine additional countries are in under negotiation. As late as 8 April 2014, Korea signed a FTA with Australia.

Besides these treaties, South Korea is now being invited to the table as an equal by its two towering neighbors. At an annual meeting in Beijing on 13 May 2012, Chinese Premier Wen Jia-bao, Japanese Prime Minister Noda Yoshihiko, and Korean President Lee Myung-bak agreed to start official negotiations on a trilateral free-trade pact within the year 2012. As it so happens, all three of these leaders were replaced in 2012, so now it is up their successors to carry through with the plan.

"Hallyu" as a sign of Korea's popularity in the global community.
Recently, the Korean pop cultural wave known as *Hallyu* has
generated worldwide interest beyond Korea and its neighboring
countries. *Hallyu* principally produces entertainment in three
different media: pop music (K-pop), television drama (K-drama), and
movies (K-movies). The movement grew out of public enthusiasm
for Korean movies and television soap operas, as well as musical
performances by Korean singers and dancers, in Japan, China,
Taiwan, and other Southeast Asian countries in the early 2000s.
Some of these smash-hit soap operas, such as *Dae Jang Geum* (*Jewel in
the Palace*), were set in the dynastic past, especially the Joseon period,
which appealed to Korean cultural nostalgia. Lee Young-ae[Yi Yeong-
ae], the actress who played the female protagonist in *Dae Jang Geum*,
has been very popular in China, Hong Kong, Taiwan, and elsewhere.
Television networks there often broadcast reruns of the show.

K-pop is also popular in African countries such as Uganda,
Ethiopia, and Kenya, where students are studying the Korean
language because of the impact of *Hallyu*. In Thailand, *Hallyu* has
also sparked an interest in learning the Korean language. There is a
Hallyu Graduate School at The Catholic University of Korea. The
CUK's e-Learning campaign to teach the Korean language to foreign
brides who married Korean men offers instruction to over 100,000
foreign brides who live in Korea and also to people around the world
over the Internet free of charge. Currently, some 8,000 people from
over 70 countries are taking the online Korean language courses. To
meet the growing demand for learning the Korean language, since 4
December 2013, under the nick name of "Quick Korean," the CUK
has developed a newly revised version of its online Korean language
learning program for people around the world. And these signed up
for this free on-line educational program and enrollment is increasing
every day.

K-pop fever has even grabbed the attention of scholars (Park 2004,
2005). Perhaps scholarly studies on *Hallyu* will help sustain the wave.

As the Korean wave washed more widely out into the world, it became more than merely a fad in its effect on Korea. More than anything else, *Hallyu* put Korea on the world map. It has helped dispel stereotypes and old clichés of Korea as an oriental isolate. Because of the wave, the number of foreign visitors to Korea reached an all-time high of 6 million in 2005, when the wave was at its peak. The wave has also had a considerable economic and political impact on Korea, though it is difficult to measure and quantify it exactly. Nevertheless, according to a May 2012 survey conducted by the Ministry of Culture, Sports and Tourism, together with the Korean Foundation, of 100 Korean corporate CEOs questioned, 95 percent responded that K-pop contributed to promoting business abroad. In another survey of 4,500 people, including foreign students studying in Korea, more than half of Asian students (51.7 percent) said they were influenced by *Hallyu* when making the decision to study in Korea. Students picked K-pop (28.2 percent) as their favorite aspect of *Hallyu*, followed by Korean food (20.9 percent), TV dramas (20.9 percent), and electronics (18.9 percent), as reported by the *Korea Herald* in May 2012.

Not only is Korean television known outside Korea, but so is Korean music. *Samulnori* is a style of music performed using four instruments, including small and large gongs made of bronze and leather, a double-headed hourglass, and barrel drums. The instruments are distinctly different in terms of musical range, timbre, and resonance, yet their sounds are brought together to form a harmonious whole. This traditional Korean farmers' outdoor musical performance was adapted in the 1970s for indoor performances. In the spring of 2004, a *Samulnori* team organized and led by Kim Duk Soo[Gim Deok-su] performed in ten cities in the United States and Canada to rave reviews. The traditional vocal music of *Pansori* is another component of popular culture regaining reputation. The songs of *Pansori* tend to be very long, some of them taking more than eight hours to perform. *Pansori* alternates between slow and fast tempos, quick and dramatic passages, and melodic passages and passages rendered in everyday

speech. Performed by a single vocalist who tells a long story, the music elicits many different emotions, ranging from sidesplitting laughter to profuse tears. Because it is a unique genre of traditional Korean music, *Pansori* vocalists were invited to perform in Lyon, France, in April 2006.

Psy and his Gangnam style. Of all K-pop stars in 2012, Psy was the one who attracted the most attention for his song and video "Gangnam Style." Psy was thirty-four years old in 2012, and his real name is Park Jae-sang. He once studied in the United States. The literal meaning of *Gangnam* is "south of the Hangang," and Gangnam style refers to the lifestyle of this most posh district in Seoul, newly developed after the Korean economy began to take off in the early 1970s. To most Koreans, Gangnam is a symbol of newfound riches and luxury, even extravagance.

The popularity of Psy's "Gangnam Style" went viral over the Internet. In December 2012, the music video became the first video in the history of the Internet to be viewed more than one billion times. As of January 2013, the music video had been viewed over 1.10 billion times on YouTube and became the site's most-watched video. Also, his inspiring dance touched off a craze in Paris, Rome, Milan, and Berlin. By the end of 2012, the song had topped the music charts of more than 30 countries, including Canada, France, Germany, Italy, Russia, and England. "Gangnam Style" is even popular among notable world leaders, such as British Prime Minister David Cameron and U.S. president Barak Obama. In fact, on 9 December 2012, Psy performed in front of the American first family at the "Christmas in Washington" event in Washington, D.C. Psy even received a Guinness World Record for his spectacular success. Psy's new video "Gentleman" had more than 100 million hits on YouTube less than five days after its release.

On 28 March 2014, the *Korea Herald* has reported that the *Hallyu* has buoyed even Korean fashion. According to the report,

hundreds of Chinese fans were frenzy at the opening of Seoul Fashion Week on 26 March 2014 when K-pop boy group EXO took the catwalk presenting the latest works by young Korean designers. It has been reported that K-pop and Korean dramas play an important role in attracting attention to Korean fashion, particularly from China and Hong Kong. The Seoul Design Foundation has reported that, "the Korean Wave, *Hallyu*, is driving the popularity of not just music, but also fashion."

Almost everyone who knows something about *Hallyu* wonders why it has received such enthusiastic support from so many people around the world. Japanese television producer for the Japanese NHK network Ogawa Junko told the *Dong-A Ilbo*, on 6 January 2004, that it has not come about simply because the actors and actresses in these movies and shows are handsome and beautiful but because the Japanese viewing audience is attracted by Korean culture itself. To me, Psy's performance, combining music with hobby-horse dance steps, seems to blend two old Korean cultural traditions: the horse-riding spirit of the Goguryeo people and the "divine wind" (*sinparam* in Korean, meaning "elation or high spirits," and *kamikaze* in Japanese) of the whirling shamanistic ritual of *gut*. Daniel Tudor (2012:124) suggests that "*Sinparam* may have a Buddhist underpinning as well as shamanist one, since it involves the acceptance of suffering (or the fact that 'life is pain') and seeing that the way around this is through transcendence rather than the pursuit of revenge or correction."

After the television soap opera *Gyeoul Yeonga* (Winter Sonata) aired in Japan, the Japanese did much to spread the wave. Many Japanese visited Korea to see the settings where the soap opera was filmed. Japanese audiences enthusiastically greeted *Hallyu* stars at the airport whenever they visited Japan. Nevertheless, compared to *Hallyu* in the early 2000s, the Japanese reception of Psy has been only lukewarm. Presumably this has something to do with the presently strained diplomatic relations between Korea and Japan, ratcheted up in 2012, over territorial disputes concerning Dokdo and the unsettled issue of

the Korean "comfort women" (or sex slaves) conscripted during World War II and sent to battle zones to work in brothels for Japanese soldiers.

Paradox of inwardness versus outwardness

In 1993 when I was living in an old missionary's house on the campus of Yonsei University as a senior Fulbright Researcher and Lecturer, my next-door neighbor, who was the great-grandson of an American missionary, told me that even though he was born in Korea and grew up there (except for a few years of college in the United States), he still could not understand Koreans' values when it came to inwardness versus outwardness. In characterizing Koreans' conception of globalization, he used the analogy of a tadpole, saying that to most, Korean globalization means being a tadpole in someone's else pond rather than having others come to your pond.

Indeed, to most Koreans, globalization means looking outside or going outside one's own country. Korea established a foothold in the Arctic by becoming a permanent observer to the Arctic Council on 15 May 2012, stepping up its foray into the region where melting ice sheets are boosting the potential for maritime logistics, resource development, and scientific research. In the case of Foreign Direct Investment (FDI), some experts say that Korea's outward FDI is much greater than its inward FDI. Before 1960, Korea did not permit inward FDI. Even when the Korean economy was in a period of rapid growth, Koreans discouraged inward FDI. Foreign investors point to the continuing importance of family connections in Korea, lack of transparency, and predictability in business environments as reasons for low foreign investment in Korea. Some believe that "the Korean economy might grow faster if Korea invested less abroad and devoted more of its scarce domestic savings to domestic investment" (Eichengreen et al. 2012:269); according to Barry Eichengreen and his associates, "Korea has one of the lowest service-sector shares of inward FDI in the OECD; of 21 OECD countries, only Norway and Italy had lower service sector shares in 2006." Perhaps Korea's

aversion to foreign investment might have something to do with the twentieth-century Japanese colonial occupation.

At any event, Koreans are preoccupied with the territory boundary concept of ours (*uri*) versus theirs. To Koreans, "hometown" (*gohyang*) has a much stronger appeal than the word does in English. Koreans are attached very strongly to their *gohyang* and inwardly directed in their emotion and sentiment, yet they act outwardly in their global activities, which is a paradox.

Environmental Conservation and Restoration

It is widely known to the outside world that Koreans are so preoccupied with economic development and industrialization that it might be supposed that they do not care much about environmental conservation. Paradoxical though it may sound, traditionally Koreans have been conscientious about environmental conservation. While Westerners tend to believe that human beings are the center of the universe and thus can control and challenge nature, up until recently Koreans have held a view of the universe in which human beings, nature, and God are equal, coexisting entities. Many Korean paintings, novels, and indigenous beliefs illustrate these views (T. Kim 1977). This worldview stipulates that human beings essentially remain integrated with nature. Koreans must have been natural environmentalists and conservationists to have maintained a balanced ecosystem for so long.

The traditional Korean worldview began to change, however, with the wave of economic development and industrialization that began in the mid-1960s. Because of the priority given to "development for development's sake," everything else, including human rights, civil liberty, and environmental conservation, became secondary. During the early stages of economic development in Korea, even some informed citizens and intellectuals tended to think that Koreans

had to accept the negative consequences of environmental problems as the price to pay for development. Air pollution was not even an issue until the 1970s. The government simply picked the sites and built the plants. Until very recently, local people had to deal with it. Anyone who advocated for environmental protection and joined rallies against various development projects was labeled an antigovernment activist. As a result, Korean ecosystems were altered and the environment seriously damaged, in some cases irreparably.

Beginning in the 1980s, an environmental grass roots movement sprang up to oppose reckless development projects throughout the nation. One example is what happened in Buan-gun, Jeollanam-do. In 2003, when the Korean government was seeking a repository site for nuclear waste, Buan-gun submitted a proposal to the central government to host its facility at Wido, a small island in the county. However, citizens of that county vehemently opposed the proposal and furious demonstrations raged on for months until the government finally cancelled the plan altogether. The conservationists have sometimes been successful in stopping the government's plans to construct a dam, as was the case with Yeongwol Dam in the Donggang.

Paradoxically, as the Korean standard of living has improved, Koreans have become increasingly aware of environmental problems. Nongovernmental organizations for environmental conservation have begun to organize, and the Korean government created an agency to regulate the environment at the ministerial level and enacting a series of environmental laws. To uphold the environmental goal of creating a "symbiotic community of all living organisms," in 1994 the Korean government promoted the Environmental Agency to ministry status and has promulgated thirty-three environmental laws as of 2002 under the new ministry's directive. Also, Korea has signed a total of forty-four environmental conservation agreements, including the United Nations Framework Convention on Climatic Change and the Montreal Protocol on Substances that Deplete the Ozone Layer.

Environmental disturbance

Mountain ranges. The most visible environmental destruction has taken place in the Great Baekdu Mountain Range (Baekdudaegan), the backbone of the Korean mountain range originating with Korea's tallest mountain, Baekdusan (2,750 meters). The steep, high mountain range and dense forests of the eastern slope sweep all the way down the peninsula to Jirisan (Mt. Jiri) (1,915 meters) in Gyeongsangnam-do and Jeollanam-do. The entire length of the Great Baekdu Mountain Range is 1,484.3 kilometers. Other Korean mountains and their ranges connect to or branch off of the Great Baekdu Mountain Range. Because of the construction of roads, dams, mining, hot springs, and the cultivation of vegetables that grow well in the cooler region of the highlands, the southern portion of the mountain range below the DMZ has been badly damaged.

To prevent further destruction, in December 2004 the Korean government introduced a bill. At the same time, the Ministry of Agriculture (currently, the Ministry of Agriculture, Food and Rural Affairs under the Park Geun-hye administration) announced a plan to restore 215 damaged sites covering 3,688 hectares by planting trees until 2015. Also, the Ministry of the Environment and the Korea Forestry Service proposed to restore 535,918 hectares of land, but local governments included in the restoration plan demanded that this be reduced to 239,479 hectares (44.6 percent of the proposal). This is an indication that, for local government, development still trumps conservation.

Restoration of the Cheonggyecheon. The 5.8 kilometer-long(3.6 miles) Cheonggyecheon (Cheonggye Stream) runs through the heart of Seoul. It had been considered troublesome for more than half a millennium because of occasional floods, ever since the capital of the Joseon dynasty had been relocated there in 1394. Several Joseon kings such as Taejong (1400-1418), Sejong (1418-1450), Yeongjo (1724-1776), and Jeongjo (1776-1800) mobilized thousands of people to clean up the stream and dig its course more deeply to control flooding. As

the stream became polluted, functioning as the city sewage system beginning in 1920 through the early 1940s, Japanese authorities planned to fill it in to make a new road, but the plan never materialized. In 1958, the road project was resumed, and in 1963, as part of a government-led industrialization project, the stream was completely covered over with concrete. On top of the newly built concrete road, an overpass bridge was built.

In 1991, a small group of academics, environmentalists (especially Green Korea United or *Noksaek Yeonhap*), writers, and informed citizens, joined later by politicians (including then mayoral candidate Lee Myung-bak), launched a methodical campaign to restore the stream by removing the concrete cover, including the overpass bridge. *Noksaek Yeonhap,* or Green Korea United (GKU), is a nongovernmental civic organization working to protect ecosystems and to promote public awareness in order to harmonize people with nature, including protecting forests and wildlife. Their headquarters are in Seoul, with some forty staff members and 15,000 members. The GKU has been monitoring the environmental effects of 93 U.S. military bases since 1996 and also campaigned against the Saemangeum reclamation project to preserve South Korea's largest and most significant wetland. The GKU built an experimental eco-village with local residents. It also works for the Baekdudaegan conservation project. Similar organizations include the Korean Association for Conservation of Nature, Seoul Free-cycle Network, Northeast Asian Forest Forum, Word from the Forest, and others.

Despite opposition by shop owners and merchants in the surrounding area, on 1 July 2003, as Seoul's newly elected mayor, Lee Myung-bak began the restoration project for the Cheonggyecheon. The project was finally completed on 1 October 2005 and included the construction of twenty-two bridges, a mixture of renovated originals and newly built replicas. The stream now looks attractive and charming, and the trees planted alongside the dikes add aesthetic beauty to the city. The restoration not only attracts many tourists from Korea and abroad,

A Scene of the Cheonggyecheon After the Restoration

but it also brought back freshwater fish, frogs, and birds such as swallows, which were not found in Seoul before the restoration due to pollution. The temperature of the areas surrounding the restored stream has been found to be cooler than it is in other sections of the city. Furthermore, the restoration boosted the business activities of the merchants who once opposed the project and increased the value of real estate in the surrounding areas. On 4 October 2005, Mayor Lee Myung-bak said, "The restoration of the environment, history, and cultural relics resulted in economic effects. The city has become livable for foreigners and friendly to foreign companies." The restoration of the stream became one of the mayor's important accomplishments and later helped in his bid for the presidency. On the downside, the stream does come with costs: it takes 120,000 tons of water per day to keep it running continuously, and it needs over 30,000 kilowatt hours of electricity a day, equivalent to that used by over 3,000 households daily. Keeping the Cheonggyecheon flowing costs about 1,800 million *won* (about $1.7 million) per year.

Nanjido ecological park. The transformation of the Nanjido Waste Repository into an ecological park is a meaningful success story from an ecological standpoint. The nearly 3 million square meters of Nanjido were created over a long period of time by the Hangang. Nanjido was an island that had drawn little attention except from some fishermen before it became the major repository of household waste for over 10 million Seoulites. From 1978 to 1993, when the site was closed because it had been filled to capacity, 92 million cubic meters of waste from the Seoul metropolitan area was deposited there. The elevation of Nanjido was originally only seven meters, but the accumulated waste raised it to a 100-meter high mountain. When the repository was in use, it created all sorts of environmental hazards, not to mention an unbearable stench. Winds often carried the odor to distant sections of the city. Because of the methane gas generated by organic particles in the lower layers, there were 1,400 fires in fifteen years, some lasting for forty-five days.

The plan to transform the waste repository into an ecological park began in 1991, two years before the site was closed, and the restoration project was completed in 2001. The 942,000 square-meter waste site has now been transformed into an attractive ecological park. The site has become a sanctuary for over 400 species of plants and insects as well as over 9 million human visitors annually.

In 1998, the Sangam-dong Soccer Stadium, the largest and most modern soccer field in Korea, was built on this site. The stadium eventually hosted the 2002 FIFA World Cup. Furthermore, the city built parks, a golf course, and other sports and recreation facilities on the site; it also established the Digital Media City there to lure high-tech industries. Some reputable high-tech industries have already moved in, and others are planning to build facilities there. On the whole, it is one of the world's most amazing projects successfully transforming a waste repository into a manmade park and complexes.

A Scene of the Nanjido Park After the Transformation
of the Landfill to an Ecological Park

DMZ as an eco-zone. The DMZ, which zigzags across the middle
of the Korean peninsula, separates North and South Korea. It was
established in 1953 when a cease-fire was declared to the Korean
War to prevent inter-Korean acts of hostility. The DMZ runs along
a line 248 kilometers (155 miles) long, four kilometers (1.25 miles) wide,
and two kilometers on each side. The DMZ and the surrounding area
within five to ten kilometers south of the DMZ remains a heavily
guarded no-man's land. Covering 992 square kilometers, the DMZ
includes mountains, fields, valleys, basins, and several rivers. The
region provides habitats and migration routes for aquatic birds and
cranes.

The inaccessibility of the DMZ for more than half a century
allowed war-ravaged forests to return to their natural state, and the
DMZ and surrounding areas now serve as a sanctuary for many
endangered species of plants and animals. It is a natural laboratory
for environmentalists and ecologists to study. Recently, for the first

School Children Take Fieldtrip Along the DMZ Fence

DMZ Serves as a Sanctuary for Many Animals and Plants,
Including Deer Shown in the Photo

time, a research team of South Koreans found eleven types of rare animals and 2,716 species of plants and animals in the area. Such ecological studies are expected to continue in the future. If North and South Korea could come to a formal agreement over the DMZ, the two Koreas could create the world's most valuable ecological park and laboratory, which would attract many visitors from all over to study an ecosystem in action.

Addressing the U.S. Congress on 8 May 2013 during her four-day state visit to the U.S., Korean President Park Geun-hye announced her hopes to establish an international park that "sends a message of peace to all humanity." She added that the DMZ had the "potential to ensure that the demilitarized zone strengthens peace not undermines it." In response to the president's address, Seoul has launched a government-wide effort to draw up plans for establishing Park's idea. According to a report made by the *Korea Herald*, 13 May 2013, "The concerned ministries that will be proposed in talks with North Korea are being drawn up." Although the government is expected to build up momentum for the plans, observers say that realizing them will be difficult due to heightened tension on the peninsula at the time this book is being written. In fact, North Korea has cut off all communication with Seoul, and its actions have resulted in the temporary shutdown of the Gaeseong industrial complex from 3 April 2013 to 16 September 2013. The industrial complex was established in 2004 as a symbol of the last active inter-Korean economic cooperation. It remains to be seen what North Korea's response will be about plans for a "peace park."

Conservation and changes in Korean burial culture. Korea's population density is rather high: twentieth in the world, with 497 persons per square kilometer in 2011. Only 20 percent of Korean land is arable. Despite the dearness of land, 1 percent of all the land in Korea is devoted to burials, and over 130,000 new burial mounds are erected yearly. Anyone who has traveled in Korea, especially to

the countryside, finds the most attractive sites occupied by burial mounds. As a consequence, living Koreans have to compete with the dead for land. Many burial mounds not only take up a large amount of space; they also disturb the environment.

To conserve Korea's available land and preserve its environment, the government and concerned citizens have launched a campaign to stop the building of large burial mounds, suggesting cremation as an alternative. Traditionally, according to Korean custom, cremation was not common, being limited to some Buddhists, including monks and nuns, and people who died of highly contagious diseases. However, since this campaign began, the rate of cremation has increased steadily from 5.8 percent in 1955, 13.7 percent in 1981, 52.6 percent in 2005, and by 2011, all the way to 71.1 percent. This emergent cremation culture will be helpful in preserving the natural beauty of mountainous Korea since burials have long been concentrated in mountainous areas. Such a conservation effort is important because mountains and hills cover nearly 70 percent of the Korean peninsula.

Yellow dust and Korean air. Despite massive development activities in Korea over the past several decades, Korean air is cleaner now than it was in the 1970s thanks to conservation efforts. However, Korea cannot control polluted air resulting from the yellow dust (*hwangsa*) that spreads over the peninsula beginning in early spring, carried eastward from the Gobi desert by low atmospheric pressure. Yellow dust clouds usually arrive more than ten times before disappearing in the summer. A thick yellow dust like this occurred on 30 March 2007, having a density of over 800 micrograms (one millionth of a gram) per cubic meter. The total amount of dust was estimated to have been from 46,000 to 86,000 tons, enough to fill four or five fifteen-ton dump trucks. On that day, downtown Seoul was nearly empty since citizens were unwilling to go outside, and many outdoor activities were either canceled or restricted.

What can Korea do about this troublesome phenomenon other than issue warnings to alert its citizens? Many people disturbed by these dust clouds can only lament, "We pray that China reaches a mature stage of development soon, so it can make every effort to deal with environmental issues such as preserving clean air, as Koreans have done."

Green growth and the economy. In another move to reconcile economic development with protection of the environment, in August 2008 Korean President Lee Myung-bak declared green growth to be the core of a new national vision for economic growth. Since the launch of the Global Green Growth Institute (GGGI) in June 2010, it has evolved from a small South Korean nonprofit into an organization with an international presence. It currently has some sixty staff members and three regional offices — in Abu Dhabi, Copenhagen, and London, in addition to its Seoul headquarters. The GGGI had an estimated 2012 budget of more than $35 billion. President Lee has envisioned that a low carbon emission, green growth strategy fits with the nation's long-term growth. To this end, President Lee contributed $83.6 billion, amounting to 2 percent of Korea's GDP. The Park Geun-hye administration's view on green growth remains to be seen.

Concurring with the green growth movement, urban farming spreads fast in Korea with growing interest in healthy lifestyle, food safety and environment. According to a feature story published in the *Korea Herald*, dated on 29-30 March 2014, ". . . Seoul has been witnessing the rise of a civic movement aimed at embracing a slow but fruitful life. All the center of the movement is an army of urban farmers who are betting on a green future for the city rather than pursuing a faster, and perhaps easier life. From abandoned plots in inner city areas and plastic boxes on apartment balconies, to rooftop gardening, a number of urban dwellers are reconnecting with the earth in the heart of metropolis. . . According to the Seoul city

government, the number of city farms surged drastically from 66 in 2010 to 2,056 last year [2013])."

In addition, Korea is now the headquarters for the Green Climate Fund (GCF), a fund within the United Nations organization to transfer money from the developed to the developing world to assist developing countries in adaptation and mitigation practices to counter climate change. The GCF is based in Songdo, Incheon, and the agreement between Korea, Incheon, and the U.N. Green Climate Fund was entered into in 2013. This organization is governed by a board of twenty-four members and initially supported by an interim secretariat. The GCF will support projects, programs, policies, and other activities in developing countries, and aims to raise $100 billion a year by 2020.

All in all, Korea has made significant progress on issues related to environmental protection and conservation despite its aggressive economic growth. It is hoped that Korea can come up with other ways to wed economic development and environmental protection in a workable relationship.

Persistent Confucianism and a Female President

Before Korea was influenced by Chinese Confucianism—with its tenets of five primary social relationships, one being that men dominate women—traditional Korean society appeared to be a society of relative gender equality. As mentioned previously, in fact during the Silla dynasty, there were three queens: twenty-seventh queen Seondeok yeowang (632-647), twenty-eighth Jindeok yeowang (647-654), and fifty-first Jinseong yeowang (887-897).

Confucianism was introduced to Korea during the Three Kingdoms period. By the fourteenth century it had become an integral part of Korean culture, and by the sixteenth century it came to dominate Korean thought. Confucianism teaches the importance

of a hierarchical order based on five fundamental social relations: father-son, ruler-subject, elder brother-younger brother, husband-wife, and friend-friend. The paternal authority of the father/husband over the mother/wife is highly valued. Confucianism became the principal ethic governing the Korean way of life, and Korean males dominated females from the end of the fourteenth century to the twentieth century.

Ever since Korea established itself as an independent republic in 1948, many outspoken Korean "sisters" have worked hard to improve female rights, but the major breakthrough came from a Constitutional Court decision. On 5 February 2005, the Korean Constitutional Court ruled that the *hojeok* system, based on male-oriented family registries, was unconstitutional, which then made way for greater gender equality. Before that, only male members could be the "head" (or *hoju*) of a household, and children had to take the surname of their fathers. Following the court decision, in March 2005, the Korean National Assembly passed a statute abolishing the *hoju* system.

The introduction of a women's rights movement has done much to change the old patterns of women's rights. In July 2005, the Supreme Court ruled that women, even married women, had an equal right to share clan property. Younger generations of Koreans today prefer to have girl children over boys. Korea's women's rights movement has come a long way from the time when Korean women put up with the "three rules of obedience." Consequently, Korea had its first female prime minister in 2006.

Finally Koreans elect a woman president

Korea has an historical reputation for adhering more staunchly to Confucian ethics than do the Chinese, with whom they originated. Nevertheless, on 19 December 2012, the day of South Korea's presidential election, sixty-year-old Park Geun-hye was elected president.

The prediction had been that the margin between Park, a member of the ruling party, and the opposition party candidate Moon Jae-in[Mun Jae-in] would be very narrow, yet Park won with a rather comfortable margin of over 1 million votes (1,080,935). Park received 15,770,926 (51.55 percent) out of 30,723,431 valid ballots cast; Moon received 14,689,961 (48.02 percent). Park Geun-hye is the daughter of former president Park Chung-hee, who led the military coup in 1961 and became president, holding power until he was assassinated by his own Korean Central Intelligence Agency chief on 26 October 1979. Park Geun-hye's misfortune started before she lost her father. Her mother was assassinated five years before her father was. On 15 August 1974, while Park's mother attended a Liberation Day celebration, she was shot dead by an assassin. At the time Park Geun-hye was studying in France. When she returned to Korea upon the death of her mother, she played the role of first lady in lieu of her mother in the presidential Blue House (Cheongwadae) until her father was killed. Because she lived in the presidential mansion for eighteen years, from 1961 to 1979, she will now be returning to a familiar place.

By winning the presidential election, Park has set several records. First, she became the first female president in the history of the Korean republic. Not only is she the first female president of Korea; New, she is the only top female political leader in East Asia–including China, Taiwan, and Japan. Second, Park became the first Korean president whose father was also president of Korea. Third, Park is the first Korean president to have received a majority of votes, with 51.55 percent, since Korea adopted direct election by popular vote in 1987. Fourth, she became the first Korean president who had never married. Fifth, Park is the first Korean president with a college degree in science, specifically electronic engineering. After the election, many people around the world were surprised, and some were even shocked, at Korea's demonstration of democracy in action. Perhaps this election will prove to be the most remarkable transformation for

The Inauguration of Park Geun-hye, Korea's First Woman President

Korea in its sixty-four-year history of democracy. Koreans have a way of surprising the people of the world!

What must also be taken into account in this watershed event is that women in Korea currently occupy only 4.6 percent of high government offices. Of 281 high civil servants, including ministers, vice ministers, and high echelon civil servants whose ranking is *il-geup* and above, only thirteen (4.6 percent) of them are women. Eight of them are *il-geup*, three are vice ministers, and two are ministers, including the Minister of Gender Equality and Family (*Dong-A Ilbo,*

4 June 2012). By organizing of the Minister of Oceans and Fisheries in February 2014, there is only one woman minister in the Park's government. Such a pattern not only holds in bureaucracy but prevails in big business as well in Korea. Seen from this perspective, President Park's victory presents an even bigger paradox than it might seem at first.

Postscript

Traditionally, most anthropological works have been written by Western anthropologists about non-Western societies. Because of cultural differences among societies, it is generally argued that doing fieldwork in an alien society has some distinct disadvantages over doing fieldwork at home. Naturally, the outside anthropologist has to learn a new language, become familiar with an alien culture, and endure many hardships. Consequently, it takes the outside anthropologist longer to research the same or nearly the same semantic categories of understanding as it would a native.

However, beginning in the mid-1960s, and especially from the early 1980s, a growing number of anthropologists began to study their own society the way they have studied others. Accordingly, the literature about the constraints and contingencies of doing research in one's own society has been rapidly expanding. Suddenly, an increasing number of anthropologists who have been doing their research at home and/or near it began to discuss the difficulties involved.

For my own part, while I was doing my research in the American South, I took advantage of being a neutral person, an Asian, in the biracial dichotomy of the South. Anthropologist Hortense Powdermaker (1966:13), an American, did her study of a rural community in Mississippi in the same community where I did my fieldwork. She felt that her fieldwork in that community was far more difficult and complex than the fieldwork she did in "exotic" cultures: "True, I did not have to learn a new language and the community

was a subsection of my culture with a known history. But I had to find my way and fit into a southern community which, even in the mid-thirties, was characterized by deep fears and anxieties of both Negroes and Whites." A friend of mine, Emiko Ohnuki-Tierney (1984a:585), a Japanese American anthropologist, has pointed out that foreign anthropologists have a tremendous advantage: "All foreigners, especially Westerners, usually receive the red-carpet treatment from the Japanese, who go out of their way to accommodate their visitors." I also found this true when I was doing fieldwork in a rural Korean village, Yeomul-ri. I was unable to compete with a Western Catholic priest who drew the attention of all the villagers. I was left alone, unnoticed (Kim 2002:51-52).

Methods courses in anthropology teach students that anthropologists have to study others societies than their own to acquire proper reflexivity. Reflexivity is the (imperfect) antidote to one's own cultural biases; reflexivity helps one to be more objective—one of the essential ingredients in scientific work. Emiko Ohnuki-Tierney (1984a:584) had this to say about maintaining reflexivity:

> I experienced this difficulty of distancing myself from Japanese culture although I had been away from Japanese society, both physically and psychologically, for two decades. . . . When I returned to Japan in 1979 to undertake anthropological research . . . among my own people in Kobe, they seemed strange, with intriguing behavioral patterns and thought processes. Everywhere I went I observed incessantly and took copious notes. Astonishingly, however, my vivid reactions became increasingly milder after only a month and a half, and I found myself becoming more and more like "them."

What Ohnuki-Tierney experienced is close to what I experienced myself upon my return to Korea after a thirty-six-year absence. After ten years or so, I believe I have become almost completely re-encultured into Korean society. I cannot pretend to be an outsider

any more.

Maintaining distance from an emotionally related issue is hard work. From the mid-1980s to the late 1980s, I conducted my fieldwork on Korean families dispersed before, during, and after the Korean War. I listened to the poignant stories of their separations on television as part of a "reunion telethon" that was meant to bring together families who had been separated by the North-South strife. As I listened to these stories, I felt it was almost impossible to maintain a cool scientific distance. In the book that resulted from that fieldwork, I confessed my struggles with objectivity:

> It has been difficult for me to write about myself and "my own people" and yet remain objective. In this book I have tried to maintain a balance between the "compassion" of being a native anthropologist doing fieldwork with "my own people" and the "detachment" of being a "scientist." In attempting to depict the struggles of millions of sundered Koreans, the anguish of the war that I also experienced tortured me day after day. It was painful to complete this book. Nonetheless, as Miles Richardson once asked, "If the anthropologist does not tell the human myth, then who will?" (Kim 1988a:145).

Having studied parts of both worlds, East and West, not only for a few years but for over half a century since 1963, I have come to the conclusion that for anthropologists, or for that matter all social scientists, there is no distinctive advantage to being an insider/native as opposed to an outsider/foreigner when it comes to doing research and writing about it. Although I have made every effort to maximize my identity as a researcher in terms of being an insider and being an outsider, I have often felt that I am neither an insider who can make good use of his access nor an outsider who can capitalize on his ethnic or racial otherness. Perhaps I am simply a betwixt-and-between.

Anyone who writes about Korea today no longer writes about

a homogeneous, uniform society with a single ethnic group and culture, as some foreign observers once considered Korea. Koreans are as heterogeneous as any other industrialized society in the world. Heterogeneity reminds me of what Emmett Grogan once said: "anything anybody can say about America is true" (Marty 1977:134) because America is so heterogeneous that everything can be discovered there if one looks far and wide. Such is also the case with the American South. As my dear friend Miles Richardson (1977:321) points out, in the South there is James Earl Ray, assassin of Martin Luther King, Jr., on the one hand, and James Earl Carter, a strong human rights advocate, on the other. The same thing can be said about Korea: anything anybody can say about Korea is true, too.

Let me bring this book to an end with a final thought on the parallels between the American South and Korea. Throughout I have described in detail Korea's rapid transformation. There is no question that Korea has transformed more quickly than some other societies. That being said, though, it seems to me that such rapid transformation is also what I witnessed in the American South, my adopted home. In the following description by the celebrated W. J. Cash (1941:x) one can easily substitute "Korea" for "the South": "The South, one might say, is a tree with many age rings, with its limbs and trunk bent and twisted by all the winds of the years, but with its tap root in the Old South." So, too, is Korea. Korea would not, could not, and should not transform into anything but itself.

References Cited

Abelmann, Nancy.

1996   *Echoes of the Past, Epics of Dissent: A South Korean Social Movement.* Berkeley: University of California Press.

Abelmann, Nancy, and John Lie.

1995   *Blue Dreams: Korean Americans and the Los Angeles Riots.* Cambridge: Harvard University Press.

Akiba, Takashi.

1957   "A Study on Korean Folkways." *Folklore Studies* 14:1-106.

Amsden, Alice H.

1989   *Asia's Next Giant: South Korea and Late Industrialization.* New York: Oxford University Press.

Bae, Ki-dong[Bae Gi-dong].

2002   *"Jeongok-ri guseokgi yujeok-ui josagwajeong-ui munjejeom"* (Jeongok-ri Paleolithic site, Current understanding). Paper presented at the International Seminar in Memory of the Excavation of Paleolithic site, Yeoncheon, Korea, May 3.

Baek, Nak-jun (George Paik).

1982   "Inchon Kim Sungsoo-wa minjok gyoyuk" (Kim Songsu and national education). In *Inchon Kim Sungsoo-ui aejok sasang-gwa geu silcheon*(The patriotism of Kim Sungsoo in thought and deed), Kwon Ogi[Gwon O-gi], ed. Pp. 207-220. Seoul: The Dong-A Ilbosa.

Bae, Kyuhan[Bae Gyu-han].

1987   *Automobile Workers in Korea.* Seoul: Seoul National University Press.

Befu, Harumi.

1971   *Japan: An Anthropological Introduction.* New York: Chandler Pub. Co.

Benedict, Ruth.
 1946   *The Chrysanthemum and the Sword: patterns of Japanese culture*. Boston: Houghton Mifflin.

Benjamin, Roger.
 1982   "The Political Economy of Korea." *Asian Survey* 22:1105-1116.

Brandt, Vincent S. R.
 1971   *A Korean Village: Between Farm and Sea*. Cambridge: Harvard University Press.

Breen, Michael.
 2004   *The Koreans: Who They Are, What They Want, Where Their Future Lies*. New York: Thomas Dunne Books of St. Martin's Griffin.

Cash, W. J.
 1941   *The Mind of the South*. New York: Knopf.

Chen, Yu-his.
 1981   "Dependent Development and Its Sociopolitical Consequences: A Case Study of Taiwan." PhD diss., University of Hawaii.

Cho, Hung-Youn[Jo Heung-yun].
 1994   "Sinheung jonggyo" (New Religion). In *Hanguk-ui jonggyo* (Korean religion), Yun Yi-heum, et al., eds. Pp. 205-231. Seoul: Mundeoksa.

Cho, Kang-hŭi[Jo Gang-hui].
 1984   "Yeongnam jibang-ui honban yeongu: Jinseong Yissi Toegye jongsoneul jungsimuro" (The marriage network in the Gyeongsang region: Focusing on the main heir of the Jinseong Yi clan). *Minjok munhwa nonchong* (The Journal of the Institute for Korean Culture) 6:79-121.

Choe, Chong Pil[Choe Jeong-pil].
 1991   "Illyuhaksangeuro bon Hanminjok giwon yeongue daehan bipanjeok geomto" (A critical view of research on the origins of Koreans and their culture). *Hanguk Sanggosa Hakbo* (Journal of Early History of Korea) 8:7-43.

Choe, Chong Pil, and Martin T. Bale.
 2002   "Current Perspectives on Settlement, Subsistence, and Cultivation in Prehistoric Korea." *Arctic Anthropology* 39:95-121.

Choe, Tae-ryong.

2002   "Jigeop wisin-ui byeonhwa" (Change of occupational prestige). In *Jigeop-gwa nodong-ui segye* (The world of job and labor), The Committee for honoring the retirement of Professor Kim Gyeong-dong, ed. Pp. 29-86. Seoul: Pakyoungsa[Bakyeongsa].

Choe, Jae-seok.

1966   *Hanguk gajok yeongu* (A study of the Korean family). Seoul: Minjung seogwan.

Choi, In-Hyuk[Choe In-hyeok].

2010   "Internet Power House." In *Korea: From Rags to Riches,* Eung-kyuk Park[Bak Eung-gyeok] and Chang-seok Park[Bak Chang-seok], eds. Pp. 353-360. Seoul: The Korea Institute of Public Administration.

Choi, Jang Jip[Choe Jang-jip].

1990   *Labor and the Authoritarian State: Labor Unions in South Korean Manufacturing Industries, 1961-1980.* Seoul: Korea University Press.

Choy, Bong-youn[Choe Bong-yun].

1979   *Koreans in America,* Chicago: Nelson-Hall.

Chun, Kyung-soo[Jeon Gyeong-su].

2008   "Seomun" (Introduction). In *Honhyeoleseo damunhwaro* (From mixed-blood to multiculturalism), Chun Kyung-soo, et al., eds. Pp. 12-34. Seoul: Iljisa.

Chung, David, and Kang-Nam Oh[O Gang-nam].

2001   *Syncretism: The Religious Context of Christian Beginnings in Korea.* Albany: State University of New York Press.

Chung, Edward Young-Iob[Chung Young-iob].

1989   "The Impact of Chinese Culture on Korea's Economic Development." In *Confucian and Economic Development: An Oriental Alternative?,* Hung-cho Tai, ed. Pp. 149-165. Washington, D.C.: The Washington Institute for Values and Public Policy.

1995   *The Korean Neo-Confucianism of Yi T'Oegye*[Yi Toegye] *and Yi Yulgok: A Reappraisal of the "Four-Seven Thesis" and Its Practical Implications for Self-Cultivation.* Albany: State University of New York Press.

Chung, Kae H., and Hak Chong Lee[Yi Hak-jong], eds.

1989   *Korean Managerial Dynamics.* New York: Praeger.

Chung, Kae H., and Harry K. Lie.

1989   "Labor-Management Relations in Korea." In *Korean Managerial Dynamics*, Kae H. Chung and Hak Chong Lee, eds. Pp. 217-231. New York: Praeger.

Clark, Charles Allen.

1961   *Religions of Old Korea*. Seoul: The Christian Literature Society of Korea.

Clark, Donald N.

1986   *Christianity in Modern Korea*. Lanham: University Press of America.

2000   *Culture and Customs of Korea*. Westport: Greenwood Press.

Cole, Robert E.

1971   *Japanese Blue Collar: The Changing Tradition*. Berkeley: University of California Press.

Collins, J. Lawton.

1969   *War in Peacetime: The History and Lessons of Korea*. Boston: Houghton Mifflin.

Cotterell, Arthur.

1994   *East Asia: From Chinese Predominance to the Rise of the Pacific Rim*. New York: Oxford University Press.

Crane, Paul S.

1978 [1967] *Korean Patterns*. Seoul: Royal Asiatic Society, Korean Branch.

Cumings, Bruce.

1981   *The Origins of the Korean War*. Vol. 1 of *Liberation and the Emergence of Separate Regimes, 1945-1947*. Princeton: Princeton University Press.

1984   *The Two Koreas: Foreign Policy Association Headline Series No. 269* New York: Foreign Policy Association.

1997   *Korea's Place in the Sun: A Modern History*. New York: W.W. Norton & Co.

2005 [1997] *Korea's Place in the Sun: A Modern History* (updated). New York: W.W. Norton & Co.

De Mente, Boyé Lafayette.

2012 [1998] *The Korean Mind: Understanding Contemporary Korean Culture*. North Clarendon, VT: Tuttle.

Deuchler, Martina.

1977a   *Confucian Gentlemen and Barbarian Envoys: The Opening of Korea, 1875-1885.* Seattle: University of Washington Press.

1977b   "The Tradition: Women during the Yi Dynasty (Joseon)." In *Virtues in Conflict: Tradition and the Korean Woman Today*, Sandra Mattielli, ed. Pp. 1-47. Seoul: The Royal Asiatic Society, Korea Branch.

1992   *The Confucian Transformation of Korea: A Study of Society and Ideology.* Cambridge: Council on East Asian Studies, Harvard University.

Deyo, Frederic C.

1989   *Beneath the Miracle: Labor Subordination in the New Asian Industrialism.* Berkeley: University of California Press.

Dix, Griffin M.

1980   "The Place of the Almanac in Korean Folk Religion." *Journal of Korean Studies* 2:47-70.

Dore, Ronald.

1987   *Taking Japan Seriously: A Confucian Perspective on Leading Economic Issues.* Stanford: Stanford University Press.

Eckert, Carter J.

1990   "The South Korean Bourgeoisie: A Class in Search of Hegemony." *Journal of Korean Studies* 7:115-148.

1991   *Offspring of Empire: The Koch'ang*[Gochang] *Kims and the Colonial Origins of Korean Capitalism 1876-1945.* Seattle: University of Washington Press.

Eckert, Carter J., et al.

1990   *Korea Old and New: A History.* Seoul: Ilchokak.

Eichengreen, Barry J., Dwight H. Perkins, and Kwanho Shin[Sin Gwan-ho].

2012   *From Miracle to Maturity: The Growth of the Korean Economy.* Cambridge: The Harvard University Asia Center.

Ember, Carol R., and Melvin Ember.

1996   *Anthropology.* Upper Saddle River, NJ: Prentice-Hall.

Farnsworth, Paul.

2000   "Identity through Beer." *Anthropology News* (February): 2000:18.

Fernandez, James W.

1980   "Reflections on Looking into Mirrors." *Semiotica* 30:27-39.

1982   *Bwiti: An Ethnography of the Religious Imagination in Africa.* Princeton: Princeton University Press.

Ferraro, Gary P.

1998   *The Cultural Dimension of International Business.* Upper Saddle River, NJ: Prentice-Hall.

Frankl, John M.

2008   *Hanguk munhage natanan oeguk-ui uimi* (Images of "the foreign" in Korean literature and culture). Seoul: Somyong Publishing Co.

Freeman, Caren.

2011   *Making and Faking Kinship: Marriage and Labor Migration between China and South Korea.* Ithaca: Cornell University Press.

Gerschenkron, Alexander.

1962   *Economic Backwardness in Historical Perspective.* Cambridge: The Belknap Press of Harvard University.

1968   *Continuity in History and Other Essays.* Cambridge: The Belknap Press of Harvard University Press.

Gibson, John.

1978   "Tone nŏmu chipch'ak handa[Don neomu jipchakhanda]" (Too much concern about money). In *Han'guk-in-ŭn nugu-in-ga: Oeguk-in-i-bon uriŭi ŭisik kujo*[Hangugineun nuguinga: Oegugini bon uri-ui uisikgujo] (Who are the Koreans? The structure of Korean thought patterns seen by foreigners), Sin Tongho[Sin Dong-ho], ed. Pp. 269-274. Seoul: Chosun Ilbosa.

Gorer, Geoffrey, and John Rickman, md.

1949   *The People of Great Russia: A Psychological Study.* London: Cresset.

Grajdanzev, Andrew, Jr.

1944   *Modern Korea.* New York: International Secretariat, Institute of Pacific Relations.

Griffis, William Elliot.

1882   *Corea: The Hermit Nation.* New York: Charles Scribner's Sons.

Habermas, Jürgen.

1994   "Struggles for Recognition in the Democratic Constitutional State." In *Multiculturalism: Examining the Politics of Recognition*, Amy Gutmann, ed. Pp. 107-148. Princeton. Princeton University Press.

Hahm, Hanhee[Ham Han-hui].

2005   "Rice and Koreans: Three Identities and Meanings." *Korea Journal* 45: 89-106.

2009   "Hanguksarameun wae geureoke haengdonghalkkae gohanda" (Tell why Koreans behave as they do?): Review of: *Kimchi and IT: Tradition and Transformation in Korea* by Choong Soon Kim, Seoul, Ilchokak, 2007). *Hanguk munhwa illyuhak* (Korean Cultural Anthropology) 42: 275-283.

Hahm, Pyong-Choon[Ham Byeong-chun].

1964   "Korea's "Mendicant Mentality"? A Critique of U.S. Policy." *Foreign Affairs* 43: 165-174.

Hamel, Hendrick, Jean-Paul Buys, tr.

2011 [1653] *Hamel's Journal and a Description of the Kingdom of Korea, 1653-1666*. Seoul: Royal Asiatic Society, Korea Branch.

Han, Kyung-Koo[Han Gyeong-gu].

2000a   "The Politics of Network and Social Trust: A Case Study in the Organizational Culture of Korean Venture Industry." *Korea Journal* 40: 353-365.

2000b   "Wigi-ui inseong-gwa 21segi hanguk sahoe" (Crisis-ridden personality and Korean society in the 21st century). In *20segi ditgo ttwieoneomgi* (Jump over by stepping on the 20th century), Hwangyeong undong yeonhap 21segi wiwonhoe, ed. Pp. 289-303. Seoul: Nanam.

2003   "The Anthropology of the Discourse on the Koreanness of Koreans." *Korea Journal* 43: 5-31.

2007   "The Archaeology of the Ethnically Homogeneous Nation-State and Multiculturalism in Korea." *Korea Journal* 47:8-31.

Han, Wookeun[Han Wu-geun].

1981 [1970] *The History of Korea*. Seoul: Eulyoo.

Harvey, Youngsook Kim.

1979   *Six Korean Women: The Socialization of Shamans*. St. Paul: West Publishing Co.

1983   "Minmyŏnŭri[Minmyeoneuri]: The Daughter-in-law Who Comes of Age in Her Mother-in-law's Household." In *Korean Women: A View from the Inner Room*, Laurel L. Kendall and M. Peterson, eds. Pp. 45-61. New Haven: East Rock Press.

Hasan, Parvez.
1976   *Korea: Problems and Issues in a Rapidly Growing Economy*. Baltimore: Johns Hopkins University Press.

Hasan, Parvez, and D. C. Rao.
1979   Korea: Policy Issues for Long-Term Development: The Report of a Mission Sent to the Republic of Korea by the World Bank. Baltimore: Johns Hopkins University Press.

Hatada, Takashi.
1969   *A History of Korea*. Warren W. Smith, Jr., and Benjamin H, ed. and tr. Hazard. Santa Barbara: ABC-Clio Press.

Hattori, Tamio.
1989   "Japanese Zaibatsu and Korean Chaebol[Jaebeol]." In *Korean Managerial Dynamics*, Kae H. Chung and Hak Chong Lee, eds. Pp. 79-95. New York: Praeger.

Henderson, Gregory.
1968   *Korea: The Politics of the Vortex*. Cambridge: Harvard University Press.

Hicks, George.
1995   *The Comfort Women*. St. Leonard, Austria: Allen & Unwin.

Hoebel, E. Adamson.
1966   *Anthropology: The Study of Man*. New York: McGraw-Hill.

Hofheinz, Roy J., and Kent E. Calder.
1982   *The Eastasia Edge*. New York: Basic Books.

Hofstede, Geert, and Michael Harris Bond.
1988   "The Confucius Connection: From Cultural Roots to Economic Growth." *Organizational Dynamics*, Spring: 5-21.

Hong, Ŭisŏp[Hong I-seop].
1975   *Han'guk chŏngsinsa sŏsŏl*[Hanguk jeongsinsa seoseol] (An introduction to the history of Korean thought). Seoul: Yonsei University Press.

Hsu, Francis L.K.

1965 "The Effect of Dominant Kinship Relationships on Kin and Non-Kin Behavior." *American Anthropologist* 67: 638-661.

1970 *Americans and Chinese: Purpose and Fulfillment in Great Civilizations.* Garden City, NY: Natural History Press.

1971 *Kinship and Culture.* Chicago: Aldine.

1977 "Intercultural Understanding: Genuine and Spurious." *Anthropology & Education Quarterly* 8: 203-209.

1979 "The Cultural Problem of the Cultural Anthropologist." *American Anthropologist* 81:517-532.

1981 [1953] *Americans and Chinese: Passages to Differences.* Honolulu: University of Hawaii Press.

1983 *Rugged Individualism Reconsidered: Essays in Psychological Anthropology.* Knoxville: University of Tennessee Press.

Huh, Soo Youl [Heo Su-yeol].

2005 *Kaebal ŏpnŭn kaebal: Ilje Chosŏn kaebalŭi hyŏnsang-gwa ponjil*[Gaebal eopneun gaebal: Ilje Joseon gaebal-ui hyeonsang-gwa bonjil] (Development without development: Reality and essence of Korean economic development under the Japanese colonial period). Seoul: Ŭnhaengnamu[Eunhaeng namu].

Hussain, Tariq, Sae-min Lee[Yi Se-min], tr.

2006 *Diamond Dilemma: Shaping Korea for the 21st Century.* Seoul: Random House JoongAng.

Hwang, Hie-shin[Hwang Hye-sin].

2010 ""Ppalli, ppalli:" Get Everything Done Early!" In *Korea: From Rags to Riches*, Eung-kyuk Park and Chang-seok Park, eds. Pp. 448-454. Seoul: The Korea Institute of Public Administration.

Hwang, Sung-hyuk[Hwang Seong-hyeok].

2010 "World's Best Shipbuilder." In *Korea: From Rags to Riches,* Eung-kyuk Park and Chang-seok Park, eds. Pp. 299-304. Seoul: The Korea Institute of Public Administration.

Janelli, Roger L., and Dawnhee Yim[Im Don-hui].

1982 *Ancestor Worship and Korean Society.* Stanford: Stanford University Press.

Janelli, Roger L. with Dawnhee Yim.

1993 *Making Capitalism: The Social and Cultural Construction of a South Korean*

Conglomerate. Stanford: Stanford University Press.

Jones, Dorothy B.
  1955   *The Portrayal of China and India on the American Screen, 1896-1955:*
          The Evolution of Chinese and Indian Themes, Locales, and Characters as
          Portrayed on the American Screen Communications program. Cambridge:
          MIT Press.

Jones, Leroy P., and Il Sakong[Sagong il].
  1980   *Government, Business, and Entrepreneurship in Economic Development:*
          The Korean Case. Cambridge: Council on East Asian Studies, Harvard
          University.

Keidel, Albert.
  1980   "Regional Agricultural Production and Income." In *Rural Development*,
          Sunghwan Ban[Ban Seong-hwan], Pal Yong Moon, and Dwight H. Perkins,
          eds. Pp. 112-159. Cambridge: Council on East Asian Studies, Harvard
          University.

Kemper, Robert V.
  2004   Review of: "One Anthropologist, Two Worlds" by Choong Soon Kim.
          The Journal of the Royal Anthropological Institute of Great Britain and
          Ireland 10: 182-183.

Kendall, Laurel.
  1985a   *Shamans, Housewives, and Other Restless Spirits: Women in Korean Ritual*
          Life. Honolulu: University of Hawaii Press.
  1985b   "Ritual Skills and Kotow Money: The Bride as Daughter-in-law in
          Korean Wedding Rituals." *Ethnology* 24:253-267.
  1988   *The Life and Hard Times of a Korean Shaman: Of Tales and the Telling of*
          Tales. Honolulu: University of Hawaii Press.
  1996a   *Getting Married in Korea: Of Gender, Morality, and Modernity.* Berkeley:
          University of California Press.
  1996b   "Korean Shamans and the Spirits of Capitalism." *American Anthropologist*
          98:512-538.

Kennan, George.
  1905   "Korea: A Degenerate State." *The Outlook*, 7 October.
  1905   "The Korean People: The Product of a Decayed Civilization." *The*
          Outlook, 21 December.

Kim, Byung-mo[Gim Byeong-mo].

1994   *Han'gukin-ŭi paljach'wi*[Hangugin-ui baljachwi] (Footprints of Koreans). Seoul: Chipmundang[Jipmoondang].

2006   *Kim Byung-mo-ŭi kogohak yŏhaeng*[Gim Byeong-mo-ui gogohak yeohaeng] (Kim Byung-mo's archaeological journey). 2 vols. Seoul: Goraesil.

2008   *Hŏ Hwang-ok route: Indo-esŏ Kaya kkaji*[Heo Hwang-ok route:Indoeseo Gayakkaji] (The route of Hŏ Hwang-ok: From India to Kaya). Seoul: Yŏksa-ŭi ach'im[Yeoksa-ui achim].

Kim, Chŏng-ho[Kim Jeong-ho].

2003   *Han'guk-ŭi kwihwa sŏngssi: Sŏngssiro pon uriminjok-ŭi kusŏng*[Hanguk-ui gwihwa seongssi: Seongssiro arabon uriminjok-ui guseong] (The naturalized Korean surname groups: The composition of the ethnic nation of Korea by surname). Seoul: Chisiksanŏpsa[Jisiksaneopsa].

Kim, Choong Soon[Gim, Jung-sun].

1968   "Functional Analysis of Korean Kinship System." Unpublished M.A. thesis, Emory University.

1974   The Yon'jul-hon[Yeonjulhon] or Chain-String Form of Marriage Arrangement in Korea. *Journal of Marriage and the Family* 36:575-579.

1977   *An Asian Anthropologist in the South: Field Experiences with Blacks, Indians, and Whites.* Knoxville: University of Tennessee Press.

1978a   Wellin's review of: "*An Asian Anthropologist in the South* by Choong Soon Kim." *Rural Sociology* 43:506-508.

1978b   "On Anthropological Studies in the American South." *Current Anthropology* 19:186-187.

1987   "Can an Anthropologist Go Home Again?" *American Anthropologist* 89:943-946.

1988a   *Faithful Endurance: An Ethnography of Korean Family Dispersal.* Tucson: University of Arizona Press.

1988b   "An Anthropological Perspective on Filial Piety versus Social Security." In *Between Kinship and the State: Social Security and Law in Developing Countries*, Von Benda-Beckmann, et al., eds. Pp. 125-135. Dordrecht, Holland: Foris Publications.

1990   "The Role of the Non-Western Anthropologist Reconsidered: Illusion versus Reality." *Current Anthropology* 31 (2):196-201.

1992   *The Culture of Korean Industry: An Ethnography of Poongsan Corporation.* Tuckson: University of Arizona Press.

1993   "Koreans." In *Encyclopedia of World Cultures*, Vol. 5 of *East and Southeast*

Asia, Paul Hockings, ed. Pp. 144-149. Boston G. K. Hall & Co.

1995 *Japanese Industry in the American South*. New York: Routledge.

1998 *A Korean Nationalist Entrepreneur: A Life History of Kim Sŏngsu*[Gim Seong-su], *1891-1955*. Albany: State University of New York Press.

2000 *Anthropological Studies of Korea by Westerners. IMKS Special Lecture Series*, Vol. 5. Seoul: Institute for Modern Korean Studies, Yonsei University Press.

2001 *Munhwareul almyeon gyeongyeong jeonryaki seonda* (If one understands the culture, one can develop business strategies). Seoul: Ilchokak.

2002 *One Anthropologist, Two Worlds: Three Decades of Reflexive Fieldwork in North America and Asia*. Knoxville: University of Tennessee Press.

2007 *Kimchi and IT: Tradition and Transformation in Korea*. Seoul: Ilchokak.

2011a "What Makes Korea Tick?: An Historical and Cultural Interpretation of Korea's Economic Transformation." In *A Glimpse into Korea: The Center for International Affairs*, ed. Pp. 96-118. Gyeonggi-do, Korea: The Academy of Korean Studies Press.

2011b *Voices of Foreign Brides: The Roots and Development of Multiculturalism in Korea*. Lanham, MD: AltaMira Press.

Kim, Dong Ki[Gim Dong-gi], and Chong W. Kim.

1989 "Korean Value Systems and Managerial Practices." In *Korean Managerial Dynamics*, Kae H. Chung and Hak Chong Lee, eds. Pp. 207-216. New York: Praeger.

Kim, Duck Choong[Gim Deok-jung].

1986 "Role of Entrepreneurs in Korea." In *Toward Higher Productivity*, D. K. Kim, ed. Pp. 51-64. Tokyo: Asian Productivity Center.

Kim, Eun Mee[Gim Eun-mi].

1997 *Business, Strong State: Collusion and Conflict in South Korean Development, 1960-1990*. Albany: State University of New York Press.

Kim, In-hoe.

1980 [1979] *Hangugin-ui gachigwan* (Korean value system). Seoul: Moonumsa.

Kim, Jay S., and Chan K. Hahn.

1989 "The Korean Chaebol[jaebeol] as an Organizational Form." In *Korean Managerial Dynamics,* Kae H. Chung and Hak Chong Lee, eds. Pp. 51-64. New York: Praeger.

Kim, Kwang-Ok[Gim Gwang-ok].

1998 "The Communal Ideology and Its Reality: With Reference to the Emergence of Neo-Tribalism." *Korea Journal* 38:5-44.

Kim, Kwang-Suk[Gim Gwang-seok], and Michael Roemer.

1979 *Growth and Structural Transformation.* Cambridge: Council on East Asian Studies, Harvard University.

Kim, Gyeong-il.

1999 *Gongjaga jugeoya naraga sanda* (The country can sustain itself if and when Confucius dies). Seoul: Bada books.

Kim, Linsu[Gim In-su].

1989 "Technological Transformation of Korean Firms." In *Korean Managerial Dynamics,* Kae H. Chung and Hak Chong Lee, eds. Pp. 113-129. New York: Praeger.

Kim, Seong-Nae[Gim Seong-rye].

1999 "Hanguk mugyo yeongu-ui yeoksajeok gochal" (Studies on the history of Korean shamanism). In *Hanguk jonggyo munhwa yeongu 100nyeon* (The hundred years studies of Korean religious culture), Kim Seong-Nae, et al. eds. Pp. 139-207. Seoul: Cheongnyeonsa.

2002 "Hanguk mugyo-ui jeongcheseong: Jaengjeom bunseok" (The identity and importance of Korean Shamanism: An analysis of the debating issues). *Shamanism yeongu* (Studies of Shamanism) 4:359-394.

Kim, Seung-Kyung[Gim Seung-gyeong].

1997 *Class Struggle or Family Struggle? The Lives of Women Factory Workers in South Korea.* New York: Cambridge University Press.

Kim, Tae-Kil[Gim Tae-gil].

1977 *Soseolmunhake natanan hangugin-ui gachigwan* (Values of the Korean People mirrored in Fiction). Seoul: Iljisa.

Kim, Taek-kyu[Gim Taek-gyu].

1964 Dongjok burak yeongu (The cultural structure of a consanguineous village). Daegu: Ch'ŏnggu[Cheongu] University Press.

1986 [1979] Ssijok burak-ui yeongu (Study on consanguineous village). Seoul: Ilchokak.

Kim, Woo Choong[Gim U-jung].

1992 *Every Street is Paved with Gold: The Road to Real Success.* New York:

William Morrow & Co.

Kim, Won-yong.
1982   "Discoveries of Rice in Prehistoric Sites in Korea." *Journal of Asian Studies* 4:513-518.

Kim Wook[Gim Uk], and Kim Chong-Youl[Gim Jong-yeol].
2005   *Mitochondria DNA Byeoni-wa hangugin jipdan-ui giwon yeongu* (Modern Korean origin and the peopling of Korea as revealed by mtDNA lineages). Seoul: Koguryŏ yŏn'gu chaedan yŏn'gu ch'ongsŏ[Goguryeo yeongu jaedan yeongu chongseo] (Goguryeo Research Foundation).

Koh, Hesung Chun[Jeon Hye-seong].
1983   "Korean Women, Conflict, and Change: An Approach to Development Planning." In *Korean Women: View from the Inner Room*, Laurel Kendall and Mark Peterson, eds. Pp. 159-174. New Haven: East Rock Press.

Krizek, Robert L.
1988   "What the Hell Are We Teaching the Next Generation Anyway?" In *Fiction and Social Research: By Ice or Fire*, Anna Banks and Stephen P. Banks, eds. Walnut Creek, CA: AltaMira Press.

Krueger, Anne O.
1979   *The Developmental Role of the Foreign Sector and Aid: Studies in the Modernization of the Republic of Korea*. Cambridge: Council on East Asian Studies, Harvard University.

Koo, Hagen[Gu Hae-geun].
1987   "The Interplay of State, Social Class, and World System in East Asian Development: The Cases of South Korea and Taiwan." In *The Political Economy of the New Asian Industrialism*, Frederic C. Deyo, ed. Pp. 165-181. Ithaca: Cornell University Press.

Kuk, Hŭng-ju[Guk Heung-ju].
1986   "Han'gukinŭn wae sŏdurŭnŭn'ga[Hangugineun wae seodureuneunga]" (Why do Koreans hurry so much?) In *Han'gukin han'gukpyŏng*[Hangugin hangukbyeong] (Koreans and Their Illness), Yi Kyu-t'ae, et al., eds. Pp. 111-119. Seoul: Ilyeom.

Kymlicka, Will.
2005   "Liberal Multiculturalism: Western Models, Global Trends, and Asian

Debates." In *Multiculturalism in Asia*, Will Kymlicka and Baogang He, eds. Pp. 2-55. New York: Oxford University Press.

2007   *Multicultural Odysseys: Navigating the New International Politics of Diversity*. New York: Oxford University Press.

Langness, L. L.

1965   *The Life History in Anthropological Science*. New York: Holt, Rinehart & Winston.

Lee, Changsoo[Yi Chang-su], and George A. De Vos.

1981   *Koreans in Japan: Ethnic Conflict and Accommodation*. Berkeley: University of California Press.

Lee Haejun[Yi Hae-jun].

1996   Joseon sigi chonrak sahoesa (History of village during the Joseon dynasty). Seoul: Minjok Munhwasa.

Lee, Hak Chong[Yi Hak-jong].

1989   "Managerial Characteristics of Korean Firms." In *Korean Managerial Dynamics*. Kae H. Chung and Hak Chong Lee, eds. Pp. 147-162. New York: Praeger.

Lee, Hi-seung[Yi Hui-seung].

1963   "Characteristics of Korean Culture." *Korea Journal* 3:13-16.

Lee, Ki-baik[Yi Gi-baek].

1984   *A New History of Korea*. Edward W. Wagner with Edward J. Schultz, tr. Cambridge: Harvard-Yenching Institute by Harvard University Press.

Lee Kwang-kyu[Yi Gwang-gyu].

1982 [1975] *Hanguk gajok-ui gujobunseok* (A structural analysis of the Korean family). Seoul: Iljisa.

1983 [1977] *Hanguk gajok-ui sajeok yeongu* (A historical study of the Korean family). Seoul: Iljisa.

Lee, Kwang-kyu, and Joseph P. Linskey, ed.

2003   *Korean Traditional Culture. Korean Studies series, no. 25*. Seoul: Jimoondang.

Lee, Man-gap.

1960   *Han'guk nongch'on-ŭi sahoe kujo*[Hanguk nongchon-ui sahoe gujo] (The social

structure of Korean farming villages). Seoul: Korean Research Center.

Lee, Man'gyu[Yi Man-gyu].

1946 *Yŏ Un-hyŏng*[Lyuh Woon-hyung] *sŏnsaeng t'ujaeng-sa* [Yeo Un-hyeong seonsaeng tujaengsa] (History of Lyuh Woon-hyung's struggles). Seoul: Minju Munhwasa.

Lee, O-young[Yi Eo-ryeong].

1963 *Heuksoge Jeo Baramsoge* (In the dirt, and in that wind). Seoul: Hyeonamsa.

2002 *Heuksoge Jeo Baramsoge* (In the dirt, and in that wind). The 40th year anniversary ed. Seoul: Munhak sasangsa.

Lee, Tai-Young [Yi Tae-yeong].

1957 Hanguk ihon jedo yeongu (A study of divorce in Korea). Seoul: Yŏsŏng Munje Yŏn'guso[Yeoseong munje yeonguso].

Lee, Taek-hui.

1991 "Pulgap'ihan sŏnt'aek: Chŏngch'i chidojaŭi kil[Bulgapihan Seontaek: Jeongchi jidoja-ui gil]" (Unavoidable choice: the way of a political leader). In *P'yŏngjŏn Inch'on Kim Sŏngsu: Choguk kwa kyo˘re-e pach'in ilsaeng.* [Pyeongjeon Inchon Gim Seong-su: Joguk-gwa gyeore-e bachin ilsaeng] (A critical biography of Kim Songsu: Dedicated Whole life for His Homeland), Sin Il-cheol, ed. Pp. 339-421. Seoul: Dong-A Ilbosa.

Lew, Young-Ick[Yu Yeong-ik].

1990 *Kabo Gyeongjang yeongu* (A study of the Kabo Reform Movement). Seoul: Ilchokak.

Lewis, Oscar.

1966 "Tepoztlan Revisited." In *Reading in Modern Sociology*, Alex Inkeles, ed. Pp. 51-64. Englewood Cliffs: Prentice-Hall.

Lewis, W. Arthur.

1966 *Development Planning: The Essentials of Economic Policy.* New York: Harper & Row.

Lim, Youngil[Im Yeong-gil].

1981 *Government Policy and Private Enterprise: Korean Experience in Industrialization.* Berkeley: Institute of East Asian Studies, University of California.

Lowell, Percival L.

1888   *Chosŏn*[Joseon]: *The Land of the Morning Calm*. Boston: Ticknor.

Marty, Martin E.

1977   "The American Tradition and the American Tomorrow." In *Tomorrow's American*, Samuel Sandmel, ed. Pp. 134-155. New York: Oxford University Press.

Mason, Edward S., Mahn Je Kim, Dwight H. Perkins, Kwang Suk Kim[Gim Gwang-seok], and David C. Cole.

1980   *The Economic and Social Modernization of the Republic of Korea*. Cambridge: Council on East Asian Studies, Harvard University.

McCune, Shannon.

1966   *Korea: Land of Broken Calm*. New York: D. Van Nostrand Company.

1976   "Geographical Observations on Korea." *Bulletin of the Korean Research Center: Journal of Social Sciences and Humanities* 44:1-19.

1980   *Views of the Geography of Korea, 1935-1960*. Seoul: The Korean Research Center.

McGee, Harold Franklin, Jr.

1977   Comment on: "Anthropological Studies in the American South" by Carole E. Hill. *Current Anthropology* 18:321.

Mead, Margaret.

1942   *And Keep Your Powder Dry: An Anthropologist Looks at America*. New York: William Morrow.

1951   "The Study of National Character." In *The Policy Sciences*, D. Lerner, and H. D. Lasswell, eds. Pp. 70-85. Stanford: Stanford University Press.

1953   "National Character." In *Anthropology Today*: A. L. Kroeber, ed. Pp. 642-647. Chicago: University of Chicago Press.

1962   Review of: "National Character and National Stereotypes: A Trend Report Prepared for the International Union of Scientific Philosophy." H.J.C. Duiker, and N.H. Frijda, eds. *American Anthropologist* 64: 688-690.

Mead, Margaret, and Rhoda B. Métraux, eds.

1953   *The Study of Culture at a Distance*. Chicago: University of Chicago Press.

Miller, John, Jr., Owen J. Carroll, and Margaret E. Tackley.

1956   *Korea 1951-1953*. Washington, D.C.: U.S. Government Printing Office.

Miller, Roy Andrew.

1980   *Origins of the Japanese Language: lectures in Japan during the academic year, 1977-78*. Seattle: University of Washington Press.

Moore, Barrington.

1958   *Political Power and Social Theory: six studies*. Cambridge: Harvard University Press.

Na, Se-jin.

1963   "Physical Characteristics of Korean Nation." *Korea Journal* 3:9-29.

Nelson, Laura C.

2000   *Measured Excess: Status, Gender, and Consumer Nationalism in South Korea*. New York: Columbia University Press.

Nelson, Sarah M.

1993   *The Archaeology of Korea*. New York: Cambridge University Press.

Nimkoff, M. F., ed.

1965   *Comparative Family Systems*. Boston: Houghton Mifflin Co.

Ohnuki-Tierney, Emiko.

1984a   "Native Anthropologist." *American Ethnologist* 11:584-586.

1984b   *Illness and Culture in Contemporary Japan: An Anthropological View*. New York: Cambridge University Press.

Osgood, Cornelius.

1951   *The Koreans and Their Culture*. New York: The Ronald Press Company.

Pai, Hyung Il[Bae Hyeong-il].

2000   *Constructing "Korean" Origins: A Critical Review of Archaeology, Historiography, and Racial Myth in Korean State-Formation Theories*. Cambridge: Harvard University Asia Center.

Park, Jung-Sun[Bak Jeong-sun].

2004   "Korean American Youth and Transnational Flows of Popular Culture Across the Pacific." *Amerasia Journal* 30: 147-169.

2005   "The Korean Wave: Transnational Cultural Flows in East Asia." In *Korea at the Center: Dynamics of Regionalism in Northeast Asia*, Charles K. Armstrong, Gilbert Rozman, Samuel S. Kim, and Stephen Kotkin, eds. Pp. 244-307. Armonk, NY: M.E. Sharpe, Inc.

Park, Myung-Lim[Bak Myeong-lim].

1996 Hanguk jeonjaeng-ui balbal-gwa giwon (The Korean War: the outbreak and its origins). 2 vols. Seoul: Nanam.

Park, Oak-kol[Bak Ok-geol].

1996 *Koryŏ-sidae-ŭi kwihwain yŏn'gu*[Goryeo sidae-ui gwihwain yeongu] (A study of the naturalized people in the Koryŏ[Goryeo]period). Seoul: Kukhakcharyowŏn[Gukhak Jaryowon].

Perkins, Dwight H.

1986 *China: Asia's Next Economic Giant?* Seattle: University of Washington Press.

Peterson, Mark.

1974 "Adoption in Korean Genealogies: Continuation of Lineage." *Korea Journal* 14: 28-35.

Poitras, Edward W.

1978 Malaedo sŏyŏl-i itta[Maredo seoyeori itta] (There is an order even in speech). In *Han'guk-in-ŭn nugu-in-ga: Oeguk-in-i-bon uriŭi ŭisik kujo* (Who are the Koreans: Structure of Korean thought patterns seen by foreigners), Sin Tongho, ed. Pp. 29-35. Seoul: Chosun Ilbosa.

Powdermaker, Hortense.

1966 *Stranger and Friend: The Way of an Anthropologist.* New York: W.W. Norton.

Pratt, Mary Louise.

1986 "Fieldwork in Common Places." In *Writing Culture: The Poetics and Politics of Ethnography*, James Clifford and George E. Marcus, eds. Pp. 27-50. Berkeley: University of California Press.

Queen, Stuart A., and Robert W. Habenstein.

1974 *The Family in Various Cultures.* 4th ed. New York: Lippincott Williams and Wilkins.

Redfield, Robert.

1947 "The Folk Society." *American Journal of Sociology* 52: 293-308.

Reed, John Shelton.

2003 *Minding the South.* Columbia, MO: University of Missouri Press.

Reeves-Ellington, Richard.
1999 "From Command to Demand Economies: Bulgarian Organizational Value Orientations." *Practicing Anthropology* 21: 5-13.

Reischauer, Edwin O., and John K. Fairbank.
1960 *East Asia: The Great Tradition.* Boston: Houghton Mifflin.

Richardson, Miles.
1975 "Anthropologist–The Myth Teller." *American Ethnologist* 2:517-533.
1977 Comment on: "Anthropological Studies in the American South" by Carole E. Hill. *Current Anthropology* 18:321.

Robinson, Michael E.
1988 *Cultural Nationalism in Colonial Korea, 1920-1925.* Seattle: University of Washington Press.
2007 *Korea's Twentieth-Century Odyssey: A Short History.* Honolulu: University of Hawaii Press.

Sahlins, Marshall D., and Elman R. Service.
1960 *Evolution and Culture.* Ann Arbor: University of Michigan Press.

Schmid, Andre.
2002 *Korea Between Empires, 1895-1919.* New York: Columbia University Press.

Serrie, Hendrick.
1999 "Training Chinese Managers for Leadership: Six Cross-Cultural Principles." *Practicing Anthropology* 21: 35-41.

Shin, Gi-wook[Shin Gi-wuk].
1997 *Peasant Protest and Social Change in Colonial Korea.* Seattle: University of Washington Press.
2006 *Ethnic Nationalism in Korea: Genealogy, Politics, and Legacy.* Stanford: Stanford University Press.

Soh, Chunghee Sarah.
1996 "The Korean Comfort Women: Movement for Redress." *Asian Survey* 36: 1226-1240.
2008 *The Comfort Women: Sexual Violence and Postcolonial Memory in Korea and Japan.* Chicago: University of Chicago Press.

Smart, Clifford E. J.

1978   Ta'inŭn modu changaemul[Taineun modu jangaemul] (All strangers' impediments). In *Han'gukin-ŭn nuguinga: Oegukinibon uriŭi ŭisik kujo* (Who are the Koreans: Structure of Korean thought patterns seen by foreigners), Sin Tongho, ed. Pp. 117-123. Seoul: Chosun Ilbosa.

Sorensen, Clark W.

1983   "Women, Men, Inside, Outside: The Division of Labor in Rural Central Korea." In *Korean Women: View from the Inner Room*, Laurel Kendall and Mark Peterson, eds. Pp. 63-78. New Haven: East Rock Press.

1988   *Over the Mountains Are Mountains: Korean Peasant Households and Their Adaptations to Rapid Industrialization.* Seattle: University of Washington Press.

Steers, Richard M., Yoo Keun Shin[Sin Yu-geun], and Gerardo R. Ungson.

1989   *The Chaebol* [Jaebeol]: *Korea's New Industrial Might.* New York: Harper & Row.

Steinberg, David L.

1989   *The Republic of Korea: Economic Transformation and Social Change.* Boulder: Westview Press, 1989.

Stone, I.F.

1952   *The Hidden History of the Korean War.* New York: Monthly Review Press.

Suh, Dae-Sook[Seo Dae-suk].

1967   *The Korean Communist Movement, 1918-1948.* Princeton: Princeton University Press.

The Center for International Affairs, ed.

2011   "What Makes Korea Tick? An Historical and Cultural Interpretation of Korea's Economic Transformation." In *A Glimpse into Korea*, The Center for International Affairs, ed. Pp. 96-118. Paju-si: The Academy of Korean Studies Press.

Ti, Uting.

1978   "Sihaeng ch'agowa nakkwanjuŭi[Sihaeng chago-wa nakgwanjuui]" (Trial and Error, and Optimism). In *Han'guk-in-ŭn nugu-in-ga: Oeguk-in-i-bon uriŭi ŭisik kujo* (Who are the Koreans: Structure of Korean thought patterns seen by foreigners), Sin Tongho, ed. Pp. 242-247. Seoul: Chosun Ilbosa.

Timblick, Alan.

2010 "Building Abroad for Dollars." In *Korea: From Rags to Riches*, Eung-kyuk Park and Chang-seok Park, eds. Pp. 167-172. Seoul: The Korea Institute of Public Administration.

Trotsky, Leon.

1960 *The History of the Russian Revolution*. Ann Arbor: University of Michigan Press.

Tu, Wei-ming.

1984 *Confucian Ethics Today: The Singapore Challenge*. Singapore: Federal Publications.

1998 "Confucius and Confucianism." In *Confucianism and the Family*, Walter H. Slote and George A. De Vos, eds. Pp. 3-36. Albany: State University of New York Press.

Tudor, Daniel.

2012 *Korea: The Impossible Country*. North Clarendon, VT: Tuttle Publishing.

Tweddell, Colin E., and Linda Amy Kimball.

1985 *Introduction to the Peoples and Cultures of Asia*. Englewood Cliffs: Prentice-Hall.

Veblen, Thorstein.

1915 *Imperial Germany and the Industrial Revolution*. New York: The Macmillan Company.

Vogel. Ezra F.

1965 "The Japanese Family." In *Comparative Family Systems*, M.F. Nimkoff, ed. Pp. 287-300. Boston: Houghton Mifflin.

1980 *Japan as Number One: Lessons for America*. New York: Harper Colophon Books.

Wade, Larry L., and Bong-Sik Kim[Gim Bong-sik].

1978 *Economic Development of South Korea: The Political Economy of Success*. New York: Praeger.

Wallace, Jonathan, and Mark Mangan.

1996 *Sex, Laws, and Cyberspace*. New York: Henry Holt & Co.

Warner, W. Lloyd., and Paul S. Lunt.
  1941 *The Social Life of a Modern Community.* Yankee City Series, Vol 1. New Haven: Yale University Press.

Weber, Max.
  1951 *The religion of China: Confucianism and Taoism,* Hans H. Gerth, ed. and tr. Glencoe: The Free Press.
  1970 "Science as a Vocation." In *The Relevance of Sociology,* Jack D. Douglas, ed. Pp. 45-63. New York: Appleton-Century-crofts.

Wellin, Edward.
  1978 Review of: "An Asian Anthropologist in the South" by Choong Soon Kim. *Rural Sociology* 43: 312-314.

Welty, Paul Thomas.
  1984 *The Asians: Their Evolving Heritage.* 6th ed. New York: Harper & Row.

Westphal, Larry E.
  1978 "The Republic of Korea's Experience with Export-Led Industrial Development." *World Development* 6: 347-382.

Whang, In-Joung[Hwang In-jeong].
  1981 *Management of Rural Change in Korea: The Saemaul Undong, Korea Studies Series,* no. 5. Seoul: Seoul National University Press.

Whiting, Allen S.
  1960 *China Crosses the Yalu: The Decision to Enter the Korean War.* Stanford: Stanford University.

Wilk, Richard R.
  1999 "Real Belizean Food: Building Local Identity in the Transnational Caribbean." *American Anthropologist* 101: 244-255.

Wilkie, Laurie A., and Paul Farnsworth.
  1999 "Trade and the Construction of Bahamian Identity: A Multiscalar Exploration." *International Journal of Archaeology* 3:283-320.

Yang, Key P., and Gregory Henderson.
  1958 "An Outline History of Korean Confucianism: Part II: The Schools of Yi Confucianism." *Journal of Asian Studies* 43: 81-101.

Yi, Chang'u[Yi Jang-u], and Min-hwa Yi.

2000 [1994] *"Han" Gyeongyeong* (The "Han" management). Seoul: Gimmyoungsa.

Yi, Kwang-su[Yi Gwang-su].

1922 "Minjok Gaejoron" (Reconstructing the nation). *Gaebyeok* (Creation) 23:18-72.

Yi Kyu-t'ae[Yi Gyu-tae].

1981 *Hangugin-ui uisikgujo* (Structure of Korean thought patterns). 2 vols. Seoul: Munrisa.

Yŏn, Kapsu[Yeon Gap-su].

2008 Kojongdae chŏngch'i pyŏndong yŏn'gu[Gojongdae jeongchi byeondong yeongu] (Studies on political change during the Gojong era), Seoul: Iljisa.

Yoo, Sangjin[Yu Sang-jin], and Sang M. Lee.

1987 "Management Style and Practice of Korean Chaebols[Jaebeols]." *Management Review*, Summer: 95-110.

Yoshida, Seiji.

1983 *Watashi-no Sensō hanzai: Chōsenjin kyōsei renkō* (My war crime: the forced transport of Koreans). Tokyo: San-ichi Publishing Co., Ltd.

Yoshino, Kosaku.

1992 *Cultural Nationalism in Contemporary Japan: A Sociological Inquiry.* London: Routledge.

Young, John.

2000 "Situation and Time: Observations on the Chinese Way of Doing Business." *Practicing Anthropology* 22: 13-17.

Yun, Yi-heum., et al.

1994 *Hanguk-ui jonggyo* (Korean religions). Seoul: Mundeoksa.

Yun, Tae-lim.

1971 *Uisik gujosangeuro bon hangugin* (Mental structure of Korean people). Seoul: Hyeonamsa.

Zenshō, Eisuke.

1935 *Chōsen-no Syōraku* (Korean villages). Seoul: Chōsen Sōtokufu (Japanese Government-General in Korea).

List of Abbreviations

AKS: Anthropologists for Korean Studies

CERD: Committee on the Elimination of Racial Discrimination, UN

CICI: Corea [Korea] Image Communication Institute

CPKI: Committee for the Preparation of Korean Independence

CPV: Chinese People's Volunteers

CUK: Cyber University of Korea, The

DAC: Development Assistance Committee

DHL: Dalsey, Millblom& Lynn

DJP: Democratic Justice Party

DMZ: Demilitarized Zone

DPRK: Democratic People's Republic of Korea

DRP: Democratic Republican Party

FDI: Foreign Direct Investment

FTA: Free Trade Organization

GCF: Green Climate Fund, UN

GGGI: Global Green Growth Institute

GKU: Green Korea United

HUGO: Human Genome Organization

IDEP: International Development Exchange Program

IMF: International Monetary Fund

IMO: International Organization for Migration

KBS: Korean Broadcasting System

KCIA: Korean Central Intelligence Agency

KDI: Korean Development Institute

KDP: Korean Democratic Party

KOICA: Korea International Cooperation Agency

KPG: Korean Provisional Government

KPR: Korean People's Republic

KRIVET: Korean Research Institute for Vocational Education and Training

MOOCS: Massive Open Online Courses

NGO: Non-governmental Organization

NSRRKI: National Society for Rapid Realization of Korean Independence

ODA: Official Development Assistance

OECD: Organization for Economic Co-operation and Development

POSCO: Pohang Iron and Steel Company

ROK: Republic of Korea

SWNCC: State-War-Navy Coordinating Committee

UNESCO: United Nations Education, Scientific and Cultural Organization

URA: Uruguay Round Agreement

USAFIK: United States Armed Forces in Korea

USAMGIK: United States Army Military Government in Korea

WTO: World Trade Organization

Index

348